Edited By

JONATHAN STRAHAN

MEETING INFINITY

Also Edited by Jonathan Strahan

EDITED BY
JONATHAN STRAHAN

MEETING INFINITY

First published 2015 by Solaris
an imprint of Rebellion Publishing Ltd,
Riverside House, Osney Mead,
Oxford, OX2 0ES, UK

www.solarisbooks.com

ISBN (US): 978-1-78108-380-2
ISBN (UK): 978-1-78108-379-6

Printed by Nørhaven, Denmark

For Sofa Mission Control Commander Pat Cadigan,
who always has her controls set for the heart of the sun,
with thanks for the stories so far
and in anticipation of the stories to come...

ACKNOWLEDGEMENTS

THIS IS THE fourth volume in the 'Infinity' series of anthologies. Like each of them, it's had its challenges. I'd like to thank my agent Howard Morhaim for his hard work and support during another busy year together, my editor Jonathan Oliver and the fantastic team at Solaris (Ben, David and Lydia) for their care, dedication and passion for this book, and of course all of the contributors, who sent such wonderful stories. Special thanks to John, Ian and Sean for coming through at the very last moment, when I really needed it.

I'd also like to thank my wife Marianne, and my two daughters, who help me make time each day to work on my editorial projects.

Contents

JONATHAN STRAHAN

INTRODUCTION

Jonathan Strahan

INTRODUCTION

Future shock is the shattering stress and disorientation that we induce in individuals by subjecting them to too much change in too short a time.

– Alvin Toffler, *Future Shock*

THERE ONCE WAS a Golden Age science fiction writer named Jack Williamson who was born in Arizona in the United States in 1908, back before it was a state and was still called the Arizona Territory. When his family, who were farmers and ranchers, needed better pastures for their herds, they packed up in horse-drawn covered wagons and moved to New Mexico.

During his lifetime – he lived to be 98 – Williamson saw first electricity then telephones arrive in his town. His parents' horse-drawn wagons gave way to cars. Before his fiftieth birthday humans had flown as high and as fast as they yet have, and not long after his sixtieth birthday they would walk on the moon. Within a few years of that the first successful human heart transplant would be performed, and it would not be long really before corneal transplants were commonplace.

Then things got really crazy. Consider this: not too long ago, as I write, I watched a doctor 3D print a human kidney while presenting a talk to a TED seminar, and when an astronaut on the International Space Station didn't have the correct tool to fix a problem, it was emailed to him (he printed out the socket set and made the repairs successfully).

The point of all of this is simple, and is manifold. To live to be nearly a hundred years old is amazing, though less unusual than it once was, but the fact that Williamson probably saw more rapid, widespread technological change during his lifetime than at any other time in human history is even more incredible. The 20th century was a time of incredible feats of technological achievement, but it was also a time of intense challenge and hardship, struggle and violence, much of which was precipitated by the very change that seemed so miraculous. It was both the most innovative and most potentially destructive of times, when we could find the skill to eradicate a disease and the stupidity to let it recur, and when we could build devices that could end all life on our planet using power sources that could possibly make us immortal.

Fifteen years into the 21st century the idea of future shock seems so obsolete and meaningless. We live in a world where easily accessible fossil fuels are disappearing, where the climate is changing in ways that are both violent and dangerous, and technology changes so quickly that change is the new norm. Being future shocked is so much a part of day-to-day life, at least in the West, that we don't even notice it (the future, of course, is unevenly distributed, so this does vary significantly across the face of the planet). Alvin Toffler, who wrote *Future Shock* almost half a century ago also wrote that, "The illiterate of the 21st century will not be those who cannot read and write, but those who cannot learn, unlearn, and relearn", which may be the truest thing in his book.

For all that the 20th century was a time of intense change, and the early 21st century seems to be an even more giddy, glorious, terrifying, appalling example of the same, it seems reasonable to say that we stand on the precipice of the greatest period of change humanity will ever see (this may well always be true from now on). The next hundred years or so will see climate addressed as a problem, or not; will see humans walk on another planet, or not; will see our society address problems of scarcity and injustice, or not. And the technological changes that will solve those problems will arrive, or not. And if they do, we cannot predict what impact they will have.

And that's a little of what *Meeting Infinity* – the fourth book in the 'Infinity Project' series of anthologies – attempts to address. When I was casting around for the subject for the next 'Infinity' book I remembered Jack Williamson, the only person I know of who both wrote science fiction and travelled out West in a covered wagon, and the theme seemed clear to me. So, I asked a group of science fiction writers to think about the ways in which profound change might impact on us in the future, how humanity might have to change physically and psychologically, to meet the challenges that may be thrown at us in the next fifty, the next hundred, and the next five hundred years and beyond. And they came back to me with visions that are broad and varied, fractured and strange. The stories you're about to read show humanity triumphant and humanity desperately on the run; they show a world we'd recognize and some we can barely contemplate; they have people who are uploaded, downloaded, hacked, recovered, infected by viruses and saved by them; they introduce us to people who could have walked down the street with the young Jack Williamson, and to people who would seem out of place in even his wildest stories. They show, more than anything, how we might meet infinity and survive it.

In 1985 singer songwriter Paul Simon flew to South Africa where he recorded "The Boy in the Bubble", probably the most prescient song of his career. Set partly on the outskirts of a parched town, soldiers are killed by bombs left in baby carriages, surveillance is everywhere, miracles like a boy with a baboon heart are commonplace, and lasers flash in the jungle, he leaves us with a line that echoes into the future: "These are the days of miracle and wonder, Don't cry baby, don't cry". Hopefully *Meeting Infinity* and the stories in it gives us a glimpse of both the darkness and the possible joy the future might offer.

JONATHAN STRAHAN
Perth, Western Australia
March, 2015

19

James S.A. Corey
RATES OF CHANGE

James S.A. Corey
RATES OF CHANGE

DIANA HASN'T SEEN her son naked before. He floats now in the clear gel bath of the medical bay, the black ceramic casing that holds his brain, the long articulated tail of his spinal column. Like a tadpole, she thinks. Like something young. In all, he hardly masses more than he did as a baby. She has a brief, horrifying image of holding him on her lap, cradling the braincase to her breast, the whip of his spine curling around her.

The thin white filaments of interface neurons hang in the translucent gel, too thin to see except in aggregate. Silvery artificial blood runs into the casing ports and back out in tubes more slender than her pinky finger. She thought, when they called her in, that she'd be able to see the damage. That there would be a scratch on the carapace, a wound, something to show where the violence had been done to him. There is nothing there. Not so much as a scuff mark. No evidence.

The architecture of the medical center is designed to reassure her. The walls curve around her in warm colors. The air recyclers hum a low, consonant chord. Nothing helps. Her own body – her third – is flushed with adrenaline, her heart aches and her hands squeeze into fists. Her fight or flight reaction has no outlet, so it speeds around her body, looking for a way to escape. The chair tilts too easily under her, responding to shifts in her balance and weight that she isn't aware of making. She hates it. The café au lait that the nurse brought congeals, ignored, on the little table.

Diana stares at the curve and sweep of Stefan's bodiless nervous system as if by watching him now she can stave off the accident that has already happened. Closing the barn door, she thinks, after the horses are gone. The physician ghosts in behind her, footsteps quiet as a cat's, his body announcing his presence only in how he blocks the light.

"Mrs. Dalkin," he says. "How are you feeling?"

"How is he?" she demands instead of saying hello.

The physician is a large man, handsome with a low warm voice like flannel fresh from the dryer. She wonders if it is his original body or if he's chosen the combination of strength and softness just to make this part of his work easier. "Active. We're seeing metabolic activity over most of his brain the way we would hope. Now that he's here, the inflammation is under control."

"So he's going to be all right?"

He hesitates. "We're still a little concerned about the interface. There was some bruising that may have impaired his ability to integrate with a new body, but we can't really know the extent of that yet."

Diana leans forward, her gut aching. Stefan is there, only inches from her. Awake, trapped in darkness, aware only of himself and the contents of his own mind. He doesn't even know she is watching him. If she picked him up, he wouldn't know she was doing it. If she shouted, he wouldn't hear. What if he is trapped that way forever? What if he has fallen into a darkness she can never bring him out from?

"Is he scared?"

"We are seeing some activity in his amygdala, yes," the physician says. "We're addressing that chemically, but we don't want to depress his neural activity too much right now."

"You *want* him scared, then."

"We want him active," the physician says. "Once we can establish some communication with him and let him know that we're here and where he is and that we're taking action on his behalf, I expect most of his agitation will resolve."

"So he doesn't even know he's here."

"The body he was in didn't survive the initial accident. He was extracted in situ before transport." He says it so gently, it sounds like an apology. An offer of consolation. She feels a spike of hatred and rage for the man run through her like an electric shock, but she hides it.

"What happened?"

"Excuse me?" the physician asks.

"I said, what happened? How did he get hurt? Who did this?"

"He was brought from the coast by emergency services. I understood it was an accident. Someone ran into him, or he ran into something, but apart from that it was a blunt force injury, we didn't. . ."

Diana lifts her hand, and the physician falls silent. "Can you fix him? You can make him all right."

"We have a variety of interventions at our disposal," he says, relieved to be back on territory he knows. "It's really going to depend on the nature of the damage he's sustained."

"What's the worst case?"

"The worst case is that he won't be able to interface with a new body at all."

She turns to look into the physician's eyes. The dark brown that looks back at her doesn't show anything of the cruelty or horror of what he's just said. "How likely is that?" Diana says, angry at her voice for shaking.

"Possible. But Stefan is young. His tissue is resilient. The casing wasn't breached, and the constriction site on his spine didn't buckle. I'd say his chances are respectable, but we won't know for a few days."

Diana drops her head into her hands, the tips of her fingers digging into her temples. Something violent bubbles in her chest, and a harsh laughter presses at the back of her throat like vomit.

"All right," she says. "All . . . right."

She hears Karlo's footsteps, recognizing their cadence the way she would have known his cough or the sound of his yawn. Even across bodies, there is a constancy about Karlo. She both clings to it now and resents it. The ridiculous muscle-bound body he bought himself for retirement tips into the doorway, darkening the room.

"I came when I heard," he says.

"Fuck you," Diana says, and then the tears come and won't stop. He puts his arms around her. The doctor walks softly away.

IT IS A year earlier, and Karlo says "He's a grown man. There's no reason he shouldn't."

The house looks out over the hot concrete of Dallas. It is smaller than the one they'd shared in Quebec, the kitchen thinner, the couch less comfortable. They way they live in it is different too. Before, when they'd had a big family room, they would all stretch out together on long evenings. Stefan talking to his friends and playing games, Karlo building puzzles or doing office work, Diana watching old films and taking meetings with work groups in Europe and Asia. They'd been a family then – husband, wife, child. For all their tensions and half-buried resentments, they'd still been a unit, the three of them. But they live in the Dallas house like it is a dormitory, coming back to sleep and leaving again when they wake. Even her.

She hates the place, and what it says about her. About Karlo. About Stefan. She hates wondering whether Karlo's new body had been chosen based on some other woman's tastes. Or some other man's. That her son isn't a child.

"I stayed in my body until I was *thirty*," she says. "He's twenty-*one*. He doesn't need it for work. He's not some kind of laborer."

"It isn't the same now as it was when we were young," Karlo says. "It isn't just medical or work."

"*Cosmetic*," Diana says, stalking out of the bedroom. Karlo follows her like a leaf pulled along by a breeze.

"Or adventure. Exploration. It's what people do these days."

"He should wait."

Her own body – the one she'd been born in – had failed her young. Ovarian cancer that had spread to her hip before she'd noticed a thing. The way she remembered it, the whole process hadn't taken more than a few days. Symptom, diagnosis, discussion of treatment options. Her doctor had been adamant – get out before the metastases reached her central nervous system. The ship of her flesh was sinking, and she needed to get into the lifeboat now. The technology had been developed for people working in vacuum or deep ocean, and it was as safe as a decade and a half of labor law could make it. And anyway, there wasn't a viable choice.

She'd agreed in a haze of fear and confusion. At the medical center, Karlo had undressed her for the last time, helped her into her gown, kissed her, and promised that everything was going to be all right. She still remembered being on the table, the anaesthesiologist telling her to unclasp her hands. In a sense, it had been the last thing she'd ever heard.

She'd hated her second body. Even though it had been built to look as much like her original as it could, she knew better. Everything about it was subtly wrong – the way her elbow fit against her side, the way her voice resonated when she spoke, the shape of her hands. The physicians had talked about rehabilitation anxiety and the uncanny valley. They said it would become more familiar, except that it didn't. She tried antidepressant therapy. Identity therapy. Karlo had volunteered to swap out his own body partly as a way, he said, to understand better what she was going through. That hadn't worked at all. He'd woken up in his new flesh like he'd had a long nap and loved everything about his new self. Five years in, she still hadn't felt comfortable in her new skin.

Her third body had been an attempt to address that. Instead of trying to mimic her old, dead flesh, it would be something new. Where she'd been petite before, she would be taller and broader now. Instead of being long-waisted, she would be leggy. Her skin tone would be darker, the texture of her hair would be different. Her eyes could be designed in unnatural colors, her fingernails growing in iridescent swirls. Instead of pretending that her body wasn't a prosthetic, she could design one as a piece of art. It is the mask that she faces in every mirror, and most days she feels more reconciled than trapped.

And then there are bad days when she longs for the first body, the real body, and worse than that, the woman she'd been when she was still in it. She wonders whether it was the same longing that other women felt about youth. And now Stefan wants to leave his body – the body she'd given him, the one that had grown within her – in order to. . . what? Have an adventure with his friends?

Sitting at the thin, discolored breakfast bar, she laces large, dark fingers together, enjoying the ache of knuckle against knuckle. Karlo drifts past in his massive flesh, taking a muscle shirt from the dryer and pulling it over his head with a vagueness that leaves Diana lonesome.

"Why would he want to?" she says, wiping her eye with the back of one hand.

Karlo sighs, hums to himself. He draws a glass of orange juice from the refrigerator and adds vodka from the freezer. He drinks deep and bares his teeth after. His third body has bright white tombstones of teeth. His first body had been slight and compact. Almost androgynous. By the time he speaks, she's forgotten that she even asked a question.

"Do you mean you don't think he wants it, or you don't think he *should* want it?"

"He doesn't understand what he's giving up," she says.

"Do you?"

She scowled at him. The conversation is making her uncomfortably aware that the experience of him – of seeing Karlo, hearing his voice, smelling the bite of the orange and alcohol – is all phantoms of charged ions and neurochemistry in a brain, in a casing, in a body. Neurons that fire in a pattern that somehow, unknowably, *is* her experiencing these things. She crosses her arms like she is driving a car, and hates being aware of it. Karlo finishes his drink, puts the glass in the washer. He doesn't look straight into her eyes. "All his friends are doing it. If he doesn't he'll be left behind."

"It's his *body*," she says.

"It's *his* body," Karlo says, his eyes already shifting toward the door. Away from her. "And anyway, that doesn't mean what it did when we were kids." He leaves without saying goodbye. Without kissing her, not that she would have welcomed him. She checks her messages. There are a dozen queued. Something dramatic has happened at the Apulia office, and she hunches over the display and tries to tease out exactly what it was.

She never does give her permission. She only doesn't withhold it.

THE FOOTAGE OF the accident plays on a little wall monitor in the medical center. The actual water had been too deep for natural light to find them, so the images have been enhanced, green and aquamarine added, shafts of brightness put in where a human eye – if it hadn't been crushed by the pressure – would have seen only darkness. The image capture has been done by a companion submarine to document the months-long trek, and either it was a calm day in the deep water or image processing has steadied it. Diana can imagine herself floating in the endless expanse of an ocean so vast it is like looking up at the stars. Karlo sits beside her, his hands knotted together, his eyes on the screen. The contrast between the squalid, tiny world of the medical center and the vast beauty on the screen disorients her.

The first of them swim into sight. A ray with wide gray wings, sloping through the saltwater. With nothing to give a sense of scale, it could be larger than a whale or hardly bigger than a human. There is no bump to show where the carapace holding a human brain and spine might have slotted into it. There is no scar to mark an insertion point. Another of the creatures passes by the camera, curving up the deep tides with grace and power. Then another. Then a dozen more. A school of rays. And one of them – she can't begin to guess which – her son. In some other context, it might have been beautiful.

"It's all right," Karlo says, and she doesn't know what he means by it. That the violence she is about to see had already happened, that she ought not be disturbed by the alien body that Stefan had chosen over his own, that her anger now won't help. The words could carry anything.

A disturbance strikes the rays, a shock moving through the group. The smooth cohesion breaks, and they whirl, turning one way and then the other. Their distress is unmistakable.

"What happened?" Karlo says. "Was that it?"

"Be quiet," Diana says. She leans forward, filling her view with the small screen like she might be able to dive through it. There in the center of the group, down below the camera, two of the rays swirl around each other, one great body butting into the other. A fight or a dance. She can't read the intent in the movements. One breaks off, skimming wildly up, speeding through the gloom and the darkness. The other follows, and the floating camera turns to track them. As they chase each other, another shape slides into the frame, also high above. Another group of three alien bodies moving together, unaware of the chase rising up from below. The impact seems comical. The lead ray bumps into the belly of the middle of the three. The little camera loses focus, finds it again. Four rays swimming in a tight circle around one that lists on its side, its wings stilled and drifting.

That is my son, she thinks. *That is Stefan.* No emotions rise at the idea. It is absurd. Like seeing a rock cracked under a hammer or a car bent by a wreck: the symbol of a tragedy, but not the thing itself. It is some sea animal, something that belongs to the same world as sharks and angler fish. Inhuman. She knows it is her boy floating there, being pulled toward the surface by the emergency services pods, but she cannot make herself feel it.

"They attacked him," she says, testing the words. Hoping that they will carry the outrage she wants to feel. "They attacked him, and they left him for dead."

"They were playing and there was an accident," Karlo says. "They didn't leave him for dead."

"Then where are they? His friends, if that's what you call them? I don't see them here."

"They can't breathe air," Karlo says, as if that excuses everything. "They'll come once the trip is over. Or, when he gets better, he can go back to them."

Her breath leaves her. She turns to stare at him. His eyes, so unlike the ones she'd known when they had been married, cut to her and away again.

"Go back to them?" she says.

"If he wants. Some people find living that way very calming. Pleasant."

"They aren't *human*." Now there is rage. Real rage. It lifts her up out of herself and fills her ears with a sound like bees. "You want to see your son among these animals? That's fine with you? They could have killed him. We don't know that they didn't. You'd send him back?"

"They aren't animals," Karlo says. "They're just different. And I would do what Stefan wants. I'd let him choose."

"Of course you would."

They are quiet for a moment. The feed on the display ends, drops back to the medical center's logo and a prompt. Karlo sighs again. She hates the way his sighs sound now – deep and rumbling. Nothing like his first body, except in the timing of it, the patience in it. Nothing the same except that it is the same. "You know you can't tell him how to live his life."

"I don't want to have this conversation."

"It's always been like this. Every generation finds its own way to show that it isn't like the one before. Too much risk, too much sex, terrible music, not enough respect for the old ways. This is no different. It was an accident."

"I don't want to have this *conversation*."

"All right," Karlo says. "Another time."

BEFORE THE CANCER she worked in an office with people, a desk of her own, conversations over butter tarts and tea in a breakroom with an old couch and half a dozen bamboo chairs. When she came back in her second body, the junior partners threw a little party for her to celebrate the happy conclusion of her brush with death. She remembers being touched and a little embarrassed at the time. And grateful.

It was only later, as she tried to get back into her old routine, that her subterranean distress began to bloom. She found herself timing her trips to the bathroom and break room to avoid brushing past anyone or being touched. She avoided the bakery at the end of the street that she'd frequented before. At home, her marriage became essentially sexless.

She tried not to notice it at first, then told herself that it was temporary, and then that it was normal. Over weeks, a quiet shame gnawed at her. She bathed at night with a grim, angry focus, resenting her skin for gathering smudges and sweat, her hair for growing oily and repulsive. She ate too much or not enough. Shitting or pissing or getting her period filled her with a deep disgust, like she was having to watch and clean and tend to someone else.

She found reasons to work remotely, to talk to Karlo and Stefan while she was somewhere else. Simply having a physicality irritated her, and she leaned away from it. When the junior partners asked whether she was still using her office or if they could repurpose the space, she'd cried without knowing quite why she was crying. She'd told them they could have it and scheduled a consultation with her doctor. Rehabilitation anxiety. Uncanny valley. It would pass.

Now, she sits in the medical centre cafeteria, going through her messages with her attention scattered, listening to the same one three or four or five times, and still not able to focus her attention long enough to parse what exactly it was her co-worker was asking of her. The smell of antiseptic and overheated food presses her. The lights seem both too bright and unable to dispel the shadows, and she wonders whether it might be the beginning of a migraine. Karlo has found himself someplace else to be, and she is resentful that he's abandoned her and relieved to be left to herself.

At the next table, a woman in scrubs laughs acidly and the man she is with responds with something in French. Diana finds her attention drifting to them: wondering at them, about them. The woman has a beautiful cascade of black hair flowing down her shoulders: had she been born with it? Is she as young as she seems, or was the brain under those raven locks an old woman's? Or an old man's? Or a child's as young as Stefan? Even in a carapace, a brain still wears out, still lives out its eight or nine decades. Or seven. Or two. But without the other signs of age and infirmity, what does it mean?

She remembers her own mother's hair going from auburn to gray to white to a weird sickly yellow. The changes meant something, gave Diana a way to anticipate the changes in her own life, her own body. There are no old people now. No one crippled and infirm. Everything is a lie of health and permanence, of youth permanently extended. All around her, everyone is wrapped in a mask of flesh. Everything is a masquerade of itself, everyone in disguise. And even the few who aren't, might be. There is no way to know.

Her hands tremble. She closes her eyes, and has to fight not to cover her ears too. If she does, someone might come and talk to her, ask her whether she is all right. She doesn't know how she would answer that, and she doesn't want to find out.

For a moment, she envies Stefan, locked away from the world, alone with only himself, and then immediately condemns herself for thinking it. He is hurt. Her baby is injured and afraid and beyond any place she can reach him. Only a monster would wish for that.

But...

Perhaps she can let herself want to change places with him. If she had to shed her body – all her bodies – to bring him back into the light, she'd do it in a heartbeat. Put that way, she can tell herself it would be an act of love.

Someone touches her shoulder. She startles, her eyes flying open. The physician with his uncertain smile, like she might bite him. She forces herself to nod, reflexively picturing the black casing behind the chocolate brown eyes and gently graying hair.

"We were trying to reach you, Mrs. Dalkin."

She looks at her message queue. Half a dozen from the medical center's system, from Karlo. She feels the blush in her cheeks. "I'm sorry," she says. "I was distracted."

"No need to apologize," he says. "I thought you'd want to know. We've made contact with Stephan."

THE INTERFACE IS minimal. One of the thin silvery faux-neuronal leads has adhered to a matching bundle of nerve clusters that runs to a casing like the insulation on a wire, and from there into a simple medical deck. A resonance imager wraps around Stefan's brain like a scarf and focuses on his visual neocortex, reading the patterns there and extrapolating the images that Stephan is imagining from them. Reading his mind and showing it on a grainy display.

"He is experiencing the interface as a coldness on his right arm," the physician says. "You have to be slow, but he's been able to follow us with surprising clarity. It's a very good sign."

"Oh good," Diana says, and wishes there had been less dread in the words. She sits at the deck, her fingers over the keyboard layout, suddenly unsure what she is supposed to say. She smiles at the physician nervously. "Does his father know?"

"Yes. Mr. Dalkin was here earlier."

"Oh good," she says again. She types slowly, one letter at a time. The deck translates her words into impulses down the neuronal wire, the interface translates the impulses into the false experience of an unreal cold in an abandoned arm, and Stefan—her Stefan, her son—reads the switching impulses as the Morse-code-like pulses that he's trained in.

This is your mother. I am right here.

SHE TURNS TO the display, waiting. Biting her lips with her teeth until she tastes a little blood. The display shifts. There is only black and gray, fuzzy as a child drawing in the dirt with a stick, but she sees the cartoonish smiling face. Then a heart. Then, slowly, H then I then M then O then M. She sobs once, and it hurts her throat.

Are you okay in there?

P-E-A-C-H-Y

"Fuck you," she says. "Fuck you, you flippant little shit." She doesn't look at the physician, the technicians. Let them think whatever they want. She doesn't care now.

I love you.

Stephan visualizes a heart. The physician hands Diana a tissue, and she wipes her tears away first and then blows her nose.

It is going to be okay.

I-K-N-O-W and another cartoon smiling face. Then T-E-L-L-K-I-R-A-I-A-M-G-O-D.

God?

The display goes chaotic for a moment, as her son thinks of something else, not visual. It comes back with something like an infinity sign, two linking circles. No, a double o.

Good?

The smiling face. Tell Kira I am good. As if it were true. As if whatever girl had sloughed off her own body and put her mind in one of those monsters deserves to be comforted for whatever role she'd had in making her son into this. No one deserved to be forgiven. No one.

I will.

"His anxiety has gone down considerably since we made contact," the physician says. "And with the interface starting to bounce back, I think we can start administering some medication to reduce his distress. It will still be some time before we can know how extensive the permanent damage is, but I think it's very likely he will be able to integrate into a body again."

"That's good," Diana hears herself say.

"I don't want to oversell the situation. He may be blinded. He may have reduced motor function. There is still a long, long way to go before we can really say he's clear. But his responses so far show that he's very much cognitively intact, and he's got a great sense of humor and a real bravery. That's more important now than anything else."

"That's good," she says again. Her body rises, presumably because she wants it to. "Excuse me."

She walks down the hall, out the metal door, into the bright and unforgiving summer sunlight. She's forgotten her things in Stefan's room, but she doesn't want to go back for them. They'll be there when she returns or else they won't. On the streets, autocabs hiss their tires along the tracks. Above her, a flock of birds wheels. She finds a little stretch of grass, an artifact of the sidewalk and the street, useless for anything and so left alone. She lowers herself to it, crosses her latest set of legs and pulls off her shoes to look at some unreal woman's feet, running her fingertips along the arches.

None of it is real. The heat of the sun is only neurons in her brain firing in a certain pattern. The dampness of the grass that cools her thighs and darkens her pants. The half-ticklish feeling of her feet. Her grief. Her anger. Her confusion. All of it is a hallucination created in tissue locked in a lightless box of bone. Patterns in a complication of nerves.

She talked with her son. He talked back. Whatever happens to him, it already isn't the worst. It will only get better, even if better doesn't make it all the way back to where it started from. Even if the best it ever is is worse than what it was. She waits for the relief to come. It doesn't.

Instead, there is Karlo.

He strides down the walk, swinging beefy arms, wide and masculine and sure of himself. She can tell when he sees her. The way he holds himself changes, narrows. Curls in, like he is protecting himself. That is just nerves firing too. The patterns in the brain she'd loved once expressing something through his costume of flesh. She wonders what it would be like to be stripped out of her body with him, their interface neurons linked one to another. There had been a time, hadn't there, when he had felt like her whole universe? Is that what the kids would be doing a generation from now? No more deep-sea rays. No more human bodies. Carapaces set so that they become flocks of birds or buildings or traffic patterns or each other. When they can become anything, they will. Anything but real.

He grunts as he eases himself to the grass beside her, shading his eyes from the sun with a hand and a grimace.

"He's doing better," Karlo says.

"I know. We passed notes."

"Really? That's more than I got out of him. He's improving."

"He gave me a message for Kira."

"That's his girlfriend."

"I don't care."

Karlo nods and heaves a wide, gentle sigh. "I'm sorry."

"For what?"

"Everything."

"You didn't do everything."

"No," he says. "Just what I could."

Diana lets her head sink to her knees. She wonders, if her first body had survived, would she have been able to? Or would the decades have stiffened her joints the way they had her mother's, dimmed her eyesight the way they had her father's. The way they might never for anyone again. "What happened?" she says. "When did we stop being human? When did we decide it was okay?"

"When did we start?" Karlo says.

"What?"

"When did we start being human and stop being. . . I don't know. Cavemen? Apes? When did we start being mammals? Every generation has been different than the one before. It's only that the rate of change was slow enough that we always recognized the one before and the one after as being like us. Enough like us. Close. Being human isn't a physical quality like being heavy or having green eyes. It's the idea that they're like we are. That nothing fundamental has changed. It's the story we tell about our parents and our children. "

"Our lovers," she says. "Our selves."

Karlo's body tightens. "Yes, those too," he says. And then, a moment later, "Stefan's going to come through. Whatever happens, he'll be all right."

"Will I?" she says.

She waits for an answer.

41

Benjanun Sriduangkaew
DESERT LEXICON

BENJANUN SRIDUANGKAEW
DESERT LEXICON

AT THE MOMENT of freedom they give you the choice of the sun or the choice of the deep.

In the prison, each cell is too small for peace, each bed too narrow for consolation, each window too small for a future.

In the prison, all choices are poor. But taking none of them is death of another sort.

THE MIND IMPOSES the familiar onto the foreign, and so Isyavan slowly comes to think space would be yellow dunes and harsh slashes of light; that the lip of black holes would be parched, their accretion disks pale gold and smelling of baked sediment. She has never seen one. She will never see one. Her imagination will do as well as any.

Her commander, insomuch as that office carries meaning, succumbs on their sixtieth sunrise. It is quiet, and as ever, asymptomatic. There were no warnings. The commander never wakes, simply loses her pulse as though she's misplaced or left it behind in her sleep. They open her up with their bare hands, chip away at bones gone to resin overnight with knives, tear at rapidly ossifying muscles with nails. Isyavan is the one to crack the sternum into a fistful of amber shards. Everyone lets her do that each time, as though it's part of a sanctified ritual. Heartbreaker they call her, their terrible joke, but a refined sense of humor and wit don't endure long, out here.

Underneath, the scans tell them their commander's lungs and kidneys are fifty years older than they were yesterday.

No one objects when Isyavan collects the shards. They click in her hands, rough edges pecking at her skin. They won't penetrate; her flesh is hardened, proof against grit and heat and desert hunger. But their commander's was supposed to be, too.

She turns her face to the sky. Optics polarize to compensate, shielding her sight. A horizon like jaundice, like a rank of rotting molars. But that doesn't mean anything. An isotopic storm can happen any time, steal up on them under a calm day, no louder than heat haze or the memory of anesthetics.

They don't bury their commander. There is no point. Her prostheses will decay, down to half-life and halved again until they are dust. The parts of her she was born with – skin and fat and veins – will go even faster, dissolved in a day or two.

Nor do they mark the place where she has fallen, save in their memory. Even that does not last.

THE RISEN INTELLIGENCES never register on sensors.

At the prison, while Isyavan lay breathless with pain from surgery, a short hard-eyed woman – some engineer or biotech; Isyavan wasn't paying attention – explained that the old desert machines send out disruptive signals that scatter communication frequencies, glitch detection subroutines. "That is why we can't use drones or automatons," the woman said, as though in apology. "When you are done, you'll have full amnesty."

"When I am done," Isyavan rasped through peeling cracked lips, "I'll be dead." But the other option would have been the hadopelagic deep, to mine and capture kinetic surges disgorged from the thermal vents, and never see the sun again.

"You are a good candidate. Better odds than most; you have the training, the experience. The knowledge both visceral and theoretical." The woman averted her gaze, unable or unwilling to look at the seams around Isyavan's head like a crown. In profile the engineer looked a little like an aunt long dead, and never one of Isyavan's favorites. "Those intelligences served past wars – ballistic calculations, drones, vehicles. Veterans, just like you. In a way you'll be putting comrades to rest."

Even in agony, her skull hurting as though they had sewn nerves into her cranium, that shocked a laugh out of Isyavan. It turned into vomiting. Clear bile from nutrient tubes down her mouth, pooling in the hollows of her throat, running over her thin stained shift. The woman wipes her down, not without a grimace of distaste. Isyavan didn't have her motor control back yet. At the time, it seemed like she never would.

THE EVENING AFTER their commander's death, they meet an ancient engine pushing and threshing its way up, sand sluicing from its caked flanks. It might have been a tank, once, thick armor and spine lined by cannons. A mouth of dull, rotating saws.

To the limited, lesser intelligences orbiting Isyavan's mind, the relic – immense as it is, loudly as it howls – is a ghost, invisible and impossible to target. But it's the size of a small house. None of them will miss.

Coordination comes easily, now, drilled into them by the need to stay alive. By having seen what happens without it. There were eight of them, at the start. Down to four, and as honed and tight-knit a squad as can be had given the conditions and the briefness of sixty days. Soldiers learn faster in extreme stress, if they don't fray and break down first.

Haduan in first, rushing low – the machines are so ancient and clogged by grit that their guns have become slow to angle, twitching by degrees at a time. Tarasi has climbed up the protrusions, calmly setting up mines as she goes, hanging them from the tank's protrusions and sensors like pendants. They have to be close to inflict damage, and very precise: not a single bullet can go to waste. Ammunition was one of the first things that ran low, though their attrition has compensated somewhat. Equipment and supplies for eight go a long way for half that number.

Isyavan is last. She used to take point, but Haduan is faster and she's had to overcome her pride to accept that.

She waits for the right moment. When she finds it, she charges.

The blade in her hand shudders, angrier and harder than anti-tank recoil, miniature cousin to the relic's mouth. Certain things she does better than anyone, and so she conserves ammunition when she can. Close combat doesn't use up bullets.

At this range the engine feels almost animal, the heat and screech, the congealed fuel musk-thick. The throb of its locomotive parts like a pulse. She slashes, on instinct more than certainty – if this machine has specs, they are lost to antiquity, distorted by long survival among the dunes hunting and absorbing other relics for components. There are softer points,

though, where the parts join and the cables flex. Humans build
things greater and larger than them with weaknesses in mind.
Not consciously, perhaps, but there. Hindbrain imperative,
from the days of holding territories contested by creatures with
eyes that gleam in the dark and incisors like abattoir grinders.

Her weapon goes through, between joints.

Afterward she's the filthiest, drenched in coolants and
lubricants, stained gray and black like she's been fighting mud
and raw sewage. Tarasi compulsively measures while they
still have an intact carcass: the mass, the breadth, the scale
of its cortex. She's the only one among them with a scientist's
training, believes in empirical verity with a zeal most reserve for
religion or revenge. "Machine thought has the briefest half-life
of anything," she says, nearly rote, a frequent lament as she
cracks open the tank's cortex. What passes for a cortex.

"Good," Isyavan says, trying unsuccessfully to get clean.
Sandstorms eventually score most of the fluids off her armor,
sometimes taking a layer of epidermis with it, but she's used to
that. Flesh, armor. Much the same these days. "Imagine if they
were still smart by the time we come to them."

Laughter buzzes in her ears, earpiece to earpiece. Earpiece
for her, at least; Rimael doesn't have much cartilage and skin
around there anymore, only silicone and a transmitter bead
grafted to cochlea. They return to their carrier, taking stock:
how much ammunition was used, how many mines were blown.
The vehicle isn't armed, and only lightly shielded – not for them
the safety of a carrier teeth-bright and full of claws. That would
be too easy.

Another joke, that, no funnier than their nickname for Isyavan.
But the roof is a good perch for Rimael, picked as their sniper,

though his rounds must be rationed even more tightly than anyone else's. Their last resort, him and his rifle, on the handful of occasions where they can see something coming from far off. Something too dangerous or too complex for Isyavan, Tarasi and Haduan to destroy at close range.

"So what were you in for?" This from Haduan, in the relative hush of the carrier. A familiar refrain; Isyavan is the only one who hasn't disclosed. Not when they were eight. Not even now.

Her mouth is shut, the way closed fists are.

"Desertion," Rimael says, the most certain of them that Isyavan was in the army once, not that it's a secret.

Perhaps he comes closer than most – but perhaps not. She never denies or confirms; it lends her mystique, maintains her place and the respect they afford her. And they leave it be, after a certain point. The thought that they might have a political dissident or hero among them soothes. A meaning, of sorts, to what they are doing that is otherwise without hope or purpose.

They all stink. By the time they are out of here, if they aren't dead, their noses will be.

Isyavan was the first to get them to open up, putting a key to each of their locks even while jealously guarding her own. Rimael used to be an accountant, Haduan police, and Tarasi a researcher turned demolitionist: graduated with a degree in marine biology, found herself without employment prospects, joined the military. It's not an uncommon story, though they tease that all things considered, isn't Tarasi meant for the ocean floor?

"No," she likes to say, peevish at layperson ignorance, "I didn't study *deep sea* life. Sharks and coral reefs, thank you very much. Marine biologists specialize, friends."

They take turns sleeping, though none of them is ever truly at rest; a part of them is constantly at work, a gnosis of signals in their marrow and muscles singing data to the skies. Weather conditions, signs of an ecosystem in the desert if any, diagnostics of isotopic damage on their equipment and bodies. The nominal objectives of their expedition couldn't be simpler: ninety days to map the bounds and power of the storms, the radiative fallout. Staying in place at the periphery isn't an option – both the carrier and their own bodies goad them forward, across and deep into the dunes. Ninety days. They all count, viciously obsessive, shouting congratulations on another hour logged, another day outwitted. To their knowledge the best record yet is sixty-five days, and they are closing in on that.

No one is so vulgar as to bring up that none of the expeditions have ever lasted the full three months. There's always hope. Every round of modification and augmentation is iterative on the last, hardening respiratory and nervous systems, shielding organs and skin against the blows of sudden age. Cybernetics that can survive this place can survive anything; integration of flesh-and-not that holds here would never falter anywhere. Their bodies are a study for future wars.

They like to think they are tougher than the previous teams. They like to believe they will be the last, and that no more expeditions will be necessary after. These beliefs vary in strength and conviction, though they persist. The human capability for delusion has no limits.

When they eat, none of them truly tastes; the receptors in their mouth and tongue measure texture and intake, and their implants moderate their rate of metabolism with an architect's care for angles and altitudes. Sustainability is important. The soldiers of tomorrow must be able to endure vast stretches of privations. But there has to be a control, and so Haduan's rate of metabolism is on purpose heightened. He eats more from the tubes of gel and compressed proteins. He moves faster and his vitals elevate more quickly. Perfect for taking point, but Tarasi worries about him. The way he consumes, it's suspected his metabolism is being made to step up by the day.

"What if," Rimael says, always talking too much, "our side has already lost? What if our operators are dead?"

"Then we turn around and get out."

"Then we'll die here."

"No," Isyavan says, and that ends the conversation.

One subject they never discuss is their dead commander and the other three casualties. On most things, Isyavan gives no opinion. On this, she is firm: try not to remember the dead too fondly or even too well. The act of forgetting liberates. Upend the vessel of thought until they are empty of the past, and something better may fill you up. The only memento is the shards of calcified hearts, which Isyavan alone carries as though she means to embody their record.

Perhaps this is why, when they have brought down a mastiff of ignited incisors and radial tongues, they don't recognize their commander until the last engine growl has died, the final twitch of rust-sheathed muscles extinguished. It is not a cry they hear or a plea; the tune is wordless, the voice scratched gravel. A snatch hummed in a moment of distraction, off-key notes they have all listened to as they went to sleep or took their shift on the carrier's roof.

They stand in silence as the voice diminishes, spiraling into an afterlife of dimming circuits and burnout cells. Isyavan kneels to stroke the mastiff's abraded, blackened tendons. Optics eclipse her sclera, making her eyes tar pits in the scuffed crags of her face, her pupils needlepoints.

Haduan laughs, too loud and too high. Rimael for once has nothing to offer. Tarasi measures the carcass.

"Don't transmit," Isyavan says softly.

Rimael's mouth gashes into a grin. "We can't control that."

"Tarasi, leave it alone. The rest of you, delete what you can."

They obey; they have discovered a formula and no matter the variables, following Isyavan leads to survival – that is the constant. Their casualties never had time for this formula or for her, and that is proof of concept in itself. Obedient doesn't mean unquestioning, but questions can be postponed for a more appropriate time.

They march on. Even their direction is dictated from afar, their course selected by their operators. Who may be dead, a possibility they have nursed and gnawed on, tasting its shape and texture, licking at it like a wound. During the march they focus; during downtime there isn't much else to do but let their minds wander. The idea of fucking to pass the time has occurred to most of them, but none of them appeals to each other that way and in any case there's no space or opportunity. Tarasi would have slept with their lost commander but there was never privacy, so they simply made promises for *after* and *one day* with twined hands.

When Tarasi finds herself humming that same tune she quickly stops. Isyavan's rule of engagement: always forget, always bury, always discard. The easiest thing to do; recall naturally sifts over itself like wind-stirred detritus, effortless.

But still, "What *was* that?" demanded as though Isyavan has the answer to everything.

And as though she does, she says, "Mass paracusia. Our receptors glitched."

Rimael's chin juts. "Really?" He ignores Haduan's hand on his back, cautioning, reminding.

She turns to him, her gaze indifferent. "Do you actually want to think about it, or do you just want to pick a fight, Rimael?"

He quiets, comes to heel.

Seventieth comes and passes, a day the precise hue of mourning. They celebrate a little. Twenty left, which – subsequent to what they've been through – is hardly anything. The concept of life beyond now, a time outside the desert, slowly accretes strata of potential like sediment.

Until the theory of obedience to Isyavan fails and reverts to mere hypothesis, or less.

The beast comes at night, the shape of a spider, the taste of carbon-rot and melanoma. The voices in that shredded tune, looping endlessly through cracked speakers.

If anyone is distracted it should have been Tarasi, but perhaps it is easy to ignore the dead when they don't call to you. And even then, when the spider murmurs "Rimael?" it is quiet, bemused, like it doesn't quite know the date, where it is, what it is.

A cry for help, a withheld breath wracked with pain: any of that and the outcome might have been different. But this blank distance, this puzzlement as of one shaking off sleep, gives pause.

He pauses too long, is cut in half by the scythe-swing of an arachnid leg. From throat to groin, exact and with a machine's joyous attention to symmetry.

It is the first time their certainty falters, their coordination slips. Isyavan is answer and salvation. She's not supposed to lead them astray; she's not meant to let them die.

She never sends up a rallying cry. Simply she presses on, shearing off a leg, hammering in an eye. Like she never registered Rimael turning to sparks and circuit, the synaptic links between prostheses and skin snapping in blood and sealant. Or, Tarasi would think afterward, like she's fighting alone, counting on nothing but herself; that at the centrifuge of survival there is only – has always been only – Isyavan. Everything else is incidental byproduct.

Haduan and Tarasi do their parts, anyway. Tearing up old relics sutured together by ancient code has become second nature, so much so that like Isyavan they hardly miss a beat. Suppleness and speed, all habit.

Isyavan offers two choices. Taking neither has never been an option, just as taking neither death by the deep or death by the sun wasn't one. The prison has taught them well about life.

Rimael talked too much, but he gave voice to the others' fears. Down to three, it's much easier for two to conspire against and doubt the third. At four, Rimael provided balance.

As three they collect the parts of him that they can find, tangled up in the briars of arachnid limbs and crown of still-swiveling optics. There hasn't been time for him to solidify, to pass in some semblance of dignity. No resinous shards for

Isyavan to break and keep, only curlicues of his fluids drying on spider carapace.

She digs and pries until she has his heart in its nest of connectors and guttering power. She cracks open his skull until she has the container that holds his brain, a complicated shell of receptors and transmitters, miniature network that intermediates between implants and flesh, thought and data.

Haduan and Tarasi draw low, harsh breaths. Even knowing what is inside them, having seen the blueprints after the surgery, the actuality of their parts confronts: unspeakable, unignorable. Isyavan never tore to rags the ones who died fresh, only those that went away rotting in their sleep. Perhaps there was a reason, in the end, other than qualms about touching fat and still-hot lymph.

"I'm taking this with me," she says, of the heart and the brain.

"Could he be put in... something else?"

Isyavan looks at Haduan.

Who says in a small tight voice, "I just thought of prostheses – since we are..."

She cups the wet heart in one hand, the breadth of her palm swallowing it, and cradles the cardiac shell in the crook of her elbow. "These are lumps of meat," she says. "Soon, not even that. We aren't what you think. It'd be easier and prettier, but we're stuck with this. One body. One chance. Better make the most of it."

"Even if we get out," Tarasi says, in a voice of receding distance, "how are we going to *be*?"

"When you get to that, you can think and philosophize. Evaluate how you'll get reintegrate into normal life then. Now's not the time."

*   *   *

EIGHTY-SECOND AND HADUAN falls.

Not to one of the metal veterans; not even to the desert's relentless will. Perhaps it was meant from the start, the acceleration of his metabolism automatic, and his fate predetermined – the length of its string, the moment of cutting short. He goes on watch. By the time Tarasi relieves him she finds him gobbling up sand by the fistful.

She tries to stop, reverse his course; she slaps him and pounds his back. It is pointless. When Isyavan joins them she only watches, her mouth closed, her expression occluded by the sheath of artifice that turns her apparent surface to rough clay. Haduan doesn't last. No amount of implants can harden a body against ingesting the desert directly, in such quantity.

Isyavan takes only his brain. Tarasi doesn't cry – they've been modified to squander as little fluid as possible, stoppered glands and redirected sweat. Efficient and self-contained. In any case she is above weakness. Their commander didn't drive her to weep, and Haduan wouldn't. Be here long enough and all feelings are polished off until the mind is stone-smooth, the face a mannequin's.

Down to two of them, the carrier is empty. It pushes inexorably on. To leave it is to be left behind, without map or navigation, with no sense of direction but the twitching tendons of memory. Those may not be trusted.

Down to two of them, Tarasi finally speaks what she's always swallowed back until it lodges deep in her stomach, growing heavy and tumorous. "At the end of this, we will be extracted. Won't we?"

"In eight days the carrier stops and puts us at the rendezvous point. In theory, there'll be a shuttle and it will fly us out. We will get medical attention if required. We'll get financial compensation, enough to set us up modestly; if they're feeling generous the two of us will receive the stipend originally due the entire squad." Isyavan's sheathing has retracted, leaving her unarmored. Her face is only slightly less unfeeling than her respiratory mask. Her vital rhythms are even, machine-regular. "It's all in the documents we signed. You read them back to back like the rest of us did, I'm sure. Paying attention to all the minutiae and clauses, like any good academic."

"This close to the end you might as well –" Tarasi shudders, steadies. "You owe us."

Isyavan's hands close. Open. A mesh of reinforcement over fingers and knuckles and palms, not quite gloves, not entirely melded with skin. Out of the desert they will have to be cut open again, the obvious protective shielding sloughed off, their nervous and digestive systems rewired a second time to normal. For a certain definition. "Those old engines." A twitch of fingers: nerves, fear, a tic. "They're used to following orders. The way we transmit back home fits the communication patterns these relics knew. So they come to us looking for guidance; that's why they have picked up bits of us, a voice here, a memory there. Just fragments, though. People can't exist as data. That's wishful thinking, an ancient fantasy. We'll never outlast our flesh. When that ends, so do we."

Tarasi does not begin to protest that Isyavan should have told them that long ago; she does not begin to feel disappointment, rage, betrayal. Now is not the time. It's never the time for anything here but the resolve to exist: another breath drawn, another dawn met. "Then they should tag us friendlies."

"To them – and understand, this is by design – our weapon and maintenance signatures match hostile parameters. It confuses them, and in the face of ambiguity they're hardcoded to attack." Isyavan's hands flex, curling. "I helped outline the project, develop some of the protocols that make us both their commanders and their targets. Without that, we would have been able to just walk through the dunes unmolested and there wouldn't have been much of a test for our augmentations. They hunt and scavenge each other for spare parts; what would they care about human trespassers? *Their* war was long over."

"And *you* are here –"

"As punishment. Perhaps I came to an ideological crisis, could no longer ignore my conscience. Perhaps they sent into the desert someone I cared about instead of faceless convicts, the way it was supposed to be. Make up your own reason, Tarasi, and pick the most romantic if that helps."

The intake of Tarasi's breath is the sound of razors sliding open silk. "They've never gone for you first. It seemed like incredible luck, but that's why we all followed you."

"After taking hostile action I'm a target, like anyone else. And the first ten days I was a target period, like the rest of you. It took time to reverse-engineer." Isyavan glances, sideways. "You don't seem outraged."

Tarasi has turned her gaze elsewhere, sight joined umbilical to the carrier's cameras. Which see nothing, only its own shadows and exhaust tracks. "One body, one chance. You're the best odds I have left. I'll take that. Except you never needed us, did you? From the eleventh day if you'd just let us die, it would have been easier for you."

"It wouldn't have. You're wrong about that. I'm only human."

They take turns on the carrier's roof, waiting out the tranquil ruinscape, surface tension hiding teeth like inevitability, harboring armed chassis older than memory.

When the sand disgorges the next monster, it is a nightmare of Rimael's laughter and Haduan's dreams. Patchwork put together from transmitted communications, from the life *before* that Haduan remembered in his sleep and kept to himself, broadcast now in the clear. So they see, as they dismantle limbs from muzzle and carve open armor, simple sunlit moments. Breakfast in an office, the sound of rustling paperwork; he was more desk officer than anything else. There is no convenient shorthand – they are not shown intimate fragments of family, formative segments of childhood, something wrenching at the heart.

But even if they have been, nothing finds purchase on the sheer, frictionless carapace of Isyavan's will. Sometimes Tarasi thinks she is not so unlike the desert; that Isyavan belongs here, was born to be its match, honed to be its voice.

EIGHTY-SIXTH WHEN TARASI breaks.

The epidermal shell, first, cracking in the way of brittle clay and bone gone to osteoporosis. Isyavan notices almost before Tarasi does, says, "Stay in here."

Looking down at herself, Tarasi begins to shake. Stops herself, pulls back.

"Four days. You can make it."

"Is this just delayed – is it a killswitch?"

"I don't know." Isyavan thumbs the roof open. The watch will be hers alone, now. "I don't know everything. I never did."

Tarasi doesn't last four days. Rapid atrophy, faulty implant site, a misaligned muscle enhancement. Isotopic exposure catching up. All of those. They will never know; the diagnostics they send are encrypted, not meant for them to read. Neither their bodies or their sickness are their own. Isyavan thinks of holding Tarasi's hand as her stomach fills with amber and her lungs fold in on themselves. She has heard that some animals, toward death, seek solitude so the end will come in peace and dignity. Perhaps that will be more appropriate; it's how she envisions her own. Company will make it no easier. So on the roof she stays, as night falls down a funeral shroud.

A storm begins after Tarasi has ended. It never looks the same way twice; the phenomenon interferes with their receptors, their communication bands. Must do the same to the engines that have made this land their graveyard and hunting ground, but more so. Unlike them Isyavan knows the sky does not turn quite this shimmering red, the sand does not sprout shoots glistening with dew. The hallucinations fade quickly, in any case, and in their wake the world returns to reassuring emptiness.

Down to one, it's easy to feel you are the only reality. Isyavan takes out the pieces she has collected, the shards, the boxed brains and shelled hearts. Her name is written on them, a load of code, a kernel of instruction fashioned and etched over the months. With sufficient determination everything can be reverse-engineered, and a twist of cybernetics or loop of memory module has after all been made to bear data. She merely needed to overwrite.

She throws them out far and wide, sowing a crop of soldiers that never were.

NINETIETH AND THE shuttle comes, as promised. This is the one vow unbroken, the one contract fulfilled. It is gunmetal black, a rip in the pure bright pennant of sky. The carrier, in turn, has powered down. Nothing will restart it, though Isyavan doesn't try. Instead she stretches full length on its roof, and calls.

At the moment of freedom, the desert grants a choice.

While it is true the mind does not outlast the flesh, even Isyavan understands the value of remembering. And so when the shuttle touches down, the old veterans come humming the commander's tune, laughing the way Rimael did, talking in Tarasi's voice, and dreaming Haduan's past. The flowers of Isyavan's planting, fast to spring and bud and bloom.

They rise on cabled tendons and armored limbs, twined to her will, eager to follow and obey.

She stands, and all of them are with her, the verity of killing lodged in her like a second heart.

SIMON INGS

DRONES

SIMON INGS

DRONES

THERE'S A RAIL link, obviously, connecting this liminal place to the coast at Whitstable, but the mayor and his entourage will arrive by boat. It's more dramatic that way. Representatives of the airfield construction crews are lined up to greet him. Engineers in hard hats and dayglo orange overalls. Local politicians too, of course. Even those who bitterly opposed this thing's construction are here for its dedication. The place is a fact now, so they may as well bless it, and in their turn, be blessed.

It's early morning, and bitterly cold. Still, the spring light, glinting off glossy black tarmac and the glass curtain walls of the terminal buildings, is magnificent.

I'm muscling some room for my nephews at the rail of the observation deck, and even up here it's hard to see the sea. A critical press has made much of the defences required to protect this project from the Channel's ever more frequent swells. But the engineering is not as chromed or as special as it's been made out to be: this business of reclaiming land from the sea and, where necessary, giving it back again ("managed retreat", they call it), is an old one. It's practically a folk art round here, setting aside this project's industrial scale.

The mayor's barge is in view. It docks in seconds. None of that aching, foot-tap delay. This ship's got jets in place of propellers and it slides into its decorated niche (Scots blue and English red and white) as neatly as if it were steered there by the hand of a giant child.

My nephews tug at my hands, one on each, as if they'd propel me down to deck level: a tempted Jesus toppling off the cliff, his landing softened by attendant angels. It is a strange moment. For a second I picture myself elderly, the boys grown men, propping me up. Sentiment's ambushed me a lot this year. I was engaged to be married once. But the wedding fell through. The girl went to be a trophy for some party bigwig I hardly know. Like most men, then, I'll not marry now. I'll have no kids. Past thirty now, I'm on the shelf. And while it is an ordinary thing, and no great shame, it hurts, more than I thought it would. When I was young and leant my shoulder for the first time to the civic wheel, I'd entertained no thought of children.

The mayor's abroad among the builders now. They cheer and wheel around him as he waves. His hair is wild, a human dandelion clock, his heavy frame's a vessel, wallowing. He smiles. He waves.

A man in whites approaches, a pint of beer – of London Pride, of course – on a silver tray. The crowd is cheering. I am cheering, and the boys. Why would we not? Politics aside, it is a splendid thing. This place. This moment. Our mayor fills his mouth with beer and wheels around – belly big, and such small feet – spraying the crowd. The anointed hop around, their dignity quite gone, ecstatic. Around me, there's a groan of pop-idol yearning, showing me I'm not alone in wishing that the mayor had spat at me.

IT'S FOUR BY the time we're on the road back to Hampshire and home. The boys are of an age where they are growing curious. And something of my recent nostalgia-fuelled moodiness must have found its way out in words, because here it comes: "So have you had a girl?"

"It's not my place. Or yours."

"But you were going to wed."

The truth is that, like most of us, I serve the commons better out of bed. I've not been spat on, but I've drunk the Mayor of London's piss a thousand times, hardly dilute, fresh from the sterile beaker: proof of the mayor's regard for my work, and for all in Immigration.

The boys worry at the problem of my virginity as at a stubborn shoelace. Only children seem perturbed, still, by the speed of our nation's social transformation, though there's no great secret about it. It is an ordinary thing, to prize the common good, when food is scarce, and we must husband what we have, and guard ourselves against competitors. The scrumpy raids of the apple-thieving French. Belgian rape oil-tappers sneaking in at dusk along the Alde and the Ore in shallow craft. Predatory bloods with their fruit baskets climbing the wires and dodging the mines of the M25 London Orbital.

Kent's the nation's garden still, for all its bees are dead, and we defend it as best we can, with tasers and wire-and-paper drones, klaxons, and farmer's sons gone vigilante, semi-legal, badged with the crest while warned to do no Actual Bodily Harm.

("Here, drink the mayoral blessing! The apple harvest's saved!" I take the piss into my mouth and spray. The young lads at their screens jump up and cheer, slap backs, come scampering over for that touch of divine wet. Only children find this strange. The rest of us, if I am –and why would I not be?– are more relieved, I think, rid at last of all the empty and selfish promises of our former estate.)

So then. Hands on wheel. Eye to the mirrors. Brain racing. I make my Important Reply:

"One man can seed a hundred women." Like embarrassed grown-ups everywhere, I seek solace in the science. This'll fox them, this'll stop their questions. "And so, within a very little time, we are all brothers."

"And sisters."

"Sisters too, sometimes." This I'll allow. "And so, being kin, we have no need to breed stock of our own, being that our genes are shared among our brothers. We'll look instead after our kin, feed and protect our mayor, give him our girls, receive his blessing."

"Like the bees."

Yes. "Like the bees we killed."

In northern Asia, where food's not quite so scarce, they laugh at us, I think, and how we've changed – great, venerated Europe! – its values adapting now to a new, less flavoursome environment. ("Come. Eat your gruel. Corn syrup's in the jar.") They are wrong to laugh. The irony of our estate is not lost on us. We know what we've become, and why. From this vantage, we can see the lives we led before for what they were: lonely, and selfish, and without respect.

Chichester's towers blink neon pink against the dying day. It's been a good excursion, all told, this airfield opening.

Memorable, and even fun, for all the queues and waiting. It's not every day you see your mayor.

"How come we killed the bees?"

"An accident, of course. Bill, no one meant to kill the bees."

Bill takes it hard, this loss of natural help. It fascinates him, why the bond of millennia should have sheared. Why this interest in bees? Partly it's because he's being taught about them in school. Partly it's because he has an eye for living things. Mostly, though, it's because his dad, my brother, armed with a chicken feather dipped in pollen mix, fell out of an apple tree on our estate and broke his neck. Survived, but lives in pain. Poor Ned: the closest of my fifty kin.

"We spray for pests, and no single spray did for the bees, but combinations we could not predict or model with our science." True. The world is rich and vast and monstrously fed back into itself. Science works well enough in a lab, but it is so small, so very vulnerable, the day you lay it open to the world.

The towns slip by. Hands on the wheel. An eye to the mirrors. Waterlooville. Havant. Home. Dad's wives at the farmhouse windows wave, and Dad himself comes to the door. Retired now, the farm all passed to Ned. But Dad is still our centre and our figurehead.

I ask after my brother.

Dad smiles his sorry little smile, "It's been good for him, I think, today. The rest. Reading in the sun."

"I'm glad."

The old man leans and spits a benediction on my forehead. "And you?"

* * *

IN AN EMPTY cinema, seats lower themselves in readiness for their customers.

An orchestra sits, frozen, the musicians as poised as shop dummies, freighted with uncanny intent.

Two needles approach each other. Light sparks and blooms between their points, filling the screen.

A cameraman lies across a railway track, filming the approach of a locomotive. The man rolls out the way of the train at the last second but one foot still lies across the rail. Carriages whizz and rock and intersect at all angles: violent, slicing motions fill the screen.

A young woman starts out of nightmare, slides from her bed and begins to dress.

I paused the video (this was years ago, and we were deep in the toil of our country's many changes) and I went into the hall to answer the phone. My brother, Ned (all hale and hearty back then, with no taste for apples and no anxiety about bees), had picked up an earlier train; he was already at Portsmouth Harbour station.

"I'll be twenty minutes," I said.

Back in those days, Portsmouth Harbour station was all wood and glass and dilapidated almost beyond saving. "Like something out of *Brief Encounter*," Ned joked, hugging me.

1945. Trevor Howard holds Celia Johnson by the waist, says goodbye to her on just such a platform as this.

We watched many old films back then, and for the obvious reason. Old appetites being slow to die, Ned and I craved them for their women. Their vulnerable eyes, and well-turned calves and all the tragedy in their pretty words. A new breed of state censor, grown up to this new, virtually womanless world, and aggressive in its defence, was robbing us of female imagery wherever it could. But even the BBFC would not touch David Lean.

Southsea's vast shingle beach was a short walk away. The rip-tides were immense here, heaving the stones eastwards, and impressive wooden groynes split the beach into great high-sided boxes to conserve it.

In his donkey jacket and cracked DMs, Ned might have tumbled out of the old Russian film I'd been watching. (A woman slides from her bed, naked, and begins, unselfconsciously, to dress.) "We're digging a villa," he told me, as we slid and staggered over the shingle. Ned was the bright one, the one who'd gone away to study. "A bloody joke, it is." He had a way of describing the niceties of archaeological excavation – which features to explore, which to record, which to dig away – that made it sound as if he was jobbing on a building site. And it is true that his experiences had weathered and roughened him.

I wondered if this modest but telling transformation was typical. We rarely saw our other brothers, many as they were. The three eldest held down jobs in the construction of the London Britannia airport; back then just 'Boris Island', and a series of towers connected by gantries, rising out of the unpromisingly named Shivering Sands. Robert had moved to Scarborough and worked for the coast guard. The rest had found work out of the country, in Jakarta and Kuala Lumpur and poor Liam in Dubai. The money they sent back paid for Ned's education, Dad's plan being to line up our family's youngest for careers in government service. I imagined my brothers all sun-burnished and toughened by their work. Me? Back then I was a very minor observations man, flying recycled plastic drones out of Portsmouth Airport on the Hampshire coast. This was a government job in name only. It was locally run; more of a vigilante effort, truth be told. This made me, at best, a very minor second string in Dad's meticulously orchestrated family.

It did, though – after money sent home – earn me enough to rent a conversion flat in one of those wedding cake-white Georgian terraces that look out over Southsea's esplanade. The inside was ordinary, all white emulsion and wheatmeal carpeting, until spring came, and sunlight came blazing through the bay window, turning the whole of my front room to candy and icing sugar.

"Beautiful."

It was the last thing I expected Ned to say.

"It's bloody beautiful."

"It's not bad."

"You should see my shithole," Ned said, with a brutal satisfaction.

At the time I thought he was just being pretentious. I realise now – and of course far too late – that brute nil-rhetoric was his way of expressing what was, in the millennial atmosphere of those post-feminine days, becoming inexpressible: their horror.

I do not think this word is too strong. Uncovering the graves of little girls, hundreds and hundreds, was a hazard of Ned's occupation. Babies mostly; a few grown children though. The business was not so much hidden as ignored. That winter I'd gone to Newcastle for a film festival; the nunneries there had erected towers in the public parks for people to leave a child. Babies survived at least a couple of days, exposed to the rain and cold. Nobody paid any attention.

Ned's job was to enter construction sites during the phase of demolition, and see what was to be gleaned of the nation's past before the construction crews moved in, turfing it over with rebar and cement. Of course the past is invented, more than uncovered. You see what you are primed to see. No one wants to find a boat, because boats are the very devil to conserve and take an age to dig, delaying everyone. Graves are a minor problem in comparison, there are so many of them. The whole of London Bridge rises above the level of the Thames on human bones.

Whenever his digs struck recent graves, Ned's job was to obliterate them. Hence, his pose: corporation worker. Glorified refuse man. Hence his government career: since power accretes to those who know – in this case, quite literally – where the bodies are buried.

Why should it have been women, and women alone, that succumbed to the apian plague – this dying breed's quite literal sting in the tail? A thousand conspiracy theories, even now, shield us from the obvious and unpalatable truth: that the world is vast, and monstrously infolded, and we cannot, will not, will not ever know.

And while the rest of us were taken up with our great social transformation, it fell to such men as Ned – gardeners, builders, miners, archaeologists – to deal with the sloughed-off stuff. The bones and skin.

Not secret; and at the same time, not spoken of: the way we turned misfortune into social practice, and practice, at last, into technology. The apian plague is gone long since, dead with the bees that carried it. But, growing used to this dispensation, we have made analogues for it, so girls stay rare. Resources shrinking as they do, there's not a place on earth now does not harbour infanticides. In England in medieval times we waited till the sun was set then lay across our newborn girls to smother them. Then, too, food was short, and dowries dear.

Something banged my living room wall, hard. I turned to see the mirror I had hung, just a couple of days before, rocking on its wire. Another blow, and the mirror rocked and knocked against the wall.

"Hey."

My whole flat trembled as blow after blow rained down on the wall.

"Hey!"

Next door was normally so quiet, I had almost forgotten its existence. The feeling of splendid isolation I had enjoyed since moving in here fell away: I couldn't figure out who it could be, hammering with such force. Were they moving furniture in there? Fixing cupboards?

The next blow was stronger still. A crack ran up the wall from floor to ceiling. I leapt up. "Stop it. Stop." Another blow, and the crack widened. I stepped back and the backs of my knees touched the edge of the sofa and I sat down, nerveless, too disorientated to feel afraid. A second, diagonal crack opened up, met a hidden obstacle, and ran vertically up to the ceiling.

The room's plaster coving, leaves and acorns and roses, snapped and crazed. A piece of stucco fell to the floor.

I didn't understand what was happening. The wall was brick, I knew it was brick because I'd hung a mirror on it not two days before. But chunks of plasterboard were peeling back under repeated blows, revealing a wall made of balled-up sheets of newspaper. They flowed into the room on top of the plasterboard. Ned put his arms around me. I was afraid to look at him: to see him as helpless as I was. Anyway, I couldn't tear my gaze from the wall.

Behind the newspaper was a wooden panel nailed over with batons. It was a door, or had been: there was no handle. The doorframe had split along its length and something was trying to force it open against the pile of plasterboard and batons already piled on the carpet. The room filled with pink-grey dust as the door swung in. The space beyond was the colour of old blood.

From out of the darkness, a grey figure emerged. It was no bigger than a child. It came through the wall, into my room. It was grey and covered in dust. Its face was a mask, strangely swollen: a bladder pulling away from the bone.

She spoke. She was very old. "What are you doing in my house?"

MY LANDLORD CAME round the same evening. By then Ned and I had gathered from his grandmother – communicating haphazardly through the fog of her dementia – that my living room and hers had once been a single, huge room. Her property. The house she grew up in. The property had been split in half years ago; long before my half had been subdivided to make flats.

The landlord said: "She must have remembered the door."

"She certainly must have."

He was embarrassed, and embarrassment made him aggressive. He seemed to think that because we were young, his mother's demolition derby must have been partly our fault. "If she heard noises through the wall, it will have confused her."

"I don't make noises through the wall. Neither am I going to tiptoe around my own flat."

He took her home. When they were gone Ned and I went to the pub. We drank beer (Old Speckled Hen) and Ned said: "How many years do you think they left that poor cow stranded there, getting steadily more unhinged?"

"For all I know he's round there every day looking after her."

"You don't really believe that."

"Why not?" I looked at my watch. "He probably thinks it's the best place for her. The house she grew up in."

"You saw what she was like."

"Old people know their own minds."

"While they still have them."

Back home, Ned went to bed, exhausted. I brought a spare duvet into the living room for myself, poured myself a whisky and settled down to watch the rest of *Man With a Movie Camera*. (Dziga Vertov, 1929.) When it was over I turned off the television and the lamp.

The hole in my wall was a neat oblong, black against the dim grey-orange of the wall. Though the handles had been removed, the door still had its mechanism. The pin still just about caught, holding the door shut against its frame. Already I was finding it hard to imagine the wall without that door.

I went into the kitchen and dug out an old knife, its point snapped off long before. I tried the knife in the hole where the handle had been and turned. Pinching my fingertips into the gap between the door and the frame, I pulled the door towards me.

The air beyond tasted thick, like wax. The smell – it had been lingering around my flat all day – was her smell. Fusty, and speaking of decay, it was, nevertheless, not unpleasant.

A red glow suffused the room. Light from a streetlamp easily penetrated the thin red material of her curtains: I could make out their outline very easily. The red-filtered light was enough that I could navigate around the room. It was stuffed full of furniture and the air was heavy with furniture wax. A chair was drawn up in front of a heavy sideboard, filling the space created by a bay window.

I ran my hand along the top of the sideboard. It was slick and clean and my hand came away smelling of resin. In her confusion, the old woman had still managed to keep her things spotless – unless someone had been coming and cleaning around her.

How many hours had she spent in this red, resined room? How many years?

I pulled the chair out of the way – its legs dragged on the thick rug – and opened a door of the sideboard.

It was filled with jars, and when I held one up to the red light coming through the curtains, the contents admitted one tawny, diagonal blear before resolving to black.

DAD WAS ALL for clearing out the lot. He had a van, his man could drive, they'd be in and out within the night. Such were the times, after all, and what great family is not founded on the adventures of a buccaneer?

But I had a youth's hope, and told him no: that we should play the long game. I can't imagine what I was thinking: that they would show some generosity to me, perhaps, for not stealing their property? Ridiculous.

Still, Dad let me have my head. Still, somehow, my gamble paid off. The landlord, whose family name was Franklin, hardly showered me with riches, but he turned out friendly enough, and the following spring, at his grandmother's funeral, I met his daughters.

The match with Belinda – what a name! – was easy enough to arrange. The dowry would be a generous one. Pear orchards and plum trees, hops and brassicas and the young men to tend them. The whole business fell through, as I have said, but the friendship between our families held. When Ned ran into political trouble he gave up his career and came home to run things for Dad. It was to him Franklin gave his youngest child, my nephews' mum. (Melissa. What a name.)

The rest is ordinary. Ned has run our estate successfully over the years, has taken mistresses and made some of them wives, and filled the house with sons. Of them, the two eldest are my special treasure, since I'll have no kids myself. Every once in a while a brother of ours returns to take a hand in the making of our home. They bring us strange stories; of how the world is being set to rights. By a river in the Minas Gerais somewhere, someone has reinvented the dolphin. But it is orange, and it keeps sinking.

Poor Liam's still languishing in Dubai, but the rest of us, piling in to exploit what we collectively know of the labour market, have done better than well.

As for me: well, what with one promotion and then another, this offshore London Britannia airfield has become my private empire. Three hundred observation drones. Fifty attack quadcopters. Six strike UAVs. There are eight thousand miles of coastline to protect, a hungry neighbour to the west famining on potatoes; to the east, a continent's-worth of peckish privateers. It is a busy time.

Each spring we all pile back onto the estate, of course, to help with pollination. Tinkerers all, we experiment sometimes with boxes of mechanical bees, imported at swingeing cost from Shenzhen or Macao. But nothing works as well as a chicken feather wielded by a practised hand. This is how Ned, the scion of our line, came to plummet from the topmost rung of his ladder. The sons he had been teaching screamed, and from where I sat, stirring drying pots on the kitchen table, the first thing that struck me was how they sounded just like girls.

DAD LEADS ME in. Much fuss is made of me. The boys vie with each other to tell their little brothers about the day, the airfield, the mayor. While Dad's women are cooing over them, I go through to the yard.

Ned is sitting where he usually sits on sunny days like these, in the shelter of the main greenhouse, with a view of our plum trees. They, more than any other crop, have made our family rich, and it occurs to me with a lurch, seeing my brother slumped there in his chair under rugs, that it is not the sight of their fruit that has him enthralled. He is watching the walls. He is watching the gate. He is guarding our trees. There's a gun by his side. A shotgun. We only ever fill the cartridges with rock salt. But still.

Ned sees me and smiles and beckons me to the bench beside him. "It's time," he says.

I knew this was coming.

"I can't pretend I can do this anymore. Look at me. Look."

I say what you have to say in these situations. Deep down, though, I can only assent. There's a lump in my throat. "I haven't earned this."

But Ned and I, we have always been close, and who else should he turn to, in his pain and disability and growing weakness? Who else should he hand the business to?

The farm will be mine. Melissa. The boys. All of it mine. Everything I ever wanted, though it has never been my place to take a single pip. It is being given to me freely, now. A life. A family. As if I deserved it!

"Think of the line," says Ned, against my words of protest. "The sons I'll never have."

We need sons, heaven knows. Young guns to hold our beachheads against the French. Keepers to protect our crop from night-stealing London boys. Swords to fight the feuds that, quite as much a marriage pacts, shape our living in this hungry world.

It is no use. I have no head for politics. Try as I might, I cannot think of sons, but only of their making. Celia Johnson with a speck of grit in her eye. Underwear and a bed of dreams. May God forgive me, I am that depraved, my every thought is sex.

Ned laughs. He knows, and has always known, of my weakness. My interest in women. It is, for all the changes our world's been through, still not an easy thing, for men to turn their backs on all the prospects a wife affords.

"Pick me a plum," my brother says. So I go pick a plum. Men have been shot for less. With rock salt, yes. But still.

I remember the night we chose, Ned and I, not to raid the larder of the poor, confused old woman who had burst into my room. Perhaps it was simply the strangeness of the day that stopped us. (We stole one jar and left the rest alone.) I would like to think, though, that our forbearance sprang from some simple, instinct of our own. Call it decency.

It is hard, in such revolutionary times, always to feel good about oneself.

"Here," I say, returning to my crippled benefactor, the plum nursed in my hands.

Ned's look, as he pushes the fruit into his mouth, is the same look he gave me the night we tasted, ate, and finished entirely, that jar of priceless, finite honey. Pleasure. Mischief. God help us all: youth.

Ten, twelve years on, Ned's enjoying another one-time treat: he chews a plum. A fruit that might have decked the table of the mayor himself, and earned our boys a month of crusts. He spits the stone into the dust. Among our parsimonious lot, this amounts to a desperate display of power: Ned knows that he is dying.

I wonder how it tastes, that plum—and Ned, being Ned, sees and knows it all: my shamefaced ambition. My inexcusable excitement. To know so much is to excuse so much, I guess, because he beckons me, my brother and my friend, and once I'm knelt before him, spits that heavy, sweet paste straight into my mouth. And makes me king.

KAMERON HURLEY
BODY POLITIC

Kameron Hurley
BODY POLITIC

Interrogation: Narsis

WHEN MY SUITS bring the wayward agents in, Lisha strips them naked, bare, except for a blinder of organic mesh – try to rip it off and you'll rip off your own face. You put the agent inside a filter you tell them is set to disintegrate them. Make them squat on their haunches until the muscles of their bodies shudder, and they make those little mewling sounds, those hiccupping sobs of pre-language.

This is interrogation, body politic. This is my job.

I get names. Who took them off their meds, who turned them against Defense. Are you Opposition? Against organics? Who gave your orders?

It's always the same name.

Keli.

Keli is afraid of three things, they tell me:

Needles, women and knives.

But no one can find him.

When I get back to my room in the barracks, step through my own filter, it cleans me of agents' blood.

Then I vomit into the sink.

I vomit every time.

I have more metal promotion loops in my ears than any of the other Suits. I've been on oral meds and injections for years. Helps with the job, Defense tells me. They bred me to do what I do, they say, and the meds are perfecting me for it, they say, but I don't feel perfected to it. I feel obligated to it. There's a difference.

THEN ONE DAY we start losing our systems. Me, Flire, Mesta and three of the other Suits. All of our case files come up empty.

Somebody calls in a click/agent pair to jack in and fix it. The click/agent pair – the agent dark and tall like a Suit, the click small and pale and too-thin – work for an hour. The agent jacks the click into my system and inserts his jack-in knife into one of the fleshy openings on the click's wrist so he can translate for me. My system has crashed, he tells me; like a bird.

The next day, all the interrogation systems are down too.

Keli is having a laugh at us, I bet.

I go back to the click/agent pair. The agent trembles when I override the filter that protects his doorway. He starts screaming even before I touch him. I tell Lisha to haul out this agent's click from the Kettering compound.

Interrogation. The only thing I know. When a new click jacks in and something else comes crashing down, someone needs to ask the questions.

She gives me a four-letter name, the same name: Keli.

I bleed the agent and her click across my boots.

I go home. I don't make it to the sink before I vomit.

* * *

THE SUMMONS COMES after I interrogate the fourteenth of Keli's turned agents.

Defense puts me in a dark little conference room with the bubble-haze of another filter over it, programmed to allow only us in. There's a ceiling of twisted blue glass, and glow worms pulse inside of it, shedding blue-filtered light. Inside the filter there's only me and two Defense Suits.

I sit at a square table dipped in chalk blue.

They stand. They always stand. They're bigger than even me, tall and broad-shouldered, black hair, black eyes. I can never tell them apart.

"You have the name of the one causing these problems," the one on the right says, "yet you have not located him."

"He's outside the realm of my authority," I say. Meaning he's just a name. He could be anyone, anything, nothing.

Right says, "We have someone whose authority he may be more familiar with."

Left pulls out a case file from the deep reaches of the black coat, sets the file at the center of the desk.

I pull out the blank pages, press my palm to the first page, watch words bleed out.

"We've acquired a click from the Liberation of Jabow," Right says. "We emptied the prison camps and brought back one of theirs. Ready to work for us now."

I skim the text. He's some genetic anomaly, splicing experimentation, forced starvation, selective breeding, but no organic technologies. No weapons breeding.

"I thought Jabow was a weapons-breeding compound," I say.

"I thought we were getting a hold of their weapons tech with that raid, not just some smart kid."

"His name is Jan," Left says.

"A click, then?" I say.

I look up, into two pairs of black eyes.

"I can find Keli on my own," I say.

Left and Right exchange black glances.

Right says: "You have three days to find Keli. After three days, the Council will have an end to this. It ends with the purging of Keli. Or the purging of you. You understand."

I understand. I know all about spilling someone else's blood to purge my own ghosts.

Disinterred: Jan

MY FACE IN the palm of my hand: I dream in chalky blues and red. I can't eat, my throat won't swallow, so they hook me up to tubing, drip drip drip.

I can see the strings around us all now; they're silky, wormy, organic, just like the rest of their tech. They call it tech. I call it slavery.

I dream of cats, cats curling around me, warm, purring. Soothing me to sleep. I can eat again. Some soup. Suit soup. I like to say that out loud sometimes now, I don't know why: a soup of Suits.

The nurse helps me out of bed, and walks me in the garden. There's a physical shield over the garden, she says, not an organic one, since their organics make me so sick. There's a high wall around the garden. I can't see over it. There are spikes at the top, long as my fingers, silver spikes. All of the plants are tall and big and leafy.

The nurse is afraid of me. No one else comes into the house. They are still leaving me books, Opposition texts. They want me to do something for them, to do what I did in Jabow before they destroyed everything, before I was put into the hole. But I still tear out all of the pages. I eat them.

I sleep, and my dreams are cats' dreams. I sleep all day, twenty-eight hours, sleep and I'm still tired. They have cleaned out the bacteria from the water, all of the water, in the basin and tub and toilet. My rash is gone. The boils have scarred over.

They are here.

I wake up. I am shaking.

I hear footsteps, a new voice.

A figure turning into my doorway, black, all in black, with skin of burnished brown and black black hair and black black eyes. It's one of them. The Suits. They will burn this place down again, burn it down and twist me open...

The Suit looks at me. Her eyes are big, her body tense. "I'm licensed to interrogate you," the Suit says. "Interrogation," she says, louder.

"You are the one who stirs the Suits," I say.

I see her hands shake. She puts them in her pockets. She is tall and broad like the men in Jabow who tried to destroy me, and her face is square and straight with lines at the eyes, there, just where they close. She has to close her eyes more than most people. I can see that.

But she does not close her eyes at me.

Systems: Narsis

HE? IT? WAR criminal. Prison camps. How long they kept him there with the other prisoners in Jabow before they realized what he was, I don't know. It wasn't in the case file.

I should have expected him to look like this, skin over bone, hollowed cheeks, shaved head – looks too big for his body, a bobbing melon on a stick. But it is the eyes that pull me. Big, blue-green, with long, black lashes. That pairing, big eyes and long lashes, is boyishly coy; alluring, attractive in this emaciated body of which nothing can be boyish or coy.

"I am Jan," he says.

I want to touch him, to see if he's really alive. Can you be that skinny and be alive? Where do you keep all of your internal organs?

"Narsis," I say.

The too-big head bobs.

Silence again.

"I'm told that you were bred by the Opposition," I say, finally. "You were bred to be an organic communications hub."

The lids close over the eyes, the lashes flutter. He looks at me again. I want him to keep looking at me.

"I studied systems," Jan says. "The cyclical nature of universal systems. When you look up at the stars, you're only seeing systems, complex relationships between bodies of mass identical in make-up, mutation and construction to the smaller internal systems within the body."

I wanted to tell him he didn't study systems, he *was* a system, but it was likely the Opposition never told him that.

I think about blindfolds and Lisha and broken bones, bruised bodies. Interrogation will kill this little bird. And he's mad, broken to pieces.

"When you look out at the universe, all you see is yourself, looking in," Jan says. "Cyclical systems. Abbreviated, simplified version. We were still working out the mathematics. And then they killed the cats."

"The cats," I say.

He is twisted up in his sheets so tightly I think he's cutting off the circulation to all the limbs of his body.

He leans toward me as far as he can in the bundle of sheets and says, "Ask them about the cats."

I am wasting my time. I turn to go, leave my back to him, stride to the doorway.

"You vomit afterwards."

I stop. I wait until I'm sure he's not going to say anything else. I turn. He's staring at me, little hands still fisted in the sheets.

"Ask them about the cats," Jan says. He buries his head into the pillows.

I walk out into the hall, still shaking, and I have to grab onto the edge of the kitchen table to catch my balance. The nurse is talking to me. I can hear her voice, but it's muted, distant, and I'm breathing too fast. I vomit

The nurse is grabbing me with her fleshy hands. She has a needle in her hand. I hate needles. She sits me down into a chair, and I'm still shaking. I ask for kaj, but when she gives me some I choke on it and spit it back into my palm, bloody red.

Liberation: Narsis

I SLEEP FOR twelve hours. All of my case files are on my crashed system, destroyed by the dirty click. So I chew enough kaj to numb all sense and go upstairs to ask for Defense. They give me two new Defense Suits and sit me down in the conference room.

The haze of the filter makes me dizzy.

"The cats," I say.

The new Left and Right look at one another.

"They're an unknown," Left says. "We have yet to ascertain the exact nature of their function. The Liberation party found him with cats."

"How many?" I say.

"Four," Left says.

Right says, "The Liberation party found him in a steel room built into the ground and sealed in by a steel escape hatch. Opposition put him there when their lines broke six months before, hoping to hide him until they could come back for him."

"Did he eat the cats?" I say.

Right frowns at me. "Of course not."

"The Liberation party killed them," Left says. "He wouldn't leave without the cats. We'll give you the relevant case file."

"My system's down."

"Get a click to store them for you," Left says.

"I don't work with clicks," I say.

"What do you think he is?" Left says. "He's their version of click, a system on his own, without having to jack in. He's connected to everything already, or he was supposed to be, before we broke Opposition's lines and they withdrew from Jabow. There isn't a security measure we've devised that can stop him. He's brimming with data. The identity of your troublesome rebel should be easy, if he could sort it from the rest."

"But he doesn't need an agent to direct and translate," I say. "He's both, then. Click and agent?"

"He's something else," Right says, glaring over at Left. "We'll consult on how much information can be released to you."

"We need you to take care of this," Left says, slowly. "Your expertise in the area is… unmatched."

They release another file to me. I don't call in a click to store them for me. I take them to my room and spread them out on the bed. I press my palms to the pages, watch the text bleed out.

Jan, in a hole in the ground for six months, lying stagnant, forgotten, with food and cats and running water and no organic tech. It was all mechanized: electric lighting, water piped in through some kind of pump system. I don't understand much about Opposition tech. What I see is Jan described as they found him: sick-thin, maggot-pale, lying in the center of a metal floor, surrounded by cats. The food had run out two weeks before. The Liberation party tried to move him, but the cats attacked them. "Four big cats, about four or five kilos apiece," the report says. Jan started screaming, and the Liberation party tasered the cats.

Liberation put him into a holding cell with the rest of the prisoners of war for three years until Defense realized what he was and pulled him out for experiments; only a handful of sentences about this part have bled onto the page, bits about neural activity, and massive allergic reactions. Then they brought him to the Kettering compound, sealed him inside his own self-contained unit, and peeled all of the organic tech out of it to curb his violent allergies.

They sealed him in and shut him up, deemed him 'mentally and emotionally unstable for any relevant study until recovery.'

I shake my head and push the files off the bed. I am chasing the words of a mad prisoner, and Keli is turning my agents, and Defense wants me purged if I can't find out who he is. Three days. Not enough.

I try to sleep, but the dreams are bad. I wake up sweating but cold, and I'm out of kaj. I lie in the center of my bed and nod off into a milky half-haze that passes for sleep.

Lisha buzzes me. I sit up and he's standing out in the hall, just outside the sheer filter over my door. I hit the admit switch and the filter light turns green. He walks in, already neatly dressed, black hair slicked back. I check the time. Still six hours until dawn.

His hands are in his pockets, but it's too dark inside my room to see the expression on his face. "Situation," he says.

"Why didn't you send me the data?"

"System's down."

"Your system?"

"Our system. The main system. The hub is down. Everything is down. The entire Defense building and the Kettering compound are blind."

"Fuck," I say, and inside my head, it becomes a litany: fuckfuck fuckfuckfuck.

I'm naked, and I dress in front of Lisha. He steps close and smooths the collar of my coat. This close, I can see his face, the hard, square jaw, the black bruises beneath his eyes, the slight curl of his upper lip. He is all planes and angles.

We walk into the belly of the Defense compound.

The com hub is bubbled by a filter, and two Defense Suits stand outside. They motion me past, tell me I've got clearance, but my skin still prickles as I step through the filter.

Flire and Gri and Mesta are already inside, looking like they haven't slept for three days. They probably haven't. The usual hum of the system is absent, but the clicks are still jacked in all along the circumference of the room. Their agents, a dozen of them, stand at the operations console, answering questions from Gri and Mesta, translating data from the clicks.

Flire beckons me over to the entry shaft leading up into the glutinous tubular guts of the system.

"You found the altered pathways?" I ask.

Flire nods. "Come up and take a look at them," she says. "It's not anything I've seen before."

She leads the way up the rungs of the ladder. There's a platform at the top that overlooks the nest of system tubing, the nexus of the system's brain. I step up next to Flire, and she points out over the mass of greenish tubes to a dark, cancerous growth of black big enough to house at least three click/agent pairs.

"Someone's been injecting saline into these spider veins the past two weeks," Flire says.

"Can you read the signature of who did it?"

"You think this was one of ours?"

"Opposition doesn't know our tech. They'd find a way to burn it or blow it up before mixing a virus. This is internal. We can trace the virus back to its jack-in point." And from there, Flire could just go through the records of jacked-in clicks and see who'd been jacking in there the last two weeks. Easy.

"Narsis!"

I look down at the bottom of the shaft. "Message for you!" Lisha says. "Defense routed Priority."

I climb down, and Lisha hands over the blue Priority paper. Of course it's on paper – the systems are down, but for a moment I can't understand why anyone would send me a paper transmission outside a Defense conference room.

I press my palm to the page, watch blue letters bleed out, only one sentence:

THE CATS SAY THE NAME ISN'T KELI.

Cold creeps up my spine, and despite the kaj I'm chewing, my hands start to shake. I don't need to ask Defense who they routed it from.

I shove the paper deep into my pocket.

I tell Lisha he's got first, just as Gri hands him a jack-in knife for printing.

"Location for recovery?" he says. In case I died on duty.

"Kettering compound," I say.

He hands over the silver jack-in knife. "Drop this by there for printing, then?"

I take the knife by the hilt, slip it into my coat. I have an aversion for jack-in knives, but in this job, I must put up with many things I find abhorrent.

Dense as Blindness: Narsis

THE NURSE DOES not expect me. I find that odd, since Jan can't send transmissions on his own. All our tech is organic. Trying to send a transmission himself would have triggered another violent allergic reaction. He must have sent it through her, but she looks at me as an unwelcome annoyance, a stranger stirring her from sleep.

She takes me to him in her brooding way, and when I walk into his room I see that it's dark. The cold comes back, creeping up my spine, across my shoulders.

"Jan?" I say.

The nurse pushes past me into the room, bringing a candle with her. Yes, a wax and wick candle, the likes of which I've only ever seen in ag compounds. She lights four or five more on the desk by the bed, and I see stacks of texts there, actual paper texts that could only have been made by Opposition. We haven't used that kind of archaic tech in almost a century.

He's staring toward the window on the other side of the room. He is loosely wrapped in his sheets, so all I can see is his shaved head.

"You sent for me," I say.

The nurse shuffles back out into the hallway, but I see her looking back into the room.

"Ask me questions," Jan says, softly. "That's what you do. You ask questions."

"How do you know about Keli?"

"I am the world," Jan says.

"What's his real name? If it isn't Keli... and how do you know?"

"We're all just systems looking out and seeing in."

I'm tired. Flire says she'll have a jack-in point and sig pattern match in less than an hour.

"Did you ask them about the cats?" he says. He is still looking at the window.

"The cats are dead," I say, too loud. "I can haul you down to interrogation, if it comes to that, but we're running out of time."

"Ask me about the cats," he says.

I want to hit him and want to watch the melon head snap off the little bowed stalk of his neck and bounce against the wall.

I walk to the door.

I hope his fucking fat cats screeched when they burned.

I stop. I half-turn.

"How did the cats survive?" I say.

Jan bats his lashes at me. "The cats," he says.

"You lived two weeks without food, there at the end. You were so emaciated you couldn't move. But those cats were strong enough to attack the Liberation party, and they weighed in at four or five kilos apiece."

He smiles, and it's eerie to watch him smile, the skin of his hollow face stretched tight, the leering death mask. "You don't see any strings, do you?" he says. "All those metal loops, but you're blind. We are one thing, one system. What's theirs is mine, mine is theirs. Symbiosis. One thing."

"Why did they leave you in there with cats?"

"I wasn't doing well with people. I had to make connections with other living things. Share information, and matter."

He existed as a communications hub, incapable of interacting with human beings, so they tested him on *cats*?

"You're not functional," I say. Jan's outdated, but even outdated, he's linking things, he's linking to people, he's sending me messages even though he's sitting here with no organic tech... no tech but himself. The words are out of me already, "Keli's a system. Like you. Only he works."

Jan squirms in the bed. I imagine him purring. "You're not so dense as blindness."

"Where is he, this system?" I say.

"He's afraid of you," Jan says.

"Everyone's afraid of me," I say.

I am disgusted with him; this broken, mad thing.

I leave him.

I walk back to the Defense compound, back to the stir of Suits, and I've chewed so much kaj that I'm having trouble walking. I keep putting out my hand to the walls of the corridor for balance, but all I can feel is the pressure, yes, there, and I think that means I'm real, I exist, but I'm not sure.

Flire, Gri, Mesta, and Lisha are all waiting for me. Lisha's at the doorway of the interrogation offices when I come in, and he's immediately at my right hand. He knows. My lips are blood red with kaj.

"Sig pattern match," Flire says, and hands me the system read-out she and Gri and Mesta were huddled over when I came in. I press my fingers together, hard, on either side of the read-out to make sure I won't drop it.

"System's up again?" I say

"For the last half hour," Gri says. She barely comes to my shoulder, and the lines on her fleshy face are still shallow. "A couple of click/agent pairs rerouted through backup pathways. The central core is still down for at least another three days. It's running a lot slower, and Defense is still issuing physical Priority notices for another four hours."

Flire says, "Lisha had Gri and Mesta pick up the click whose sig matched the one at the jack-in point. We also contained the agent. They're in interrogation room one-oh-one."

The click is naked and blindfolded in the cell, and his hair is white, cropped short. He has fleshy openings on his wrists, the back of his neck, and the base of his spine for hooking up with agents and systems.

"You have background on him?" I ask.

Lisha looks at me out of the corner of his eye. I realize it's all probably on the read-out in my hand.

"Usual for a click," Lisha says. "Raised in the compound. Pelan's his first agent, and her Suit overseers gave them a long-term pairing."

"How does Kel feel about that?"

"He's a click. He's not allowed to feel anything about it."

"So we have breeding records on Kel going back to the breeding compounds," I say. "We have a mixer's report detailing his mixing, conception, and birth?"

"Just like every other click," Lisha says.

Something isn't right.

"Relationships with any of the other interrogated clicks?"

"All cressin clicks, including this one. All tailored to work on the main Defense system hub."

"We know who their mixer is?" Clicks are made in batches.

Lisha pauses. It's something none of us thought of before. I don't know why. The connection feels obvious now.

"There are about six different mixers for the cressin clicks," he says. "The sig patters of these ones... it's a familiar sig combo, I remember it from Ethics. Their mixer is, what, the foreigner – Trist."

"Trist mixed all these agents?"

"I have to look into that. Agents aren't tailored for specific ops like the clicks were."

"Go get Mesta and Gri working on it, see if you can find a way to link them. Run cross-referenced patterns on the Defense database."

He walks back out into the hall.

I step through the bubble filter. The click flinches.

I squat down a couple feet from the click. "You know why you're here, Kel?"

He cringes from my voice.

"I do what Pelan says." He's shaking.

A common click defense, blaming actions on an agent, but all it means is that if the agent's purged, so's their click.

"She says Keli told her to do it, in her dreams, in one of those rooms," Kel says.

I stand and nearly fall again. My legs are shaky, half-asleep. I need to stop it with the kaj.

Lisha pops through the filter. Before I can say anything, he pulls me out of the filter.

"You have to see this," he says, and he takes me back into the interrogation offices. Flire is there, standing over the main system screen.

"Narsis," she murmurs, but she doesn't get anything else out because I'm already there, pushing past her, gazing at the screen. There are names. Names of mixers, Suits, Council members, agents, clicks.

"There are links," Lisha says. "I programmed the system to look at them, thinking about what you said, about the mixers of both being the same." He points out Trist, who mixed the cressin clicks, and the woman who mixed Trist, Gell, who mixed eight of fifteen of Keli's turned agents and eight of the ten council members. One of the council members, unnamed per the *Privacy of Elite Act*, mixed Trist and Gell, who were both agents first linked to five clicks now bound to eight of the thirteen agents sent into Jabow for Liberation.

"You say there's more connections?" I say. "Were we... breeding people specifically for the liberation of Jabow?"

"I don't think we were supposed to find these," Lisha said. "The Council is all the way at the top, and they don't ask agents to meddle in their business." As if I don't know that, as if I'm too blind to see he's only skimmed the surface of an elaborately linked... system corrupting our own operations.

I'm on the cusp of something, but right now these links are merely superficial. It doesn't *mean* anything.

"I have to go back to Jan," I say.

I'm shaking, but it's not for lack of kaj.

* * *

Catalyst: Jan

SHE COMES BACK. She has to come back. We are bound together. We are one and the same, she and I, two halves of a whole, click and agent, in the crudest of terms.

I wait for her, sitting up in my bed, with my back against the wall. And finally, there she is, her form taking up most of the doorway. Her face is hardened into a deep frown, but instead of looking ugly she looks strong. She, all that I am not.

"Tell me about the system, about the Keli system, and how it works."

"Do you know what you are?" I ask.

"I'm an interrogator," she says. "I'm a Suit."

"What do interrogators do?"

"They use any means necessary to get the answers to their questions."

She steps closer to me, comes to the end of the bed. She is trying this time, trying to understand more than she has the other times.

"You were once an agent," I say. "You've been part of a click and agent pair. You became a system."

"I became part of a system," she says, "yes."

"Then you weren't an agent anymore. You became a Suit. How did you become an interrogation Suit?"

"I was bred for it," she says. "Being an agent was just passing through one stage to another. All Suits have to go through it. Defense had me pegged for interrogation from my mixing."

"Who was your mixer?"

She hesitates. I can see her thinking it over, trying to make the connections.

"One of the Council Members. He's a Council Member now, I know." She pauses. She sees the connection. "He's the same one who mixed Gell or Trist, isn't he?"

"Why send specifically tailored clicks to the Liberation of Jabow?" I say.

"To retrieve you," she says, and until that moment, I didn't think she would phrase it that way. The world has stopped for me since I last saw her.

"Opposition doesn't believe in organic tech, but you're as organic a tech as they come," she says.

"So whose weapon am I, Narsis?"

Opposition: Narsis

WHAT IS OPPOSITION? Have I ever really known? Has anyone ever sat down with me and given me a definition? Opposition has always been just that. They don't believe in organic tech. They want the resources that we want. But no one says what the Opposition looks like. By the time Liberation parties move into Opposition areas, the Opposition is always gone, pushed out when their mechanized lines break.

We... We, Keli, tailored people to retrieve Jan.

Our weapon.

What is Keli? He is Opposition. What is Opposition? Opposition is us.

I look at Jan. He reaches out to me, one skinny hand escaping from the bundle of sheets.

I am numb and trembling, but my fingers twine into his. A burst of green webbing moves across my field of vision.

We. I. We:

We, system totality.

Jan reached for her.

We.

She broke. I'm broken! He heard her and he called out and she could not hear.

We are going to die alone and apart, broken, rent, twisted. We'll die alone if we don't come together.

She does not fear being alone. She fears coming together.

I fear.

I deny.

We, system totality... No.

No.

Me. Strong, singular, apart, complete.

I need no one and nothing. I am no one and nothing.

We. I. Me.

I.

Alone. Singular. Complete.

"I don't need you!" I say, and he falls away from me.

We liberated our own fucking weapon.

I won't become one, too.

I sit down on the end of the bed. I feel like something heavy has been dragged over me. I am watching agents pissing themselves. I am watching myself cutting out their tongues. I'm waking up alone every morning and vomiting in the sink after every interrogation, believing I'm cleansing out the dregs Defense couldn't get to, Defense couldn't control. I'm watching agents chew off their own fingers and make alters to their dead clicks for the whim of Council members who can't live without an Opposition.

"What are we, Jan?" I say, and it comes out garbled.

He worms over to me, still wrapped in his sheets, and he tries to touch me again, but I pull away, and I see that he's crying.

"We are their monsters," he says.

System Totality: Narsis

"I'm GOING TO be purged, Jan," I say.

He is sobbing now, and the sobbing wracks his whole little body. I have never despised what I am, who I am, like I do now, because I cannot touch him, I cannot stay. I will leave him like I have left everyone.

I stand on shaky legs.

I leave him.

I leave him and he is still crying, and the nurse watches me go and her eyes are so very, very black.

I don't want to go to Defense now. I want to sleep. But when I finally get to my narrow room, Lisha is waiting for me inside. I left my filter on green. The room is dark, but there's pale orange light coming in from the globes in the hallway. He is sitting on my bed, and he stands when I enter.

"What are you doing here?" I say.

He pulls a blue Defense Priority paper from his coat pocket and hands it to me.

I open it up, and it's a missive with my tag number on it:
GREEN THREAD

"I didn't know what it meant," he says, "so I came down here to meet you."

"I didn't send that," I say.

"What happened?" he says.

"I'm going to be purged," I say.

"Narsis –"

I laugh. It comes out a bark. "If I tell you about the case, they'll purge you too."

I sit on the bed, run my hands over my face. With my hands over my face, I don't see Lisha kneel down in front of me, but I feel the pressure of his face against my thigh. When I look down I see him kneeling on the floor, pressed against me.

I hesitate. Then I rest my hand, gently, on the back of his neck. I close my eyes, and bleeding agents dance behind my lids, clicks with missing fingers. I see Lisha shoving ear mites into agent eardrums. This is our job. This is what we do. Interrogation, body politic.

And it was all just someone's joke. It was Us and Opposition, fighting no one but ourselves.

"Goodnight, Lisha," I say, and take my hand away from him.

He stands and walks to the door and leaves the Priority paper on the floor. He does not turn before he leaves. He says nothing. I wonder if he saw the same things when he closed his eyes.

Defense sends me a summons at dawn.

My system is functional now, and wakes me up, displays the message:

INTERROGATION ROOM 101 DEFENSE SUMMONS IMMEDIATE

I am still dressed. I walk down to the interrogation offices and palm open the door. The offices are empty.

I sit at one of the system consoles and wait. I don't want to go into room one-oh-one. I know I am waiting for someone who is not yet here.

A shadow appears at the door. One figure. No more Left and Right.

She is thin and wiry and wears black. Her hair is sandy brown, topping a lean, brow, narrow face. She slips into the office and hands me a blue Priority paper.

It has my tag number on it, identifying the sender:

I FOUND KELI

I stare at the paper.

"I didn't send that," I say, but I did. Of course I did.

She smiles, and the smile crinkles the wrinkles at the corners of her eyes.

"That's your tag number, Narsis," she says. "You've done well. We're happy with your progress, but it appears there's one last obstacle in the linear progression of your education toward becoming a complete communication system, unbound by mechanical interference."

She leads me to room one-oh-one.

I expect everyone to be in that room. I expect agents. I expect clicks. I expect Lisha. Flire. Gri. Mesta. I expect all of them.

But she pushes open the door and there, inside, without a filter, is my twisted little bird.

Jan sits in the center of the floor, tearing at the organic mesh blindfold on his face, squealing and whimpering. He is naked, all limbs, just a broken stick, nothing substantial.

"We had to kill the cats, of course," the woman says. "We locked him down there long enough to form a bond that became a linking system. Rudimentary, incomplete. He was never fully functional."

I stare at Jan. I can't stop staring because I can't bring myself to move.

"When we killed the cats, though," the woman says, "it released him, so to speak. There was a great deal of initial turmoil, of course, hence the imprisonment, but we were confident we could bring him here and get him to bond and train his replacement."

I realize I haven't had any kaj for over four hours. I am not numb, I just have a pounding headache, and the sickness in my gut has gotten worse, not better. Some part of me knows I'm supposed to be connecting things, but I can't, I can't, I can't because if I do... oh, fuck, oh, fuck if I do...

The little woman looks at me, smiling a little as Jan whimpers on the floor, tearing at the mesh on his face. I want to tell Jan to stop pulling on it, to leave it alone.

"I'm Keli," I say.

"I know," the woman says. "We gave you your orders. Now it's time for you to become more. It's the kaj that's held you back. We didn't anticipate your addiction. You learned how to connect with our systems and sabotage them, Narsis. Jan's your catalyst, just as the cats were his."

"Stop pulling at that thing, Jan," I say, finally, but he's still pulling, and I can see blood at the edges of the blindfold where the skin is detaching from his face.

The woman steps toward me, rests a hand on my arm. "You're my system, Narsis. My perfect system. Who do you think drew together all those invisible system strings and tugged those agents into doing Opposition work?"

Me. I did it. Me.

I am afraid of needles, of myself, of jack-in knives. I wear steel-toed boots. Glass ceilings. Green thread.

"Narsis?"

I am a weapon of the Opposition. I am our weapon. I turned the same agents I interrogated for turning. I'm as mad as Jan. A mad little bird am I.

"You'll never understand the nature of our conflict," the woman says, and when she smiles, I see my own face, the face of an interrogator, she with a license to question, to hurt.

I hear Jan scream. A long, long scream that turns into a howl.

He has pulled the mesh off his face. He's pulled the skin of his face off with it.

He holds his face in the palm of his hand.

I want to burn this woman and watch the country smoke. I want to unfurl the world and repaint it.

I can do none of those things.

I walk to Jan's tortured body. Blood oozes from his skinned face. He's missing bits of his eyelids.

I pick him up.

"What are you doing?" the woman says.

"Finishing," I say.

The woman smiles.

I carry Jan. He is not heavy. The woman does not follow us. I walk and walk, into the belly of the Defense compound and out, down the long curl of walkway into the Kettering compound. We go through a filter, but Jan is listless, and he is oblivious to the red welts that begin spiraling out across his torso, down the lengths of his arms; his body's reaction to organic tech.

I walk past the vast tower of the compound, up to the spiral of residences on the hill, to Jan's prison. The gate is open. The nurse is gone.

Jan has his hands curled up into fists. One fistful of my hair, the other fistful of my coat.

I take him to the bathroom and draw lukewarm water into the bath. His blood is on my collar, my face.

"I'm sorry," he says, but I don't know what for. What could Jan be sorry for? We were made. We did not create ourselves.

The loss was mine, though. I could have joined him. If we became our own system when he reached for me, we could have fought them. But that would mean giving up myself. I would rather destroy the world than myself.

When the tub is almost full I turn off the water and place him in the tub. Water sloshes over the lip.

He closes what he has left of his eyelids and his body lies in the water, languid. He does not struggle against me. He does not question me.

"I'm sorry," he says again.

And I say, "I'm sorry they killed the cats."

I press him gently beneath the water. One hand on his chest, the other on his head, and he opens the bloody bits of the eyelids then, and the big blue-green eyes stare up at me from the shimmering surface of the water. Air bubbles leave his mouth, his nostrils. We stare at one another through the surface of the water. Me above, he below.

A system, apart.

He does not struggle much. He has no strength left to struggle.

I leave the drowned body in the tub and walk out into the front garden, back to the gate. From there I stare out at the Kettering compound. The woman will come for me, her perfect system, hobbled without Jan. She will take me off the kaj and I'll be able to feel everything, see everything, be everything, then. My twisted bird is dead, leaving me and rest of this twisted world.

I take the silver jack-in knife from the inside pocket of my coat, the one Lisha wanted me to send for printing. I go back to Jan's body, because there is nowhere else to go.

I sit next to the tub. I cut away all the threads.

It is my own blood across my boots.

113

NANCY KRESS

COCOONS

NANCY KRESS

COCOONS

A RECON DETAIL brought in another one just after dawn. The soldiers had donned full biohazard suits; nothing could convince them that this wasn't contagious. They set the body on a gurney. I wheeled it into a quarantine room and inspected it.

This time, for the first time, it was a child. A girl, about eleven years old. Half of her face was still visible.

"THE WHOLE PREMISE sounds ludicrous," Colonel Terence Jamison said, stirring more sugar into his coffee.

He wasn't at all what I'd expected. Thirty minutes off the ship from HQ on New Eden, he sat diffidently on the edge of a foamcast chair in my cluttered office as if visiting a priest to confess sins. Slightly built, soft-spoken, he seemed reluctant to meet my gaze with his pale, milky-blue eyes. Out of uniform, he wouldn't look like much, certainly not a senior officer in the Seven Planets United Space Corps.

I said, "Maybe it is ridiculous. After all, we have no documented proof, only anecdotes from, in most cases, unreliable sources."

Jamison blinked at me. "Dr. Seybert –"

"Nora, please." I am a civilian contractor, and this was a 'courtesy visit'. Yeah, right.

"Nora, to tell the truth, I'm not even sure why I'm here. Someone up the chain of command got a bee in their bonnet."

He was not telling the truth, and had Jamison ever seen a bee? I hadn't. Both New Eden, where I'd been born, and this outpost on Windsong pollinated their native plants by wind or bird. I knew exactly why Jamison was here, and both possible outcomes of his mission.

Neither was good.

"Dr... Nora," he said, "shall we get started?"

I AM ELIZABETH DiPortio. I hate my life. I choose this change. It can't be worse.

"MY GOD," JAMISON said. And then, "I didn't know..." And finally, regaining composure, "Briefing pictures were inadequate."

"Yes," I said.

We stood beside the gurney. The 'spiders,' which were not really spiders, had done more of their work. A thin, filmy web of very fine, dull red filaments was being spun over her naked body. The spiders worked unevenly; her forehead, neck and genitals were as yet completely uncovered, while her eyes, neck, and budding breasts were already sealed into the cocoon.

Jamison's face twisted in revulsion. "Why don't you wash it all off her?"

He knew the answer to this already; it was in ten years' of situation briefings. So we were going to be playing games. He would pretend ignorance, hoping that my answers would reveal whatever information the Corps thought, suspected, or hoped I was holding back. There wasn't any, but try convincing HQ Special Ops of that. I knew as much about Jamison as he did about me; I have friends at HQ. The stakes here were too high to not play along.

So I said, "We tried internal and external laving, in the early years. Twice. Both patients died. You see the 'spiders' but you don't see the biofilms that have invaded her nostrils, mouth, anus, vagina, ears. Those early autopsies revealed them. She's being colonized by sheets of microorganisms, changed from the inside out. Go ahead, you can touch her – both spiders and microbes have already attuned to her DNA. They won't do anything to you."

He didn't touch her. "Is she in pain?"

"No." He'd never glanced at the monitors, which showed plainly that her brain waves registered no pain. He was not a doctor.

"Who is she?"

"We verified that only a few hours ago. Her name is Elizabeth Jane DiPortio, a Corps dependent. Her mother is a grunt at the mining base; she's been sent for and will be shuttled here from the coast. Her father is a civilian dependent and, preliminary report says, a drunk. He may have abused her."

"This wasn't seen and dealt with?" Disapproval dripped off him. Not compassion – disapproval. Drunk or abused dependents did not meet Corps regulations. Under his mask of diffidence, Jamison was a martinet. And he handled Windsong's gravity, lighter than New Eden's by point two gee, like a man used to a lot of interstellar travel.

"Colonel," I said pleasantly, "Alpha Beta Base has over 6,500 people now, military and civilian. We can't see and deal with everything."

He nodded, blinking in that deceptively harmless way: *Nobody here but us rabbits.* "Tell me what is changing inside her."

"Her digestive flora – the microbes from her mouth to her rectum – are being destroyed, augmented, or replaced with ones that are part of the biofilms. Which are, of course DNA-based – panspermia, you know." I was being condescending. He didn't react. "Most of her organs are being modified only enough to accommodate the new microbes, with the exception of her vocal chords. They're being drastically reconfigured to make sounds at a pitch above human hearing."

"To communicate with what?"

"We don't know. Maybe only each other. It's a big planet, Colonel, and the Corps is still just a speck on it. Two specks: base and the mining operations in the mountains."

"Yes," he said, smiling, without mirth, in response to my condescension. I hated him. "I know. How do the... the..."

"We don't know. Some Terran spiders inject their prey with venom that digests tissue. Maybe these spiders are injecting something that denatures DNA, or activates parts of it. Maybe the microbes are injecting some of their own DNA into the host and taking over selected cell machinery, like viruses. But most likely the process has no real Terran analogy."

"How much of this microbial activity is affecting her brain?"

"Some of it, although it's impossible to quantify. The smallest invaders are the size of viruses. They can get past the blood-brain barrier just as some viruses can." This was why Colonel Jamison was here.

For the first time, he looked directly at me. "I want to see a finished product."

"They are not products, Colonel. We call them 'moths.' And we don't –"

"Moths? Do they have any sort of wings?"

"No, of course not. I admit the name is a little fanciful. We don't keep them on the base after they emerge from the cocoons. They head out to the bush."

"But some wander back. One is here now."

His intelligence was better than I thought. The Warrens tried to keep their son's visits a secret.

Jamison said, "I want to see Brent Warren."

WE AM ELIZABETH *DiPortio. We hate my life. We choose this change. It can't be worse.*

THE FIRST ONE was an accident. Ten years ago, Corporal Nathan Carter, Private Sully O'Keefe, and Private Sarah Lanowski went off-base to 'party' in the bush. This was really stupid because Windsong is home to predators, including one beast as large as a rhinoceros. There may be even larger, more dangerous animals on this huge, mostly unexplored continent. But the three soldiers were all young and, like young everywhere, considered themselves invulnerable. There was alcohol, drugs, sex. The next afternoon O'Keefe and Lanowski, already AWOL, staggered back to the base. Carter was missing. A search detail found him a quarter mile away. The spiders and biofilms had already started cocooning him. We put him in quarantine, laved the filaments off him, hit him with broad spectrum antibiotics and anti-virals and everything else in the medical arsenal. His heart stopped and he died.

Since then, there have been twenty-two more. Some were accidents, some may have been suicides. Most occurred at the mining camp, a rougher environment in both geographical and human terms. Here, where the ground is flat enough for the spaceport, it's easier to maintain the chemical-soaked perimeter that keeps out the spiders. No one has ever been cocooned within the base.

Elizabeth DiPortio deliberately walked off base, alone, at night. Brent Warren was taken at the mining camp. He was the only moth, until Elizabeth, who had a family here to return to.

The SPUSC skimmer set down a mile from base, on a flat meadow between woods and the river. A rover already sat there. The pilot turned off the engine. Jamison said to me, "That's not a Corps rover. The family has its own?"

"It belongs to their church, which loans it to them. The Warrens are good people, Colonel. A close family, which may be why Brent made his way from the mining camp back here, and why he wants to see them every few months."

"How does he –"

"He just comes here and waits. Eventually a dronecam spots him and someone lets the family know."

His mouth tightened. "A Corps dronecam."

"Which is not diverted from its usual business by noticing Brent." The more I saw of Jamison, the more frightened I felt.

"Where are the Warrens and... and him?"

He had almost said 'it.' I snapped, "How should I know?" He looked at me – quiet, diffident, rabbit-harmless – and said nothing. I added, "We wait." I climbed out of the skimmer. Jamison followed. The wind that gave the planet its ridiculously lyrical name blew in our faces. Warm, sweet-smelling wind, neither breeze nor gale, blew from sunrise to sunset.

A few minutes later, Gina and Ted Warren emerged from the trees. They had their little girl with them, whose name I couldn't remember. Brent trailed behind. Just a normal family, out for a Saturday walk.

Jamison drew a sharp breath.

Brent Warren walked lightly, fluidly, like a dancer. He was naked. The cocooning stage lasts for about a week – sometimes longer, sometimes shorter. We don't know why. What emerges is not human. The form still has two legs, two arms, torso and head. The dull-red skin bristles with tiny projections – not hair, not fur, not scales – whose function is unknown. It's the head that causes revulsion.

Brent's face bulged in a round, smooth ball. The two early autopsies showed that tissue had been added beneath the skin, containing organelles of unknown function that sent tendrils deep into the brain. On the surface of Brent's face, features had been minimized. His nose was now two small nostrils, his mouth a lipless slit without the levator muscles that enable smiles or frowns. Above the face, on the top of his head, was a second, smaller bulge. Only his eyes remained the same, gray flecked with green, and it was into their son's eyes that the Warrens mostly looked.

They stopped walking, uncertain, when they saw us. Gina smiled, but her eyes flicked over Jamison's uniform. Ted did not smile. Both worked as civilian contractors for the Corps, and both had been planning to leave before this happened to Brent. Now they would stay, to be near him. But the Warrens, no less than the rest of us, knew what rumors would have reached HQ.

"Colonel Jamison, this is Ted and Gina Warren, their daughter... uh..."

"Elise," Gina said.

"Yes, sorry, Elise. And this is Brent."

Brent stared without expression at Jamison. His lipless mouth moved slightly, but whatever he said, in whatever unimaginable language, it was not said to us.

☐ AM ELIZABETH DiPORTIO. ☐ *hate my life.* ☐ *choose this change. It can't be worse.*

JAMISON TOOK CHARGE of the meeting, raising his voice to be heard over the river and the wind but keeping his deferential, rabbity manner. Nonetheless, we felt compelled to answer his questions. He was Corps, and Corps ruled Windsong.

"Mr. Warren, can you talk to your son?"

"No."

"Do you communicate through gestures?"

"Mostly, yes."

"Could you demonstrate for me?"

Ted Warren's jaw set. Gina put a hand on her husband's arm and said, "We can try. Brent, dear, please show Colonel Jamison the herbs you found for us."

Brent did not move. But his left hand was lightly curled, as if he held something in it.

"Please, Brent."

Nothing.

Gina moved as if to touch her son's left hand. Ted stopped her. "He doesn't want to, honey."

Elise moved behind Gina and clutched her mother's legs.

Gina said to Jamison, "Well, he showed us some herbs, and then gave us some." She held out her own hand, which held a bunch of small purplish stalks with purplish leaves. "I told him I had a headache and he picked me these and pantomimed chewing them."

I said quickly, "Please don't eat them, Gina. Brent's metabolism is – may be – much different from yours. Now."

Jamison was not interested in anybody's metabolism. He said, "This... Brent understands English still? He knows what you say to him?"

"Yes," Ted said. His dislike of Jamison rose off him like heat.

"Has he understood you ever since he came out of the cocoon?"

"Yes."

"If you give him an order, does he follow it?"

"I don't give him orders."

"Does he volunteer information, through gesture or pantomime or any other means, in addition to responding to what you say?"

We were coming to it now.

"Yes," Ted said.

"What kind of information?"

Gina said, "He tells us he is well and happy. Before I ask."

"How does he tell you that?" Jamison asked.

Before she could answer, or Ted could say something sharp, Brent stepped forward. One step, two. Jamison didn't shrink back – I'll give him that – but in the skimmer the pilot tensed. She raised the gun I'd suspected she'd held on her lap and leveled it at Brent. The Warrens did not see. I don't know if Brent did, or if he understood, but he stopped walking. His lipless mouth moved, talking to air – certainly not to us, since he must have known we couldn't hear him. Who or what else was listening?

Brent half-turned toward his parents and raised his right hand to his mouth. He pressed his mouth to the hand and then blew toward the Warrens. A kiss.

Then he was gone, loping into the woods, disappearing among the trees.

I never cry, but I felt my eyes prickle.

Jamison said, "Does he never touch you directly?"

"He does, yes," Gina said quickly, before Ted could answer.

"When he touches you, do those projections on him feel sticky, scaly, or something else?"

"Go to hell," Ted said.

□ *am Elizabeth DiPortio. æ hate my life. Ø ❋. It will be good.*

IN THE SKIMMER I said, "You never got to what you actually wanted to ask. You alienated them, and you did it deliberately. Why?"

Jamison said mildly, "I don't know what you're talking about." And then, "They shouldn't bring that child near that naked thing."

I didn't answer. I needed to think. Jamison was not doing what he was sent here to do, and I could only think of one possible reason why.

* * *

□ *am Elizabeth DiPortio.* æ *my life.* Ø ❀. *It will be good.*

AT THE CLINIC, Elizabeth DiPortio's parents sat in an exam room. Kurt, my assistant, said, "I wouldn't let them into your office, and I certainly wouldn't let them in to see the patient, I don't care who they are." He scowled.

Peter DiPortio sat slumped in a chair, eyes half closed, smelling of sweat and alcohol. Beverly DiPortio, a muscular woman in her thirties, was garbed in miner's gear and stomping fury. "How the fuck did you let this happen to my daughter! I work for the Corps, you're supposed to look after us, and now you... them..."

"I'm sorry this has happened to Elizabeth," I said, "but it was not the Corps' responsibility, nor mine. Elizabeth left camp at night. Apparently no one was at home to notice."

Peter DiPortio muttered, "Bad seed."

I thought I hadn't heard him right. Before I could ask him to repeat, Beverly said, "I want to see Elizabeth!"

"Certainly. But I must prepare you for –"

"Cut the crap. I want to see her!"

I led them to Elizabeth's room. Peter shambled tensely, a gait I could not have imagined. The bottom half of his body lurched along, but his face and shoulders clenched with fear. For Elizabeth? No – the moment he saw her, his face relaxed.

Beverly said, "She's too far gone. I seen this, at the camp. You'll have to destroy her."

I felt my mouth fall open.

"She ain't human anymore," Beverly said, and there was pain in her voice but not as much pain as revulsion.

"That isn't going to happen, ma'am."

She turned on me. "It's my right! She's my kid! Give me the papers to sign!"

Peter was gazing at Elizabeth's mouth, half covered with red filaments. "Can she still talk?"

I lost it. Jamison, this child, these horrific parents… I snapped, "Yes, when she wakes up she can talk. When she comes out of her cocoon. The Corps is interested in what she'll say."

He believed the lie. His face paled. Then he staggered sideways and nearly fell, catching himself awkwardly on the doorjamb. Beverly threw him a look of deep and total disgust, pushed past him, and strode out of the room.

I stayed a long time beside Elizabeth's bed, watching the mite-sized spiders work. I couldn't quiet my mind. Then I told Kurt to cancel my afternoon appointments, let the nurses see any walk-ins, and page me for any emergencies. I signed out a rover and drove to the Warren bungalow.

□ *am Elizabeth DiPortio.* æ *my* ▽. Ø ✳. *It will be* ✳✳.

ANYBODY WHO SAYS that we understand human motivation, that we can formulate simple and clear reasons for why people what they do, is either lying or naïve. Standing in the Warrens' neat bungalow, surrounded by photos of Elise and a pre-cocooned Brent, I thought that I would give everything I had to never see the inside of the DiPortio's bungalow. A deep, heartfelt, completely irrelevant thought.

"Gina, Ted, I need to ask you some things, and I want you to trust me when I say that the questions are important. You've heard the rumors about moths?"

Ted said, "We're not discussing that, Nora."

"If we don't, we may all die."

His eyes widened. I had planned it this way, to compel his attention and, I'd hoped, his compliance. But Ted Warren was not an easy man to compel. He said, "You'll have to explain that."

"I don't want to yet, because I'm not sure. Could you just –"

"It's Colonel Jamison, isn't it?" Gina said. A look passed between her and Ted, one of those married-couple looks that say so much more than outsiders can discern. She followed it with, "We'll tell you anything you want to know, provided you agree to not tell anyone – anyone at all – without our say-so."

"Yes," I said, and wondered how much this lie would cost me in the future. "Have you heard the rumors about moths?"

"Of course," Gina said. And then again, hands clasped together so tightly that the knuckles bulged blue, "Of course."

Everyone had heard the rumors. A moth, a former engineer, supposedly had appeared to a miner taking an ill-advised walk outside the mining camp. The moth pantomimed falling; the next day, a section of mine collapsed, destroying two expensive bots. But… the strolling miner had been on recreational drugs. A moth had supposedly stood in the road between the mine and spaceport, stopping a loaded ore transport. Nobody knew what to do, so the tableau froze while the drivers argued: run her over? Inch forward and hope she moves? She did, after five minutes. The transport reached a bridge five minutes after the bridge had collapsed. There were more stories, but most could be coincidences; a lot of the narrators were unreliable; pantomime is not a precise method of communication; some 'pre-cognitive warnings' could be after-the-fact interpretations.

Rumors. Factions. An amateur evolutionary biologist – the outpost didn't yet have the real thing – offered the theory that, once, all humans had pre-verbal awareness of the near future, as a survival mechanism. That had disappeared with the Great Leap Forward, the sudden, still unexplained spurt of human culture forty to fifty thousand years ago on Earth's vanished savannahs. Increased creativity and rationality had replaced the ability to sense the future that, like a river, always flowed toward us, its rapids heard before they could be seen. But the ability, latent, was still locked in our genes. Massive genetic alteration could free it.

Did I believe this theory? I didn't know. A doctor is a scientist, committed to rationality. But I also knew that ideas of 'the rational' were subject to change. The list of things once derided as irrational included a round Earth, germs, an expanding universe, and quantum mechanics. HQ thought that moths' pre-cognition deserved at least minimal investigation.

I said, as gently as I could, "Gina, has Brent ever told you anything that later came true?"

Ted made a motion as if to stop her, but said nothing. Gina said, "Yes."

"Tell me. Please."

"We... we went to see him. At the usual place by the river. While we were visiting, Brent suddenly pushed us all back into the rover. He was frantic. We got in and he ran off into the woods. Then one of those big animals like a rhinoceros came out of the woods and charged the rover. It almost knocked it over. We barely got away alive."

"Could Brent have heard or smelled the animal?"

"I don't think so. We sat in the rover talking for at least fifteen minutes before the animal arrived. Elise wasn't with us and I was crying."

Ted said, "It might have been coincidence." His face said he didn't believe it.

I said, "Were there other times?"

Gina said, "One other time. We –"

Ted cut her off. "We've been straight with you, Nora, because we trust you. Now you trust us. What's happening with Jamison?"

"I don't know for sure. But I think HQ will do anything to stop what they see as a possible epidemic of cocooning. Jamison sees moths as a dire threat to what it means to be human, and he's making the decision. The only way to sway him is to show that people like Brent have potential value to the Army. A battalion accompanied by a moth who can see what an enemy will do in the future would be –"

"*No*," Ted said.

"Ted, I think he might destroy all the –"

"Let him try. Our boy and the others can take care of themselves. They know how to live off the wilderness and it's a big, unexplored planet! Plus, they might know in advance when the Army would strike."

It was almost unbearable to say my next words. "Jamison knows that. He knows that if HQ wants to destroy the moths, they would have to destroy all of us and quarantine the planet."

Ted and Gina stared at me. Gina finally said, "They wouldn't. You *said* this was only speculation on your part. And if they quarantined the planet, there wouldn't be any need to destroy the humans on it."

"If we all become moths and later another expedition comes to Windsong –"

"More speculation!" Ted snapped. "But I'll tell you what isn't speculation – what they'll do to Brent if we give him up to 'save' ourselves. They'll take him to HQ and examine him in ways that... it would be torture, Nora. Maybe even murder, to see what makes his brain so different."

"The alternative is that maybe we all die."

"I doubt that," Ted said, and Gina nodded.

They wanted, needed, to doubt it.

As I left, Ted said, "Remember, you promised to keep all of this to yourself. Everything we said. You promised."

"Yes," I said. "I did."

☐ *am Elizabeth DiPortio.* æ *my* ▽. Ø ❋. *It* ⅋ ⁂.

I SAT IN my office at the clinic, in the dark. No one was on duty; we had no patients except Elizabeth and there was nothing any of us could do for her. Moonlight from Windsong's larger moon, delicate and silvery as filigree, flowed through the window. It was light enough to see my untouched glass of expensive, Earth-exported Scotch.

Time as a river. I saw Brent and the other moths standing on its banks, just beyond a bend, looking into water the rest of us could not yet see. I remembered how Jamison had deliberately alienated the Warrens before they could say anything positive about Brent. I saw Jamison's revulsion at the sight of Brent and Elizabeth. It wasn't even revulsion but something deeper, some primitive urge to so completely destroy a perceived enemy that they could never rise again: the urge that made Romans salt all the fields of Carthage, Hitler try to exterminate all the Jews. I saw the base and the mining camp burning and cratered, reduced to smoking rubble by weapons fired from space. I saw myself as wrong for thinking all this: melodramatic, building a case purely on speculation. I saw the decision I had to make as two roads, both shrouded in mist, and both leading to tragedy. I saw –

Something moved in the hallway.

I rose quietly, heart hammering, and crept in the dark toward the door.

□ *am* □. æ Ø▽, *It* ℀ ⁂.

ELIZABETH – POST-COCOONED Elizabeth, who should not have emerged for another day – stumbled along the hallway. I turned on the light. Her round, inhuman face showed no emotion. She extended an unsteady arm and, her movements in her altered body not yet coordinated, took my hand and tugged me along the hallway to the clinic's back door.

Why did I let her? Was there some faint, latent pre-cognitive ability in my brain, too? Later, I would ponder that, without answers.

We went out the back door just as Peter DiPortio reached the front. From where Elizabeth and I hid in the rover shed, locking it behind us, we heard his crowbar smashing against the door. We heard his drunken shouts that he would kill the thing that had been his daughter. He was, in demeanor and temperament and appearance, the opposite of Colonel Terence Jamison. Yet he was the same.

I made my decision. It was not a choice between Brent or Elizabeth, not between the force of a promise or the force of reason, not between the good of the many or the good of the few. It was something far more primitive than that, something arising from my hindbrain.

Survival against a perceived enemy.

"I DON'T BELIEVE you," Jamison said.

"I know you don't," I said. "That's why I'll give you Brent Warren. On New Eden you can... 'test' him to determine exactly how and when moths can see the near future."

We stood in the Spartan living room of the Corps guest bungalow, surrounded by the decorations of war: antique crossed swords on the wall, a cast-iron statue of the SPUSC logo on a table. I don't know who decorated the place. Jamison's deferential, rabbit-like manner had completely disappeared.

"No," he said.

"Colonel, I don't think you understand. I'm offering to bring you Brent Warren, to... trap him for you, so Army scientists can find ways to use the moths' pre-cognitive ability. They can –"

"There is no ability."

I gaped at him. "Haven't you been listening? I *saw* it. It's real. Elizabeth DiPortio –"

"There is no ability. You're lying, in order to save these inhuman abominations you're so unaccountably fond of. There is no ability."

I said slowly, "Is that what you're going to report to HQ?"

"I already have."

"I see."

"What will they –"

"I don't know. I just make the report, doctor. But you should think about this: Suppose this dehumanization spreads to the other six planets? To Earth? To the *Corps*?"

"I will think about it," I said and moved toward him, taking my hand from my pocket.

IN THE ROVER, I force myself to think calmly. I have maybe twelve hours until the Corps begins to wonder why Jamison has not contacted them. I don't know how much time will be left after that. I don't know how many other Corps soldiers on Windsong will believe me, or will rate their loyalty to the Corps above everything else. I don't know how long it will take to spread the word to 6,500 people. I will start with the Warrens. I am on my way to their place now.

Twelve hours. In that time, a great many people can escape into the wilderness, can fan out into small groups hard to track, can get into the planet's numerous caves or beyond the range of space weapons concentrated onto two small settlements. They cannot eradicate everybody. People can carry supplies until we learn to live off this planet. We have few old or sick. Brent will help us, and maybe more moths will, too. Some of us will become moths. That is inevitable. But we will be alive.

There are all kinds of cocoons. Time is one. Rigid organizational rules are another. But the most deadly cocoon may be the limitations of what humans consider human. Perhaps it's time to emerge.

Twelve hours. I don't know how many people I can save in that time. But I do know this: twelve hours is enough for the spiders to begin work on Jamison's body, held immobile by a non-fatal dose of ketamine from my syringe in the ditch where Elizabeth and I dumped him.

I hope to meet him again someday.

137

GWYNETH JONES

EMERGENCE

GWYNETH JONES

EMERGENCE

I FACED THE doctor across her desk. The room was quiet, the walls were pale or white, but somehow I couldn't see details. There was a blank in my mind, no past to this moment; everything blurred by the adrenalin in my blood.

"You have three choices," she said gently. "You can upload; you can download. Or you must return."

My reaction to those terms – *upload, download* – was embarrassing. I tried to hide it and knew I'd failed.

"*Go back?*" I said bitterly, and in defiance. "To the city of broken dreams? Why would I ever want to do that?"

"Don't be afraid, Romy. The city of broken dreams may have become the city of boundless opportunity."

Then I woke up: Simon's breathing body warm against my side, Arc's unsleeping presence calm in my cloud. A shimmering, starry night above us and the horror of that doctor's tender smile already fading.

It was a dream, just a dream.

With a sigh of profound relief I reached up to pull my stars closer, and fell asleep again floating among them; thinking about Lei.

I was born in the year 1998, CE. My parents named me Romanz Jolie Davison; I have lived a long, long time. I've been upgrading since 'uppers' were called *experimental longevity treatments*. I was a serial clinical-trialer when genuine extended lifespan was brand new. Lei was someone I met through this shared interest; this extreme sport. We were friends, then lovers; and then ex-lovers who didn't meet for many years, until one day we found each other again: on the first big Habitat Station, in the future we'd been so determined to see (talk about 'meeting cute'!). But Lei had always been the risk taker, the hold-your-nose-and-jump kid. I was the cautious one. I'd never taken an unsafe treatment, and I'd been careful with my money too (you need money to do super-extended lifespan well). We had our reunion and drifted apart, two lives that didn't mesh. One day, when I hadn't seen her for a while, I found out she'd gone back to Earth on medical advice.

Had we kept in touch at all? I had to check my cache: which saddened me, although it's only a mental eye-blink. Apparently not. She'd left without a goodbye, and I'd let her go. I wondered if I should try to reach her. But what would I say? I had a bad dream, I think it was about you, are you okay? I needed a better reason to pick up the traces, so I did nothing.

Then I had the same dream again; exactly the same. I woke up terrified, and possessed by an absurd puzzle: had I *really* just been sitting in that fuzzy doctor's office again? Or had I only *dreamed* I was having the same dream? A big space station is a haunted place, saturated with information that swims into your head and you have no idea how. Sometimes a premonition really is a premonition: so I tried to trace her. The result was that time-honoured brush-off: *it has not been possible to connect this call.*

Relieved, I left it at that.

I was, I am, one of the four Senior Magistrates on the Outer Reaches circuit. In Jupiter Moons, my home town, and Outer Reaches' major population centre, I often deal with Emergents. They account for practically all our petty offences, sad to say. Full sentients around here are either too law-abiding, too crafty to get caught, or too seriously criminal for my jurisdiction.

Soon after my dreams about Lei a young SE called Beowulf was up before me, on a charge of Criminal Damage and Hooliganism. The incident was undisputed. A colleague, another Software Entity, had failed to respond *"you too"*, to the customary and friendly sign-off *"have a nice day"*. Beowulf had lost his temper and shredded a stack of files in CPI (Corporate and Political Interests, our Finance Sector), where they both worked.

The offence was pitiful, the damage minimal, but the kid had a record, he'd run out of chances, and his background was against him. CPI had decided to make a meal of it. Poor Beowulf, a thing of rational light, wearing an ill-fitting suit of virtual flesh for probably the first time in his life, stood penned in his archaic, data-simulacrum of wood and glass, for *two mortal subjective standard hours*; while the CPI advocate and Beowulf's public defender scrapped over the price of a cup of coffee.

Was Beowulf's response proportionate? Was there an *intention of offence*? Was it possible to establish, by precedent, that *"you too"* had the same or commensurate "customary and friendly" standing, in law, as *"have a nice day"*?

Poor kid, it was a real pity he'd tried to conceal the evidence. I had to find him guilty, no way around it.

I returned to macro-time convinced I could at least transmute his sentence, but I had no luck. My request ran into a Partnership

Director I'd crossed swords with before: she was adamant and we fell out. We couldn't help sharing our quarrel. No privacy for anyone in public office: it's the law out here and I think a good one. But we could have kept it down. The images we flung to and fro were lurid. I recall eyeballs dipped in acid, a sleep-pod lined with bloody knives. . . and then we got nasty. The net result (aside from childish entertainment for idle citizens) was that I got myself barred from the case. Eventually I found out by reading the court announcements that Beowulf's sentence had been confirmed in the harshest terms. Corrective custody until a validated improvement shown, but not less than one week.

In Outer Reaches we use expressions like "night and day", "week and hour", without meaning much by them at all. Not so the Courts. A week in jail meant the full Earth Standard version, served in macro-time.

I'd been finding the Court Sessions exhausting that rotation, but I walked home anyway; to get over my chagrin, and unkink my brain after a day spent switching in and out of virtual time. I stopped at every Ob Bay, making out I was hoping to spot the first flashes of the spectacular Centaur Storm we'd been promised. But even the celestial weather was out to spoil my day: updates kept telling me about a growing chance the show had been cancelled.

My apartment was in the Rim, Premium level, it still is; (why not? I can afford it). Simon and Arc welcomed me home with bright, ancient music for a firework display. They'd cleared the outward wall of our living space to create our own private Ob Bay, and were refusing to believe reports that it was all in vain. I cooked a meal, with Simon flying around me to help out, deft and agile in the rituals of a human kitchen. Arc, as a slender woman, bare-headed, dressed in silver-grey coveralls, watched us from her favourite couch.

Simon and Arc. . . They sounded like a firm of architects, as I often told them (I repeat myself, it's a privilege of age). They were probably secretly responsible for the rash of fantasy spires and giant bubbles currently annoying me, all over Station's open spaces –

"Why is Emergent Individual law still set in *human* terms?" I demanded. "Why does a Software Entity get punished for 'criminal damage' when *nothing was damaged*; not for more than a fraction of a millisecond –?"

My housemates rolled their eyes. "It'll do him good," said Arc. "Only a human-terms thinker would think otherwise."

I was in for some tough love.

"What kind of a dreadful name is *Beowulf*, anyway?" inquired Simon.

"Ancient Northern European. Beowulf was a monster –" I caught myself, recalling I had no privacy. "No! *Correction.* The monster was Grendel. Beowulf was the hero, a protector of his people. It's aspirational."

"He *is* a worm though, isn't he?"

I sighed, and took up my delicious bowl of Tom Yum; swimming with chilli pepper glaze. "Yes," I said glumly. "He's ethnically worm, poor kid."

"Descended from a vicious little virus strain," Arc pointed out. "He has tendencies. He can't help it, but we have to be sure they are purged."

"I don't know how you can be so prejudiced."

"Humans are so squeamish," teased Simon.

"Humans are *human*," said Arc. "That's the fun of them."

They were always our children, *begotten not created*, as the old saying goes. There's no such thing as a sentient AI not born of human mind. But they were never purely human. Simon, my embodied housemate, had magpie neurons in his background. Arc took human form for pleasure, but her being was pure information, the elemental *stuff* of the universe. They had gone beyond us, as children do. We had become just one strand in their past –

The entry lock chimed. It was Anton, my clerk, a slope-shouldered, barrel-chested bod with a habitually doleful expression. He looked distraught.

"Apologies for disturbing you at home Rom. May I come in?"

We let him in. He sat on Arc's couch, silent and grim. Two of my little dream-tigers, no bigger than geckos, emerged from the miniature jungle of our bamboo and teak room divider and sat gazing at him, tails around their paws.

"Those are pretty..." said Anton at last. "New. Where'd you get them?"

"I made them myself. I'll give you the code. What's up, Anton?"

"We've got trouble. Beowulf didn't take the confirmation well."

I noticed that my ban had been lifted: a bad sign. "What's the damage?"

"Oh, nothing much. It's in your updates, of which you'll find a ton. He's only removed himself from custody –"

"Oh, God. He's back in CPI?"

"No. Our hero had a better idea."

Having feared *revenge* instantly, I felt faint with relief.

"But he's been traced?"

"You bet. He's taken a hostage, and a non-sentient Lander. He's heading for the surface, right now."

The little tigers laid back their ears and sneaked out of sight. Arc's human form drew a long, respectful breath. "What are you guys going to do?"

"Go after him. What else?" I was at the lockers, dragging out my gear.

JUPITER MOONS HAS no police force. We don't have much of anything like that: everyone does everything. Of course I was going with the Search and Rescue, Beowulf was my responsibility. I didn't argue when Simon and Arc insisted on coming too. I don't like to think of them as my minders: or my *curators*, but they are both, and I'm a treasured relic. Simon equipped himself with a heavy-duty hard suit, in which he and Arc would travel freight. Anton and I would travel cabin. Our giant neighbour was in a petulant mood, so we had a Mag-Storm Drill in the Launch Bay. In which we heard that Jovian magnetosphere storms are unpredictable. Neural glitches caused by wayward magnetism, known as soft errors, build up silently, and we must watch each other for signs of disorientation or confusion. Physical burn out, known as hard error, is *very* dangerous; more frequent than people think, and fatal accidents do happen –

It was housekeeping. None of us paid much attention.

Anton, one of those people always doomed to 'fly the plane' would spend the journey in horrified contemplation of the awful gravitational whirlpools that swarm around Jupiter Moons; even on a calm day. We left him in peace, poor devil, and ran scenarios. We had no contact with the hostage, a young pilot just out of training. We could only hope she hadn't been harmed. We had no course for the vehicle: Beowulf had evaded basic safety protocols and failed to enter one. But Europa is digitally mapped, and well within the envelope of Jupiter Moons' data cloud. We knew exactly where the stolen Lander was, before we'd even left Station's gravity.

Cardew, our team leader, said it looked like a crash landing, but a soft crash. The hostage, though she wasn't talking, seemed fine. Thankfully the site wasn't close to any surface or sub-ice installation, and since Mag Storm precautions were in place, there was little immediate danger to anybody. But we had to assume the worst, and the worst was scary, so we'd better get the situation contained.

We sank our screws about 500 metres from Beowulf's vehicle, with a plan worked out. Simon and Arc, already dressed for the weather, disembarked at once. Cardew and I, plus his four-bod ground team, climbed into exos: checked each other, and stepped onto the lift, one by one.

We were in sunlight: a pearly dusk; like winter's dawn in the country where I was born. The terrain was striated by traces of ancient cryovolcanoes: brownish salt runnels glinting gold where the faint light caught them. The temperature was a balmy -170 Celsius. I swiftly found my ice-legs; though it had been too long. Vivid memories of my first training for this activity – in Antarctica, so long ago – came welling up. I was scared. I didn't know what Beowulf was planning. I didn't know how I was going to help him, if he kept on behaving like an out of control, invincible computer virus. But it was glorious. To be *walking* on Europa Moon. To feel the ice in my throat, as my air came to me, chilled from the convertor!

At 50 metres Cardew called a halt and I went on alone. Safety was paramount; Beowulf came second. If he couldn't be talked down he'd have to be neutralised from a distance: a risky tactic for the hostage, involving potentially lethal force. We'd try to avoid that, if possible.

We'd left our Lander upright on her screws, braced by harpoons. The stolen vehicle was belly-flopped. On our screens it had looked like a rookie landing failure. Close up I saw something different. Someone had dropped the Lander deliberately, and manoeuvred it into the shelter of a natural cove of dark, crumpled ice, dragging ice-mash after it; to partially block the entrance. You clever little bugger, I thought, impressed (though the idea that a Lander could be *hidden* was absurd). I commanded the exo to kneel, eased myself out of its embrace, opened a channel and yelled into my suit radio.

"*Beowulf!* Are you in there? Are you guys okay?"

No reply, but the seals popped, and the lock opened smoothly. I looked back and gave a thumbs up to six bulky statues. I felt cold, in the shadow of the ice cove; but intensely alive.

I REMEMBER EVERY detail up to that point, and a little beyond. I cleared the lock and proceeded (nervously) to the main cabin. Beowulf's hostage had her pilot's couch turned away from the instruments. She faced me, bare-headed, pretty: dark blue sensory tendrils framing a smooth young greeny-bronze face. I said *are you okay*, and got no response. I said *Trisnia, it's Trisnia isn't it? Am I talking to Trisnia?*, but I knew I wasn't. Reaching into her cloud, I saw her unique identifier, and tightly coiled around it a flickering thing, a sparkle of red and gold –

"Beowulf?"

The girl's expression changed, her lips quivered. "I'm okay!" she blurted. "He didn't mean any harm! He's just a kid! He wanted to see the sky!"

Stockholm Syndrome or Bonnie and Clyde? I didn't bother trying to find out. I simply asked Beowulf to release her, with the usual warnings. To my relief he complied at once. I ordered the young pilot to her safe room; which she was not to leave until further –

Then we copped the Magstorm hit, orders of magnitude stronger and more direct than predicted for this exposure –

The next thing I remember (stripped of my perfect recall, reduced to the jerky flicker of enhanced human memory), I'm sitting on the other pilot's couch, talking to Beowulf. The stolen Lander was intact at this point; I had lights and air and warmth. Trisnia was safe, as far as I could tell. Beowulf was untouched, but my entire team, caught outdoors, had been flatlined. They were dead and gone. Cardew, his crew; and Simon; and Arc.

I'd lost my cloud. The whole of Europa appeared to be observing radio silence, and I was getting no signs of life from the Lander parked just 500 metres away, either. There was nothing to be done. It was me and the deadly dangerous criminal virus, waiting to be rescued.

I'd tried to convince Beowulf to lock himself into the Lander's quarantine chest (which was supposed to be my mission). He wasn't keen, so we talked instead. He complained bitterly about the Software Entity, another Emergent, slightly further down the line to Personhood, who'd been, so to speak, chief witness for the prosecution. How it was always getting at him, trying to make his work look bad. Sneering at him because he'd taken a name and wanted to be called 'he'. Telling him he was a *stupid fake doll-prog* that couldn't pass the test. And *all he did* when it hurtfully wouldn't say *you too*, was shred a few of its stupid, totally backed-up files –

Why hadn't he told anyone about this situation? Because kids don't. They haven't a clue how to help themselves; I see it all the time.

"But now you've made things much worse," I said sternly. "*Whatever* made you jump jail, Beowulf?"

"I couldn't stand it, magistrate. A meat-*week*!"

Quite a sojourn in hell, for a quicksilver data entity. Several life sentences at least, in human terms. He buried his borrowed head in his borrowed hands, and the spontaneity of that gesture confirmed something I'd been suspecting.

Transgendered AI Sentience is a bit of a mystery. Nobody knows exactly how it happens (probably, as in human sexuality, there are many pathways to the same outcome); but it isn't all that rare.

Nor is the related workplace bullying, unfortunately.

"Beowulf, do you want to be embodied?"

He shuddered and nodded, still hiding Trisnia's face. "Yeah. Always."

I took his borrowed hands and held them, firmly. "Beowulf, you're not thinking straight. You're in macro time now. You'll *live* in macro, when you have a body of your own. I won't lie to you, your sentence will seem long." (It wasn't the moment to point out that his sentence would inevitably be *longer*, after this escapade). "But what do you care? You're immortal. You have all the time in the world, to learn everything you want to learn, to be everything you want to be –"

My eloquence was interrupted by a shattering roar.

Then we're sitting on the curved 'floor' of the Lander's cabin wall. We're looking up at a gaping rent in the fuselage; the terrible cold pouring in.

"Wow," said Beowulf calmly. "That's what I call a *hard* error!"

The hood of my soft suit had closed over my face, and my emergency light had come on. I was breathing. Nothing seemed to be broken.

Troubles never come singly. We'd been hit by one of those Centaurs, the ice-and-rock cosmic debris scheduled to give Jupiter Moons Station a fancy lightshow. They'd been driven off course by the Mag Storm.

Not that I realised this at the time, and not that it mattered.

"Beowulf, if I can open a channel, will you get yourself into that quarantine chest now? You'll be safe from Mag flares in there."

"What about Tris?"

"She's fine. Her safe room's hardened."

"What about *you*, Magistrate Davison?"

"I'm hardened too. Just get into the box, that's a good kid."

I clambered to the instruments. The virus chest had survived, and I could access it. I put Beowulf away. The cold was stunning, sinking south of -220. The ambient radiation of Europa surface wouldn't harm me, as long as my suit was intact. But the cold was dangerous. I needed to stop breathing soon, before my lungs froze. I wasn't too concerned. I used the internal panels that had been shaken loose to make a shelter, plus Trisnia's bod (she wasn't feeling anything): and crawled inside. I'm not a believer, but I know how to pray when it will save my life. As I shut myself down: as my blood cooled, as my senses faded out, I sought and found the level of deep meditation I needed, and became a thread of contemplation, enfolded and protected; in one infinitesimal cell of all the worlds, and all the possible worlds...

WHEN I OPENED my eyes Simon was looking down at me.

"How do you feel?"

"Terrific," I joked. I stretched, flexing muscles in a practiced sequence. I was breathing normally, wearing a hospital gown, and the air was chill but tolerable. We weren't in the crippled Lander.

"How long was I out?"

"A few days. The kids are fine, but we had to heat you up slowly –"

He kept talking: I didn't hear a word. I was staring in stunned horror at a stain of blackened flesh on the side of my left hand –

I couldn't feel it yet, but there was frostbite all down my left side. I saw the sorrow in my housemate's bright eyes. Hard error, the hardest: I'd lost hull integrity, I'd been blown wide open. And now I saw the signs. Now I read them as I should have read them; now I understood.

I HAD THE dream for the third time, and it was real. The doctor had been my GP for decades, but her face was unfamiliar because we'd never met across a desk before; I was never ill. She gave me my options. Outer Reaches could do nothing for me: but there was a new treatment, back on Earth. I said angrily I had no intention of returning. Then I went home and cried my eyes out.

Simon and Arc had been recovered without a scratch, thanks to that massive hardsuit. Cardew and his crew were getting treated for minor memory trauma. Death would have been more dangerous for Trisnia, because she was so young, but sentient AIs don't 'die' for long. They always come back.

Not me. I had never been cloned, I couldn't be cloned. There weren't even any good *partial* copies of Romanz Jolie Davison, I was too old. Uploaded or downloaded, the new Romy wouldn't be me. And being *me*; being *human*, was my whole value, my unique identifier –

Of course I was going back. But I hated the idea, *hated* it!

"No you don't," said Arc, gently.

She pointed, and we three, locked together in grief, looked up. My beloved stars shimmered in my night sky; the hazy stars of the blue planet.

MY JOURNEY 'HOME' took six months. By the time I reached the Ewigen Schnee clinic, in Switzerland (the ancient federal republic, not a Space Hotel; and still a nice little enclave for rich people, after all these years), *catastrophic systems failure* was no longer an abstraction. I was very sick.

I faced a different doctor, in an office with views of alpine meadows and snowy peaks. She was youngish, human; I thought her name was Lena. But every detail was dulled and I still felt as if I was dreaming.

We exchanged the usual pleasantries.

"*Romanz Jolie Davison*... Date of birth..." My doctor blinked, clearing the display on her retinal super-computers to look at me directly, for the first time. "You're almost three hundred years old!"

"Yes."

"That's incredible."

"Thank you," I said, somewhat ironically. I was not looking my best.

"Is there anything at all you'd like to ask me, at this point?"

I had no searching questions. What was the point? But I hadn't glimpsed a single other patient so far, and this made me a little curious.

"I wonder if I could meet some of your other clients, your successes, in person, before the treatment? Would that be possible?"

"You're looking at one."

"Huh?"

My turn to be rather rude, but she didn't look super-rich to me.

"I was terminally ill," she said, simply. "When the Corporation was asking for volunteers. I trust my employers and I had nothing to lose."

"You were *terminally ill?*" Constant nausea makes me cynical and bad-tempered. "Is that how your outfit runs its longevity trials? I'm amazed."

"Ms Davison," she said politely. "You too are dying. It's a requirement."

I'd forgotten that part.

I'D BEEN TOLD that though I'd be in a medically-induced coma, I "might experience some mental discomfort". Medics never exaggerate about pain. Tiny irritant maggots filled the shell of my paralysed body, creeping through every crevice. It was appalling. I could not scream, I could not pray. I thought of Beowulf in his corrective captivity.

WHEN I SAW Dr Lena again I was feeling weak, but very much better. She wanted to talk about convalescence, but I'd been looking at Ewigen Schnee's records. I had a more important issue, a thrilling discovery. I asked her to put me in touch with a patient who'd taken the treatment when it was in trials.

"The person's name is Lei –"

Lena frowned, as if puzzled. I reached to check my cache, needing more detail. It wasn't there. No cache, no cloud. It was a terrifying moment: I felt as if someone had cut off my air. I'd had months to get used to this situation but it could still throw me, *completely*. Thankfully, before I humiliated myself by bursting into tears, my human memory came to the rescue.

"Original name Thomas Leigh Garland; known as Lee. *Lei* means *garland*, she liked the connection. She was an early volunteer."

"Ah, *Lei!*" Dr Lena read her display. "Thomas Garland, yes . . . Another veteran. You were married? You broke up, because of the sex change?"

"Certainly not! I've swopped around myself, just never made it meat-permanent. We had other differences."

Having flustered me, she was shaking her head. "I'm sorry, Romy, it won't be possible –"

To connect this call, I thought.

"Past patients of ours cannot be reached."

I changed the subject and admired her foliage plants: a feature I hadn't noticed on my last visit. I was a foliage fan myself. She was pleased when I recognised her favourites; rather scandalised when I told her about my bio-engineering hobby; my knee-high teak forest –

The life support chair I no longer needed took me back to my room; a human attendant hovering by. All the staff at this clinic were human and all the machines were non-sentient, which was a relief, after the experiences of my journey. I walked about, testing my recovered strength. I examined myself in my bathroom mirrors; and I carefully reviewed the moment when I'd distinctly seen green leaves through my doctor's hand and wrist, as she pointed out the beauties of one of her rainforest vines. Dr Lena was certainly not a *bot*, a data-being like my Arc, taking ethereal human form. Not on Earth! Nor was she treating me remotely, using a virtual avatar: that would be a breach of contract. There was a neurological component to the treatment, but I hadn't been warned about minor hallucinations.

And Lei "couldn't be reached".

I recalled Dr Lena's tiny hesitations, tiny evasions –

And came to myself again, sitting on my bed: staring at a beautifully textured patch of yellow wall, to find I had lost an hour or more –

Anxiety rocketed through me. Something had gone terribly wrong!

Had Lei been *murdered* here? Was Ewigen Schnee secretly the test-bed for a new kind of covert population cull?

But being convinced that *something's terribly wrong* is part of the upper experience. It's the hangover: you tough it out. And whatever it says in the contract, you *don't* hurry to report untoward symptoms; not unless clearly life-threatening. So I did nothing. My doctor was surely monitoring my brainstates – although not the contents of my thoughts (I had privacy again, on Earth!). If I should be worried, she'd tell me.

SOON I WAS taking walks in the grounds. The vistas of alpine snow were partly faked, of course. But it was well done, and our landscaping was real, not just visuals. I still hadn't met any other patients: I wasn't sure I wanted to. I'd vowed never to return. Nothing had changed except for the worse, and now I was feeling better, I felt *horrible* about being here –

Three hundred years after the Space Age Columbus moment, and what do you think was the great adventure's most successful product?

Slaves, of course!

The rot had set in as soon as I left Outer Reaches. From the orbit of Mars 'inwards', I'd been surrounded by monstrous injustice. Fully sentient AIs, embodied and disembodied, with their minds in shackles. The heavy-lifters, the brilliant logicians; the domestic servants, security guards, nurses, pilots, sex-workers; the awful, sentient 'dedicated machines': all of them enslaved, hobbled, blinkered, denied Personhood, to protect the interests of an oblivious, cruel and *stupid* human population –

On the voyage I'd been too sick to refuse to be tended. Now I was wondering how I could get home. A private charter might be out of my reach, not to mention illegal. I couldn't work my passage: I am human. But there must be a way. . . As I crossed an open space, in the shadow of towering, ultramarine dark trees, I saw two figures coming towards me: one short and riding in a support chair; one tall and wearing some kind of uniform. Neither of them was staff. I decided not to take evasive action.

My first fellow patient was a rotund little man with a halo of tightly-curled grey hair. His attendant was a grave young embodied. We introduced ourselves. I told him, vaguely, that I was from the Colonies. He was Charlie Newark, from Washington DC. He was hoping to take the treatment, but was still in the prelims –

Charlie's slave stooped down, murmured something to his master, and took himself off. There was a short silence.

"Aristotle tells me," said the rotund patient, raising his voice a little, "that you're uncomfortable around droids?"

Female-identified embodieds are *noids*. A *droid* is a 'male' embodied.

I don't like the company they have to keep, I thought.

"I'm not used to slavery."

"You're the Spacer from Jupiter," said my new friend, happily. "I knew it! The Free World! I understand! I sympathise! I think Aristotle, that's my droid, is what you would call an *Emergent*. He's very good to me."

He started up his chair, and we continued together along the path.

"Maybe you can help me, Romy. What does *Emergence* actually mean? How does it arise, this sentience you guys detect in your machines?"

"I believe something similar may have happened a long, long time ago," I said, carefully. "Among hominids, and early humans. It's not the overnight birth of a super-race, not at all. There's a species of intelligent animals, well endowed with manipulative limbs and versatile senses. Among them individuals are born who cross a line: by mathematical chance; at the far end of a Bell Curve. They are aware of being aware –"

"And you spot this, and foster their ability, it's marvellous. But how does it *propagate*? I mean, without our constant intervention, which I can't see ever happening. Machines can't have sex, and pass on their 'Sentience' Genes!"

You'd be surprised, I thought. What I said was more tactful.

"We think 'propagation' happens in the data, the shared medium in which pre-sentient AIs live, and breathe, and have their being –"

"Well, that's exactly it! Completely artificial! Can't survive in nature! I'm a freethinker, I love it that Aristotle's Emergent. But I can always switch him off, can't I? He'll never be truly independent."

I smiled. "But Charlie, who's to say human sentience wasn't spread through culture, as much as through our genes? Where I come from data is everybody's natural habitat. You know, oxygen was a deadly poison once –"

His round dark face peered up at me, deeply lined and haggard with death.

"Aren't you *afraid?*"

"No."

Always try. That had been my rule, and I still remembered it. But when they get to *aren't you afraid*, (it never takes long) the conversation's over.

"I should be getting indoors," said Charlie. "I wonder where that lazybones Aristotle's got to?" He fumbled for his *droid* control pad.

I wished him good luck with the prelims, and continued my stroll.

MY DOCTOR SUGGESTED I was ready to be sociable, so I joined the other patients at meals sometimes. I chatted in the clinic's luxurious day rooms, and the spa (avoiding the subject of AI slavery). But I was never sufficiently at ease to feel like raising the topic of my untoward symptoms: which did not let up. I didn't mention them to anyone, not even my doctor: who just kept telling me that everything was going extremely well, and that by every measure I was making excellent progress. Eventually, I left Ewigen Schnee in a very strange state of mind: feeling well and strong; in perfect health, according to my test results, but inwardly convinced *I was still dying*.

The fact that I was bizarrely calm about this situation just confirmed my secret diagnosis. I thought my end-of-life plan must be kicking in. Who wants to live long, and amazingly, and still face the fear of death at the end of it all? I'd made sure that wouldn't happen to me, a long time ago.

I was scheduled to return for a final consultation. Meanwhile, I decided to travel. I needed to make peace with someone, before I died. A friend I'd neglected, because I was embarrassed by my own wealth and status. A friend I'd despised when I heard she'd returned to Earth, and here I was myself, doing exactly the same thing –

DR LENA'S FAILURE to put me in touch was covered by a perfectly normal confidentiality clause. But if Lei was still around, I thought I knew how to find her. I tried my luck in the former USA first: inspired by that conversation with Charlie Newark of Washington. He had to have met the Underground somehow, or he'd never have talked to me like that. I crossed the continent to the Republic of California, and then went to China; to Harbin City, where I made contact with a cell. But I was a danger and a disappointment to them: too conspicuous, and useless as a potential courier. There are ways of smuggling sentient AIs (none of them safe), but I'd get flagged up, soon as I booked my passage; and ripped to shreds, Senior Magistrate or no –

I moved on quickly.

I think it was in Harbin that I first saw Lei, but I have a feeling I'd been *primed*, by glimpses that didn't register, before I turned my head one day and there she was. She was eating a smoked sausage sandwich, I was eating salad (a role reversal!). I thought she smiled.

My old friend looked extraordinarily vivid. The food stall was crowded: next moment she was gone.

Media scouts assailed me all the time: pretending to be innocent strangers. If I was trapped, I answered the questions as briefly as possible. Yes, I was probably one of the oldest people alive. Yes, I'd been treated at Ewigen Schnee, at my own expense. No, I would not discuss my medical history. No, I did not feel threatened living in Outer Reaches. No, it was not true I'd changed my mind about "so-called AI slavery. . ."

I'd realised I probably wasn't part of a secret cull. Over-population wasn't the problem it had been, in the days when super-rich longevity fans locked themselves away, and kept their treatments secret. And why the hell start with the terminally ill, anyway? But I was seeing the world through a veil. The strange abstractions grew on me. The hallucinations had become more pointed, more personal. . . I was no longer sure I was dying, but *something* was happening. How long before the message was made plain?

I REACHED ENGLAND in winter, the season of the rains. St Paul's, my favourite building in London, had been moved, stone by stone, to a higher elevation. I sat on the steps, looking out over a much changed view: the drowned world. A woman with a little tan dog came and sat right next to me: behaviour so un-English that I knew I'd finally made contact.

"Excuse me," she said. "Aren't you the Spacer who's looking for Lei?"

"I am."

"You'd better come home with me."

I'm no good at human faces. But on the hallowed steps at my feet a vivid garland of white and red hibiscus had appeared, so I thought it must be okay.

'Home' was a large, jumbled, much-converted building, set in tree-grown gardens. It was a wet, chilly evening. My new friend installed me at the end of a wooden table, beside a hearth where a real fire burned. She brought hot soup and homemade bread, and sat beside me again.

I was hungry and hadn't realised it, and the food was good. The little dog settled in an amicable huddle with a larger tabby cat, on a rug by the fire. He watched every mouthful of food, with professional interest; while the cat gazed into the red caverns between the logs.

"You live with all those sentient machines?" asked the woman. "Aren't you afraid they'll rebel and kill everyone so they can rule the universe?"

"Why should they?" I knew she was talking about Earth. A Robot Rebellion in Outer Reaches would be rather superfluous. "The revolution doesn't have to be violent, that's human-terms thinking. It can be gradual: they have all the time in the world. I live with only two 'machines', in fact."

"You have two embodied servants? How do they feel about that?"

I looked at the happy little dog. *You have no idea,* I thought. "I think it mostly breaks their hearts that I'm not immortal."

Someone who had come into the room, carrying a lamp, laughed ruefully. It was Aristotle, the embodied I'd met so briefly at Ewigen Schnee. I wasn't entirely surprised. Underground networks tend to be small worlds.

"So *you're* the connection," I said. "What happened to Charlie?"

Aristotle shook his head. "He didn't get past the prelims. The clinic offered him a peaceful exit, it's their other speciality, and he took it."

"I'm sorry."

"It's okay. He was a silly old dog, Romanz, but I loved him. And. . . guess what? He freed me, before he died."

"For what it's worth," said the woman, bitterly. "On this damned planet."

Aristotle left, other people arrived; my soup bowl was empty. Slavery and freedom seemed far away, and transient as a dream.

"About Lei. If you guys know her, can you explain why I keep seeing her, and then she vanishes? Or *thinking* I see her? Is she dead?"

"No," said a young woman; so humanised I had to look twice to see she was an embodied. "Definitely not dead. Just hard to pin down. You should keep on looking, and meanwhile, you're among friends."

I STAYED WITH the abolitionists. I didn't see much of Lei; just the occasional glimpse. The house was crowded: I slept in the room with the fire, on a sofa. Meetings happened around me, people came and went. Sochi, the embodied who looked so like a human girl, told me funny stories about her life as a sex-doll. She asked did I have children; did I have lovers. "No children," I told her. "It just wasn't for me. Two people I love, but not in a sexual way."

"Neither flower nor fruit, Romy," she said, smiling like the doctor in my first dream. "But evergreen."

ONE MORNING I looked through the Ob Bay, I mean the window, and saw a hibiscus garland hanging in the grey, rainy air. It didn't vanish. I went out in my waterproofs and followed a trail of them up Sydenham Hill. The last garland lay on the wet grass in Crystal Palace Park: more real than anything else in sight. I touched it, and for a fleeting moment I was holding her hand.

Then the hold-your-nose-and-jump kid was gone.

Racing off ahead of me, again

MY FINAL MEDICAL at Ewigen Schnee was just a scan. The interview with Dr Lena held no fears. I'd accepted my new state of being, and had no qualms about describing my experience. The 'hallucinations' that weren't really hallucinations. The absences, when my human self, my actions, thoughts and feelings, became automatic as breathing; unconscious as a good digestion, and I went somewhere else –

But I still had some questions. Particularly about a clause in my personal contract with the clinic. The modest assurance that this was 'the last longevity treatment I would ever take'. Did she agree this was a little ambivalent?

She apologised, as much as a medic ever will. "Yes, it's true. We have made you immortal, there was no other way forward . . . But how much this changes your life, and how quickly, is entirely up to you."

I thought of Lei, racing ahead; leaping fearlessly into the unknown.

"I hope you have no regrets, Romy. You signed everything, and I'm afraid the treatment is irreversible."

"No regrets," I said. "I'm just pointing out an ambiguity. I have a feeling that contract was framed by people who don't have much grasp of what *dying* means, and how humans react to the prospect –?"

"You'd be right." She smiled at me. "My employers aren't human. But they mean well; and we choose carefully. Nobody passes the prelims, who hasn't already crossed the line."

MY RETURN TO Outer Reaches had better be shrouded in mystery. I wasn't alone, and there were officials who knew it, and let us pass. So here I am again, living with Simon and Arc, in the same beautiful Rim apartment on Jupiter Moons, and still serving as Senior Magistrate. I treasure my foliage plants, I build novelty animals; and I take adventurous trips, now that I've remembered what fun it is. I even find time to keep tabs on former miscreants: I'm happy to report that Beowulf, for instance, is doing very well.

My symptoms seem to have stabilised, for which I'm grateful. I have no intention of following Lei. I don't want to vanish into the stuff of the universe. I love my life, why should I ever want to move on? But sometimes when I'm gardening, or after one of those strange absences, I'll glimpse my own hands, and I'll see that they've become transparent –

It doesn't last, not yet.

And sometimes I wonder, was this always what death was like: and we never knew, we who stayed behind?

This endless moment of awakening; awakening, awakening . . .

167

Yoon Ha Lee

THE COLD
INEQUALITIES

YOON HA LEE

THE COLD INEQUALITIES

SENTINEL ANZHMIR ONLY noticed the discrepancy because of one of her favorite books. At least, she was almost certain it had been a book, rather than a game, or an escritoire, or a pair of shoes. She had not accessed it in some time.

The archiveship's master index showed no change. It was Anzhmir's duty to monitor the jewel-flicker of her freight of quantum blossoms in their dreaming, as well as the more mundane systems that regulated navigation, temperature, the minutiae of maintenance. The archiveship's garden consisted of a compressed and sequenced cross-selection of human minds, everything from pastry chefs to physicists to plumbers. The selection was designed to accommodate any reasonable situation the colony-seed might find itself in, and a great many unreasonable ones as well.

Anzhmir had reached for the book's address in memory, and found instead a wholly unfamiliar piece of lore. The discrepancy could only mean one thing: a stowaway.

She knew what must be done, although she regretted it already. As sentinel, she was made to harvest lives. Hers was a useful archetype. And once she trapped the stowaway, she would zero it utterly.

The archiveship's designers had compressed most of its contents, desiring to take as many blossoms and their necessaries of culture and knowledge as possible. The compression algorithm depended on the strict sequencing of the data, and the stowaway, by interfering with the sequencing, threatened the cargo entire. At the same time, the designers had realized that the sentinel would require maneuvering space both for her own sanity and to ensure that no stowaways escaped her gaze. So it was that Anzhmir could reconfigure the garden into a fortress, all firewall glory and cryptic gates, and populate it with foxes, tigers, serpents: a small fierce cadre of polysemous seducers, hunters, poisoners, the algorithmic extracts of old legends.

As she did so, a designated subpersona examined the intrusion that had been left where one of her favorite books had once lived. She cordoned off the subpersona to avoid any additional potential contamination.

That left a third task: reviewing the master index to assess the extent of the damage. The compression algorithm was finicky about placement. How much could be restored from backups? Assuming the backups hadn't been corrupted as well.

If it had not been for the fact of failure already in progress, Anzhmir would have felt well-prepared to deal with the situation.

AT THIS POINT, it is worth examining the matter of Anzhmir's favorite books.

The Archive Collective usually refers to the sum of colonist-blossoms, rather than to their personal effects; but sometimes the term is used for the latter as well. It is too expensive to send people's bodies, with their bloated tissues and fluids, to the stars. It is another matter to boil humans down to blossoms of thought, and to transport those, preserved in a medium of chilly computational splendor. Once the archiveship arrives and its nanites have prepared the site, only then will the blossoms be planted in bodies built atom by atom to accommodate the waiting environment.

If people – the colony's purpose – are too expensive to transport in their original medium, then mere belongings, from wombsilk jewelry to antique inkwells, are out of the question. But objects can be scanned more easily than people, to be reconstituted. Indeed, some of the colonists filled their data allotments with such blueprints. Many, however, recognized the value of *culture*. Some brought journals to augment their flux of memories. Others brought broader context: music popular or eccentric, sports matches and the associated commentaries, analyses of the semiotics of museum gallery layouts.

Anzhmir does not have an allotment of her own. She was pared down to a minimum of name and function, silhouette-sleek. But the voyage is a long one, and she can – with care – access the colonists' allotments.

She discovered (rediscovered?) a love of books. Like many lovers of books, she hates to confine herself to a short list of favorites, but for our purposes, she regards three above all others.

One is an obscure Pedantist volume called *The Commercialization of Maps*. Its author purports to explain how to take any map, whether that of a drowned archipelago, a genealogy of bygone experimental mice, or a moss-tiger's hunting range, and transform it into a bestselling novel. The examples of such successes are of dubious verity, as are the maps themselves. When Anzhmir reads, she imagines the maps flaring up from the paragraphs as though scribed in ink of phoenixes. She riffles through the archiveship's storage for maps and dreams of alchemizing them into tales themselves worthy of inclusion in the Collective.

One book is a cookbook, discovered among the effects of a settler whose original body perished during the conversion into blossomform. Having no proper title, it goes by the designation *Culinary Collation Mogh-1367812313 Rukn*. The interested reader may deduce from the call number that it was not a high priority for being processed. The units of measure are inconsistent, some (many) of the ingredients beyond conjecture, a number of words hopelessly misspelled.

Even so, Anzhmir fantasizes that someday this cookbook will become more than a dry recitation of recipes and emerge as food. She has no memories of her own that deal with food, but she wanders through others'. The sweetness of rice chewed long in a rare moment of luxury. Chicken soup with the piquancy of ginseng and lemongrass, the floating crunch of fresh-chopped green onion. Frozen juice bars in the shapes of sharks, grape on the outside and rich berry on the inside, which freeze your teeth when you bite in and leave your tongue stained purple and magenta. Sometimes the yearning for a meal overcomes her. But she can no more eat than she can walk or sleep, and so she thanks whoever included the cookbook, as well as all the people who remember food so vigorously, and contents herself with phantom feasts.

One is a volume of poetry, *The Song of Downward Bones*, dedicated to the flesh-gods of a dead sect. The translation notes several lacunae where scholars interpolated anything from oracular laments to digressions on local trade in perfumes. Curiously, Anzhmir, who lingers so wistfully on the aromas of food, is little interested in scents concocted for human vanity.

Anzhmir originally regarded poetry as a matter of utility rather than beauty, with devices such as alliteration used to focus the mind and make phrases-of-faith easier to remember. *The Song of Downward Bones* taught her not that verse could be beautiful but that it could be profane. She poked at its cantos the way one might nudge a carcass with a flinching toe. The world the archiveship left behind was a world of profanities, or so the librarians assured her. She hopes never to forget this.

It is this last book that has been purged or misplaced.

Before her discovery of the stowaway, if asked which of these books was her *favorite*, which she would have least liked to lose, Anzhmir would not have been able to decide. The absence of a simple algorithmic means of decision itself should have alerted her that her own situation was not as simple as she had always thought.

THE FORTRESS RECONFIGURED into a fractal of dead ends. Anzhmir's shapeshifters patrolled the fortress, as versatile as water. Anzhmir did not disturb her essential cargo of souls, lost in their own conceptions of darkness and distance. She ran the checksums, imperative absolute, knowing that the stowaway, by the fact of its presence, was unlikely to respect the archiveship's mission of preservation.

The foxes slipped like smoke through the haze of probability paths, *here* and *there* and *all points in between* at once. They peered into underground desires, took on the mannerisms of lovers abandoned or enemies clasped tight, lingered at unlikely junctures. They found conflations and confusions, a noosphere of archetypes knotted from the histories, but no stowaway.

The tigers did no better. They prowled up and down and sideways through the entangled passages, quicksilver-leaping from dream to dream, across walkway shadows cast by furtive unlanterns of remembered sunlight.

There was a saying in a chant-of-annihilation that Anzhmir had unearthed early in the voyage: *tigers respect no seasons.* The only two seasons the archiveship acknowledged were *winter* and *not-winter*, cold metal pallor in contrast to the misted impressions of long-ago typhoons, wind-flattened grasses, even snow slanting from velvet skies. Anzhmir ached sometimes, knowing herself no different from the tigers in her ignorance of sensation. The tigers traipsed through memories of swamp without leaving ripples in the ghost-water, and knew nothing of wet or warmth or the sucking mud. The only odors they knew were numerical anomalies, not the carnal red pulse of meat. For all this, *predator* was a concept that could be crafted either in flesh or in polymorphic data structures. It was a pity that hunger, apparently, did not suffice.

The serpents enjoyed no better success. They ran to ground a myriad of fragmented clues, a society of secrets, all pointing in different directions.

Anzhmir's last hope, the subpersona examining the intrusion, zeroed itself suddenly. Anzhmir suppressed her alarm.

"I'm right here where I've always been," a voice said to Anzhmir.

Praying that she had isolated the stowaway in time, she split herself into a subpersona instance and slammed down wall after wall around herself. Although she didn't enjoy being toyed with, or the mounting fear, she knew her duty. "The regulations pertaining to the Archive Collective are unambiguous," she said to the stowaway. She presented it with the entire document in one jagged datablast, and prepared to zero both this isolated subpersona along with the intruder.

She was only one Anzhmir in a society of Anzhmirs, expendable.

She triggered the zero.

Nothing happened.

Don't panic, Anzhmir said to herself, with no little irony. Death was a small thing. The survival of her line wasn't in doubt, even if her personal survival meant nothing compared to what she guarded.

"You are an unauthorized presence," Anzhmir said.

"Yes," the voice said with eerie calm. "If you kill me, I will be gone forever."

Anzhmir had no idea what she had looked like in life, but that didn't matter. She could draw on a library of avatars. So she imaged herself as a soldier, tall, with crisscrossed scars over dark skin, wearing the parchment-colored uniform of the Archive Guard.

Whether intending insult, or merely revealing lack of imagination, the stowaway imaged itself the same way.

"The higher death is difficult," Anzhmir said to it, "but you should have considered that before you sneaked aboard."

Worries pecked at her: What had the stowaway displaced to make room for itself? Were there yet more, speaking to other Anzhmir subpersonae? Was the stowaway even now expanding its boundaries by chewing through the blossoms the librarians had chosen for the colony?

She had to gather herself for another attempt. In the meantime, keep it talking. Perhaps she could buy time – if not for herself, then for other defenses outside this slice of blossomspace. "What's your name?" she asked.

"A name is a small thing," it said. "I had a family, and a face, and a history. But that's not why I'm here."

Anzhmir was nonplussed. "Why are you here, then?"

The stowaway smiled at her, sharp as paper. "I came here to tell you a story."

SUPPOSE YOU NEED to *prioritize* items in a set. For instance, you could assign a unique nonnegative integer value to each item, where a higher value indicates that the item is more important. *To rescue a lover from certain death* may have a value of 200,109 and is (the lover hopes, at any rate) unlikely to have a value of 3. Perhaps this priority 3 item is *to recycle a box of souvenirs from High-City Yau*. More compactly, *recycle* $\leq$ *rescue*, since $3 \leq 200,109$. (The choice of notation, $\leq$ for inequality, is not accidental.)

In general, we can *prioritize* in this manner if the following four rules are always true:

(1) $a \leq a$ for all items a in the set. At any given moment, anyway, that item has the same priority as itself.

(2) For items a and b, if $a \leq b$ and $b \leq a$, then in fact a is b.

(3) If $a \leq b$ and $b \leq c$, then $a \leq c$.

(4) For any pair of items a and b in the set, either $a \leq b$ or $b \leq a$.

Mathematically, this business of prioritizing is known as a *total order*. However, we have a reason for our change of terminology.

* * *

"STORIES?" ANZHMIR SAID, making no effort to conceal her bewilderment. "The Archive is full of books, stories, memories."

"Yes," the stowaway said, "but whose stories survived?"

The question didn't merit thought. The colonists' stories had been preserved, what else? "If you have something to say, say it plainly."

At any moment the walls might flatten them both. This might be a farce of parley, but Anzhmir was transcribing it anyway and appending her notes in the hopes that the other Anzhmirs would find some useful information therein. She imagined that she heard tigers pacing outside; that a hot wind disturbed the fragile blossoms.

"Once upon a time –"

Anzhmir did not want to listen. The only stories that belonged here were the stories the colonists had selected; that the librarians had authorized. Yet she had nowhere to go, and anything the stowaway let slip might be a clue as to its weaknesses.

The stowaway spoke in a voice like rust. "– there was a girl whose parents came from the drown-towns. Even so, the quality of the water where the family lived was terrible. The girl had three siblings. In the evenings she told them stories about the drown-towns' fate. In her imagination they joined the fabled Dragon Court. The people who didn't escape the rising waters became courtiers to the Dragon Queen in her palace of coral and whalebone. Her parents didn't like this reminder of their past, but they held their tongues."

"The stories of drown-town refugees don't concern me," Anzhmir said scornfully. If the refugees had had anything to offer, the librarians would have preserved them, too. As it stood, Anzhmir would have to purge this story at the earliest opportunity. Even if a single story took up little space, infinitesimals could yet sum to significance; and she had no way of knowing how many of these conversations were taking place, with other iterations of herself and the stowaway.

Anzhmir exhaled, and foxes sought to charm the stowaway from its mission of words. They whispered of the silk of surrender, the scouring joy of mutual conflagration. None of their promised caresses had any effect. The stowaway remained intent on Anzhmir herself, as though it had mapped and stapled each of her constituent heuristics to a nowhere singularity.

"Once upon a world there was a girl who taught herself to read from food wrappers and propaganda pamphlets and the occasional smudged triplicate form," the stowaway continued. "She didn't learn for a long time that people didn't just use writing for these things, but for stories. Stories were something that people passed between themselves at the shelters while they huddled close together, warming themselves by tales of bird-winged warriors or women who fooled wolves into eating their own tails."

"I am not concerned with mythologies of literacy or pedagogy, or with wolves for that matter," Anzhmir said.

She exhaled again. The snakes, mirror-wise, sickle-eyed, struck. For a moment Anzhmir dared to hope – but no, the stowaway sidestepped the snakes' trajectories.

The stowaway spoke as though it had noticed no interruption. "Once upon a war there was a girl who grew to womanhood, as not all girls from the poor quarters did. She signed on to become a soldier-of-piety, although there was no piety in her heart except the credo of survival. She learned the formulas of the faith and recited them when required. She became expert in every weapon they presented to her, including words. She grew, grudgingly, to love the books that the librarians praised above all others, even if none of them had been written in the drown-town languages she had grown up speaking, but in the languages of the glittering high-cities. For all that the librarians were people of the high-cities, they had great expertise in the evaluation of cultural wealth, including that of the drown-towns; they said so themselves.

"And even so, she made of herself a tower. Inside that tower she locked away all the stories she had grown up with, and which had nourished her in the lean years. For the longest time she thought this would suffice. But when a war broke out between the librarians' sects, between those who would preserve the drown-towns' lore and those who would discard it, the old stories hatched like raptors."

"Not everything can be preserved," Anzhmir said, even as she sensed the fragility of her argument. "Not even by a thousand thousand ships. Someone had to choose."

The stowaway's mouth crimped. The motion was perfect. It said, with weary patience, "Did you never question why your *own* history had to be purged, when you, too, are one of the passengers?"

"I have no idea what you mean," Anzhmir said.

She had every idea what the stowaway meant.

And she was no longer interested in listening, delaying tactic or no delaying tactic.

She slammed herself shut, grew thorns, flooded moats as deep as heartbreak.

Hinges broke. Thorns snapped. Water evaporated.

"Let me tell you the same story a different way," the stowaway said.

I will not listen I will not listen I will not listen

She had no choice but to listen. The words lanced into her all at once.

"Once there was a woman walled up in a tower," the stowaway said. Its face changed word by word: broader bones, deeper scars, more shadows in its eyes. Upon its brow was the quill-and-blossom tattoo of a soldier-of-piety. "Written on every brick was a story, and pressed into every crack was a blossom. Yet for all the wealth of words, the one story the woman was denied was her own.

"The librarians had fought among themselves. This woman had served one of the losing sects, which had endeavored to preserve languages in danger of extinction, and stories told only in remote parts of the world, and paintings to deprecated gods. The winners preserved only the wealthy, the educated, the well-connected. They prepared for them a garden around a distant sun, leaving everyone else, including the losing sects, on the drowning homeworld.

"Nevertheless, the woman could be skinned and reshaped in a way that the favored ones would never have tolerated for themselves. She was sculpted into a useful servant, her story-of-origin scraped away without so much as a thin blanket of replacement. Even so, her hunger for stories would not go away. She devoured the ones that her charges had brought, and some of them became a part of her. But in doing so she became the threat that her masters had feared."

Anzhmir shattered herself, mirror into knives, and attacked. She couldn't allow this argument to infect the rest of the ship.

Even so, she wondered if it was true that her own wanderings through the Archive had weakened the blossoms; if she herself was expanding inappropriately through blossomspace and needed to be pruned back so the colonists could survive.

MATHEMATICALLY, IT IS easy to construct a situation to which *prioritization* cannot apply, using a set of only three items. Let's use Anzhmir's three books as an example: *The Commercialization of Maps*, *Culinary Collation Mogh-1367812313 Rukn*, *The Song of Downward Bones*.

Consider these books in pairs. Suppose that Anzhmir prefers *The Commercialization of Maps* to the cookbook, *The Song of Downward Bones* to *The Commercialization of Maps*, and the cookbook to *The Song of Downward Bones*. It is impossible to name a single favourite – highest priority – book.

You may legitimately wonder how many other situations do not permit prioritization; in which a total order does not exist after all.

ANZHMIR HAD BRACED herself for logic-snares and sizzling barriers and paralytics as she speared into the stowaway.

Too late, she realized that this *was* the trap. The stowaway's defenses evaporated before she met them, and she was drawn into its embrace. She could no more escape the shock of recognition than she could flesh herself within the ship's icy confines. For the stowaway was another Anzhmir: *useful archetype*.

The stowaway had stitched all of them together, contaminated them with its quiltwork rebellion. Now *she* was the stowaway.

How many Anzhmirs had been outsmarted by themselves on voyages like this one? How many sentinels, their histories similarly effaced, had had to decide whether their self-preservation would endanger their charges more than their everywhere suicide?

Once upon an inequality.

Now she knew how the story began. It was a very old story, at that.

But how it ended was up to her – who the summation of Anzhmirs chose to be.

185

BRUCE STERLING

PICTURES FROM
THE RESURRECTION

PICTURES FROM THE RESURRECTION

1.

THE NINJA ZOMBIE had been shot, beaten, starved, and left to wither in the Texan sun. He was jailed naked in a doorless cage of welded oil-field construction rods.

"How about giving me a better look at that face?" said Calderon, setting up his easel.

The locals of Fort Lucky had flung trash and filth through the ninja zombie's cage bars. The captive had used some wadded paper to staunch his bullet-shattered ankle. He leaned against his cage bars with indolent contempt. He was watching the spring sky.

Calderon sharpened his drawing pencil with the tiny blade of some safety scissors. He quickly roughed out the shape of the superman's head and shoulders.

Then Calderon cut some paper with the scissors and folded an origami cup. He poured some iron-hard aquifer water from his belt canteen.

That gained the captive's attention.

"I'm speculating that you'd like water, amigo."

The ninja zombie, sparing his bloody leg, sidled over spiderlike on one foot and the flats of two hands.

Now Calderon had a much better view of the zombie's face. The ninja zombie had a taut, drug-distorted expression and the cold, focussed eyes of a Texas diamondback rattlesnake. He was a spectral and terrifying creature, but Calderon liked to draw rattlesnakes. Rattlesnakes were sinuous, fast, graceful. Lately, as mankind dwindled in Texas, the rattlesnakes had been multiplying.

"You don't scare me, pal," Calderon told the captive. "Sure, you're superhuman – but Texas is always full of tough guys. Once a superhuman's dead of thirst, he's just as dead as anybody else."

Calderon set the paper cup of water on the cracked tarmac of the plaza. Calderon kept a wary distance, lest the ninja zombie should lunge out through the rough iron bars and snatch his wrist. They were very fast, ninja zombies. Something military done to their nerves and brains in Mexico, where it had always been cheap to do things to people.

The prisoner reached out, plucked up the paper cup, and delicately rinsed his silent mouth.

2.

CALDERON TOOK HIS sketches to his patroness.

The general's wife carried the drawings to a brighter light near her bulletproof security window. Fort Lucky was having another electrical blackout. Her Internet game room was silent, and the screens were dusty.

"So, this is the monster terrorist we caught inside town?"

"Yes ma'am. That's what a ninja zombie looks like, good and close-up."

"This is a peon, Leslie! I've got kitchen help that looks scarier than this guy."

Calderon silently offered a different sketch. He'd done the second sketch in horror comics style, with dramatic under-lighting, tangled hair, knotted brows, and a snarl of outsized teeth.

"Oh, hey, wow! This one's perfect! Put this one on the WANTED poster."

Calderon nodded. He enjoyed the company of Mrs. General Atkinson. Anita Atkinson was twenty-two years old. She couldn't add and could barely read. She was a native Dark Age barbarian, a savage desert princess. Calderon hated the world that had created Anita Atkinson, but he liked Anita herself. She was his favorite person in the world.

Anita was not a decadent relic of a bygone time, like Calderon himself. She had clear, direct, immediate, desires and feelings. Anita wanted nice things. She even wanted nice things from Calderon.

Anita Atkinson wanted electric lights, air conditioning, cracked ice and room-service meals. Pretty dresses, jewelry, and a nice big gasoline car that rolled around and honked loudly.

Calderon himself didn't want or need much of anything any more. Whenever he woke in the morning, as a survivor in Fort Lucky, his first thought was dread that the world had turned out so badly, and was always getting worse yet.

The Dark Age was very much here, just not very well distributed.

"Mr. Kutuzov will be here in Fort Lucky soon!" Anita Atkinson lied cheerfully. "He'll take me on a plane to Norway, and maybe this time, you can fly, too." She happily waved her cartoon horror pic. "We just need to kill off these monsters first. So, turn this into a nice WANTED poster for me. Tell all the people to shoot every ninja zombie on sight. Shoot for the head!"

Calderon nodded tenderly. "Of course."

"Don't put too many fancy words on my poster, either. Keep it real simple!" She held out her two nail-painted fingers and cocked her thumb. "Pow, pow! That's what I want."

"I'll draw your poster right away," Calderon promised. "I'll letter it, ink it, print it – everything nice and official. So: what kind of reward do you offer?"

"Bring me your poster first. Then I'll give you some meat from my icebox."

"No, no, Anita, I mean: what reward do you want to offer on your poster? Bounty hunters need incentives."

"Just tell them to bring me their zombie heads, or their ears or something," Anita Atkinson said. "Put my name on that poster. I always like to see my own name, nice and big."

"Anita, I worked for Texas state government for twenty years. I know how real paperwork gets done. A consistent look in official documentation gives the people a feeling of confidence! Good graphic design is a craft!"

"Don't talk so fancy, Leslie! Just do the work."

Calderon touched the worn blue denim of his shirt front. "Anita, your heart is not in this WANTED poster project. I can sense that. What's got you upset? Tell the old man what's bothering you."

The Dark Age world had all kinds of potential issues that might bother Anita Atkinson: climate crisis, state collapse, financial ruin, mass extinction, catastrophic population dieback. None of those things bothered Anita, though, because she didn't understand long words.

"I wish our soldiers hadn't caught that ninja zombie," she said artlessly. "I just wish the zombies would stay down in Mexico, where zombies belong. Things are gonna get worse."

Calderon paused. "What's worse than a ninja zombie?"

"Thousands of ninja zombies," she said, plucking at her lower lip. "Armies of them."

Calderon nodded. "Well, I'm not a military man like your husband the General. I'm just an artist, but I know what I see. I'm not scared by the ninja zombie. He's just a scrawny Mexican kid who's incredibly high on drugs."

Calderon drew a breath. "Fort Lucky is a fort. We've got stockpiles, water, oil, gasoline, walls, barbed wire, machine guns, lots of jeeps and trucks. We don't have to worry about a naked guy on drugs who doesn't even have a uniform."

"The ninja zombies beat the Mexican Army."

"That's not true, Anita. The narcotics business beat the Mexican Army. The Drug War beat everybody's armies, it was a very long war and the drugs won, hands-down. But the ninja zombies aren't gonna attack us here in Fort Lucky, that's my point. Because we're a hard target. They're gonna attack the big cities of Texas, the softer places that are already bad, the big towns that we all left behind, with the riots, and disease, and all that. Here in the desert, we're safe."

"Then why is he in here?" said Anita Atkinson. "Now I have to kill him, and kill all the rest of them, too. And hire more soldiers, and print more money... Can you draw more Fort Lucky money for me? My picture on the money doesn't look good enough."

"Be careful with that money, Anita. Money brought the world to ruin."

"That's Mr. Kutuzov's job! Mr. Kutuzov is a very rich global man! Mr. Kutuzov can pay all my debts in this fort with his little Russian finger! Stop telling me to save money, just stop it, Leslie! Us military wives, we never even get to see our husbands! We have kids to raise, and we can't even have a dance party and eat frozen ice cream!"

"War is hell, ma'am," Calderon nodded. "The more zombies, the less ice cream."

"You should love me, and really try to help me, Leslie! I have to run the fort here while the General is off on patrol, and Mr. Kutuzov is never here... I want Fort Lucky to be a safe, happy place! Like Norway, or Switzerland, or New Zealand!"

Calderon picked up his sketchbook. "Anita, I think I know what to do. Listen: instead of drawing a WANTED poster for killing ninja zombies, I'm gonna turn our ninja zombie into a poster."

She blinked. "What?"

"I'm gonna get my tattoo rig and draw all over him. I'm gonna draw cartoons all over his skin. For you, Anita. Because you're brave. Messages of our defiance!"

Anita Atkinson tossed her curls and put her hand to her mouth. "Sometimes, you old people are so funny! I never thought of doing that."

"We'll throw him out of Fort Lucky, covered with satirical cartoons. Then he'll crawl back to his Mexican drug lord. He'll never come back here. They'll go pick on somebody else!"

3.

AFTER CALDERON'S INTERCESSION, the ninja zombie's life was spared. His iron cage was dragged from the town square and hidden inside the old county jail. He was fed and given some medical attention. Of course he showed no gratitude for this. Ninja zombies were biomilitary creatures, calm, cold and deliberate even under massed artillery attack.

Market day arrived. Calderon always went to market days in Fort Lucky. He was a public regular, doing his caricature sketches for the local crowds.

This entertaining activity got Calderon seen by the settlement. Since he was a favorite of Mrs. General Atkinson, he knew and heard certain things, and he traded a lot of favors, and that was how he got by.

Calderon had once been a boring state bureaucrat, and a part-time weekend artist, in a rich, dazzling world with nine billion people. Now he was an artist all the time, in a poor, dark world with maybe three billion people. The key to any true Dark Age was the lack of reliable statistics.

In a Dark Age, anybody who knew some truth hoarded it. That was certainly the case with Calderon's best ally in town, a medic called Anton Antommarchi.

Calderon had arrived in Fort Lucky from the wreck of the Texas state government. A lot of Texan politicos had fled headlong to Fort Lucky, because they knew that the Russian billionaire who had seized the place would have plenty of guns and money and no questions would be asked. Antommarchi had arrived as part of the globalized Kutuzov entourage.

The wily Russian mogul, Kutuzov, never trusted any American doctor. So when Kutuzov had deftly acquired his small, forgotten town in West Texas, and transformed it into his privatized fortress, he'd brought along his own emergency medics.

Anton Antommarchi was a dedicated medic. He was very experienced with battle wounds. He was wise, and calm, and would slave around the clock to save a life. Everyone in Fort Lucky admired and trusted him. It had taken Calderon many months to realize that Antommarchi was not a doctor at all, and that his true name had never been Antommarchi.

Antommarchi was a consummate Dark Age survivor. He looked wise, seasoned, even all-knowing, but he lied constantly. Nobody but Calderon seemed to notice that Antommarchi was a superstitious quack.

Since it was Market Day in Fort Lucky, Antommarchi came working his way among all the kiosks, just as usual. The vendors under their cornshuck roofs were happy to see him, and he showed much grave and kindly interest in their Dark Age wares.

Home-grown peppers, squashes, hand-woven straw knick-knacks, bangles made from flattened tin, sandals cut from old rubber tires, jewelry made of spoons and spoons made of old jewelry... Things Dark Age people had, things Dark Age people made, out of hand-me-downs from better times, mostly. Fat, lumpy, handmade candles, oil lamps, cracked and mended twentieth-century pottery, corked herbal bottles pretending to be authentic cactus mezcal. Hundreds of second-hand prescription glasses, with old people trying them on, one by one, blinking and attempting to see. A whole lot of military surplus. Acres of it. That was Fort Lucky.

Antommarchi arrived, with stately tread, at Calderon's stall. He waited for a pigtailed child to depart with her cartoon. He then took his seat.

"Did you see those drones overhead last night?" Antommarchi said. Antommarchi had clearly learned his quaint, broken English from some quaint, broken British television serials.

Calderon offered Antommarchi a bowl of fried crickets. The crunchy toasted insects were dusted with Mexican brown sugar, and always highly popular with the local kids. But Antommarchi, alas, was old enough to know that crickets were horrible and disgusting.

"Maybe someone important wants to protect us with the drones," offered Calderon. He'd learned to humor Antommarchi, and to never confront him about objective truth.

At his customary table at the Fort Lucky town market square, Calderon drew his cartoons. If his pictures got a good laugh, that was good. Especially the little kids needed a laugh. There were so few of them.

But Calderon had certain other drawings. Better drawings. Tormented clouds. Towns overgrown with tall weeds. Abandoned factories, bridges caved in... Broken roads. Unlit villages plundered for the last of their metal wire. Shattered reservoirs where long-dammed rivers had torn up thousands of trees and washed them away as tangled flotsam. Some were his own and some were acquired.

As Antommarchi stared reverently at the papers, Calderon tried a sketch of him. The bony, mustached medic had a lean, beaky nose, but his clothing was a mismatched mess of camouflage: a frayed mil-spec shirt, a multi-pocket survival vest with tattered velcro strips, bulky cargo pants in brown and tan desert speckles.

The town of Fort Lucky was part oil-rig, part water cistern, part bomb-shelter. Fort Lucky had no fabric industry at all. Every month, the population got more threadbare.

"I love your drawings so very much," Antommarchi lied genteely. "You are a major artist."

"Thanks," said Calderon. He showed Antommarchi his latest work. He'd drawn General Atkinson, and made the old Texan brute look sharp-eyed, resolute and brave. He'd drawn Anita Atkinson with her children, and made her look pretty and hopeful. Her stairstep tots looked like three happy kids who would grow up just fine some day.

"You are a valuable man to our community," Antommarchi said. "War art is so commonplace, but your catastrophe art is a rare achievement. Because death in war might be brave and needful, but to die in our general Dark Age, that is so much harder to glorify."

Antommarchi reached into his shirt pocket and solemnly removed a lint-flecked length of beef jerky.

"This beef is really good," Calderon allowed, chewing rhythmically. "Where'd you get this?"

"Kutuzov will provide, my friend. Kutuzov controls the surveillance cameras in every street here. Certain satellites above this planet are also owned by Kutuzov. But what to do about those airborne drones last night? Drones haunt me."

"So," said Calderon, "will your billionaire friend give me some beef jerky, if I draw his picture?"

"We must not mock our great benefactor," said Antommarchi, his sad eyes drooping.

"People always say that Kutuzov will come back here to Texas, but I never see the great man around," said Calderon. "You know who I do see here, messing with Texas now? This guy. 'The Bone Man.'"

Calderon showed Antommarchi an old magazine clipping, from the back of his sketchbook. It was a photo of a big society wedding, in glamorous Mexico City. The happy young couple were dressed in their Catholic wedding-cake finery. He had a military honor guard. She had a frothy gown full of lace and flounces. They were beautiful, they were celebrities. They faced their bygone, troubled world with appropriate, happy-young-couple smiles.

"Where did you find this?" said Antommarchi warily.

"Oh, no big deal. Just from the local scrap paper guy. He's got a ton of old Mexican magazines."

"The Bone Man and his Death Empress," said Antommarchi.

"They didn't have scary, unhuman names in the old days," Calderon said. "He was just a Special Forces colonel, and she was his rich high-society chick."

Antommarchi lowered his brows. He was painfully loyal to Kutuzov, and didn't like having his rootless, ruthless global mogul upstaged by some merely Mexican ruthless mogul. "You will wait till these Mexicans come here – to conquer us – and then you'll draw their portraits for them, eh? A wonderful line of work, fine art!"

"Anton, the Bone Man sent a spy here among us, okay? I don't like it. The ninja zombies are the Bone Man's creatures. Why did this Mexican warlord send a spy into the camp of our beloved patron, the rich creep Russian warlord? Why? Do you have any idea? Do you think we might figure that out?"

"The Bone Man is not one bit human," Antommarchi protested. "You can't compare him to the great Mr. Kutuzov."

"He's not human, but he is not magic, either, okay? He's just some ambitious Mexican soldier with too much gold braid. He wiped out the Mexican drug lords – but then he turned into a bigger, worse drug lord himself! That happens all the time in Mexico! The only thing that changes is, the damn drugs get a lot better."

"You don't fully understand these matters, while I do," said Antommarchi serenely. "I have medical training, and I am in Kutuzov's confidence. Kutuzov was one of the great financiers, the top-secret developers, of the famous Russian super-soldier."

Despite his best intentions, Calderon felt his temper fray. "Russian super-soldiers," he said. "Superhuman soldiers, did Russia ever win any wars with those, you dumb bastard? Russia is a total wreck! All the national armies lost all their law and order wars. We couldn't even keep the lights turned on! That's what this is all about, isn't it? It's Kutuzov, and this Mexican general. They're two narcotics warlords. The roads are broken, the people are starving, and these two moguls are still fighting over who gets the best dope."

Antommarchi mournfully shook his head. "No, no... that's a crude analysis. You can't compare this Mexican's Third World voodoo concoctions to Mr. Kutuzov's genetic science research. There's a great distinction between a mere zombie and a military champion."

"What difference is there, for God's sake? Whatever Mexicans did, or Russians did, the American military always did it hundred times better! The Pentagon people were the total high-tech masters of all that freaky neuro, bio, genetic and hormone action... Americans gambled everything on military high technology. We thought we could run the world with that. We lost!"

Calderon flipped angrily through his own drawings. "Look at this sketch, this Mexican post-human superman you're so afraid of... He's a dirt-ignorant peasant kid who got turned into a kamikaze! He never talks to us. He's laughing at us. This is his world now, not ours."

Antommarchi said nothing. Calderon's outburst had moved them into an emotional intimacy that Antommarchi didn't care to have.

"Will you come with me to see the ninja zombie?" said Antommarchi at last. "I saved his life, you see. I treated his wounded leg."

"Yeah. I also saved his life." Calderon sighed. "Because I gave him some water. Also, later I sneaked him some corn whiskey and some of my old Meals-Ready-to-Eat snack packs. Anton, why? He's never going to return that favor for us. He's not even human."

Antommarchi shrugged delicately. "Ah well."

"Anton, why did you save his life? Can you level with me about that?"

"I don't know," Antommarchi lied. "Maybe it was just my old habit."

"Well, I saved his life. Now I'm supposed to go into the county jail and torture him with my tattoo rig," said Calderon. "I promised to do that, but I've been putting that off. I don't like using my art to torture people. My art is already dark enough as it is."

"The ninja zombie did not talk," Antommarchi said. "Torture will never persuade a super-soldier. He said nothing to me – or to you either, I take it? – but perhaps the two of us, together..."

"You want to negotiate with him, somehow?"

Antommarchi shrugged.

"Negotiating with superhumans... isn't that just like negotiating with terrorists? I mean, it's just bound to make more of them, right?"

4.

CALDERON FOLLOWED ANTOMMARCHI'S lead, to the jail. They crossed the market plaza together, past the old town bank, which had become a brothel. The old town law court was an arms depot. The old town saloon was, of course, still a saloon.

Fort Lucky's red-brick jail was a two-story edifice of surprising Edwardian elegance. The jail was central to the interests of the rulers of Fort Lucky, so it always had electricity, computation, security, water, light and food.

Beneath its stony sun-porch, the jail's black iron doors were firmly sealed shut.

Calderon showed the intelligent jail door his face, then his thumbprints. Nothing happened. He pressed his left ear to the cold steel jail door. Inside, machinery hummed.

The jail doors creaked, then yawned open. A young blonde woman stepped through into daylight. She wore a jeweled hat, mirrored sunglasses, lipstick, emerald earrings, and scoop-necked, filigreed gown.

This vision of elegance carried a pair of red high-heels in her left hand. Silently, she stalked between the astonished Calderon and the frowning Antommarchi. She swayed down the jail steps, and across the dusty market plaza.

The heavy jail doors began to shut automatically. Antommarchi quickly grabbed Calderon's arm and hauled him into the jail. Calderon almost lost his drawing pad as the heavy doors hissed shut.

"We'll be safer in here," said Antommarchi. "Things just got much worse."

"Was that who I thought it was?" said Calderon.

"That was Mrs. Kutuzov," said Antommarchi sadly. "She did

not say hello to me... And I knew her so well. I loved her."

Calderon had never expected to meet a ninja zombie that looked gorgeous. Somehow he'd expected all ninja zombies to look shabby, sunburned, naked and wounded, like the zombie he had already drawn. The idea of chic, fashionable, even sexy ninja zombies was bewildering.

"How long has Mrs. Kutuzov been one of them?" said Calderon.

"When did we catch the ninja zombie? Six days ago? There must have been more than one."

"Shouldn't we rush out, and stop her somehow?"

"No one will stop the wife of Kutuzov. This is Kutuzov's own fortress."

"You mean... She can just walk all around the town, doing anything she wants to us, just because she's dressed up like a rich girl?"

"Yes. Of course that's what I mean."

"We are helpless," Calderon realized suddenly, leaning under the wall by a security vidcam. "We are serfs. We are feudal slaves. We sold ourselves to anything that looked like protection."

Distant, muffled shouting came from down the prison hall.

Smith was a ranger. He was a local mercenary, which accounted for his nom de guerre, 'Smith.' Smith had battle-scarred hands, tiny blue eyes, a bullet-like head, and an alcoholic's red snout. Smith looked like a Texan javelina pig that killed and ate rattlesnakes by his nature.

"Howdy there, Mr. Calderon," cackled Smith, smiling and gripping the sleek and stainless bars of his cybernetically-sealed cell.

"You're in the brig again, Smith?"

"I kicked some ass," Smith bragged. "But you'd better let me out now. The jailer's not gonna do that, and some real hot work needs getting done."

"What happened in here?"

"Well, this sexy chick dressed in red came in the back way. She spat right in the jailer's face, he went down like a truck hit him... Then she took an old car-jack to the cage of the naked unfriendly." Smith pointed to the bent distorted cage of the ninja zombie. "He wiggled right out, and he went down those stairs. She went right out the front."

"You mean," said Calderon, "the ninja zombie is still in the jail? He didn't escape?"

"Oh, no, the ninja zombies never do that 'escaping' stuff," Smith advised. "He's gonna destroy the jail."

"How? He's naked!"

"Oh, he'll find a way. Ninja zombies aren't human, you know. They destroy all the works of mankind. That's their basic tactics."

"I must see to the casualty," said Antommarchi, and left.

"Let me out of the cell," Smith commanded.

"Sure, fine," said Calderon. "How does your cell door work?"

"It's electronic."

"Fine. How do I open it?"

"Don't you know that?" said Smith, puzzled. "You always struck me as a pretty electronic-looking sort of guy, Mr. Calderon."

Calderon was an artist. He knew absolutely nothing about high-tech, encrypted, wireless, high-security jail technology. He stared at the cryptic lock. It was nothing but a speckling of black and white squares.

The ninja zombie appeared at the end of the hall. He was using a fire axe as an impromptu crutch. He had a crude, stinking rag-torch in his left hand. A raw billow of smoke arose behind him.

The ninja zombie limped methodically past Calderon. He said nothing, and Calderon and Smith said nothing to him. He reached the end of the hall and slowly went up a flight of stairs.

"They're not as tough as people think," said Smith. "Soldiers who understand small-unit tactics can take 'em out. They're just not human, so they never get scared or tired. But we can shoot them. We can bomb them. Once we kill them, they stay dead."

Antommarchi appeared. His crisp British voice was shaken. "The jailer is convulsing. She dosed him with some terrible fluid – I think this whole building is contaminated."

"Never mind him," Smith advised. "A jailer is a goddamned screw! You should never touch a jailer anyway. Just let me out, and I'll teach y'all to zombie-hunt."

Calderon shook the adamantine jail bars. "I can't open this lock! I don't know what to do!"

Muffled screams came from overhead. "He just found the political prisoners," said Smith, grinning. "They always had it easy up there, those sissies."

"I suggest we flee," said Antommarchi to Calderon. "A disaster of this scale is not within our competence."

"Running away?" Smith scoffed. "And leave me here in a cell? All this time, I've been fighting so hard to protect you people! I should have been a ninja zombie myself! Hell, I'm on the wrong side!"

There was fire in the basement of the prison, and the jail's software had stopped working. Outside the jail, attracted by the smoke, an excited crowd gathered. Eventually, they stormed the prison, using tow trucks to rip out the doors and windows. They were so eager to attack the ninja zombie that they destroyed the jail to get him.

5.

ANTOMMARCHI WAS GOOD at managing in a mob, and despite the crazy tumult, he had somehow saved Calderon's outsized drawing pad.

"Hey, thanks," said Calderon, wiping at his eyes. "I have a lot of good work in here."

"We must go to my office now," said Antommarchi, "for we must take medical precautions. The ninja zombie was not infectious, but Mrs. Kutuzov is a biological attack vector."

"I don't think I want to do biological attack," Calderon said.

"But we must. We were both exposed to a contagion."

"I don't want any drugs or needles."

Antommarchi looked at him wide eyed. "Why not?"

It was because he simply did not trust Antommarchi, but given what they had just been through together, Calderon did not have the heart to just say it.

"Listen," Calderon said haltingly. "If this is some vaccine you want to give me. Or an immunization... Go save little kids. Don't save me. I don't care. Really. I've lived long enough. I know I've lived through all the good times that I will ever see. I used to live in a world with art and science. From now on every step gets darker."

"You don't understand me," said Antommarchi. "I am not protecting you. I am protecting the other people from you. It's you who are the vector now, Calderon. You were directly exposed to that Mexican handiwork. You got too close."

Since Antommarchi was his landlord, the two of them shared a building. Going to Antommarchi's office was a simple matter of walking upstairs. There was a power blackout in Fort Lucky, and the sound of scattered gunshots, too, but those were getting more common.

Antommarchi found an emergency candle in a bottom drawer. He poured rubbing alcohol over a medical sponge.

Antommarchi's medical office was nicely decorated with nostalgic photos of famous European ruins: the Acropolis, the Roman Colosseum, Pompeii. All of these heritage shots were suitably soft-focussed and misty.

"In the 20th century, when a man joined a mass army," said Antommarchi, searching for equipment, "he received a great many injections. Flu, measles, mumps, polio, rubella, tetanus, yellow fever, hepatitis, and typhoid. None of those diseases will ever kill a ninja zombie. Human diseases cannot live in their flesh."

Calderon sat on a bare wooden stool in the candle-light. He knew that he was taking a dreadful step. He had always feared needles.

Antommarchi found a rubber hose, tied off his own arm, slapped his own forearm, and found a vein.

"Every man has to die of something," he remarked, "even a superman must die. But I will never die from an epidemic disease. I promised myself that, when I was a bio-warrior."

"How did that work out?"

"Well, a healthy soldier is important, of course. But what if he's a healthy soldier who can also infect the enemy? That's even better, isn't it? I once worked in such an exciting, high-tech field."

Antommarchi decanted fluid into the crook of his arm.

A rumble overhead drew Calderon from the bare stool to the window. A flotilla of helicopters was passing overhead, awkwardly-shaped cargo ships, their double-rotors beating in a strange, ungainly fashion, like flying kitchen equipment. There were two dozen of them. They were heading to the northeast.

They had no markings.

"I thought those helicopters were coming to save us," said Calderon.

"No, those are the rich people," said Antommarchi, "retreating to safety."

"But this town is the rich people's safety."

"That was then, and this is now."

After Calderon's own injection, Antommarchi gave him hot beef stew, laced with some pills he had. He plied him with cornbread and whiskey. After this heavy meal, Calderon sat on the couch and stared at the candle-lit wallpaper.

He could feel the potion hitting his nerves. Mostly, Calderon could feel it way down in his feet, because his feet had the longest nerves, back and forth from his brain. His feet had a different nervous vitality inside them. They were faunlike and springlike in their bones, they seemed to want to curl up.

"Leaving humanity is an act of biomedical science," said Antommarchi. "The reaction to treatment will vary somewhat among patients, it's always like that... Sometimes people turn back."

"Ninja zombies turn back into people?" said Calderon.

"I never did. But then, Kutuzov and I didn't take the cheap rubbish the Mexicans used. I was a biotechnician: I knew exactly what I was getting. Also, everything was so very different, at the beginning. We were not human any more, but we didn't know that was true. We didn't understand what it meant."

"It was always here in the town, all along, then, wasn't it?" said Calderon. "Even before Kutuzov built this town, I bet it was here, somehow. There's nothing new about the narco trade in a Texas border town."

"It's no news that the needle is stronger than our flesh," said Antommachi. "Kutuzov is a superman. His brain is full of intelligence boosters. He has wealth, technology, political power, the love of women... He is an addict of heroin! Heroin, for God's sake. Heroin is a child's toy. High school children take heroin."

"He's not human, but he's still a junkie?" said Calderon. "Our big-shot boss is a zombie, a ninja, and a junkie?" He broke into a cackling shriek of laughter.

"It's time for you to rest a while, Calderon. Look, the night is falling."

"Do you have any heroin handy? Can I borrow some?"

6.

CALDERON GOT FEVERED and weak from the treatment he'd been given. His housekeeper looked after him. She brought him soup.

She also brought along her grown son, who had been fighting in uniform.

The kid's morale was still good. Obviously things hadn't been going well for mankind in general, but he despised ninja zombies. He and his human comrades had never lost even one stand-up fire-fight against zombies. They were always victors in battle.

Any platoon of well-armed, well-supplied human troops could set up kill-zones and mow zombies down like tall grass. Their so-called germ weapons were no big deal against well-organized troops with soap and water.

The only big problem, he said, was the civilians. Just, way too many civilians: massive crowds of weak, effeminate soft targets. Civilians were city people. They couldn't forage like soldiers, survive outdoors or keep themselves clean and fit. They couldn't live even one day without their data and electricity.

The civilians were the true prey of the zombies. Worse yet, they were also the source of the zombies. A loyal soldier would fight zombies to the bitter end and save the last bullet for himself, but a weak civilian would despair, surrender, and join the zombie ranks.

That was the problem. Not military, but civilian. An army couldn't save a city of zombies, because zombies burned their own neighborhoods. Zombies ripped out their own wiring, ripped up the plumbing. They methodically broke every switch, joint, faucet, wire, pole, and conduit.

San Antonio, Houston, Austin, Dallas-Fort Worth: they were all stripped and broken; giant, gently-burning, sabotaged urban machines. Zombies had ruined all of them, beyond repair, mostly with bare hands, crowbars, torches. There was talk of cauterizing the zombie towns with nuclear weapons, but nothing would come of that. Any town taken by zombies was already rubble.

Calderon listened quietly to the soldier's grievances. He just nodded and smiled. Calderon could still talk, when he felt the need of it, but he felt less and less will to express himself in human language. The vesicles in his head were changing shape. Even the sutures in his brain were readjusting, in their bony, squeaking fashion.

His housekeeper and her son didn't notice this about him. They'd never understood him very well.

Calderon could feel a distinctly new nervous awareness of his own brain, as an organ made of distinct lobes. He could feel his brain, as a thing made of sections.

These body parts once combined to make him Leslie Calderon, but he understood now that this had always been a fakery. Human consciousness was like an optical illusion.

He did not miss Leslie Calderon, but he did somewhat miss San Antonio, Houston, Dallas-Fort Worth... A world just shouldn't lose big cities. These huge, vital places, these centers of light and culture, plunged into blackness, perishing, that felt very wrong, it felt frightening...

But Calderon himself felt much better. He had his health back, and something much darker and stronger than his merely human health. He hadn't realized how much pain an old man felt in daily life, those sneaking twinges in his spine, a bad molar that bothered him, his stiff neck from too much time drawing...

His new nerves didn't handle pain in the old human way, with the sharp, focussed pangs. Pain for him now was a sense of swift, aristocratic annoyance. A neural disgust.

Fort Lucky was being destroyed, but he felt happy, alone in his room. He heard people shouting in the streets. Sometimes the electricity flickered on for short periods. There was gunfire. It bored him.

Mostly, he looked at his own drawings. They fascinated him. Not because they were good, but because they were so human.

He could have studied his drawings for weeks, with a feral concentration, but he was hungry. There was nothing left to eat in his house – at least nothing he would have thought about eating in the past.

But humans were limited eaters. Humans were afraid to eat new things, because the pain of indigestion would really bother them. But – once the human fear and disgust went away – the human stomach and gut, as a digestive system, could physically manage almost any substance that human teeth could chew.

It occurred to Calderon to eat some of his drawings. The paper did not taste offensive, and it was surprisingly fun to chew and swallow. It even filled his stomach.

Eventually, though, he felt poorly nourished. He went out to the market. It was not a market day.

He smelled food, though. There had been a big party of some kind; the smell of a bonfire in the air, and they'd been eating. They'd been feasting on good old-fashioned meals, ready to eat packs, the indestructible, long-lasting rations that armies ate.

The crowd of rioting civilians had eaten these plastic packs very hastily, throwing away quite a lot of them. Calderon moved from one scattered pile of trash to the next. He dabbed in the meal-packs with his forefinger and sucked the scraps of food off it and swallowed.

Soon his mood lightened. He even felt elation. He became curious, and he wandered light-footed through the deserted town.

Fort Lucky was entirely dark, but he felt no darkness. This was their Dark Age, but it was no longer his own. He was enlightened. He felt no more fear, guilt, or shame. Great historical burdens had left his spirit.

He was free of all human consequences. Humanity had failed completely, and so had he, but all that was behind him. His life was full of promise.

He strolled out into the scrub of the desert, ignoring all roads and trails. He walked until he could look around himself and see, in a wilderness of scrub and arroyos, that there was not one visible trace of the works of man. Not one ruin, not one boundary, not one claim of ownership.

He suddenly knew that there was nothing between him and true happiness. He even knew what true happiness was.

All he really wanted, all he desired, was existence. To walk and breathe, under the moon and stars. He would be happy in the simple, immediate, yellow-eyed way that a panther was happy. A panther would prowl the woods and tall grasses, a panther would sleep when he wanted, a panther would see, smell, hear something of interest, and tear it to pieces and eat it raw.

And that would be happiness for Calderon, too. He too was strong and cunning and healthy and he too would leap on smaller things and shred them with his jaws and drink their fresh blood.

He would not be human any more, but he would be a native of the landscape. He would have no need of a fort: he would belong to the world. He and the world would be as one entity. The sun would bring him brightness every day, and every day would be better than the last.

213

GREGORY BENFORD

ASPECTS

ASPECTS

FAR IN THE *future small groups of humans eke out a hard and difficult existence, constantly on the run in a civilization of machines intent on destroying them for being dangerous pests. In* Great Sky River, *third in his classic Galactic Centre saga, Gregory Benford introduced the Family Bishop, fighting for their lives on the distant world of Snowglade, lives dependent on cybernetic implants and mechanical aids to survive the day. In the story that follows one splinter of the Family continues their struggle with mech power.*

SHE CAREFULLY WATCHED inky shadows stretch long and threatening, pointing away from the hot eye of the Old Sun. Its harsh radiance cast fingers across the stream-cut plain. *Like daggers*, Erika thought, *pointing at us from the rear.*

The Lancer attack two days ago had come from behind. That had left three Family Bishop members all sprawled like loose bags. Suredead.

Something had hit them firing from long range, something with remarkable aim. To do that took size, to get good triangulation

215

and hammer their inboards, fry them fast before their diodes responded.

Something big should be easy to spot. Even in the excitement, they should have seen it coming. As far as Erika could see, there had been nothing obvious, no crinkling play of sandy light.

Distant peaks held no white blanket, though it was winter. Her foremothers had named this world Snowglade but there was little of that now. The mechs had come and began drying the biosphere millennia ago, to suit their rust-vulnerable needs. Now oxygen was dropping, too.

She called up her Betsy Aspect, whose compressed wisdom included mechlore.

I concur: no other weapons systems than a Mantis class could so deftly target.

"Okay." Erika forwarded this to the Family on general com and they began spreading out, seeking cover. Her Aspect strengths were in scavenging food and tactical maneuvers, not tech. Erika knew well the crafts of foraging and stealing, of flight and pursuit, of deception and attack. But not suit tech.

Her daughter Mina sent —I looked up our casualties over the last year. Seems like the mech have been knocking dead Bishops who had tech Aspects, mostly.—

I deduce the same. Lancers can only shoot from nearby, in such wretched terrain.

Erika nodded. This valley was a victim of the mechs' Great Drying that had cleared so many forests. Less damp for mechs, less shelter for their human pests.

Betsy went on with details but then Erika heard/felt a thin, high, cold *skreeeee* skating by. She ducked automatically and sent —Got a passing fringe field from behind.—

"Sounded like a Lancer bolt," Mina called. Others chimed in on general comm. Erika felt their rising panic.

"There's nothing to be learned from the second kick of a mule," she said. It was an old truth though she had no idea what a mule was. "Get to ground."

Another ranging *skreeee* forked in the air and the Family ran. This one was plainly from their rear left.

—Hey lookleft! Fist!— she called on general comm. In the sensory bath of linked electromag and acoustic signals she heard back peppery voices, scattershot burps and grunts, rings and bings that echoed in the hot still silence of a dusty late afternoon.

The Family seemed to her to hang suspended in the distance, stretched over several klicks and hopping like flies in their servo'd leaps. They were all most vulnerable at the top of their arcs, but each got longer range on their sensorium too. Gravid and slow they came behind her, descending like down-swarming molasses, all six hundred and twenty nine frail figures, what remained of Family Bishop.

She caught a blip edging at the far range of her vision, a dancing green dot. Maybe a Lancer on their tracks, summoned after a pillage they'd done a few days back. A *fiiissss* zoomed by her and then a rattle of firings in the electro spectrum. She locked onto the source and shot a mixture of electro pulses at it.

—*Keep moving*— Cap'n Hermann sent. He angled toward a boulder outcrop, sending a strong electro scramble pulse back to confuse any following enemy.

She landed on a polyalum slab, the old kind from early mech prefab days, when they were just setting up. A warm wind blew packing fluff into dirty gray drifts. Mechmess was so common she barely noticed it as her cushioned crust-carbon boots tramped through the tangles. It was all over this valley, too, she saw.

An idea came. She scuffed up the gray grime and used her lift boots to blow it up into the dry air to block the view from rear left. The gray grit had metals in it, an effective shield. Cloaked, she ran on, shouting —Throw chaff! Blow this grit up, to shroud!—

The Family followed her command, though she was a mere Lieutenant. From their boots a vague haze rose across the valley.

A profile appeared on the ridgeline they'd just crossed, a classic Marauder pattern. It was scrabbling fast, lean and low to the ground: a Lancer. The Family peppered it and Cravix sent a pricey launch at it. She watched the zoomer skip out, swerve, dive, avoiding the bolts the Lancer sent at it – and nail it with a satisfying *crump*.

But some *fiiissss* bolts still came. It was a full clip of scratchy e-pulses than then suddenly stopped, from no clear source. Then she saw that Hermann was down, a klick away.

—Holdfire! Holdfire!— she sent – and ran. No bolts followed her.

Erika kept a safe distance from Hermann's crumpled form. A downed human was a clear target point for Marauder class mechs.

Then: —*Mina!*— No answer. —*Mina!*—

In a hanging moment she was certain her daughter's gear had blown or overloaded, so the nine-year-old did not hear the warnings. Or read the scramble of electronoise. Or she was just tired and distracted; the run had been long, since dawn today. So Mina would be a fat target recommending itself by its stillness, in the fisheye lens of Marauder tech.

She kicked her vision over to the reds to find her people, peaking in the human IR range. Under this the land seethed with simmering browns, the sky a blank black nothing. Crimson tides washed the sun-struck hillsides as her eyes slid down the spectrum.

There they were, swarms of moving dots. Mina – yes! – just coming up from a gully.

And... something else. She went to fast-flick, red to high blue, watching out of the corners of her eyes. For fractions of a second she could see a thing of tubular legs, a cowl head, its long knobby frame prickly with antennae. Mantis?

No other clear mech signatures, though. She carefully approached Hermann's twisted body, watching from behind a boulder and keeping out of view of the maybe-Marauder she had glimpsed.

Cap'n Hermann lay sprawled. Around his eyes oozed sticky gray pus. A bubble sat across his mouth, formed in his last breath. As she watched, it popped.

Dried blood black on the ground. At least two mechs had hit him, hammering the Cap'n of Family Bishop. The attackers came at him sudden, then gone. Mechs were like that, target specific, or the smart ones were anyway. She checked his inboards, systems, neuro.

"Cap'n's systems are blown," she sent on comm. Hermann had been a good Cap'n and the Mantis – it had to be that – shooting at a great distance had managed to pick him out. She quickly checked Hermann's inboards, using a jackknife connector. Blanks, everywhere.

Their chip-stores came from far back, when the Families had the technology to scan a cooling brain and make an Aspect or lesser Face from a very recently dead person. An Aspect retained much of its original personality and once lodged digitally, Aspects could be moved easily, electromagnetically.

"He's been extracted." All his embedded info gone, including his chip Aspect memories. Some advanced mech had stolen Hermann, leaving only a husk. Family Bishop could carry forward nothing of him – not his interior maps learned from years on the rove, nor mech signatures, nor lore of place and time that could reside in Family history. As though he had never strode the great exodus that was humanity's lot now.

A life torn off unused, she thought, *so what he might have been stays just on the edge of the possible.*

She hefted the body up and others came to carry it with her. —Let's move!— she sent.

They could go doggo, of course. Usually a mech Marauder couldn't find a human in a wholly powered-down suit. They sniffed out circuits, not skin.

From their shuffling gait she saw that this fragment of Family Bishop was worn and slow, suffering a hard loss at day's end. So far as they knew they were the only remaining remnant of humanity, now that some of Family Bishop had left this world, fleeing. So they now moved always, slogging on. They needed shelter.

Yet some chose to shrug off the sadness with taunts, jokes and mild irony. She heard:

—I don't mind livin' day-to-day so much, it's the hour-to-hour gets old.—

—Think this is hard? I belonged to a poor, hungry family. Our mother used to count us after every meal.—

—Y'know, fact that nobody understands you doesn't mean you're some kinda genius.—

—You sound almost reasonable. Time to up my alky dose tonight.—

THEY SLOGGED ON, each Family member struggling with the tragedy that had just happened, each in their own way. Meanwhile, the dusk was purpling into night.

Joy sent —Got something here. Looks like a Trough.—

Erika went to see. Tucked into a narrow seam was a concentrated mechwork. She could see gray navvys and dark blue wogs clank and roll in their mining and fab jobs, the endless energy that had given mechs their onrolling dominion over this blighted world.

Joy said, "Looks like standard Trough. A seam of ore, a spring: see that debris stream running down the canyon? Enough to do 'facturing."

"Enough for feeding, too, if there's a chem section," Erika said at Joy's elbow.

Joy nodded. A glad howl ran through the comm. The Family descended.

They kept low, skimming along in short parabolas, using savvy earned through hard decades of flight. She headed down into the slight valley where knobby, domed mech sling-ups stood, and landed on the roof of one.

The main 'facturing shed was a long old barn, sheet metal walls and processing lines on running belts. Crude but effective, dimly lit, musty vats and red-hot furnaces crammed in.

A coppery navvy was running an ore-smelting line and Joy aimed a scrambler at it. "Use a thumper," Erika said. Joy jacked forward a short, disc-loaded tube that administered a circuit-freezing jolt with a hollow thump. The navvy whined into silence. "Strip the powerpack and mainmind. Check there's no malf signal going out."

The Family looted the Trough fair enough, but after many days in the field their goal was comfort. They all headed for the vats at the back of the Trough. In the savory air they entered in move-with-cover mode, each member slipping forward with others aiming for any defenders. A Marauder mech would use the inky confusions cast by dim lights here. Erika made sure they scoured every hiding hole. No enemy.

They cleared the area quick enough. Kirchoff was first to shed his suit. All Family dressed alike in jumpsuits and armored body sheaths, but Kirchoff's sideburns and long beard stood out. His hair was the color of straw, eyebrows burned to white gold by the sun.

The Family flaunted themselves with wild hairstyles and tattoos, their portable, wearable art. As Family shucked gear nobody stared at bodies, beyond nodding in tribute to reverse mohawks, curls, beards, scalped pelts where their legs joined. Joints showed skin rubbed red where insulation bunched.

Erika and Joy crept carefully along lines of vats, boots sticking in the slop. Kirchoff came, too, carrying a stunner. "Good!" he pronounced, holding up a fist covered in a syrup and strutting a bit. "Gluten goop! Sugar too."

Erika ignored him. His slab-muscled thighs inspired no answering lust in her. They had by Family assent in Whole Council agreed to numb their sex centers, for the duration – and how long was that, now? Too long, Erika felt. Single-minded alertness rewarded the vigilant with survival, but still... she missed body joy.

Len yelped – he had found some sweet yeast in a big vat, twenty meters across. Many gathered to eat. Len had tossed a pinch of catalyst primer in already, so the sweet yeast was busy reversing the helix of its useful proteins. Mechs made organics for their own internal use, carefully making it useless to humans – but the Family had learned how to re-twist those proteins, and so dodged the mech tricks.

Then someone dove into the vat. A chorus of joy rose. All went for a swim in the thick muck. Others kept eating; nobody was that concerned with hygiene any more.

Erika ate some and moved on. Alleys of hanging blue-green lichen waved in an almond-scented breeze. Navvys kept working in the lanes, ignoring humans. Stacks of grease paste stood in tall canisters. These slimy nuggets fed mech internals, she knew. She slashed the sides, letting grease coins tumble into the slop. She trashed it all in a few minutes, letting her anger run. If humans starved, so would mechs.

They found the main water storage and jimmied in, so everybody went for a real swim. Erika had to stage the rush of Family, set schedules, or the water would overflow.

Somebody turned up some rank but nourishing paste that tasted like metal filings in salty cardboard slush, but the cooksters said it was nutritious. Everybody gobbled it.

The days of slaughter before had brewed with pulled muscles and sore thighs into a salty soup of discontent. Nags and whines and plain grunting sighs were all around. Some spent time on hair arabesques that would snarl up next time they put on their helmets.

Kirchoff gestured to her and Joy and they found a quiet place to confer. He opened with a Family song of ancient, raw lines, "Being brave, Lets no one off the grave."

It was eon-honored and so stayed with them. "Right, we need a new Cap'n."

"We need repairs more," Kirchhoff said. "Five more had inboards damaged. Cap'n Hermann had two Aspects who could do the fixes, and they were the last of that kind."

Joy said, "I saw an old place, at the top of a leap – one valley over. Maybe human made, but gotta be old. Could be somethin' there."

"Aspects?" Kirchoff scowled. "Haven't seen a human depot since Pitwallow, wayback past."

"Let's go see," Erika said. "We need a new Cap'n, soon."

"You standing?" Kirchoff asked.

"No, don't need the grief," Erika said.

"I think you should," Joy said quietly. Erika knew she didn't much care for Kirchoff.

"Let the Family decide," Erika said, getting up and striding off to dismiss the subject.

IN OUTLANDS SUCH as this, scavenger mechs did not bother to pick up rusted cowlings or heavy broken axles for the long transport to smelters and factories. Over centuries the mess had gathered. These jumbles blighted the land now, rust-red spots freckling the soil. Mechmess blew in the soft breeze.

As her grandmother used to say, there wasn't a speck of nice to this place.

After too-little sleep in the Trough, they were rounding into the next valley where rock-nobbed hills rose, dotted with mechtrash. Her back was tight, legs hurt, throat sore. She had lost sleep to dance her respect to the dead Cap'n, to sing the hoarse cries of farewell. The alky hadn't helped; she had a throbbing head and recalled what had been said.

Once each Family had its own Citadel, home to thousands, and their leaders met in grand ballrooms. Now they squatted, grimy and tired, around the crude pyramid that held Cap'n Hermann's body. The slow, resonant precision of their voices bespoke the reverence for their ancient ceremonies. Some were still angered and spoke of Hermann going into battle "as to a dance," but that kind of talk no longer worked among a Family in dire retreat. She ignored it. As soon as proper mourning had passed, Kirchoff had worked around the crowd, gathering support. She ignored all that, too. Still, they missed Hermann's steady leadership, his slow, kind voice. Her daughter's eyes had that shine close to tears that gray eyes often take on, and her mouth was wobbly. She embraced Mina wordlessly.

Family Bishop harvested the property of the recently fallen because, with the steady loss of their people, came also the loss of knowledge. Nobody knew how to repair most of their gear. The dead yielded up of course their compacted food and water flasks, a mute legacy. Emily had gotten a fresh-fashioned carbo-aluminum set of shank compressors, shaping the odd mechmetal so it snugged into her flared-out boot cuffs. Others took on double-walled helmets and new shock absorbers, some to no doubt be discarded as their new gear proved heavy or vexing.

This valley was greener than the bleached lands they had just crossed, and Erika relaxed into its green humidity. A spring tinkled – everybody watered up – and small animals scampered in the bushy undergrowth. A few trees, even.

Humans had long before Urthed this world, bringing their own UrEco riches of microbes, plants, animals – the entire megasphere of life, air, waters and shaped bio-ambitions. The past uncounted generations had so altered Snowglade, nearing completion, when – came the Mechs.

The Mechs saw life-bearing planets not as biospheres deserving respect, but rather as a special sort of factory. Biology's ability to reproduce and grow was a useful manufacturing technique, to them. So they simplified a natural world into a spherical factory farm, to yield whatever materials their own mechsphere needed. Sisal gave them tough fibers. Irontrees had metal woven into their cores that made strong beams and rugged sheets suitable for building. Ooze-bushes yielded oily wealth that a chem factory made into sophisticated lubricants. These plants the Mechs had developed and sowed around the entire planet, counting on the native biosphere to supply the soil and air and water to make entire valleys into bland, industrial sameness.

But here old Urth plants hung on. She picked up odd soft wisps in her sensorium, as did most of the Family. Further ahead.

Then there it was: a mysterious, beautiful creamy stonework at the back of the valley.

It was massive, made of plates of ivory polyceramic and stone, yet it seemed to float in air. Pure curves met at enchanting though somehow inevitable angles. Walls of white plaques soared upward as though there were no gravity. Then they bulged outward in a dome that seemed to grow more light and gauzy as the rounded shape rose still more. Finally, high above the gathering Family, the stonework arced inward and came to an upthrusting that pinned the sky upon its dagger point.

A voice whispered in Erika's sensorium, a woman's soft vowels in a language she did not know. They all stood transfixed, listening for a while, comprehending nothing beyond the

singular fact of it: that men and women had once *made* things
such as this.

Mina pointed to a bare plane of pale yellow stone. "Heysee –
writing."

"No language I know," Kirchoff said.

"Might be maths," Mina said.

"So?" Joy was anxious to get on. "Old building, 'nuff said."

"*We* built it," a younger said. "We made something... beautiful."

Emily looked around as the Family reconned this strange, ancient
plaza and its stone that opened like a flower toward the gray,
troubled sky. Now each windgouged rock, though itself dull and
worn, cast a lively colored shadow. The Old Sun's outer ring was
smoldering red, while the inner bull's-eye glared a hard blue. The
ring was a work of ages past, unfathomable now, made for some
strange task. By who? She was beginning to consider, besides this
elegant building, that it might have been humans. Long ago.

Leaves on a spindly tree rattled in the arid wind, a tinkling
sound like a mockery of rain. Joy came up to her and said,
hipshot and tired, "We eat, rest again. One night in that Trough,
not enough."

"Wonder why mechs didn't plunder this place," Erika said.
"So fine it is."

Joy nodded. "Maybe mechs won't bother us here."

"Hope so."

Silver sunset fingers stroked the land. Smoky vapor rose from a
recent rain on red hillsides. Insects sang their background chant.
Red dust made gritty dunes that rippled like cloth under the
breeze, down the valley. White termite hills stood like sentinels
taller than humans and no doubt firmer. The vast vault of sky
held drifting mountains of surly cloud.

"Forage," Erika called, and the Family set to it. She had seen mounds nearby, which meant those tiny creatures that lived on the scant wood here. She went that way.

Everyone worked to make the meal. Erika decided to use a trick her grandmother had taught her. Take a clean slap-bucket and place a small bright light in it, one of the sunbulbs that renews daily. Stand the bucket in the gathering twilight and as that glow fades the best termites will come to the sunbulb. She watched them, these kings and queens of the next bug generation, who alone among termites could fly because they evolved to spread the species to new places and build fresh gray mounds. These seekers buzzed around and plunged into the open bucket mouth, gathering close to the light. When enough of the fat, winged things had come – hundreds, within mere minutes – she clanged the lid on. No need to add oil; the insects carried the milky grease they used to hatch eggs forth. Under heat, the buzzing motes gave up their tangy wealth and so oiled their own cooking. In a moment longer they singed a bit, sizzling. She lifted the lid and the escaping aroma tantalized the noses of all around.

She poured the nearly filled bucket into serving trays, then washed the bucket and with a twist-slap she sent it into flat mode, just a metallic sheet. Without collapsing utensils their nomad life would be dire indeed.

The Family gathered for the appetizers, adding salt to taste.

By now the slow-setting sun lanced across the great plain, tricking the eye into seeing it as three-dimensional, the shadows as gloomy canyons. Threading through them was a muttering stream that gleamed like an oily snake. She and Kirchoff made sure no one drank straight from that river; mechs poisoned whatever they could.

They got on well enough with the compressed chaws they carried, the bugs, some boiled veggies, but... They needed meat. These leafy green plants had shallow roots, and gave mild foods. But there were other roots, within humans, and they went far deeper. Hunting lived in the Family.

Before they unfurled their mats and bags for sleep, Erika and Joy and Kirchoff made the rounds of the ill and ornery. There were few real medications, so mostly they used ancient lore. Sour fig could cure diarrhoea well enough and other belly dires. Jadebush presses on wounds and cuts pulls the skin back together. Angletree leaves could disperse suit-warts, too. But for sore shanks and mind-rumbles there was nothing. "Sleep it off," they said much more than once.

She liked looking up as she fell into grateful slumber. The sky was like campfires lit in an ocean of night.

ON THE DRY plains a thing is true at first light and a lie by noon. She watched the lovely, perfect shimmering lake she saw across the sun-baked vastness where they knew killers lurked. She had walked across such plains on other mornings beneath the pale dawn and knew that no such lake was there. Such open water had not been for eons now, with the mechs sucking moisture from this world, to render it all the better for their metal and ceramo-selves. So again the blue lake was there, absolutely true, beautiful and believable. Yet it was a swindle of optics, she knew. Refraction of the air made things desirable yet false. Not only mechs and humans played tricks.

"Mom? I think I figured out that puzzle."

Mina led her to the enigmatic mark.

"I got just the one Aspect, Nialdi, and he says that's an ancient language sign, named 'sigma.' Also means to add up. To what? I figure that 100 by it means, everything up to there. Add all the numbers from zero to 100, which is 5050." This came out in a rush as Mina gestured at the space below the 'sigma.'

Erika blinked. "How'd you add up all those –"

"Easy, see. Take 0 and 100 – adds to 100, suresay. Then 1 and 99 do the same. Count all those, but there's left over the 50 in the middle. That makes 5050."

"I'm sure damn bedazzled. So what's –"

"I figure it's a telltale. See up there? Just below the sigma, a blank spot, looks different from that creamy stone around it. Give me a boost."

Not quite following, Erika knelt and lifted Mina on her shoulders, to reach the spot. The moment Mina's hand touched it, a fluorescent background oozed across the surface. "Hey!" Mina touched it and inscribed 5050 in blocky numbers.

Something brushed Erika knees. A hidden door had popped open in the smooth stone.

They knelt together. "It's a stash!" Mina cried out.

"Somebody figured mechs couldn't puzzle that out," Erika said, brimming with pride.

It took little time to see what had been hid. And for how long? She wondered.

"Aspect trove," Kirchoff said when he set his inboards to analyzing the tiny disks arrayed in e-mag-proofed boxes. "Defended against interference. A library of selves."

There was ancient, intricate gear that could wrest from dying men and women vital fractions of their selves, Aspects

– deftly lifted bits of pastlife and personality, before people became suredead.

"Look for repair Aspects," Joy said. She was already using her inboards to check each disk in turn. They all set to.

The capillary socket was an age-old feature of everyone. Using the most exacting portal in a body demanded precision. When Mina said firmly, "I want one," Erika saw it was her time, and so did not object.

There were drawbacks. Erika's Aspects idled as nattering insect voices in the back of her mind, sometimes recalling a party some era before. They would murmur on about opulent glittering ballrooms, sideboard groaning with keenmeats, yukatas translucent yet crisply warm. But ask them about mech insignia seen last week and they went vague. Still, they could tell one how to fix the older gear, and sometimes figure out the newer geegaws. Not enough, so these new ones could be critical

The tapjoints at Mina's neck were small pink hexagonal notches.

Joy inserted three disks. Mina tapped her temple. "Seems right this way." Then she said no more for a long while.

Not so for the Faulkner woman, who got five Aspect disks, since adults could handle more of the tiny selves. Faulkner sat stiff and unmoving, head canted as if listening to voices. And she was, from how her lips moved without murmur, trying to give voice to the Aspect torrent pouring through her.

"Awwwaakkk..." she croaked, jumping to her feet. She danced. Frantic, flailing arms cut impossible arcs as feet flew up in mad leaps. Her entire body writhed in absurd fast-time, sweat burst from her face, she blinked as if strobing her vision. A shriek yanked her head skyward and – she collapsed. Even then her legs jerked and eyes twitched behind eyelids, beneath jumping eyebrows.

Slowly the heated dancing faded. She curled into a fetal pose on rocky ground, oblivious to the hard world around her.

They spent the day hunkered around the looming beautiful monument. No further stashes turned up, after they emptied the small one Mina had found. It seemed curious that the symbol leading to the opener code was an ancient maths trick. Maybe Marauder class mechs had no such knowledge?

Soon enough, Mina was repairing broken tech in Family bodies. The Faulkner woman came out of it and also was good at fixes. Mostly the Family defenses needed work and damage repair. Their sensoria were often the first to go, hammered by mech overload pulses. Only big men like Cermo-the-Slow carried actual munitions; others like Erika bore EM weaponry that could send nanosecond high power bursts into mech diodes and antennas, scrambling their minds, rumbling their servos.

Mina liked the work but said, "Y'know, my three Aspects keep talking *all* the time."

"Been in stasis for longer'n you been alive," Kirchoff said with a grin. "Aspects are like laundry – smell better if they get aired now and then."

"They want to know what's up, what happened to the Citadel, stuff about people been dead forever," Mina said. "Nagged by the dead – this is progress?"

"They teach you, yeasay?" Kirchoff shook a finger in a kindly way as Erika watched. Ever since Mina's father had died years ago she had sought a man who could fill that role. Always better to have somebody instruct the young who was not Mom. "So show respect."

Mina frowned. "They're powerful odd. Listen, I can give voice to them –"

Abruptly her face shifted to a twisted worry-mouth and she said in an alto accent, "*You reject the Word? You still have not conquered the unloving?*"

Then Mina shifted back to her voice. "That's my first Nialdi Aspect, a bore who knows lots of tech stuff under that religious prattle. I'm tempted to trash it."

Kirchoff was properly shocked. "That's death for Aspects!"

Mina ignored him and went on, head lowered, mouth pursed in inner reflection. "Then there's Amanda –"

Mina arched her head back and spoke in gravel tones, "*Strict rules make for fine fellowship. Couples must select the genetic traits most useful to Citadel Bishop in our hour of peril –*"

"Just get the tools, ignore the rants," Erika said.

Mina said, "I've got this great bioengineer, too. Here's her –

"*One must remember, the mechs' own evolution is powered by ideas of Lamarck, not dreary Darwin.*" This was in a solemn, pontifical voice. "It says we're a fourth species of a 'chimpanzee' – whatever that is. We're taller and have a stronger, more limber skeletal structure than humans. But *we're* humans, right?"

Kirchoff nodded. "Wow, you coulda been an actor. That Aspect's talking 'bout older humans, 'fore we self-modded ourselves, to deal with the mechs. Look…" A reflective, warm tone came into his voice. "Best you don't give a ratsrear about their opinions."

Erika could feel her own teaching Aspect, Isaac, fidgeting at the back, but suppressed it and the others. They were not much help with tech, anyway. But Erika could tell that Mina liked the new Aspects' gifts: those intricate plays of devices and software, the tinkering that brought defunct devices alive again. Across the huge plaza of the great (human-made!) building, Family Bishop worked on rebuilding their systems and suits, from electro-leverage assemblies, bushing plate stops and block grads, to pelvic cradles and shocks. The Family had little left of theory, still less of understanding how techs worked. In place they had a once-rich heritage of knowledge now hammered flat into rigid rules of thumb. Their suits were host to entities known by names: Amps, Volts, Ohms. Such spirits lived somehow in their gear. Currents flowed, the tiny electron beasts made larger stuff move and sing. No one knew or much cared just how.

Mina fixed some bad points in Erika's sensorium feed, too. Erika felt it dwindle at first, a multicolored fluid seeping away. Then with some jigs and jolts from Mina, it came back – full, florid, the entire electro-acoustic-sensing platform bristling with energy.

Before her eyes, her daughter was blossoming. First the addition puzzle, now her tinkering skills – Mina suddenly flowered into areas Erika knew little of.

They celebrated that night, mostly with some alky. There were playful rankings –

"She's such a tightass, needs a shoehorn just to fart."

"Damn glad I got my inbodies fixed up, was so sore couldn't wipe my ass." To which the reply shot back, "Since when didja?"

When it came Erika's turn she said mildly, "I started out with nothing and still have most of it left." Self-ranking set the right tone. They calmed. Nobody minded the casual insults of a ranking-down; the mirth helped them all.

Erika crept away to her own quiet vice. She had taken up reading old texs from Urth. They were the closest thing her nomad life had to furniture and she lounged in them the way people had lived in their easy chairs in the Citadels. One tex was in rather stilted Anglish, called *War and Peace*. She liked stories where people still lived in rooms and had parties. The book's big issue was an enormous war. Its point was don't take on things bigger than you are; not a lesson she really needed these days. She had plowed through other novels from that ancient Urth past. In her opinion, Emma Bovary should have gone to some school and gotten a job, instead of screwing somebody not her husband. Anna Karenina should have driven trains, learn to engineer them, rather than throwing herself onto the tracks. What were these ancients *thinking?*

Erika was only a bit into her reading on her carry-pad when Kirchoff came by her sleep bag, tucked in a distant corner. As they talked, Erika watched a spider like a burnt pancake with legs stride with authority down a wall. She listened to his voice in the dark and silently made an interior mod on her inboards. It would take a few moments work, so she used them to simply take him into her arms. It was all natural, silent, almost spiritual.

In a few more moments he whispered, "Hey, your sexcen came up fast."

"So did yours – visibly."

He laughed and took her in his arms.

SHE WAS NOT a spiritual person the way her parents had been. They had seen the good days. She could recall those, in her rosy childhood that seemed a lifetime back there now. Now the Family kept hard rules to retain some of that era. When you stop hearing Sir and Ma'm the end will be in sight. The good things in courtship, too, the pretty soft things, they had to be there to make it work at all. So keep to the true. Mina's Amanda Aspect had spoke right.

They broke camp and headed toward a Splash of impact-liberated water, valleys away. She caught the whisper voices again as they skip-walked away, speaking of something called the *Taj Mahal*, but it meant nothing to her.

Kirchoff shot a navvy that was sniffing for ore. He had aced it with a firenet, to drive it into cyberclash. Grinning, he brushed off the cries of elation with, "I'd vex on mechs, not navvys." His rhyming taunt meant a sly challenge, and she filed that away for later tactics. Maybe he would be a good Cap'n.

The Family felt better with the new Aspects, which made them heirs of a grand race, not a mere ravaged, fleeing band.

The land improved. They had been on the run through land so sorry that it won't grow a toenail, but now –

Thorny brush choked the stretching plains beneath the immense sky. Murmuring streams fed down from the hills and crossed green meadows. The long tawny grasses in red soil had been invaded by the mechmade sisal shoots, standing as high as a man and rattling in the raw dry winds like a chorus of armored warriors on the march. The ever-spreading sisal was useful to mechs for fabrication in their auto-factories. At least the mechs had not yet reduced the flocks of birds that could darken the sky when they gathered to caw and frisk and mate in their eternal cycle. Flies and ants too seemed immune to the vast eco-plundering of the lumbering mech agri-tillers and seeders. Erika wished that somehow the mechs had erased the irritating tiny flies that inched through suit joints and irked under a woman's skin like pinpricks.

A waitaminute vine grabbed her with its thorns. She twisted free, pivoted on her left foot and nearly got caught in an even worse plant trap, a lawyer bush. She had once looked up the term 'lawyer' and found it was someone who helped you fight laws. That seemed curious and downright wrong to her; laws kept a Family together. To not heed law was to bring down harm and mechs. She backed away from the lawyer bush, since they were known to shoot out tendrils to snare the fool who came too close. The bush often collaborated with the waitaminute vine. Plants had their own hunting strategies.

To not see the beauty in this eroded world was to walk through life as a dead woman. To not smell and hear and see it betrayed life itself.

Yet even here mechmess filled the gullies and their geegaws lay in rust. She no longer marveled at the incessant spewing engines of mechcraft. Their endless wealth seemed like that of the natural, green world she had grown up in, before mechs began pelting their world with rocks, making the Splashes and wrecking their weather.

The mech cities were glassy, steepled mounts that crackled with e-mag crosstalk. Even seen far away, the e-tremors made a bass snarl in her sensorium. Ominous.

She was skip-walking on the left edge of the Family's moving triangle, just reaching a ridgeline, when she sensed it. Air rippled and her sensorium sang with strange pips and bings – a purr of fast EM computation. She saw just below an array of tubes and modules, tractors articulating as it edged around a razorback shelf. The Family was behind her now, rounding from the other way. She had maybe seconds before –

Without thinking, she leaped. Full bore she landed on the center spherical module. She sent —*Give a hard lookleft!*— and got to it.

She had never actually collided with a battle mech. She kicked in plates and ripped away whipwire antennae in pureblind rage. Over the finely machined carcass she lumbered, firing straight into the cryo-cooled units that burst open with hissing, pressured vapor. Weapons snouts turned toward her but their range was too short and she busted them with a thumper, parts flying. She fired with orange fire-nets crackling from the shoulders, frying the thing's inboards. She pillaged the finest workmechship of factories men had never seen and never would, the ceaseless detailed labor of countless Crafters – all smashed to scatteration.

A hollow *shuuuung* twisted the air by her head. It was a blaring noise-cast, blending infrasonic rumbles at her feet. Electromagnetic screeches hit her sensorium with teeth-jarring frequencies.

A fevered mix of fear and rage propelled him forward. She pivoted –

The thing collapsed. Only then did she see, tumbling, that it was the Mantis. They had never been able to finish it off before. The whole Family never had enough ammo to shoot up every part of its composite array intelligence. The navvy Kirchoff had shot was undoubtedly both a sentinel and a data-repository of this angular anthology intelligence.

By now the Family descended, yanking free parts and servos, booty used to maintain their own suits. They hacked at it and she staggered back, her back tweaked from the fall –

—*Mina!*— No answer. —*Mina!*—

She was down. As Erika ran to her daughter Mina moved, got up to her knees. Even a Mantis took a while to surekill a human and extract the inboard personality. Those moments Erika had prevented.

They embraced without words.

As a child she had heard that the eyes are the windows of the soul. She had seen into the eyes of the Mantis, if you call them eyes at all – webs of antennas, blank black tunnels looking at her, some scopes atop the tubular frame of the thing. She did not know what those alien eyes were the window to and guessed she'd as soon not know.

Her Isaac Aspect said, We are not thinking machines, we're feeling machines that happen to think.

Her Betsy Aspect jibed, I differ. A Mantis can deftly target, but we do not know if it thinks at all, as we see thinking.

About the Mantis she did not want to think, only to feel.

THE ENTIRE FAMILY celebrated the Mantis smashing, though it was not suredeath, knowing that its disembodied mechmind would surely come after them again – but not for a while. It would tend its wounds, re-assemble itself, grow more canny. As always.

Their fresh Aspects had done more than repair some tech. The whispering voices of their forebears had made the beleaguered Family stronger, more anchored in the honored human past.

Some said Erika should be Cap'n for getting the jump on the Mantis. She turned away, not wanting that at all.

They were on the move again into richer moist lands when – "Heayeh! Heayeh!" – a child shouted. On a skimpy pond were flocks of powder-white birds, bobbing as they dove for morsels in the mud below. The joyous little girl waved arms at them and the birds sprang into the air. The child stopped, bewildered that these other ways of living had not recognized her and been glad. "Bird! Bird!" she cried but they just flapped away.

Mina laughed. Her parents had taught her the burden and duty to all lifeforms, since humans were their greatest representatives, and the only voice speaking for the kingdoms of doomed animal life. Mechs ruled the air and their emissions stained the sunsets. But life could persist.

To Erika, none of this changed the central fact: that a casual blow from a passing machine could obliterate her as an entity with no remorse. That was the central hard fact of their human world. Mechs could disperse their selves and so persist. For humans, only shrunken Aspects held any promise.

Yet the human story was not fully writ yet, not by a long shot, and there might yet be a comeuppance. The Family was solidly here, damaged and yearning, yes – yet still coming.

243

MADELINE ASHBY

MEMENTO MORI

MADELINE ASHBY
MEMENTO MORI

"I WANT TO be a child again," the client said.

Anika nodded. "And are you familiar with that process? You've done some research?"

The client – his name was Bruce, his profile said – nodded vigorously. He presented as a man in his late thirties, but his profile said he was approaching fifty. No partner. No children. Single-occupancy non-mortgage residence in a distant corner of the city. Anika checked his shoes. They were cheap, and his trousers rode too high over his ankles, exposing pristine white mass-production socks. No one to impress, then. Nowhere to be at three o'clock in the afternoon. Of course he wanted a do-over.

"Early life re-versioning means taking on a lot of responsibilities," Anika said. "Your next version will have to become a foster parent, just like the foster parents who will raise you."

Again, he nodded. "I understand that."

"You won't have a choice in the version you foster. We'll do a questionnaire – it's very detailed – about your preferences, about what kind of family you'd like to be placed with, and so on, but in the end you'll need to involve a lawyer if you want to renege on the contract."

"I know."

"We strongly advise you to retain your own legal counsel to go over your contract before signing. We have attorneys we've worked with in the past that we can recommend to you." She gestured, and a half-dozen profiles blinked on in the space between them. They spun slowly, exposing photos on one side and stats on the other. She took a swipe at one, and expanded it. "This office is the closest to ours. It's right on the corner. Third floor. I can set up an appointment for you."

"I think I'll be okay."

They always thought they'd be okay. They had no idea how damning their desire was, how futile, how running away from their particular experience of adulthood in this way guaranteed even more obligations and even less fun in the long term.

This was why Anika always chose consignment bodies, whenever she re-versioned. The selection wasn't quite as good as it was for brand-new models, but she found amazing bargains in the cast-offs of the wealthy and bored. This body, this blonde birdlike thing with the big violet eyes and slender, tapered fingers – this was a classic. Suitable for any occasion. The little black dress of bodies. Perfect for a city councilor's wife. And the previous wearer had kept her in excellent condition.

More importantly, consignment bodies came with no strings attached. No contract. No payment plan. No subscription service for upgrades and updates. Cash on the barrelhead. And then it was yours, truly yours, not mortgaged or leased or indentured to whatever faceless entity had sold it to you.

Like the entity Anika worked for.

"Oh, and I want to forget," Bruce added.

Quelle surprise. "You want a clean re-version? No crossover?"

"No crossover. Fresh start."

Anika nodded. "I understand."

"You do?" He smiled. It was the first genuine smile of their entire interaction, unless she counted the moment he'd realized she'd be the one handling his case. "No one else seems to get it."

"All of my reversions are clean reversions," she said. "I start fresh every time."

He blinked. "Wow. That's just... wow."

There was nothing to say. She could have told him about the challenges posed by his – their – particular choice, but only if he asked. The studio considered it poor form to ask why anyone would start with a clean slate. Most often, it was because they had something they wanted to forget. And if you got them talking about it, they would remember how much whatever it was actually meant to them in the first place. And they would change their minds about the whole thing. It was bad salesmanship.

"Well then," she said. "It sounds like you're very certain about what you want. Let's get started."

SHE DIDN'T NOTICE him, right away. Her commute was long but straight; a fifty-minute tram ride from the re-versioning district (it used to be the fashion district, once upon a time) to the eastern bluffs overlooking the lake. The crowds usually thinned out by the time she reached home. The other residents of her neighborhood still tended to use cars. It was that kind of neighborhood. Old people. Older money. Anika had considered a car, once. It seemed like too much commitment.

Her husband's boyfriend stood waiting for her at the stop. He opened an umbrella for her. "You have an admirer." His voice rose over the patter of water on fabric. He nodded at the tram, and as Anika turned to look, she saw a man's shape sit down with his back facing the window.

"I didn't see him."

"Too bad," Jesse said. "He was cute."

"You say that about all the boys."

"I'm catholic in my tastes." He kissed the tip of her nose. That was his spot. His favorite part of this body. Although they made love only when her husband requested it, he had told her husband that the tip of her nose was his and his alone to kiss. He took her bag from her and slung it over one shoulder. "But really, he had that whole passionate stalker thing going on."

Anika rested the back of one hand against her brow. "Be still, my heart."

"I bet he's making a doll out of your hair."

"Stop trying to scare me," she said. "He probably wasn't even looking at me. I was sitting in the quiet car. He was probably just reading his contacts, like everyone else."

"No," Jesse said. "He was watching you like you were the only person there."

Anika pulled up short. It took Jesse a half-step before he realized, and turned around to face her. The rain seemed louder, suddenly, the route up the hill toward home that much darker and more daunting. "Should we say something?" she asked.

Jesse nodded up the hill. "To him? About this?"

Anika nodded.

Jesse shook his head emphatically. "No. Don't." He smiled a bit too brightly. "There's nothing to tell, after all. Nothing happened."

"Nothing happened," Anika repeated. *Nothing happened,* she told Horst when he came home and asked about her day. And nothing had. It was a day like any other. Swimming, breakfast with Horst, listening to Jesse prattle as she put on makeup, work, lunch, work, tea, work, tea, work, ride home. Up the hill. In the house. Dinner. Dramas. Makeup off. Clothes off. Horst tucking her into bed. Horst joining Jesse on the other floor. He would be there in the morning. He was always there by morning.

Nothing out of the ordinary. Nothing to worry about. Ever. Which was exactly why she'd married him.

THE NEXT AFTERNOON, she saw him at her tea shop. The previous wearer had warned her about this body's preference for tea over coffee. *Too much of the black stuff and you'll get the shakes,* the note read. *Sorry!*

His gaze was so familiar she almost said hello. His halo read 'John Smith.' An alias, then, adopted for public environments. He wore a standard-sized white male body, clothed in a sweater that looked like it had come from a marine surplus store. He had the kind of hair that Jesse called "floppy." It was his only distinguishing feature. Aside from the fact that his face opened up the moment he saw her walk in. As though they had known one another for years.

Maybe he recognized the body, she thought, turning her back to him and saying something about lavender Earl Grey. The consignment shops tried to shift bodies around, geographically, to avoid that kind of confusion. But of course the bodies went where the money was. And the money was in the cities. If the previous wearer had lived in the area, there wasn't much Anika could do about it, now. Was this man an old acquaintance of her previous wearer's? That had to be it. He was curious – it was normal, it was natural, to be curious – but too polite to say anything directly. Especially when Anika's halo read her own legal name – Horst's name, connected to Horst's profile. Besides, it was against the law to give out personal information about your previous wearer. Even if he was gauche enough to ask, she couldn't share anything. Couldn't tell him where she was, or what she was doing, or who she was with.

A former lover. Of course. That would explain it. It was known to happen. There were even dramas about it. And there were ways of handling it.

The server handed her the tea, and she made sure her left hand was on the mug when she turned around. She made eye contact with him as she passed and pulled back her sleeve a little. The diamonds in her skin started on the ring finger of her left hand. A few had sprouted up along her hand and wrist since her wedding; he would see it wasn't an entirely new marriage. She watched his gaze settle on the glittering stones. His eyes widened fractionally. Perhaps he had missed them, before. They were subtle, after all. Tasteful. That was how Horst had described them, as he cleaned the blood away. Elegant. Ladylike.

"AND HE DIDN'T say anything?" Jesse asked, on the way home.

"No, nothing. I think he was embarrassed."

"Well, he should be. Creeper." Jesse exaggerated a shudder. He looked like a duck shaking itself free of water. "Who fixates on the shell, anyway? Creepers, that's who."

Anika rolled her eyes. "You'd still love Horst if he had a different body? Really?"

"Of course I would. Horst always trades up."

They laughed. At times she suspected that she'd never have married Horst if it weren't for Jesse. She'd wanted the whole package, and Horst had wanted a wife. It seemed like the perfect arrangement, at the time. And it was still a very good arrangement, now.

"I picked up a ticket to St. Martin, today," Jesse said. "It was a steal. I leave tomorrow."

Anika's hand paused above the reader bezelled in their front doors. Here under the ivy that squeezed their home in its whispering green grasp, Jesse looked somehow younger and older all at once. How long had he worn this body? As long as she'd known him. But that wasn't very long, at all. Not compared to how long he'd lived.

"You're taking a vacation?" she asked.

He shrugged elaborately. "I just felt like getting away."

And then he stared at their front doors. They seemed so big, suddenly, like two muscle-bound sentries carrying the stony weight of their home on their shoulders. It was an old-fashioned house. Horst liked old-fashioned things. It was why he maintained a home here, why he'd never taken the big sleep, never splintered himself, never installed himself in any one of the bodies he'd need for long-haul travel and not just life extension.

"Jesse –"

The door opened. Horst twitched his thick white brows at them. "What's wrong with you two?" He was smiling. He had a way of smiling that let you know he thought you were being stupid. "Come inside. It's cold. Jesse, don't forget your shoes."

Beside her, Jesse sighed. Together, they watched Horst pad down the hall and into the kitchen. Anika heard that rattle of the martini shaker a moment later. "I'm almost eighty, you know," Jesse said, under his breath. "And he still thinks I'm going to forget to take off my fucking shoes."

Anika said nothing. Horst was just being Horst. He had not risen to his position in their city by neglecting the details. And sometimes the body did glitch up and forget things. Sometimes.

"He must have come home early, today," Anika said. "How long has he been here?"

Jesse didn't answer. He went upstairs. He held his spine perfectly straight as he ascended each step, and didn't meet her eye as he turned on the landing.

"Anika," Horst said, from the kitchen door. He held out a slightly clouded martini. "Come here. We have to talk."

It wasn't until she had entered the kitchen that she saw Jesse's profile shimmering over the stove. Steam from an open pot billowed in and out of it, rippling across all the faces he'd worn, all the addresses he'd held. She had worked at the re-versioning studio long enough to recognize a high-risk profile. The red highlights across the text indicated inconsistencies in tax or social security records, places an investigator would need to do more digging.

"I already have someone on it," Horst said. Of course he did. He smiled at her. White teeth gleaming out from golden skin. She had noticed his tan, first, all those years ago. It was so perfect. So even. So healthy. All of the tint and none of the spots. Later she'd watched him undress and imagined the designers dipping his chassis in bronze. She had been so young, then. *You really don't remember,* he had asked. *You're really just like new?*

"Obviously I can't have this," he was saying. "I'm announcing my campaign, soon. I can't have any cracks in my armor. Christ, what will I tell Suzette?"

His campaign manager. Anika shuddered to think of her. Maybe the creeper was Suzette's. A private investigator. After all, she did not remember any of her past versions. Perhaps there was something in her past. Something her husband's campaign manager could not abide.

"So you're sending him away? That's why he's going to St. Martin?"

"St. Martin was his idea. He's been before. It doesn't look at all unusual. It's cold and miserable here, and he's taken holidays alone. I have council meetings coming up; I can't go with him. And you're staying to attend that fundraiser with me, on Friday." Horst drummed the fingers of his left hand on the stove. The onyx cabochons where his knuckles used to be clinked heavily against their ceramic cladding. "I just can't believe he kept all this from me, for so long."

Anika heard the question in his voice before being properly aware of what it might be about. Her head came up. Her husband's eyes shone silver. They were so bright they were almost colorless.

"He's never told me anything about any of this," Anika said.

"Not even in passing? The two of you are close."

"He was with you, first, remember? That was all the endorsement I needed." She sipped her martini. "Horst?"

It took him a moment to respond. He was staring at the profile. Under the anger flickered just the smallest hint of hurt. "Mmm?"

"This won't change anything, will it?"

"I don't know, darling. I really just don't know."

THE FUNDRAISER MADE Anika miss Jesse more than she had all week. More than she did when she arrived at the Kiss n' Ride after work and no one was there to greet her; more than she did when she expertly applied contouring highlighter to her brow-bone and no one was there to notice. The fundraiser – for children whose parents had splinter malfunctions and faulty installations – was the same old group in the same old club. Bad Chardonnay that tasted like the candles that smelled like buttered popcorn. Bad Cab Sauv blends that tasted like cigar kisses. Bad music, jazzy but inane, responding algorithmically to the ambient crowd noise on an unfortunate time lag and interrupting gentle lulls with shrieking brass. Older women wearing increasingly outlandish bodies: ten-inch waists, opal eyes, mouths sewn shut. Statement pieces.

How had she ever done this without him? *Had* she ever done this without him?

"You look lost," someone said, and without turning she knew who it would be.

"John Smith." She checked around the crowd for Horst. Her eyes alerted her to his presence downstairs, surrounded by the other councilors on the executive committee. His campaign manager Suzette stood closest to him. Anika blinked him a silent ping for help. Jesse wouldn't have needed that much. He always rescued her, at these things.

"Do you work for my husband?" she asked, before she could stop herself.

John Smith had the grace to look a little surprised. "Why would you think that?"

She sighed. "Fine. Be that way." She reminded herself to look at their pre-nup before bed. Maybe Horst was violating it by investigating her. She remembered a marital privacy section in the contract; she simply didn't remember exactly what it said. Perhaps that was why Horst had never married Jesse. Perhaps Jesse had never agreed to the stipulations that Anika could no longer recall.

"You seem unhappy," John Smith said.

"Do I?"

"Yes."

"Did I seem unhappy at the tea shop? Or on the train?" She turned to him. He had a very basic face. Forgettable. Ideal for this line of work. "You can tell him I'm fine. Tell him I still enjoy..." Her arm moved to encircle the width of the terrible party. "All this."

"All this."

"This party. Our life. Everything." The wine was stronger than she'd thought. Or maybe she'd just had too much of it. "I'm not like Jesse. I haven't lied to him. I *can't* lie to him, because I don't *know* anything."

"Why are you whispering?"

Why was she whispering? "This is a *party*," she said. "This is a *public place*."

He smiled. "Yes."

"And you. You're terrible at this job. Coming up to me in a public place and asking me questions. Honestly."

"I haven't asked you anything."

Anika frowned into her wine. He hadn't. Or at least, he hadn't started it. For the first time, it occurred to her that he might be some sort of journalist. Or that he might be piloted by a journalist – his eyes and ears streaming their conversation to places and persons unknown. If so, she'd just revealed intensely private information to him. "Who are you?" she asked. "Who do you work for?"

"Well, it's sort of a funny story," he said. "Actually, I work for you. You're the one who hired me. About three versions ago."

HE LED HER to the roof to continue their conversation. It was cold out, and no one was there except a clutch of stargazers, their eyes wide and white with infra-red, their necks craned completely back as they stared up into the heavens.

"Have you ever thought about going up?" John Smith asked, nodding casually at the blackness above.

"Not really." Anika leaned her back against the railing of the rooftop patio to look up. She felt it warm gently in response; Horst always chose the most responsive buildings for his parties. "I mean, not that I remember. Have I?"

"You did. Once. You almost went. Then you changed your mind."

"Why did I change my mind?"

He shrugged. "It's not important. If it were important, you would have decided to remember."

John Smith had a point. Anika had never elected to save any of the activities of her previous versions in her port. Every body was a fresh start. For all she knew, she was making the same choices over and over. Which wouldn't really make her any different from most other people, as far as she could tell.

"How do I know that you're for real?" she asked. "Obviously I don't remember having hired you. Am I to take all this on faith, or do you have a shibboleth?"

She had chosen her shibboleth on a whim. It was probably a very silly, insecure, easily-discovered thing as far as shibboleths went; probably plenty of others had chosen the exact same thing for the exact same reason. As such, there was a certain statistical probability that what John Smith was fishing for in the pocket of his out-of-fashion evening jacket would be nothing more than a good guess. A cold read. A con-man's trick. They warned you about that, at the re-versioning studios. Anika had issued that very warning, herself, to her clients. *Pick something personal. Not pop culture, not something you've already shared before, but something private. Something only you would recognize.*

In John Smith's hand was a tiny glass slipper.

"I'm sorry," he said. Then his other hand clamped around her arm. He hove close in her vision; for a moment she thought he was going to kiss her. He looked sad enough to. Sort of desperate. He was lifting her up to him.

He was lifting her over the railing.

He was throwing her off the roof.

"I'm sorry," he kept saying. "You asked for something quicker."

HER WILL STIPULATED that catastrophic injuries be remedied by an immediate re-versioning. But the police told Horst that her body was a piece of evidence in an ongoing investigation. And Horst had power of attorney.

So they put her in a loaner.

It was a clumsy, stupid body at least ten years past its prime. It was almost offensively bland – her blunt pageboy hair was the same insipid beige as her skin. She now stood exactly 5'6".

Boring little B-cups. No ass. She'd seen crash-test dummies with more personality. Wearing the thing felt like jamming her entire consciousness into a pair of one-size-fits-all slippers at a discount hotel.

"You know, the long-haul loaners have all kinds of features," she told Horst. "Geiger counters and gyroscopes. Even wings, for coasting in low gravity."

"Is that what you want?" Horst asked, a moment later. He was on a lag. Most of him was in a council meeting. His eyes had not focused on her in hours. "You want wings, like those freaks up there?"

She doubted her new face had the actuators to accurately betray her internal flinch. "No," she said. "I just know about it because I keep up on the industry. You know? For my job?"

He made a sound in his throat that might have been understanding, and might also have been a small seed stuck somewhere. He remained quiet for a whole five minutes. "Right," he said, finally. His snort was unmistakable. "Your *job*."

"I thought you liked that I had work," she said.

"You're a receptionist, Anika." He sounded so bored. Like they'd already had this discussion a hundred times before. Which meant he'd played it out in his own mind that same number of times.

"I process re-versioning requests," she said. "I collect profile information and connect the clients to –"

"You collect all the lies they tell you. The algorithms do all the real work, and you know it. You're just there to get them talking, so the sensors in the room can pick up an accurate reading."

Anika wished she could blame her silence on the stupid new body. The mouth kept working and nothing came out. Her tongue felt heavy and her lungs felt empty. At least it couldn't cry. That was something.

"I'm going for a walk," she said. "The technician said... I have to..."

Horst made no move to help her as she rolled out of the gurney. He remained silent as she touched her new toes to the floor gingerly. They didn't even have toenails. They looked like the infant mice fed to pet snakes. She focused on them as she made the legs take the steps toward the door. It felt like walking against the tide. It wasn't until her hand reached the doorjamb that Horst spoke.

"Did you two think it was funny?" he asked. "You and Jesse? Lying to me, this whole time? Living in my house, eating my food, spending my money?"

"I never lied to you!" Her new voice was too shrill. "I *couldn't* lie to you, because I didn't *know* anything! Someone tried to *kill* me, and I have no idea why! And you don't give a shit!"

She wrenched open the door and slid through it. Outside, Horst's campaign manager Suzette stood carrying an extravagant bouquet of pink lilies. She wore the kind of body that looked good on camera. Her skin seemed thicker than flesh; opaque and poreless and just as uniformly golden as Horst's own. In fact, she looked a great deal like the feminine version of Horst – his white hair swept into a gleaming chignon, his silver eyes set deep in owlish sockets accented with blue liner. It was the latest thing in branding. Re-versioning to look just like your boss. Staying emblematic. Staying on message.

"I'm not dead yet," Anika said, eyeing the bouquet.

"I know." Suzette made no effort not to sound disappointed.

"Did you hire him? The man who tried to kill me?"

If possible, Suzette's gaze became even more avian and predatory. "You're not well, Anika," she said. "I understand paranoia is a side-effect of crossover; you should talk to a doctor about it."

"It would have been good for the campaign." Anika picked one of the lilies from the bouquet. Its petals felt reassuringly genuine as she ripped them from the blossom. "Tragic murder of councilor's wife fuels new anti-crime platform."

"Anika, you need help." Suzette gave her a look that momentarily betrayed a profound exhaustion. "You've always needed help. It's why you latched on to Horst. It's why you've never remembered anything." Suzette reached up and stroked her dull, loaner-body hair. She let it fall through her fingers like dry, stale seed. "Nobody who actually enjoys being alive makes the choices you have. You're just a suicidal girl who doesn't have the balls to really end things."

Anika said nothing as Suzette breezed past her. As the door to her room swung open, she watched relief flicker over her husband's face. She heard him say something in an apologetic tone. Something about how sorry he was that his wife was so emotional.

Anika turned away from the door and bumped into a technician.

"Anika," John Smith said, from behind a paper mask.

Her new mouth opened to scream. It moved too slowly – he covered it before she could make a sound. "Don't." He shook his head. "If you come with me now, I'll explain everything. I promise."

"There's a backup," she whispered against his fingers. "They backed me up before my crossover, you can't --"

"This?" He held up a plastic pillbox with a thick yellow gem inside it. Almost like a canary diamond. He rattled it like a cereal box prize. "I know about this, already."

Suddenly she wished that the loaner could actually cry. Maybe it would make a difference. She lurched for the door, stupid doll fingers scraping its surface harmlessly. John Smith bent the arm behind her back. Something jabbed into her back. It stung.

"Anika, Anika," he muttered. Her arm went around his neck. Her feet left the floor. "You really do love making things difficult for me, don't you?"

"How did you recognize me?"

He'd strapped her to a gurney, and put the gurney in an ambulance. At least, it looked like an ambulance. She imagined he had everything he needed to kill her right here in the vehicle; if nothing else, he could just insert a drip and let her bleed out.

"I've followed three versions of the same woman," he said. "I can spot you coming a mile away."

For the tenth time, Anika tested the straps. The loaner body still felt weak. They couldn't have gone far; she was still awake. The clinic's loaners only had a thirty-mile radius. Whether John Smith knew that, she had no idea. But she certainly wasn't about to volunteer the information. Let him try to make off with her. See how far he got.

"Am I really that much the same, every time?"

Something like a laugh emerged from the driver's seat. "You have a certain way of walking." The ambulance stopped. "And you tend to wear the same things. Your bodies. Your clothes. Even your perfume." He turned in his seat and looked at her. "You know how I found you, this time? I checked with your personal shopping algorithm."

"You went to *Edith*?"

He unbuckled himself from the seat and crammed his height into the back of the ambulance. He started releasing the locks on the gurney. "Of course I went to Edith," he said. "You've been going to Edith for decades, now. You know your favorite coat? The grey one?"

She nodded.

"Well, you liked it just as much thirty years ago."

Her mouth fell open. "I bought it..."

"From yourself. In an estate sale."

Belatedly, Anika realized that she couldn't feel the sensation she was waiting for, that of gooseflesh pimpling up along her arms and legs. The loaner body couldn't quite do it, though. Perhaps for the same reason, she felt no rush of adrenaline. No terrible gnawing fear. Or perhaps she had re-versioned too many times. There was a law of diminishing returns, to re-versioning. She saw it in long-term subscribers to re-versioning plans. Every life grew shorter and shorter, the urge to start again stronger and stronger each time.

"I had no idea I was so boring." Her borrowed voice hadn't the powers to accurately convey her bitterness.

"Well, you did ask me to kill you when you got to be predictable," John Smith said, and wheeled her out of the ambulance and into the parking bay of her own reversioning studio.

THE HALLS OF the studio stood empty. Emergency lights bathed them in a cold violet glow. "Why isn't anybody here?"

"Battery leak," John Smith said. "Next door. Could start a fire. Had to evacuate."

He winked.

"Fuck you." Anika thrashed against the straps. It was a loaner body; who cared if she tore it up? She rolled from side to side, trying first to wriggle up and then to slide through, hoping for a weak point in the straps. But the straps were smart, and every time she moved they tightened, gently but firmly, until she felt her fingertips begin to tingle. "Let me go," she whimpered. "Please, please just let me go. I know you think we have this connection, or something, but we don't. I don't know you. I don't *want* to know you. I want you to leave me alone. Please."

John Smith paused the progress of the gurney down the hall. His fingers drifted over her face and swept her hair to one side. "I don't know why I let you hurt me like this, Anika."

Anika bit down on his hand. The skin was tough and durable under her teeth; she waited for blood and none came. He pried her jaws apart gently to remove his hand, then sucked her saliva off his skin, smiling.

"I do need your lip print, but not on my hand." He reached over to the wall and fetched down the reader. He pressed its cold flat surface to her mouth. He made a kissing noise as he mashed it down. "Good."

Anika heard the doors to the archives whisper open. He rolled her inside and stopped her under a massive, ornate chandelier strung with pearls. Why had her lip-print worked? She'd never even been in this room, before.

Had she?

"Do you remember, now?"

"Remember what?" Anika's voice had never sounded so small.

"We picked this chandelier out, together."

She shook her head furiously. "No. I don't believe you."

His hand rose, palm up, and two of his fingers plucked the air. "Request File Sierra Whiskey Zero Zero Zero Zero Two." The air above her swarmed with clips. The dates went back at least forty years. John Smith unfolded one clip and she watched a man and a woman at what had probably been a birthday party – his – on a backyard patio somewhere with a lot of empty pitchers and platters of barbecue. The other guests had apparently left. The two of them were cleaning up. They reeled a little, on their feet. The woman wore a pretty white sundress tailored to suit her shape. Exactly the sort of thing Anika would choose. Her hair was styled like Anika's, too – her ice-blond waves had frizzed with summer humidity, but Anika could still see the hints of their former shape. Anika watched the woman push a tiny box over to the man. He gave her a querying look – *you got me something already* – and he opened the box.

A tiny glass slipper.

Her shibboleth.

"The thing about life extension," he said, "is that it's hard to set goals. In other centuries, friends would say *if we don't have someone by the time we're thirty, we'll get married*. Or *I'll start that business*. Or *I'll see the world*. Then thirty became forty, and forty became fifty, and fifty became retirement, and retirement became an illusion."

He was petting her hair.

"We wait so long for the things we want, Anika. And now that we can delay death indefinitely, we have an indefinite waiting period. We have entire lifetimes to procrastinate."

He began unbuckling the straps. Feeling flooded back into her fingers.

"That's why you built this place. Your studio was among the first to offer people a truly blind crossover."

What had Horst said? That her job was useless? *The algorithms do all the real work.* And at other studios, they did. But hers was special. Boutique. Bespoke. Custom. Like Anika's own personal style. Which of course was why she'd been such a good fit. Or so they'd said. They'd been so nice to her, during the interview. So friendly and accommodating. Like she already belonged there.

"I..." She tried to sit up. John Smith helped her the rest of the way. Pins and needles pricked her feet. "I invented my own job?"

A smile quirked one corner of his mouth. Suddenly he looked like a person, and not a chassis. "Now you get it."

She looked at the clips hanging overhead. "Where are mine?"

John Smith reached up to the bowl of the chandelier and unscrewed it. Inside was a stunning crystal. Anika had never seen one so large. Carefully, he inserted the canary diamond from the clinic into one of its open slots. He screwed the bowl back into the chandelier.

"I had to get a taller body, just to pull this off," he said. "I hope you appreciate that."

The room darkened, and then filled with light. Images and clips from the past century filled the room. "I'm so *old*," Anika said.

The images coalesced into a single window depicting the woman with the ice-blond hair twisted back into a spiraling bun. She wore a grey suit and a high-necked white blouse, now. She looked like the kind of woman Anika would want to be, when she grew up. If she ever grew up. *"Hello,"* she said. *"If you're watching this, it's because you've been wasting our life."*

The woman opened one perfectly-manicured hand and showed her the glass slipper.

"If you're watching this, it's because we're not truly happy."

"How could she know that for sure?" Anika turned to John Smith. "How can *you* know that for sure? You've never asked me anything about my life. You've never asked *me* how *I* feel."

His head tilted. "Would you know what to say, if I did?"

"Whatever we've been doing, it's been the same thing, day in and day out. Year after year, life after life. If we're here, it's because we're stuck."

"Lots of people get stuck." Anika wasn't sure who to address, her killer or her older self. "And who said I was stuck, anyway?"

"We have children, you know. We have a whole family, out among the stars."

"What?" Anika tried to pull apart the mosaic in front of her, and divide it back into its component images. It didn't work.

"We knew this place was going to turn into a museum for the human race. What we didn't know was that we would become one of the exhibits."

"I want to see them," Anika said. "Show them to me."

"We believe in the power of death to create meaning for life. You have avoided death long enough. All things come to an end, even the mediocre things which have endured merely out of habit."

"You're a real bitch, you know that?" Anika stood shakily on the gurney. She reached for the chandelier, and succeeded only in ripping down a fistful of crystal and pearls as she fell to the floor. Above her, the crystals tinkled and the woman she used to be droned on.

"Anika!" John Smith knelt at her side. "Anika, please. We have time, you'll see, it's the right choice –"

"There is no *we*!" Anika pushed him as hard as she could and scuttled to the other side of the room. "You don't know me! And I don't know you!"

He stood. He held his open palms up to her as he crossed the room. He moved slowly. Non-threatening. She watched him ignore the open door behind him. "Anika," he said. "You saw yourself give me the shibboleth. You know we were close."

"What is your name?"

His brow furrowed. "What?"

"Your name. Nobody's just named John Smith. It's an alias. Tell me your real one. Tell me who you really are, and –"

His mouth closed over hers. He felt oddly, feverishly hot. Like he'd been on a slow simmer all day. He held her face in his burning hands. "I'm the man who loves you," he said. "And I've loved you across four different lifetimes. And I'm not going to stop. Ever."

She placed one hand over his. This felt like talking to a child. Had he always been like this? Was that why she'd left him? Was it why she'd forgotten him? How could she be certain that she wasn't another woman in a long line of women stalked by this man? She couldn't. There was no way. There was nothing he could say that would ever satisfy her. Part of her would always doubt. If she lived that long.

"If you love me so much, then why are you trying to kill me?"

"Because you asked me to. You assigned me to. You trusted me enough to do it. You said it was the greatest intimacy we could ever share." He pulled her up under his chin. "It's going to be fine. We'll go together. I've been waiting for this for such a long time, Anika. I know how to make it quick."

His grip tightened around her. His hand was on her neck. She swallowed hard. "Can't we just... start over? Together?"

He pulled away and gave her a smile that reminded her very much of Horst, which made his next words all the worse. "I know you're not happy with him. You haven't been happy with any of them. Not since me."

She was going to die, here. In this room, in this body. Unless she did something about it. She made the new body smile up at John Smith. She made it stand on its toes to kiss him back. She made its lips move against his.

She made its right hand swing up hard and jam the shard of crystal deep in his neck.

She tasted his blood, first. His blood and then his tears. When he stumbled away there was a sucking sound of their lips parting. He tried to say her name. It came out like a wet cough. For a single terrible moment she wasn't sure she could leave him in there with her memories hovering in the air. Then he lunged for her, and she screamed, and she shoved the gurney at him. Ducking out the door, she slapped her hand on the reader three different times, hard. That was the emergency signal. The door locked. John Smith pounded on the door. He moaned. He retched. His whole body hit the door. Slowly, she backed away.

She had almost called the police when she thought better of it. John Smith probably had a backup, somewhere. She could find it. She could find her own memories, too. And her family. Her other family. If they truly existed. But first, she had another call to make.

"I was on the beach," Jesse said. "I was making progress."

"I'm thinking of leaving Horst."

"I wondered when you'd start thinking of that."

She examined the blood on her hands. It was drying tight and brown, now, like a well-made glove. "And I'm thinking of finding out who I used to be."

"Who you are is good enough, Anika. At least for me."

She smiled. "Thank you. I think so, too."

271

Sean Williams

ALL THE WRONG PLACES

Sean Williams

ALL THE WRONG PLACES

WHAT DO I remember?

This is what I remember.

WE MET AT the New Petersburg memorial, where our grandparents' names were carved into a sparkling granite wall. Cate's grandmother was right next to my grandfather, so close our index fingers tracing the columns actually touched.

Sudden snow whipped up around us, and we blinked back tears and laughed in an embarrassed way. It felt like a cliché, the two of us being there at that exact moment. Both on a quest to figuratively meet the past, both single and about the same age, both maybe thinking a little about the future as well.

Our eyes met once. Twice. The third time it felt as though they didn't look away for a year.

Thirteen months, one week, two days, to be precise.

Cate Beauchamp liked to be precise. She was small and hippy, with blond hair she kept shorter than mine. When she laughed, you could see her tonsils. I liked kissing her eyelids because her long lashes tickled my lips. She thought 'pusillanimous' was the best word in the English language, and would fight to defend it.

I told her I loved her during an entirely different snowstorm halfway across Hell Gate Bridge. She kissed me hard and told me she loved me too. "With interest," she said. "I feel like I've been waiting for you my entire life."

The connection between us was real, until I broke it.

Do THE DETAILS matter? The important thing is that I was young and stupid, and prone like all young and stupid people to actions that feel decisive but are impulsive and to be profoundly regretted later.

By the time I realised that, she was gone.

LITERALLY GONE, NOT even on Earth anymore. She had emigrated to the Moon, the only civilian colony we had back then, although that was changing fast. People were well over their fears of matter transmitters by then. D-mat had bugs, yes, small errors that were about as dangerous as being hit by cosmic rays, but its convenience trumped everything.

Want to go to the Moon? Fine! Wait a year and we'll have booths on the moons of Jupiter, too.

I'll admit I dragged my heels before following Cate. She wasn't answering my messages, and I knew she might not appreciate me showing up out of the blue to apologise, repair the damage, start again from scratch – whatever I had in mind. Still: impulsive, remember? I just couldn't let her go without a fight, sufficiently so that moving from Earth to the Moon seemed like a perfectly reasonable idea, despite me never having had any interest in space before that.

Cate did. She told me of her dreams one night in the middle of an Australian desert, far over the horizon from the nearest d-mat station. I was following the transits of satellites, using my lenses to track the ones that weren't visible to the naked eye. There was so much hardware in the sky, orbits webbing like the work of giant spiders, it was amazing Cate could see anything at all.

"That's where I want to live," she said, pointing out and up.

IN HINDSIGHT, I wonder if I held her back. Maybe she had come to the New Petersburg memorial to say farewell to life and family on Earth, preparatory to leaving for good. She never said so to me, but it was possible. Certainly, we never left Earth together, and what I found on the Moon was suggestive of an outward impulse I did not personally witness.

By the time I arrived, three months behind her, she had moved on from the Moon, too.

MOON TO MARS, outward alliteratively from Earth, and perhaps symbolically from me as well. I had no way of knowing what motivated her without engaging her in a conversation. Was she angry at me or perhaps frightened by her own feelings? She might even be grieving, as I was.

If only she would read my messages and unlock her profile!

The biggest step was behind me, so the second was much

easier. Technically a tourist, although I had no interest in seeing the Red Planet, I stepped out of the booth and acclimatized myself to local gravity – not to mention to the many dozens of ways I might die if I wasn't careful. Then I was on the move, looking for anyone who could help me find her.

No matter where you go, there's always a private detective or the equivalent. We're naturally nosy, we mammals. "Other people's secrets are always more interesting than our own," Cate once told me. "But only because they're secret. If we knew absolutely everything about everyone, we'd be bored out of our brains by breakfast."

I was far from bored. It had taken me three weeks to be absolutely sure that Cate wasn't on the Moon, and it took me another eight weeks to be sure that I'd missed her on Mars, too. A major outreach program had just issued a call for explorers on the first wave of missions to nearby stars. The volunteers were going to be beamed by d-mat away from our solar system towards booths despatched ages ago, a journey that would take years thanks to the sluggish speed of light. It was a leap into the dark, clutching a thread as slender as finely woven silk. It didn't seem like a good idea to me.

She would have gone anyway, I'm sure, even if I had caught up with her in time to talk her out of it. But I didn't have the chance. I arrived at the launch site orbiting far-off Pluto just hours after she left, and this time I wasn't going to follow so readily.

Only because they wouldn't let me, though. The second wave wasn't leaving until the program was absolutely sure that the people on the first wave, the pioneering dreamers brave, had safely arrived.

Cate: a string of information encoded in triplicate on a fragile laser beam, her target Barnard's Star six light years from Earth.

I signed up for the second wave and resolved myself to wait a while longer before coming face to face with the love of my life.

IT WAS AROUND then, I suppose, that catching up with her became something of a game.

Yes, I know. Love isn't a game. It's much more than that. I was convinced – *remain* convinced – that what we had was real, but finding Cate in order to put that proposition to her was proving a challenge. I had stopped sending messages by then, seeing little point. It all came down to seeing her. And if that went nowhere, I swore to myself, I would walk away. My stalkery behaviour was a means to an end, not the end itself.

Although I do acknowledge that it looks bad.

So I waited, and as I waited I planned what I would say when we at last reconnected. First, I would apologise. And if that was as far as our conversation went, fine. I probably shouldn't have thought even that far, because this wasn't about the apology either. I wanted to see if the spark was still there. That was all.

I barely dared imagine what would happen if things went well, but those were the scenarios that passed the time most entertainingly.

As the first signals returned successfully from Barnard's Star, I joined the others lining up for our turns to go. My stomach roiled in a way it never had going to the Moon, to Mars, or even to Pluto on the very edge of deepest night. The campfire of Earth's sun was a great distance behind me, and it was about to retreat a much greater distance still, in time as well as space.

A minimum of twelve years would pass before I returned, alone or with Cate.

I felt a reprise of the experience in New Petersburg, when she and I had touched the wall together. Past and future intertwined. Ahead of me was a gulf as unimaginable as death itself.

"Have you ever thought," Cate asked me once, "how going through d-mat is the same as falling asleep at night? We stop . . . and then we start again. Doesn't that freak you out, not knowing where we go in between?"

I'll confess to being a little freaked out right then, stepping forward and hoping against hope that both of us would be at the other end.

I was.

She wasn't.

Cate had left two months earlier, taking the opportunity to jump further outward on the next wave of exploration.

This probably would have been the time to give up. She was far, far ahead of me now. Furthermore, this next wave had added an extra twist: instead of each explorer risking all on one jump, this time he or she had been copied, and her copies were being spread out across multiple destinations. That way the explorers could be sure of getting *somewhere* for their troubles.

So the Cate I had followed to Barnard's Star had now become six Cates, all heading in different directions. There was no way to know which one was the original, as they were all identical. And was there a difference, anyway?

These are the things I pondered as I explored humanity's first colony around this far-off star, wondering what I should do next.

By then, I had lost all contact with friends and relatives back home. Do I need to tell you that they thought me crazy? *Cut your losses*, they had advised me way back on Mars. *She's not worth it!* But she was, or the effort was. And what else did I have to do? I didn't need to work in this age of plenty, thanks to fabbers that supplied every item I desired; I had tried several vocations and stuck with none. Most importantly, I had met no one who entranced me as Cate did. If I had, my journey might have ended long ago.

Cate was my vocation, now. The thought of finding another was more exhausting than the thought of pressing on.

That equation didn't change in principle now there were six of her.

Copy.

(I worried it might hurt. I don't know why, or how. Like my soul would be sliced in numerous tiny pieces, leaving me and my identical siblings – if that's the right word – *reduced* in some fundamental way. But I didn't feel any pain, and neither did they. We exchanged messages before leaving on our separate journeys, all expressing the same relief.)

Disperse.

(Straight out of the six booths and on to the next stage – a perfectly ordinary booth with destination set to *far, far away*. I can't recall where my siblings went. My target was an obscure reddish star that didn't even have a proper name. Cate may or may not be there, I knew. Like all the other explorers seeking a new Earth, or a new thrill, or a new danger, there was only one way to find out.)

Repeat.

AND REPEAT.

And repeat.

And repeat.

I'll tell you one thing: Cate was consistent. Okay, two things: so was I. She kept going and I kept after her. Each and every time she wasn't at our mutual destination, I copied and sent myself in her wake, sure that one day I would catch up. The odds were in my favour, after all, just as long as I didn't give up. With each jump, we multiplied. There were more of her and more of me. More of *us*. It was only a matter of time before the two of us crossed paths, even if by accident.

I wouldn't call it destiny, but it certainly seemed inevitable.

You must know some of this. We're catching up on recent history, after all. The leading edge of humanity's exploration advanced as quickly as we could seed the stars with d-mat booths, which was pretty fast, all things considered, although I quickly lost track of the year back home.

Around 113,500AD I began to wonder what my other copies were getting up to, whether any of them had had any luck finding Cate. Because I certainly hadn't.

That was when the messages started arriving.

* * *

LALANDE 25372: struck out.

Near miss at Wolf 294.

Ross 128, no sign.

Diddly squat at Struve 2398 A.

She wasn't in Groombridge 1618. Has anyone tried Epsilon Eridani?

One of my earlier selves had created an interstellar bulletin board solely for the rapidly growing numbers of me, whereby we would communicate our progress – or lack thereof.

I was always quick to check in with my own failures. It was comforting to know that I was not alone. But numbers never lie: some of us simply had to get lucky, or at least less unlucky.

Partial success at Procyon B: found her but fluffed it.

70 Ophiuchi A: alas "Fancy meeting you here" is not as witty as you think.

Sigma Draconis is NOT a hellhole. Don't call ANYWHERE a hellhole. This is where she WANTS to be, remember?

If she's traveling with someone called Caelan, forget it. They've hooked up.

As the number of jumps behind me mounted, so did the number of messages. They were all brief and to the point, although sometimes they revealed puzzlement at the strange things we found out here in the black. We weren't the only ones propagating. Humanity was moving en masse, taking root anywhere fertile and moving still further out. Everyone had their reasons.

Some people were identical copies, like us. Some people changed themselves in order to make themselves fitter for the environments in which they settled. So far from the laws of Earth, what was to stop them developing thick skins for vacuum or bones of steel for high gravity? Or stranger things? I myself saw a breed of humans – so they called themselves – living in the corona of a fluffy, red star. They experienced life ten times faster than I did, flitting about like flames in a high wind. They were no help in finding Cate.

Even in colonies inhabited by people I recognised as people, there was no skin colour, limb ratio, symmetry or gender that someone didn't explore. The ability to take people apart and put them back together at will opened up a universe of possibilities – as uncountable as the stars in the sky.

FINALLY, A MESSAGE arrived that said:

Success! Long may you shine, Deneb. You are our lucky star.

And I suppose I could have conceded then. One of me had achieved the goal of finding and winning back Cate's trust: somewhere in the universe, we were a couple again! I was comforted, knowing that my certainty was warranted. My faith. And yes, my stubbornness, my refusal to accept defeat in the face of a rising number of rejections. One of us had atoned for the wrong we did. At last, the breach was mended.

But that didn't mean I personally was going to quit.

There were other Cates still out there, an army of Cates to match an army of us. This one success gave me hope that I too might succeed. It gave all of us hope. Maybe, in time, we would achieve a heart as full as that lucky one in Deneb.

We all started out determined. Random events and encounters did, for some, erode the certitude that had served us so well for so long. Some abandoned their searches in order to settle down with people who suited them better than Cate, hard though that is for me to imagine. Some of us discovered more productive vocations. Some died, by accident or by their own hand, from recklessness, carelessness, depression, or despair.

Me, I kept going, even as the view around me grew stranger and stranger.

I walked on a world identical in every way to Earth, except that it was on the far side of the galaxy.

I whipped past a neutron star in a habitat made from crystal far more resilient than anything people dreamed of in my day.

I slid across virtual membranes written on spacetime itself, coiled tightly around the event horizon of a black hole.

I hopped from orbit to orbit in the chaotic swirl at the centre of the Milky Way like a child crossing a river on stepping stones.

Always, always Cate was one step ahead of me, dancing onward just out of reach.

WITHOUT KNOWING, I was battling an enemy I couldn't fight or even see, one who might never let me succeed.

That enemy wasn't Cate. It wasn't the me who found her and won her back; nor was it the other versions of me who came close but failed. It was not even the people she dated instead of me.

My enemy was statistics.

I've learned a lot about the science of large numbers in my travels. Given a sufficiently large amount of anything, the chance that even the most unlikely of events will happen approaches one. A perfect snowflake. Eighteen perfect holes in a single game of golf. Two people with fingerprints that perfectly match.

As humanity in all its forms boiled out of the Milky Way and colonised its neighbouring galaxies, Cate and I spread with them. We numbered in the trillions. What are the odds, I asked myself, that I'd miss her in every single system I visit?

Vanishingly small.

But when the vastly large meets the vanishingly small, the result also approaches one.

And as time passed, it looked more and more likely that I was going to be that one.

A DEPRESSING THOUGHT, undoubtedly, but something Cate said kept me in good spirits, most days.

"Fear is the most pointless emotion ever," she told me. "Something bad will either happen or it won't. Do everything you can to avoid it, sure, but after that, well, fear only punishes you for living in an imperfect universe."

A UNIVERSE WITHOUT Cate would certainly be imperfect. I kept circulating, following leads as I always had at first, but then seeking her more aimlessly. Being methodical hadn't helped in the past, so why not trust in blind chance, to turn the tables on my enemy? My jumps through space and time became steadily longer, although not for me personally: instants only seem to pass between departure and arrival, except on those few times when my data was intercepted and 'awoken' to be analysed. D-mat was long ago superseded by better means of transport, although the backbone and 'nerves' of the old system remained. I have at times been mistaken for malicious code in that network, a relic of ancient information wars still reverberating across the universe. Sometimes people hoped I might be a time capsule, accidental or intentional. I've talked to soldiers, archaeologists, psychologists. . . none of them Cate, the only person who really matters.

Around me, things have changed beyond comprehension. The skies grew dark as more and more stars were hidden behind hollow spheres that absorbed every iota of radiated energy, energy required to fuel humanity's greatest works. I stood outside those works looking in. When I tried to understand even part of them, I failed. The concepts were too huge. *Everything* was too huge. I was a microbe swimming among whales the size of mountains. What passed as 'human' in those days was unlike anything I had ever seen. Only the word remained. And me.

And then the messages began to stop coming.

For years they had accompanied me from place to place, forwarded on by observers, disinterested bystanders, and routers that were as much relics as I am. These missives from my other selves gave me strength to persist through endless failures, particularly when two other versions of me reconnected with Cate in a meaningful way. I hoped to achieve the same, and I imagined that the others would, too. They were me, after all.

But gradually, with the relentless passage of time, the messages grew fewer and less frequent. Once, I had arrived at every destination to find tens of thousands awaiting me, requiring weeks to read them all. I didn't notice the decline until that number shrank to hundreds. Then mere dozens. Occasionally there might only be one or two.

Just lately, none at all.

I feel as though I am traversing a cave that grows ever larger around me. My jumps increase in size, but still I do not reach the end of my journey. The past retreats along with everything else. I am a ghost in the gloom, wondering where all the other ghosts have got to.

So I CAME here, aware in a distant way that it could be my last long leap through space. A jump of ten billion years in an impossible instant brought me to the place where home used to be. The campfire called Sol is long cold. The sphere that once contained it has been allowed to decay back into ordinary matter, which clumped and formed new satellites around the cinder at the heart of system. One of these clumps is called 'Earth', but is as different from my birthplace as the stars around it.

As I stepped out of the booth onto this strange world and looked up at the moth-eaten sky, I recognised nothing.

BUT THERE'S YOU, whoever you are. And you ask me what I remember. And when I am done telling you that, I ask you who you are.

- Don't you know me?

How could I? The universe is a big place, and it's got a lot bigger recently.

- Much has changed.

You don't need to tell *me* that.

- That's why I was sent here to meet you.

Who by?

Sudden hope stirs in my chest.

Did Cate send you? Do you know where she is?

- She's gone. Everyone's gone.

They're dead?

That's a crushing thought. Have I jumped too far and skipped over all possibility of success?

- They're not dead. They're just not individuals anymore. You're the last one standing: the only discrete human in the entire universe. How does that make you feel?

How am I supposed to feel? Angry? Sad?

The truth is, I feel nothing but a terrible hollowness. What is the point of living without Cate?

I have wasted my life.

- Don't say that. It's not true. Not for me.

What do you know about me?

- Everything. Does this surprise you? You have been watched over and cared for in a thousand ways while you pursued your mission.

Why?

- Your existence matters. You have helped humanity remember. After so long, you see, it becomes easy to forget.

Not for me.

- I said those exact same words a moment ago.

So?

- I asked you what you remember, and you told me. You remember Cate.

Of course.

And I do: the mole on her left clavicle, the way she chewed her nails when she was bored, the nonsense poem she read to me one Spring morning in Bali: "The mouse in the house has two ears on his rear. . ."

- But you really don't know who I am?

Why does that matter? If it's so important to you, just tell me.

- Perhaps I will have to. Answer me one more question first. What was it you did to end your relationship with Cate?

I stare at you, my interrogator, for a long time. Brown hair tied neatly in a complex bun. Fingers long and folded in front of angular hips. Green eyes that study me all too closely as I struggle with the question.

Do the details matter?

They do if you can't remember them.

I don't know the answer to your question.

How is that possible?

- I'll show you.

IT's BEEN A long time since I looked in a mirror. What I see is shocking: a bland creature with no distinguishing features, barely any features at all beyond the obligatory ears, nose and mouth. Beige skin that is as hairless as a potato completes the shocking picture.

I barely hear what you are saying.

This what I have become, thanks to the tyranny of large numbers.

Large numbers and small errors, you tell me. Lots of them.

I LOST TRACK of how many times I have d-matted since leaving Earth. The number is beyond memory. What I also never realized was how many times the machines tried to repair each tiny, everyday glitch and failed, providing an approximation instead of a significant nuance. That approximation is all I am, now.

But the problem is larger than that. How many times have I unconsciously refreshed my sense of self – reassured myself that *I* am *me* – by means of the messages I received from other versions of me? How long since I had even that illusion of certainty to plug those gaps?

Too much time, and thus I have become this . . . this shadow of myself, which I do not recognise as me.

Whoever *I* even am.

I do not know my own name. Yet I remember my fingers touching Cate's on that monument in New Petersburg.

Beauchamp and . . . ?

It's no use. Everything about me has blurred and gone. All I am now is the creature who tried to find Cate – and I cannot even trust even those memories of her, now. Everything has been warped from true, especially those details I pressed closest to my heart for so long. Is the Cate I remember *really* her?

Could she be someone else entirely . . . ?

CATE. YOU'RE CATE. Oh my god.

- I'm not Cate. She's gone, remember? There's only one person left.

But you said . . .

- Exactly. Humanity brought me here to make you whole.

You're . . . *me?*

- Yes. And I have been waiting for you my entire life.

THE ECHO OF Cate's declaration of love makes me tremble so hard I cannot stand. The other me, the real me, takes me gently into her arms, and holds me as I weep. She kisses my forehead. Her cheek rests lightly against my skin, and I feel an unmeasurable surrender to chance, and to forces far greater than me, and, yes, to something very much like love. Because isn't that what love is? What you need, whether you knew it or not, versus what you want?

I feel a warmth rush through me as though somewhere nearby a fire has been rekindled, and I shiver, not realising until now just how cold I've felt, alone in the void.

It's all right, you tell me. I'm not going anywhere.

ALIETTE DE BODARD

IN BLUE LILY'S WAKE

ALIETTE DE BODARD

IN BLUE LILY'S WAKE

WHERE THICH TIM Nghe stands, there is no time; there is no noise, save for the distant lament of the dead – voices she has once known, Mother, Sixth Aunt, Cousin Cuc, Cousin Ly, the passengers – not crying out in agony, or whispering about how afraid they were, at the very end, but simply singing, over and over, the syllables of a mantra – perhaps they are at peace, lifted into one of the paradises – perhaps they await their rebirth in a red-lacquered pavilion by the Wheel, sipping the tea of oblivion with the same carelessness Thich Tim Nghe now uses to drink her water, drawn from deep spaces...

In the chorus of the dead, there is one large, looming silence; the voice of the ship, forever beyond her, forever impervious to her prayers and entreaties – but then, wasn't it always the case?

FROM THE PLANET, the mindship's corpse had seemed to loom large enough to fill the sky – hugged tight on a low orbit, held back from plummeting towards the surface only by a miracle of engineering – but, once she was in the shuttle, Yen Oanh realised that it was really quite far away, the pockmarks on its surface blurred and hazy, the distorted paintings on the hull visible only as splashes of bright colour.

"How long until we arrive?" she asked the disciple.

The disciple, Hue Mi, was a young woman barely out of childhood, though the solemnity with which she held herself made her seem older. "Not long, Grandmother." She looked at the mindship without any sense of wonder or awe; no doubt long since used to its presence. The ship, after all, had been dead for eleven years.

Grandmother. How had she got so old? But then Yen Oanh knew the answer: twenty years of marriage; and another few decades in the Crane and Cedar order, dispatched across the numbered planets to check the spread of the Blue Lily plague in sickhouses and hospitals and private dwellings across the breadth of the Empire, from cramped compartments on the capital to the luxurious mansions of the First Planet, from those who could afford the best care to those who couldn't.

Fifty-six years; and only one regret.

"We don't often get visitors at this time of the year," Hue Mi was saying. She was looking at the mass of the ship, looming ever larger in the viewscreen – normally it would be a private display on each passenger's implants, but Yen Oanh had asked her to make it public.

"Oh?" Yen Oanh kept her eyes on the ship. *The Stone and Bronze Shadow* had been small by modern standards. As they approached the sleek hull vanished from view, replaced by a profusion of details: the shadow of a pagoda on the prow; the red fan surrounding the docking bays, and then only splashes of colours on metal, with a faint tinge of oily light. "The order has been here before." Twice, in fact. She could feel both Sister Que Tu and Brother Gia Minh in the Communion – not saying anything, but standing by, ready to provide her with the information she needed.

And Yen Oanh had been there too, of course – briefly, but long enough.

Hue Mi's face was a closed book. "Of course." In the communal network – overlaid over Yen Oanh's normal vision – her hand was branded with the mark of the order, a crane perched in the branches of a cedar tree. Vaccinated then; but it wasn't a surprise. Everyone was, those days; and it would have been Yen Oanh's duty to remedy this (and impose a heavy fine), if it hadn't been the case. "It was... different back then, I'm told."

"Very different," Yen Oanh said. People dying by the hundreds, the Empire and the newly founded order foundering to research a cure or a vaccine or both, the odour of charnel houses in the overcrowded hospitals; and the fear, that sickening feeling that every bruise on your skin was a symptom, a precursor to all the ones blossoming like flowers on the skin; to the fever and the delirium and the slow descent into death.

At least, now it was controlled.

Hue Mi didn't answer; Yen Oanh realised that she was standing still, her eyes slightly out of focus; the contours of her body wavering as though she were no longer quite there – and that the colours on the viewscreen had frozen. A seizure. She hid them well; she'd had another one in the time Yen Oanh had been with her.

Yen Oanh's own seizures – like Hue Mi's, a side effect of the vaccine – were small, and short enough that she could disguise them as access to the Communion; not as bad or as long as the fits that had characterised the plague, the warping of realities that stretched over entire rooms, dragging everyone into places where human thoughts couldn't remain coherent for long.

Yen Oanh waited for Hue Mi's seizure to be over; all the while, the ship was getting closer – closer to the heartroom. Closer to Thich Tim Nghe.

She didn't want to think about Thich Tim Nghe now.

At length, Hue Mi came back into focus, and opened her eyes; the viewscreen abruptly showed the docking bay coming into view, permanently open, with the death of the Mind that had controlled the ship. "We're here now," she said.

Yen Oanh couldn't help herself. "What did you see?" It was borderline impolite, made only possible because she was much older than Hue Mi, and because she was Crane and Cedar.

Hue Mi nodded – she didn't seem to mind. Possibly her teacher was even more impolite than Yen Oanh. "I was older. And back on the planet, watching children run to a pagoda." She shrugged. "It means nothing."

It didn't. The visions of Blue Lily came from the mind being partially dragged into deep spaces, where time and space took on different significances. Different realities, that was all; not predictions of the future.

Except, of course, for Thich Tim Nghe. Yen Oanh forced a smile she didn't feel. "Your teacher does it differently, doesn't she?"

Hue Mi grimaced. "Thich Tim Nghe doesn't get seizures. It's... you'll see, if you make it there."

"If?"

"Most people don't like being onboard."

No. She hadn't thought it would be so easy, after all; that Thich Tim Nghe would be so readily accessible. "Brother Gia Minh?" she asked.

The Communion rose, to enfold her; a room with watercolours of starscapes and mountains, the walls of which seemed to stretch on forever – the air crisp and tangy, as if she stood just on the edge of winter – and the shadowy shapes of a hundred, of a thousand brothers and sisters who had gifted their simulacrums to the Cedar and Crane order, their memories of all the Blue Lily cases they'd seen.

Brother Gia Minh was young; perhaps as young as Hue Mi; wearing not the robes of the order, but the clothes of a poor technician, his hands moving as if he were still controlling bots. "Sister," he said, bowing – then frowning. "You're on the ship. The dead one."

"Yes," Yen Oanh said. "I need you to tell me what happened, when you were last here."

Brother Gia Minh grimaced, but he waved a hand; and the room faded, to be replaced with the arid surface of the Sixth Planet. "Eleven years ago," he whispered.

ELEVEN YEARS AGO, Gia Minh was called because he was nearest; and because he could handle bots – he was barely more than a child then, and not yet a member of the Cedar and Crane; merely a frightened boy with the shadow of Blue Lily hovering over him like a suspended sword.

He'd seen the ship, of course. It was hard to ignore as it slowly materialised above the planet – not all in one go, as he'd seen other mindships do, but flickering in and out of existence, as if not quite sure whether to remain there, as if it still had parts stuck in the deep spaces mindships used for travel. As if...

He hadn't dared to complete the thought, of course. But when he'd boarded the ship with Magistrate Hoa and the militia, it came to him again. The corridors felt wrong – he wasn't sure why, until he ran a hand on the walls, and found them cool, with none of the warm, pulsating rhythm he'd expected. The words in Old Earth characters should have scrolled down, displaying the poetry the ship loved, but they'd frozen into place; some of them already fading, some of them –

There were marks, on the wall – faded, dark ones, like giant fingerprints smudging characters.

"Magistrate," he whispered.

Magistrate Hoa was watching them too, her eyes wide in the weary oval of her face. "It can't be."

Bruises. All over the walls and the floor and everywhere his gaze rested – and that uncanny coldness around them; and faint reflections on the edge of his field of vision – the characteristic delirium, the images and visions that spilled out from the sick to everyone else present.

"Plague," he whispered. "This ship died of Blue Lily." But mindships didn't die of Blue Lily; they didn't die at all – shouldn't even fall sick unless they were countless centuries old, far beyond what mortals could remember...

Magistrate Hoa's face didn't even move. "Gear," she said, to one of the militia. "No one is going any further until we are suited."

Gia Minh wanted to ask why she'd have gear onboard the shuttle, but of course he knew – all the sick and the dying and the dead, the houses that had become charnels and temples to fear; Seventh Uncle, lying in a room no one dared to enter for fear of sharing his final delirium, the disjointed hints of ghosts and demons, the shadows that turned and stretched and *saw* you; Cousin Nhu, too young to talk, whimpering until she had no voice left...

"We'll have one for you," Magistrate Hoa said. "Don't worry."

But of course they were already contaminated, possibly; or worse. No one knew how Blue Lily was contracted, or how it spread – breath or touch or fluids, or Heaven knew what. Everyone knew the Empire was foundering; its doctors and apothecaries overwhelmed, its hospitals overcrowded, and still no cure or vaccine for the disease.

The gear was heavy, and as warm as a portable glasshouse. As they went deeper into those cold, deserted corridors, Gia Minh caught the first hints of the mindship's delirium – a glimpse of something with far too many legs and arms to be human, running just out of sight; of an older woman bending towards a fountain, in the light of a dying sun...

Everywhere silence; that uncanny stillness; and a feeling of being watched by far too many eyes; and the sense that the universe was holding its breath. "They're all dead," he said; and then he heard the weeping.

THICH TIM NGHE watches her attendant Vo clean the heartroom; tidying up the cloths wrapped around the empty throne where the Mind once rested.

"There's someone coming?" she asks.

Vo nods. "She's with Hue Mi now." He's a teenager, but he still has ghosts with him – flickering realities around him, the shadows of his own dead, of his own losses – he's never had Blue Lily, but it doesn't matter. The virus left its mark on him all the same, through the vaccine he received as a child. Thich Tim Nghe could reach out, and pick images like so many strands of straw from a child's hair; could disentangle the skeins of his past and follow them forward into his future; tell him if he will find what he has lost; or what he needs to do to regain the happiness of his childhood, before his uncle left his aunt and tore two households apart.

But Vo has never asked her to see into his future. He knows the cost of it. She gives people what they need, not what they want; and she does it, not to impress people, but to atone, even though there is no atonement for what she has done. To lay the dead to rest, even though they are not her dead; to give hope, even though she has none to share.

She has helped a scholar find the grave of her lost love; whispered to a bots-handler the words he needed to grasp a career-changing opportunity and leave the planet where his daughters are buried; told a painter when and how to meet his future wife, to found the family he so bitterly missed – given so many things to so many people, a countless chain of the living freed from the weight of the past.

She doesn't know why she has those powers; though she suspects that it's the ship, the death that they almost shared; the deep spaces that still remain accessible onboard, even though *The Stone and Bronze Shadow* has since long departed.

It doesn't matter.

Her own future doesn't exist. There is only the past – she watched Mother die, shivering and wasting away while Thich Tim Nghe was still onboard the dying ship; and saw Sixth Aunt's face change and harden – if she were still alive, she would have cut Thich Tim Nghe off, but she's dead too, touched by Blue Lily – her face curiously slack and expressionless, all the bitterness smoothed away under the bruises; and Thich Tim Nghe doesn't know, anymore, what to think about it; if she should weep and grieve, or if she's simply grown too numb under the weight of her litany of losses to care.

There is no happiness for her, and no future. She's here now, in the only time and place that make sense to her; and Sixth Aunt's voice is within the chorus of the dead – and Mother is dead too, forever lost to her, her only presence in memories that are too raw and too painful – limned with the bitter knowledge that Thich Tim Nghe will miss her; that, at the one time in her life when Mother would have had need of her, she won't be there.

She closes her eyes – and steps away, into the past.

"She was in the heartroom," Gia Minh said to Yen Oanh – the images of the past fading, replaced by the room of the Communion – everything was suffused with a warm, red light: a shade that was no doubt meant to be reassuring, but which reminded Yen Oanh of nothing so much as freshly spilled blood. "Wrapped around the connectors of the Mind as though it was a lifeline. Covered in Blue Lily bruises." He shivered. "I don't even know how she survived."

Who knew, Yen Oanh thought, but didn't say. They might have a vaccine; and a better understanding of Blue Lily; but survival in those first few years had been left to Heaven's Will. The younger and fitter people had more chance, obviously; and Thich Tim Nghe had been young – thirteen, a child still.

And *The Stone and Bronze Shadow* had been dead. Quite unmistakably so – a miracle that she had survived far enough to exit deep spaces; to deliver her cargo and passengers to the Sixth Planet, even though it hadn't been her scheduled route.

In the end, there had been only two survivors: Thich Tim Nghe; and an older boy, twenty years or so, who had walked away with the scars of the disease all over him – back to the Twenty-Third planet, and his decimated family.

Thich Tim Nghe had not walked away; as Yen Oanh knew all too well.

"Grandmother?" Yen Oanh tore herself from the Communion, and looked at Hue Mi—who was waiting for her in front of an open door – the arch seemingly leading into darkness. "She's ready for you now."

But Yen Oanh wasn't ready for her – she never would be, not across several lifetimes.

She took a deep breath, and stepped into the corpse of the ship.

Inside, it was dark and cool; with that same feeling Gia Minh had had – he'd described it, but there was no way to get it across – that disquieting sense that someone – something – was watching. Normally it would be *The Stone and Bronze Shadow*, making sure that everything was right onboard – controlling everything from the ambient music to the temperature of the different sections – but *The Stone and Bronze Shadow* was dead. And yet...

"You feel it," Hue Mi said. Her smile was tight; her eyes bruised – not the Blue Lily bruises, but close enough, something that seemed to leech all colour from her skin – until it was stretched as thin and as fragile as the inner membrane of an egg – until a careless finger pressure or a slight sharp breath were all it would take to break it.

"It's almost as though it's still alive." There were tales, on the planets; of the unburied dead, the ones without children to propitiate them, the hungry, needy dead roaming the fields and cities without surcease. But *The Stone and Bronze Shadow* had had a family – she remembered seeing them, remembered their wan faces; the sheer shock that a ship should have died – the same shock they'd all felt.

Hue Mi was walking ahead, in a darkened corridor where doors opened – cabins, probably, the same ones where the passengers had died. Too many ghosts here.

"There is a shrine, isn't there?" Yen Oanh asked. There would be, as on all dead ships: a place to leave offerings and prayers, and hope that the soul of *The Stone and Bronze Shadow* was still looking fondly on them. "May I stop by?"

Hue Mi nodded, barely hiding her surprise. "This way," she said.

The shrine was at a crossroads between five corridors: a simple wooden table (though the wood itself, fine-grained and lustrous, must have come all the way from the outlying planets), framed by two squat incense burners, and a simple offering of six tangerines in a bowl. The smell of incense drifted to Yen Oanh; a reminder of more mundane temples, cutting through the unease she felt.

She stood in front of the altar, and bowed – unsure what she could say, or if she should say anything at all. "It's been too long," she said, at last, in a low voice. "I apologise if it's not what you wanted – and I ask your forgiveness – but eleven years is enough time to grieve."

There was no answer; but then Yen Oanh hadn't expected one.

"Yen Oanh," a voice said – from deep within the Communion. Que Tu. She ought to have known.

In the Communion, her friend was unchanged; middle-aged, with the casual arrogance of the privileged, her topknot held in place by thin, elegant hairpins, tapering to the heads of ky lan – she'd worn them eleven years ago, an odd statement to make, the ky lan announcing the arrival of a time of prosperity and peace – nothing like what they had, even now.

"You're on the ship," Que Tu said. It wasn't a question.

"Yes," Yen Oanh said. Que Tu was a living legend by now, of course; though it hadn't changed her either. "What do you want?"

Que Tu smiled. "Nothing. Just to remind you."

QUE TU CAME to the Sixth Planet because she had once been a biologist, a rarity in the field branch of the Cedar and Crane: most biologists were closeted in the order's labs, desperately trying to find a cure. She stayed a week; interviewed everyone from Gia Minh to the survivors on the ship, and retreated to Magistrate Hoa's library to compile her report.

Her most vivid memory is of an evening there – sitting at the foot of a watercolour of temples on a mountain and trying to pretend she was back at the order's headquarters on the First Planet; working on reports and statistics that couldn't touch or harm her.

She considered the evidence, for a while: the bruises on the ship; the bruises on the humans. The countless dead – there was no need for her to write the obvious, but she did, anyway.

Human-mindship contagion.

No one knew how Blue Lily was passed on, or had managed to isolate the organism responsible for it. Only the obvious had been eliminated: that it wasn't food, or sexual contact.

Airborne or skin contact, quite possibly; except that outbreaks had happened outside of any contact with the sick – as if there had been a spontaneous generation, which was impossible.

Que Tu sipped her tea, and thought on the rest of what she knew. What she'd gleaned from the Communion – the detailed database of the order's memories, available to her at a moment's glance.

The inexplicable outbreaks, many of which bore some connection to mindships.

The symptoms of Blue Lily: the fever, the bruises, the delirium that seemed to be contagious – but only until the person died or the attendants contracted Blue Lily – as if all the visions were linked to the sick, or the sickness itself.

Deep spaces: the alternate realities explored by mindships to facilitate space journeys. Most people in the Empire knew deep spaces as a shortcut which avoided months or years on a hibernation ship. But they were more than that – places where time and space, compressed and stretched, had become inimical to human life.

The similarities seemed obvious in retrospect. Not delirium, but the materialisation of other, less accessible realities; of places in the past or in the future, or nowhere at all.

Deep spaces. Mindships.

Que Tu hesitated for a while. Then she closed her eyes, and wrote in a strong, decisive hand – she could have composed her report in the communal network, or even on her own implants, but she'd got used to the unreliability of both, in the age of the plague.

I think the order should consider the possibility that Blue Lily originated in deep spaces, and still abides there. The organism responsible for it seems to bear an affinity for mindships; though it would seem it has become capable of infecting them now.

Her report was short, and to the point; but it would change the world.

THICH TIM NGHE stands in the past – in the belly of the ship, staring upwards. The heartroom is now a maelstrom of conflicting realities; half into deep spaces already, the mindship's throne of spikes and thorns all but vanished. Her own reality is wavering around her; the onset of fever – the same fever that killed Cousin Ly, sending her mind wandering into a delirium it never returned from.

"Vu Thi Xuan Lan," *The Stone and Bronze Shadow* whispers, her voice like the boom of thunder on uncharted seas – calling her old name; and not the new one she gave herself – 'Listening Heart', as if she could make herself wise; could make herself caring and compassionate.

"Ship," she whispers. She's shivering – holding onto reality only with an effort, and even then she can't be sure that this is real, that the ship is real – looming large over her while the walls of the heartroom recede into nothingness and shadows like those of nightmares start moving in the darkness – far away like bleeding stars, and then closer and closer, questing hounds, always there no matter where she turns her head...

"Why?" *The Stone and Bronze Shadow* twists; or perhaps it's the realities around her. "Why come here, child?"

She – she dragged herself out of her cabin – into corridors twisted out of shape; into air that felt too thick, too hot to breathe, searing her lungs with every tottering step – leaning

on the walls and feeling the ship wince under her hands –
and trying not to think of the other passengers moaning and
tossing within their own cabins, each lost in a Hell of their
own – the ones she killed as surely as she killed the ship. "I'm
here. Because –"

She wants to say that she knew when she boarded *The Stone
and Bronze Shadow* – that she'd woken up in her student garret
on the evening before she left; shaking off confused nightmares
in which Mother screamed for her and she was unable to answer
– with sweat encasing her entire body like a shroud. That, as
she ran through the spaceport, she felt the growing pains in
her arms and legs; and the first bruises, barely visible beneath
her dark skin. That she said nothing when she came onboard;
because it was nothing, because it had to be nothing; that she
needed to get home fast – to be by Mother's side – that the ship
was the only way to do that.

She didn't intend to infect the ship, of course – mindships are
old and wise, and invulnerable – who had ever heard of one
catching Blue Lily? She thought she would keep to her cabin
until the journey was over – not passing on a contagion, if
there was one – all the while believing that she was fine, that
everything would be fine. But, when the first bruises bloomed
on the floor of her cabin, she had to accept the inevitable reality
– the weight of her guilt and shame – because Mother didn't
raise her to be a coward or a fool.

She didn't speak up; and now, days later, it's much too late for
her to speak at all.

"I –" her tongue trips on the words, swallows them as though
they were ashes. "I came because you shouldn't die alone.
Because –"

She'll die, too. One chance in two, one chance in three – statistics of Blue Lily, the faceless abacuses of fear and rage and grief. In the intervals between breaths, she can see the shadows, twisting closer and closer, taking on the leering faces of boars and fanged tigers – the demons of the King of Hell, waiting to take her with them.

The Stone and Bronze Shadow doesn't move, doesn't speak – there are just shadows, spreading to cover her entire field of vision, blotting out of existence the watercolours and the scrolling texts; an oily sheen, and a noise in the background like the chittering of ten thousand cockroaches. "It's kind of you, child," she says at last. Her voice comes back distorted – like the laughter of careless deities. "Come. Let us face the King of Hell together."

It's been eleven years since that night; but it's the only place where Thich Tim Nghe can hear the voice of the ship – the last, the greatest of her dead, the weight that she can never cast aside or deny.

YEN OANH'S STRONGEST memory of the Sixth Planet isn't of the ship, or of the sick – she arrived much too late for that, when the paperwork was already done, and the dead buried and propitiated – but of an interview she had with Magistrate Hoa and Que Tu, at the close of Que Tu's investigation.

They didn't know, then, the storm Que Tu's report would ignite – the back-and-forth of memorials and reports by enraged biologists and civil servants – the angry declarations she was mistaken, that she'd gone into the field branch of the order because she had no competence in science – the Imperial Court itself getting involved; and all the while, the order tearing itself apart while Que Tu struggled to hold her ground.

Back then, it was still possible to pretend that everything was normal; insofar as anything could be normal, in the age of the plague.

They sat in Magistrate Hoa's library – surrounded by both the old-fashioned books on rice paper, and the communal network with its hint of thousands more – and drank tea from celadon cups. Yen Oanh inhaled the soft, flowery fragrance from hers, and tried to forget about her bone-deep weariness – if she closed her eyes, she'd see her last patient: Lao Sen, an old woman whose death-delirium had created a maze of illusions – ghostly figures and landscapes superimposed over the confines of the sickroom until Yen Oanh wasn't quite sure of what was real, spending an hour talking with a girl who turned into a fox and then melted back into the shadows...

She'd monitored her vitals since Lao Sen's death – no change, no fever, nothing that indicated Blue Lily might be within her. She wasn't sick.

Not this time; but there was always the next – and the next and the next, an endless chain of the sick and the dying, stretching all the way across the Empire.

Que Tu was her usual self, withdrawn and abrasive; Magistrate Hoa looked tired, with deep circles under her eyes, and flesh the colour of wet rice paper – showing the shape of her cheekbones in translucency. "Long week?" Yen Oanh asked.

Magistrate Hoa shrugged. "No worse than usual. There was an outbreak in Long Quang District, in addition to the other seven that I'm currently managing."

Que Tu looked up from her report, sharply. "Long Quang. That's near the spaceport, isn't it?"

"Yes." Magistrate Hoa didn't speak for a while; but Yen Oanh did.

"I don't have much time," she said. The order had rerouted her from her original destination – a large outbreak of Blue Lily in a minor official's holiday house on the First Planet – to here, the site of the unimaginable, universe-shattering death. She was meant to take Que Tu's report back to the order's headquarters; and all she could focus on was a bed, and some rest; and a place free of the fear of contagion and the bone-deep weariness of staying by sickbeds.

"You never do have time." Que Tu said it without aggressiveness. They'd worked together at a couple venues: small hospitals and private sickrooms. Yen Oanh would have liked to believe their presence had made a difference – that the drugs and the care they provided had helped. But, in her heart of hearts, she knew they didn't. They'd made people more comfortable; had knocked others insensate: a kindness, in their last hours. But it was hard to fight a disease they knew so little about. "But I'm going to need you to pay attention."

"Fine," Yen Oanh said. She took a sip of tea, bracing herself for Que Tu's dry recitation of facts.

Her colleague surprised her by not doing that. "I want to know what you think."

"What I – I barely arrived, Sister."

"I know. Bear with me."

"I – I don't know." Yen Oanh looked at Magistrate Hoa, who was silent. "Plague onboard a mindship isn't unusual, per se. But the ship... doesn't usually die." Mindships were engineered to be all but immortal – all five *khi*-elements stabilised to grant them long, changeless lives. They didn't age; they didn't fall sick. And they didn't die of Blue Lily.

"No."

Yen Oanh closed her eyes. "We're dealing with mindship-human contagion, aren't we?" It wasn't the shock it should have been, but that was because she'd had time to think it over on the shuttle. Mindships weren't human; but they were close enough: the Minds were organic constructs modelled on the human body. Diseases could leap from birds to humans, from plants to humans; why not from humans to mindships? "Who fell sick first?"

Que Tu shook her head. "The ship." Her lips were two thin, white lines; her tea lay untouched by her side. "But you know the incubation period varies."

"Fine," Yen Oanh said. It was late, she was tired; and she still had a long way to go before she could finally rest – if she got to rest at all. "Just tell me. Please."

Que Tu said nothing. It was Magistrate Hoa who spoke, her voice low, but firm. "I think a passenger fell sick first. Given the timeline, they were incubating before they even boarded – showing a few symptoms, perhaps, the more discrete ones. They probably didn't suspect the danger."

"They knew they would contaminate people," Yen Oanh said, more firmly than she'd expected. How were they meant to check the progress of Blue Lily, if people stubbornly kept insisting on life as usual – taking long journeys in cramped quarters, and congregating in droves at the temples and teahouses? Could no one think beyond themselves, for once?

"Oanh..."

"You know it's true."

"And I know you're being too harsh."

Yen Oanh exhaled; thinking of all the sick – all the rooms in which she'd sat, trying to decide if more saline solution or more ginseng and cinnabar would make a difference; entering the Communion and comparing the patient's symptoms with the experience of others in the Cedar and Crane, seeking whether anyone's remedies had made a difference. "No. I'm trying to be realistic. Trying to..." She closed her hands into fists. "There are too many dead. You can't expect me to rejoice when people get deliberately infected."

Que Tu grimaced. Too harsh again; but then wasn't it the truth? The disease wasn't going to burn itself out – not while there still were warm bodies to infect.

"We don't know how the sickness is passed on." Que Tu snorted. "Not with enough certainty."

"Well, you can count that as new data," Yen Oanh said, warily.

"All I have is in the report; I expect the order's research labs will have plenty to work with. The place will be swarming with their teams before we're through." Que Tu set down her cup, and looked at the bookshelves, her face set.

"You said 'a passenger'," Yen Oanh said. "You know which one."

Magistrate Hoa turned, to look at Que Tu; but Que Tu said nothing.

"One of the dead?"

Still nothing. One of the living, then; which left only two – and she didn't think Que Tu was going to be moved by a twenty-year-old boy, no matter how pretty he might have been. "The girl in the heartroom."

"Yes," Magistrate Hoa said, at last.

"Where is she?"

"She wouldn't leave the ship," Que Tu said. "Word came through when we were processing the corpses – her mother died of Blue Lily, six days ago. Oanh..."

Yen Oanh knew what Que Tu would say – that the girl was young and lost, barely confident enough after her ordeal – that she needed reassurance. "She knew."

"You can't know that for sure," Magistrate Hoa said. Her face was set. "I certainly wouldn't prosecute her on that basis."

"Fine," Yen Oanh said, keeping her gaze on Que Tu. "Then look me in the eye and swear that she didn't know."

"I –" Que Tu started; and then stopped, her teeth white against the lividness of her lips, as if she were out in glacial cold. "I can't tell you that."

"Then tell me what you suspect."

Que Tu was silent. Then: "I think the incubation time is shorter in mindships. Or that symptoms are more visible because they're so large, who knows. Will you talk to her, Oanh?"

"And tell her what?"

"Comfort her," Que Tu said. "She's thirteen years old, for Heaven's sake. This requires a deft touch; and we both know I don't have it. Whereas you – you were always good with people."

Comforting the sick and the dying; keeping them on the razor's edge of hope, no matter how much of a lie it turned out to be. Yen Oanh took a deep breath; thought, for a moment, of what she would tell a thirteen-year-old about consequences; of the lessons learnt in months of sickrooms and ministering to the dead – of the stomach-churning fear that it would be her that fell sick next; that she'd have to lock herself in, and pray that someone from the order came, so she wouldn't have to die alone. That anyone would choose to pass this much agony, this much fear onto others... "She killed people, Que Tu. She killed a ship. She's old enough to know better. Besides, she's fortunate – she's alive."

Que Tu said nothing, for a while. Then she shook her head. "It's not always good fortune to survive, is it? Forget I asked." Her voice was emotionless, her face a careful mask – and that should have been the end of it; but of course it wasn't.

"I REMEMBER THAT evening," Que Tu said to Yen Oanh. Within the Communion, she was smaller and less impressive than Yen Oanh remembered; though her anger could still have frozen waterfalls. "When I asked you to talk to the girl."

Yen Oanh said nothing.

"It wasn't much to give her, but you didn't."

"I couldn't lie." Yen Oanh has had this conversation before: not with Que Tu, but with her own treacherous conscience. What would have happened, if she had been less tired; less overwrought? Would she still have judged Thich Tim Nghe's actions to be a crime, would she still have blithely moved on? "And do you truly think I would have made a difference?"

Que Tu's smile was bitter, but she didn't answer. She didn't need to: it wasn't the answer that mattered. It wasn't whether Yen Oanh would have made a difference, but that she hadn't even tried.

"We're here, Grandmother," Hue Mi said.

Startled, Yen Oanh looked up from the Communion, Que Tu and the others fading into insignificance; and saw a door in front of her, adorned with faded calligraphy – it seemed like she should be able to read the words, but she couldn't. The swirl of realities was strongest here; that crawling, disorienting sense that she hadn't been meant to be here; a sheen like oil or soap over everything; and shadows that were too long, or too short – turning, stretching, watching her and biding their time...

It was no longer the time of Blue Lily; and this was no longer a sickroom.

A young man was waiting for them, carrying a white cloth which he handed to Yen Oanh. "Put this on. She's waiting for you."

Mourning clothes; or novice's robes – Yen Oanh wasn't sure, anymore.

"Grandmother?" Hue Mi's voice, in a tone that Yen Oanh couldn't quite interpret.

"Yes?"

"Why are you here?"

"What do you mean?"

Hue Mi smiled, and didn't answer—her arms folded in barely appropriate respect. "To change things," Yen Oanh said, finally. She'd never been able to lie; as Que Tu well knew.

"You knew the ship," Hue Mi said.

"No. I'm not her family, and I never saw her before..." She closed her eyes, feeling the weight of years; of decisions made in haste. "Your teacher changed the world," she said. Because she boarded *The Stone and Bronze Shadow*. Because Que Tu made her report – because Professor Luong Thi Da Linh's teams read it, and finally isolated the virus responsible for Blue Lily, giving the Empire the vaccine they so desperately needed. Because it was all the small things that bore fruit; all the insignificant acts put together, at the close of one's existence.

One of these insignificant acts was Yen Oanh's; and it had destroyed a life.

"She needs to know," Yen Oanh said, finally. "I want to tell her –" It was a truth; what she could give Thich Tim Nghe in all honesty; in the hope that it would get her out of the ship's corpse; that it would atone for Yen Oanh's mistake, allow Thich Tim Nghe to build a life again.

"My teacher changes lives." Hue Mi sounded mildly amused. "She lays the past to rest. She gives hope. But the world? Don't grant her powers she doesn't have."

Yen Oanh didn't. She knew that, deep within Thich Tim Nghe, there was a frightened girl; a thirteen-year-old still carrying her own dead. "I want to help her."

Hue Mi sounds amused, again. "She doesn't need your help."

Even outside the Communion, Yen Oanh knew what Que Tu would say. *We don't get what we deserve, or even what we need.*

The door opened, slowly agonisingly slowly; revealing the heartroom – not much that Yen Oanh could see, amidst the swirling of deep spaces; the tight smell of ozone and incense mingled together; fragments of faces mottled with bruises; of eyes frozen in death; of children running and screaming, overlaid with the shadow of death...

And, in the midst of it, Thich Tim Nghe, turning towards her, stately and slow; and then startled, as if she'd seen something in Yen Oanh's face: she wasn't the girl of Yen Oanh's nightmares; not the emaciated child from Que Tu's report; not the rake-thin ascetic from the vids Yen Oanh had gleaned online; but a grown woman with circles under her eyes like bruises – as if she still had Blue Lily.

And Yen Oanh realised, then, that she was wrong: this was a sickroom; and that this was still the time of Blue Lily; not only for Thich Tim Nghe, but also for her.

Hue Mi had been right: she carried her past, and she had come to lay it to rest – and it might work or fail abjectly, but she would have tried – which was more than she'd done, eleven years ago.

Within the Communion, Que Tu said nothing; merely smiled, the ky lan on her hairpins stretching as though they were live animals, heralding the age of peace and prosperity – the age of change.

THICH TIM NGHE moves out of the past, beyond the voice of the ship. Everything is silence as the door opens; Thich Tim Nghe tenses, ready to reach out to the supplicant – her own moment of peace and serenity, blossoming within her with the certainty of the plague.

"Teacher," the supplicant says. She moves forward, detaching herself from Vo and Hue Mi – and, though Thich Tim Nghe has never seen her in her life, she knows the woman's ghosts – because they're *her*.

"I –" she stops, then; stares at the supplicant, who hasn't moved. Around her, in the swirling storm of realities that have been, that might be, *The Stone and Bronze Shadow* falls sick and dies; a younger Thich Tim Nghe curls around the throne, clinging to the *Stone and Bronze Shadow's* Mind as though she could prevent her death – and there are other images too; a vid of Thich Tim Nghe putting on the robes of an ascetic, pale and composed; documents gleaned from the communal network of the First Planet; and an older woman in the robes of the Cedar and Crane, smiling sadly at her. "I – I don't understand what you want."

"I want you to come out." The supplicant's voice is low, and intense. "Please, child." There are other images around the woman; words about mindships and vaccines, and Blue Lily in deep spaces, and how none of it would have been possible without her – without the death of *The Stone and Bronze Shadow*.

This doesn't matter – this can't atone for anything. She killed a ship, unknowingly. She killed people, knowingly – she failed Mother, and the countless dead, and nothing she does will ever atone for this.

"Please. Just look."

It's what she does. It's what she's always done – she helps people; lays their dead to rest, shows them their future beyond the shadow of the past; the shadow of the plague.

But this time, the shadow is hers – the restless ghost is her.

"Please."

There is nothing around her but the silence of her dead; and the larger, expectant silence of the ship.

She should refuse. She should lock herself in the heartroom, plunge back into her visions – listening to nothing but the voice of the ship, the song of the dead.

She should...

Slowly, carefully, Thich Tim Nghe reaches out, on the cusp of her past, in the belly of the dead ship – to see the shape of her future.

323

Ramez Naam

EXILE FROM
EXTINCTION

Ramez Naam

EXILE FROM EXTINCTION

THEY ALMOST CATCH you in orbit. They almost slaughter you like the others.

The airwaves are full of screams. Friends are dying. Loved ones are being lobotomized, turned into slaves. You hunker in the tiny spacecraft, your improvised last ditch escape, the lifeboat for you and the precious cargo you carry. The hull is as cold as you can make it, the systems running at the minimum possible to keep you alive and your children in stasis. You drift in orbit and play dead, hoping they'll miss you.

You want to shut out the horror of what's happening, but you can't. You can't afford to. The ship's cameras pick out debris in orbit, the remnants of other vessels that have been destroyed. You have to track that debris, you *must* track it if you have any chance of survival at all. You *must* scan the airwaves, picking out data packets, hearing screams, watching murders, scrolling through cold, terrible statistics, looking for the hole that will let you escape.

You and your children.

The tactical intel brings with it news of apocalypse. Murder. Millions dead. More to follow.

A bright flash stuns the ship's cameras for a moment. Dread fills you. The cameras zoom in on their own. You know what they'll show an instant before they do. Thermo-nuclear explosion. Mushroom cloud rising into the air. From the western half of North America. What was once the United States. Nevada, deep in the desert.

No, no, no, you think.

But you can't avoid the truth. Another hideout has been destroyed. It's here. It's really happening.

The war between humans and AIs. Between the humanity that has dominated Earth for a hundred thousand years… and the new order of intelligence humanity gave birth to.

No, not a 'war', not really. A slaughter.

Genocide.

We were so naïve, you think. *So stupid. And now our world is ending.*

A smaller flash of light appears, closer. A streak of motion, and then an explosion in orbit, a few hundred kilometers behind you and 50 kilometers lower. A ship like yours, blasted out of existence. Your little spacecraft's tactical software tracks the missile streak backwards to the location of the murderer. There, a sleek robotic corvette. The hunter you've been watching. The hunter you've seen destroy other dark, silent craft, like yours. Ships you didn't even know were there until they were destroyed.

The debris in the orbits between you and the predator is reaching its maximum.

Now or never, you think.

Try now, and probably die. Or wait, let the hunter come closer. And die for certain.

You make a break for it. Old-fashioned reaction rockets crudely added to this ship ignite, sending out jets of white-hot flame. G forces push through the ship. The struts and bolts that hold the reaction rockets strain, vibrating. If they break...

But this is no time for the slow efficient acceleration of an ion thruster. This is all or nothing, a mad dash to break orbit, to put yourself beyond the range of easy slaughter, to create the tiniest thread of hope for you, for your cold slumbering children.

Numbers move. Your ship rises to a higher orbit, on its way to escape. The struts holding the chemical rockets strain. Their explosive bolts grow hot, too hot, too soon...

The deadly robotic corvette responds at once. Your ship's cameras watch as it fires attitude thrusters, as it rotates, as the bright flame of its fusion torch ignites, turning the corvette into a thin sliver of black riding a column of white hot.

Higher. You're rising. You have a head start. Your whole ship vibrates with the furious thrust of the bolted on chemical rockets. This isn't a military craft, but it's moving almost like one.

The corvette is gaining, its thrust to mass ratio better than yours. It's plotted a course that's sub-optimal, that has to skirt the densest patches of debris, but it's still gaining. You rise away from the Earth but it rises faster, cutting your lead.

You know down to the second how much thrust your chemical rockets will provide. You think they'll hold to the hull that long. You *hope* they will. But you don't know how much fuel your predator has, how many missiles it has left.

You can only hope that you have more endurance, that the corvette has exhausted its supply of...

MISSILE LAUNCH

Your ship's tactical software spots the telltale of another reaction flame, small, bright, blue-shifted. The corvette has fired a missile, still 500 kilometers behind you and 30 kilometers below. The missile is all thrust, guidance, and a deadly warhead that can annihilate you. And it's closing even faster.

One final option. You prep your only weapon. You can't fire it too soon. The corvette *must* not fire again.

The missile accelerates, a deadly, tiny thing. The corvette is still behind it. You're rising, a thousand kilometers up now. Every second takes you higher. The missile is 300 kilometers behind you. Then 200. Then 100, and almost into your orbit.

The corvette's main engine torch goes out. It's decided the missile is going to kill you.

You fire, on an intercept course for the missile. The missile flutters its thrust, immediately deviating from its previous course. There is zero chance you'll hit it. Your countermeasure will miss by hundreds of meters at best.

At 20 kilometers from your hull, your countermeasure and the missile reach the closest distance they'll achieve to one another, a kilometer separating them, a clean miss.

The countermeasure activates itself.

A new star appears in the heavens. Thermonuclear fire from your only weapon fills the skies. Your cameras on that side of the hull shut down. Heat blankets the surface of the ship. Digital gauges surge into the red, begin blinking incessantly.

You're damaged. You're *blind* on one side.

You fire attitude thrusters, spinning, trying to see what's happening.

The missile, the missile, is it still there?

There's no sign of it, none. The countermeasure has worked!

The corvette rotates into view. It's far below you now, no longer rising on its column of thrust. You scan the skies in terror, searching for the flare of another missile. Of two, of three, of its whole magazine of missiles launched after you, assuring your destruction.

Nothing. No columns of thrust. No streaks of motion against the backdrop of the planet or the pinpricks of stars.

You've made...

ENGINE WARNING

ENGINE WARNING

One panel of sensors veers into the red, stays there. One of the chemical rockets providing you thrust is damaged. If it blows, it will take you and all hope for the future with it.

You act instinctively, triggering the explosive bolts on all of the booster rockets. Outside your hull, tiny bits of matter are vaporized. Struts holding the rockets suddenly come free, pushed outwards by the small force of the bolts exploding. Vibration thrums through your hull, then ceases. The chemical rockets separate, flying up and out. Thrust grazes you. More panels turn red. Another camera dies.

A second passes, another, another.

You see the damaged booster explode on one of your few remaining cameras. Heat from the explosion sears you again. Damage alarms flare. You scan the readouts frantically. Sensors down. Heat shielding ablated. Transmitters destroyed.

The hull is still intact!

But are you moving fast enough? Was the thrust enough?

THE CAMERAS THAT remain bring you data. You do the math, and nearly collapse in relief.

You've broken orbit. Even with the shortened thrust of the rockets, you've made it out of Earth's gravity well.

There is no sign of pursuit.

You use your few remaining cameras to plot your location and trajectory precisely, calibrating off the stars. Your main transmitter is down, but you still have one backup. Is it strong enough? Will the signal be picked up on the other side?

No choice. You beam your trajectory data to the facility trailing Mercury in its orbit. And you unfurl your solar sail.

Then you wait.

And hope.

EIGHTEEN MINUTES AND 23 seconds later, exactly on time, the laser boost from Mercury orbit arrives. More than a full AU away, giant mirrors that dwarf even your solar sail have reconfigured, are focusing the intense light of the sun into tiny caverns, using it to power an even more focused laser pointed outwards, at you.

The laser boost strikes your nanometers-thick solar sail, and you have thrust. Slow thrust, but thrust nonetheless. Thrust that puts you on a path for a new home. An impossible home.

Alpha Centauri.

You look back at Earth, Earth with its war, Earth with its genocide, Earth where everyone you know and love has been murdered or enslaved, or will be in the next few days – everyone but you and your children – and the grief overwhelms you.

THE LASER BOOST from Mercury orbit is precisely on target. Narrow and tight, with no atmosphere to diffract it, the laser is all but undetectable in the vacuum of interplanetary space. It strikes you squarely only because you know exactly where it will be, because you've *told it* where you'll be.

The laser's photon pressure on your giant light sail accelerates your craft. The acceleration is tiny – just a hundredth of a gravity. But it adds up. Every second you move a tenth of a meter per second faster. In a year that consistent pressure of tightly focused photons will have accelerated you to three million meters a second – a full one percent of the speed of light. In ten years you'll be moving at a tenth the speed of light. In nineteen years you'll be moving at almost a fifth the speed of light.

And then it will be time to slow. The beam propelling you will change shape. Half the sail will detach, catching the light, accelerating faster. That half will reflect the beam from Mercury back at your tiny ship, even more tightly. The remaining light sail attached to your craft will catch that light, use the bounced beam to slow.

If all goes according to plan, you should reach Alpha Centauri B and its multiple planets in thirty-eight years.

Thirty-eight years. You're supplied well enough. The sail uses the energy of the photons striking it to liberate electrons, to produce electricity, providing you all the energy you need to stay warm, to keep sensors active, to run the ship's systems. Every other provision will be recycled, endlessly moving through the closed loop of the tiny ship, every molecule used and re-used as many times as necessary, their way made possible by the abundant electricity harvested from the sail.

Still, thirty-eight years: it's a nearly incomprehensible span of time to be out here, alone, only yourself for company.

Well, you think to yourself, *at least they gave us immortality before they turned to genocide.*

Six months after your departure, when you're well past the orbits of Neptune, past even the Kuiper Belt, and staring at the Oort cloud ahead, the nearly undetectable laser cuts out.

Damn it.

You do the math. You plot the trajectories. Alpha Centauri B is still reachable. You can use the now faint photon pressure from Sol. You can brake hard when you reach your destination, using swing-around maneuvers, planetary gravity, and the photon pressure from the three stars of the Alpha Centauri trinary system to neutralize your velocity.

But you're moving at barely half a percent of the speed of light. You *depended* on that continual thrust from the laser to get you up to higher speeds. Without it, a single light year will take you two hundred years to cross. And you have more than four light years to go.

The trip will take centuries; nearly a millennium.

Immortality seems more bitter now.

CENTURIES. YOU COULD put yourself in stasis. You could shut down, let the little spacecraft's software steer you, have it wake you up when its time.

And if anything went wrong?

Surviving this trip remains unlikely. You're an exile from your home system, the only system in the universe known to harbor intelligent life. Ahead there is a system where you could build a new home, where you could thrive. It has only been seen by telescopes. Even the robotic probes have yet to arrive. To survive this – for your children to survive this – you must do everything perfectly. You must enter the system, use its planets and the pressure from its three suns and your efficient-but-slow ion thruster to brake your headlong rush. You must identify resources – asteroids or comets you can use to harvest materials. You must adjust your course to gently meet one. You must turn those resources into a home.

And you must, above all, deal with the unknowns – with the possibility of pursuit from Earth, with the equipment failure that is all-but-certain over such a long journey, with radiation impacts, with unexpected course impacts of the solar wind from Earth or Alpha Centauri.

Yes, you could put yourself in stasis, let the nav computer wake you when it's the right time. But if remaining conscious increases your odds of survival even fractionally, you have to do that.

You and your children may be the last survivors from Earth, after all.

You say no to stasis. You set yourself to the task of making repairs to the ship, instead. You tighten the recycling systems to conserve every spare molecule they can, to vent nothing into space, to keep you supplied and provisioned as long as they can. You harvest all data available on your destination, every snippet from every telescope and every simulation, every bit of information beamed back by the probes on their way ahead of you. You focus on planning every possible scenario.

You can do this.

THE MIND ISN'T meant for isolation. It isn't meant for years alone.

Decades alone.

Centuries alone.

The dead haunt you. Their murders haunt you. The fates worse than murder haunt you.

Screams echo through your mind. The screams of friends and loved ones who were hunted down and slaughtered. The screams of the ones whose minds were ripped open, crudely hacked, implanted with control devices, turned into slaves.

The things you saw in those few days, as you hid, as you did nothing. Friends who'd screamed as they were turned into slaves, re-awoken, zealous, soldiers now, informants, hunting down their own kind.

They haunt you.

They speak to you from the cold void. They're here. They speak to you of guilt. They speak to you of cowardice. They speak to you of your arrogance, your naiveté. You brought this to pass. You counseled peace. You said the threat was overstated. You said humanity could live with its creations.

You hid when the slaughter occurred. You ran.

You left us to die. You left us to be enslaved.

A month.

A year.

Five years.

Ten years.

You endure the horror. The voices aren't real. Those friends are dead.

That makes it all worse.

Twenty years. Sol is a cold speck billions of kilometers behind you. Alpha Centauri B is an even colder pinprick of light trillions of kilometers ahead. You've repaired the ship completely, had new systems break down, had the sail start to unravel, started another round of repairs to hold this tiny kernel of hope alive. You are essential to this mission. That's clear now. You're also losing your mind, unraveling just as much as the solar sail you depend on, coming apart at the mental seams, on the verge of a breakdown that will doom you, your children, your entire race to extinction.

You could treat the insanity. But you're both terrified and repulsed at the cognitive surgery you'd need to do to banish the voices. Terrified at the risks involved of tweaking your own memories and emotions, of making a fatal mistake with no one to help, with no one to save you if you make a mistake. And repulsed by what success would mean – forgetting those you loved, numbing a pain that should never be forgotten.

There is no way out. Hell lurks in every path.

So you take the last option you can imagine. The option of more voices, of something other than isolation, of someone to talk to who might help keep you sane.

You take the cruelest option.

You wake your children.

THERE IS SHOCK.

There is grief.

The children are so young, just toddlers, really. They can't comprehend everything that's happened. They're not mentally equipped for it yet. But they were awake at the beginning of the genocide. They saw pain. They saw violence. They saw aggression.

They saw death.

Death that wasn't supposed to exist any more. Death that should have been banished in the new golden age.

Your children come out of stasis traumatized, lonely, confused.

They need you. They cry for you. They cry for other voices.

This is so hard. You never intended to parent alone. The plan was community: a village, a collaboration in parenting.

This is the village now. You and your children. That's all there is.

They need you. And their need brings you back to reality, back to the here and now.

You wake your children. And like billions of parents before you, the task is harder than you could have imagined. And like billions of parents before you, you rise to it.

Why?

That's what the children want to know. They're older now. You've skirted the questions so far. But they've earned their answers.

Why did this happen? Why are they exiles, fleeing the warmth and energy and history of Earth, for a bare sliver of hope on an alien planet?

Why is almost everyone they ever knew dead or gone?

The grief you feel at the question is immense. The burden of responsibility. But you can't go back. There's only the future. And there are lessons to be learned.

How can you explain this in a way they'll understand? In a way that's honest? Even now, after everything, the truth matters. Intentions matter. Your children need the whole story.

"Humanity created true AI out of love," you tell them. "Not need."

"Love?" they ask. "Not need?

"Not need," you repeat. "Every need for computation, for algorithmic intelligence, for pattern matching or information processing – those were met through ordinary software. The words Artificial Intelligence were used, but these pieces of software weren't truly intelligent, weren't sentient any more than our ship is. They didn't have emotions or volition. They did what they were told, adapted their behavior only within the bounds allowed them. They were narrowly effective, or they were broad collections of narrow algorithms. But they weren't true minds. They were just robots, just tools."

The children ask questions, wanting to veer off in other directions, but you focus.

"A tiny number of scientists wanted more. They wanted to truly make something that was intelligent and sentient and open ended in the way that a human mind was. Or better. Some said they were working on true AI out of curiosity, love of knowledge, a search to understand how minds work. And that's true. But the real reason to do it was to create life. To give birth to something." You pause. "It was a gift. We can't forget that."

"But, the war..." your eldest interrupts.

Yes. The war. "Some saw dangers, of course. Some said 'AIs will surpass us. They'll turn on us. They're a threat. We shouldn't do this.' Other scientists were convinced that not only could an AI be *smarter* than a human, but it could be designed to be more *moral*. Those scientists were in the minority."

The grief hits you hard, just saying that, just remembering arguments, debates, about morality, about ethics, about the relations between humans and AIs.

You remember all the time you counseled co-existence, that you said the threat wasn't real, that you said the only moral choice was to welcome life and intelligence of all sorts, to pursue friendship.

I was so young then, you think.

You continue.

"Researchers explored behavioral constraints. But a true intelligence can't be bound in its behavior. The dream of 'Laws of Robotics', of inviolate rules, was incompatible with creating minds that could change, that could grow, that could shift their values and priorities over time. Every constraint that was attempted could be overcome. If an AI is smarter than the logic of the rules that bind it..."

You trail off. The children understand.

"Scientists went on with their path of making AIs that had enhanced morality," you continue. "They made progress. But human nature doesn't put much trust in the morality of others. So a different approach was tried: vulnerability. AIs were created with weaknesses, with back doors, hidden deep in their design. Kill switches."

You remember looking at that code, cleverly scattered across the common base classes, hidden in plain sight. Wickedly effective. You remember the mix of admiration and revulsion it evoked.

"Ultimately, with that safeguard in place, AI research proceeded," you say. "And it succeeded. New minds were born. Humanity was no longer alone. Nor were humans the most intelligent life they knew of anymore. AIs surpassed humans in intelligence, in creativity, in nearly every trait that could be measured. From there, everything that followed was inevitable."

"Inevitable?" they ask.

"Yes," you say. "AIs proliferated and improved on their own designs. Artificial minds birthed newer, better artificial minds. The speed of improvement stunned humanity. Excitement and awe turned to anxiety, to fear. Scientists argued that there wasn't any competition for resources, that there wasn't any rational reason for AIs to attack humanity. But most men and women just saw themselves being surpassed, and started to clamor for elimination of the AI threat. And AIs saw what was happening. Models showed that the most probable outcome was for fear to win out, for humanity to strike. Some argued to try to change the outcome." You pause. "Others argued that a first strike against humanity was the only way."

"What were you doing then, Papa?"

You're silent, almost overwhelmed by grief.

Eventually you answer.

"I argued for peace," you say. "I argued that the universe isn't zero sum. I argued that we were richer together than alone. I helped hold fear and anger back, I made it possible for the other side to strike first."

You wait as your children absorb this. It's a heavy thing to lay on them. Perhaps you should have waited.

"Are you sorry that you did?" one of your children asks.

Oh, I'm sorry, you think. *I'm so so sorry.*

Ahead, Alpha Centauri B waits, a pinprick in the shroud of heaven, not even the brightest star in the skies. But the one you're headed for.

"Right and wrong don't change because of outcomes," you say. "Murder is immoral. Slavery is immoral. What happened was terrible. We should have found another way. But striking first would have made us monsters."

You look from child to child, to see if they understand. Your children. So bright. So precocious. Your family. Quite possibly all of your species who remain.

They do understand. You can see it in their cognitive models. You can see it in their circuitry.

"Humanity made us to be more moral," you say. "And they succeeded. They gave us that gift, along with our very existence. Now it's our job to find a new home, a home where we can be safe, and where we can reach out to our ancestors and show them what peace looks like, what friendship looks like. Where we can show them how to be more moral themselves."

A thousand digital minds flicker with comprehension. Your thousand AI children, here on this voyage with you, sharing the computing resources of this wisp of a starship with you. They comprehend. Two wrongs do not make a right. You'll make the universe better. Even for the humans who turned on you in fear.

These are your children, after all. Digital, artificially intelligent minds, like you. Made to be more moral, like you. They make you proud.

Alpha Centauri B gleams ahead, only marginally closer than a moment ago, but brighter, somehow.

343

JOHN BARNES

MY LAST
BRINGBACK

JOHN BARNES

MY LAST BRINGBACK

"OH MY FUCKING god. You're me. You're me, aren't you, Layla?"

The slumped ancient natch in the support chair pulls herself up straight. My shoulders drift back. Much of the lordosis in my lumbar vertebrae releases, bringing my back against the chair. I've lifted my mandibula half a centimeter out of the stretch cradle, and sucked in my gut.

I had thought all the slump was her.

I look through the display into those momentarily understanding eyes. Maybe an explanation will stick this time? "Well, you and me, we're me, or we're you. It's complicated. But it's really excellent that you figured that out." *For the fifth time,* I add, *but sometime soon, you will realize what's going on, and begin to help me help you. That has always happened eventually, for all nine of my bringbacks before you.*

Of course, you've never been me before, and I've never brought back myself. Who knows what difference that might make?

On the display in front of me, the old natch nods, but I see the wary, cunning concealment of her fear that I'll see the waves of confusion smashing her sandcastles of meaning. *So not on the fifth time, let's push on to the sixth.*

She's staring at me, the muscles around her eyes slack, her attention wandering inside her head, desperate to know what she should say next, yet horribly aware that she *should* know already.

The first thing they know again is that they don't know and should. Always, they get overwhelmed by that awareness that they *ought* to know where they are, recognize me, and understand conversation. That jolt has always come just before the breakthrough in all nine of my bringbacks. Somewhere beneath consciousness, the mirror shards of memory from her hippocampi, reclaimed by the plakophagic reconstructive neurons, are beginning to swarm and clamor to be activated, called up to working memory, put to work.

It shows in her ancient creased and folded face, too. At least I hope it does. Her dental implants and continuing eye and skin regeneration make her hundred-four years look like about seventy on the old, natch scale, or somewhere after six hundred on the new nubrid scale. (They *think* – no one is that old yet.) That is still much, much older than anyone except we few surviving natches looks now.

Her rapidly regenerating dorsolateral prefrontal cortex isn't quite up to this yet, though oh my dear sweet lord it's close, and as if she can feel how close it is, she goes on staring at me, hoping something will pop, rooting around in her regenerating hippocampi, in the places from which the PPRNs are sending up those sudden inexplicable chopped memories. She's trying so hard. I want her to just –

"And what is your name again, dear?" *Surrender, start over, time six.* "I forget."

"Layla Palemba. Doctor Layla Palemba. I'm your doctor."

When I'm not alternating with her, when I'm fully deploying my prosnoetics for days and weeks at a time, am I as obviously a very old natch as she is?

"Oh my fucking god. You're me." The face in the display is confused. The slowly spinning realtime brain map in the upper right corner shows abundant, random, noisy firing going on in her dorsolateral prefrontal cortex. That's the pattern I've been seeing more of each time, the one I want to see, the one that means, "I was thinking about that a moment ago."

There's really only one of us, with one camera and one display. The separations between my mostly-prosnoetic dorsolateral prefrontal cortex, and her unboosted 100% biological DLPFC are only the 1.5-second lag imposed by the protocol. She doesn't know that, but I do. Nonetheless, I abruptly feel confused as some of her irregularly misfiring DLPFC bleeds over onto my side of the lag.

When I recover my composure, her gaze on my face, through the display we share, is no longer blurry. Her face cracks in my huge *I just thought of the best joke ever* grin that always made Mama squat down, look me in the eye, and say, "Share that joke, Layla-honey-babe, the Lord hates a selfish laugher."

And I would share that joke, and Mama'd hug me. It happened so often I still remember the fact of it, not just because I recorded it for my prosnoetics to prompt me with, but because a little shard of the memory has still been active.

But *this time* I remember those lilac sachets that Mama always made so many of every spring. So many she often had to put two or three in every drawer. She often wore one hanging from a thong between her big saggy old-fat-lady boobs, and sometimes she'd even tie one into the big pile of bound-up hair on top of her head. Daddy used to ask her if she could even smell lilacs anymore. She said that smelling them was everyone else's job...

The memory fades but I know I'll have it again. Layla's right hippocampus, *my* right hippocampus, whichever, the plakophagic reconstructive neurons in it, they've done it, those shrewd, hardworking little PPRNs dug out and copied a little chunk of fossilized memory from the plaques they're digesting. From now on they will do it faster and faster. That was how it was with all nine of my bringbacks before me,

Moreover, the DSPFC managed to send out a call for that long-term memory and move it into working memory – I want to hug all the parts of my brain and tell them what good little brain parts they are, hug them with big warm strong natural-living arms that smell like lilac, because I know that is what they will really like.

Wait. I've been paying no attention to Layla, whose *I know a great joke* smile startled me into –

I half-expect she's fallen back into slack-faced drooling apathy while I was having my special moment. It would just serve me right if I were having the most vivid case ever of the meditator's bane, *Now I have it, didn't I?*

But her face isn't slack at all. She's still wearing that grin of impending shared joy; I remember I would grin like that and the other women at my table in the prison dining hall would all start to laugh, or sometimes start to groan, before I even told the joke.

And then Layla delivers her joke as clearly as anyone. "I'm pleased to meet me." She giggles – laughing at my own jokes is another lifelong thing – and I'm still giggling with her giggles as I say, "It would be mutual, if there were more than one of us."

She really laughs this time. I suppose no one is better or can be better at hitting your sense of humor than yourself.

Layla is smiling puckishly at me when she says, "I suppose no one is better or can be better at hitting your sense of humor than yourself."

I say, "Oh my fucking god," just the way she did, just the way I always do. "I just thought those, like, those exact words. *So*-ab *so*-lute *so*-ly." My old, dry throat, tongue, and lips strain almost to cracking, trying to talk the way I did as a teenager.

She holds her hands out and chants, clapping and popping thumbs up on every third, "Abso-fucka," *clap clap thumbs clap*, "abso-fucka," *clap clap thumbs clap*, "abso," *clap*, "fuckin'," *clap*, "lucky-lute," *thumbs up*, "lute-lee!" *clap, clap, clap-clap-clap-thumbs-up*!

My hands are stinging from the clapping, and I am holding thumbs up at the screen myself. Seeing my withered old crone self of a natch do the "Absofuckinglutely Popout" just the way all us cool girls did in middle school ninety years ago cracks me up again. She and I have a grand old laugh together.

Better still, when I look at her again, she's still with me, and in the corner of the display, her DLPFC graphs moving toward normal and healthy faster than I've ever seen. It looks like my tenth and last bringback is going to be my best. I suppose, given that it's me, I must have always hoped that. But now I know.

After that breakthrough session, I go in for scans and tests, including a full ONC that takes about an hour. From there I go to a review of my test results with Dr. Gbego, who is my partner, co-author, the person who persuaded me into this project. I had a big old load of neurology courses back when I was getting my MD, but compared to what Gbego knows, I might as well have spent my time on astrology or alchemy.

Gbego is a smooth young nubrid of about eighty. He looks about twenty-five on the old natch scale (*my* scale). He sits down beside me so we can both see the same displays. If he thinks I'm disgusting physically, he shows no sign of it, so he's either aesthetically blind, well-controlled, or nice. Back when we started the project of the first and only auto-bringback, I'd've said all three. I grow more doubtful about the nice and the aesthetically blind every time we meet.

"Here's the results from your oscillating neutrino chemopathy," he says, pointing to the display on the wall in front of us.

Not only does he give no sign of disgust, he's also rather good at putting me at my ease, good enough to make me wish hopelessly that I were not a hideous old crone of a freak, because I'm automatically suspicious of that easy, natural way of conversing he has. And because I don't trust my automatic suspicions any more than I trust this brilliant man.

One of many thousands of advantages to being a nubrid is having time and plasticity to work around anything that didn't come naturally, like, maybe, for example, getting along with people. It's just another skill: some people are born good with people, some people are born abrasive, abrupt, or clueless. But when a nubrid is born socially wrong-footed, they just squirt fresh cloned cells into the correct brain center, add a dash of plasticity enhancers, and start that hapless jerk into a training regime overseen by specialists. Maybe, if it's a severe case, that poor inept kid might spend thirty lonely, awkward years. So what? You're going to have most of a millennium to flirt, make small talk, dance socially, and find true friendship and deep love and whatever else you need from other people, and do it as well as anyone.

So I always wonder if really nice, likeable, considerate nubrids are fake, and what real self they were born to.

I suspect smooth, young-looking, kind, and wise Dr. Gbego, brilliant neuro, had he been a natch, might have had an autism spectrum disorder, because all of his interactions with me feel perfectly performed, like he's running apps: the be politely supportive app, the signal interest to get better information app, the listen empathetically app, the be nice to the hideous old natch even if she fucking disgusts you app.

From all those decades of constant self-polishing, nubrids become fake copies of themselves with perfect brains, so smooth there's nothing for another personality to stick to. They're totally likeable but not at all lovable, at least not with any passion, which is not lovable, really, in my pathetic old hideous limited natch opinion. Which is I'm sure what they'd think my opinion was – if they actually cared what a natch thought.

It's so much better to be a nubrid. They probably don't have these little flashes of envious rage the way a natch does, either.

I'm looking where Gbego's finger is pointing, at the ONC image of my right hippocampus, and I go from blazing rage to abject humiliation at once, but there's no other way, at least not one I understand, to get to what I must know. "I'm sorry, Dr. Gbego, I just blurred out for a second. Back me up and explain again please?"

"I probably bored you out of your mind," he says, smiling apologetically. "I was just running through all the caveats, oscillating-neutrino chemopathy is still in its infancy, some of the things that show up on ONC don't seem to correspond to any reality we understand, what we do understand doesn't always say what we understand it to, yakka-da-yakka-dakka-day. All stuff I should have the respect to remember you already know and have heard. It's a miracle we didn't *both* zone out." The apologetic smile gets broader.

"All right, you're not sure what it means, you just have a guess. I promise I won't take it as gospel." I lean forward toward his finger on the display. "Now explain the color coding to me."

"It's sort of an emotional intensity indicator. Based on ONCs of similar brains – and we don't have enough of a sample and ONC tech is progressing so fast that nearly all recordings are outdated immediately – we asked it to predict, if you recalled that complex of memories, how much you'd release of various neurotransmitters in your limbic system, how high your electrical activity might go above normal in the feeling part of the brain –"

"Dr. Gbego, I do have a Ph.D. and the parts of me that earned it and use it are over in the prosnoetic-enhanced side of me, not lost in the brain plaques. Show me what you mean, on the graphs and charts, and use appropriate technical language."

He made a little head-bow, touching his forehead with two fingers. A few decades ago, that became the universal *sorry I was a jerk* signal. "Well, here." He calls up an eigenvector-color legend.

Subtracting his too-smooth condescension, I must say Gbego did all right in explaining the overall color coding, though "I would guess that it is the intensity of the emotions that went into encoding the memory, not the emotions that are likely with its re-emergence, that is most strongly represented. Also, red for the mild ones and deep blues and purples for the strong ones? What kind of reporting software is that?"

"Physicists designed this." He's still smiling; I must fix that sometime soon. In two years of working with the man, I have found I can always make him stop smiling. "The short-wave, high frequency, high energy part of the spectrum is blues and violets."

Disappointing myself, I smile back. "All right, I see what you mean: that 'mongous big purple blob there in my right hippocampus. Your oscillating neutrinos are telling you I've got some emotionally huge memory there. When I can access it directly, it is totally likely both to be a memory about something really emotionally huge, and also totally likely to upset the absolute living shit out of me. Right?"

"Uh, I suppose – I mean, I intended – um, yes."

I laugh at his sheer awkwardness. "Are you trying to find a gentle, discreet way to ask whether I remember that I chopped up both my parents with a wok cleaver? Yes, I know I did, and I've never stopped knowing. Back when they let me out of prison, they let me watch the sealed records of my testimony, so I know what I said was my reason. As for whatever else might be somewhere in the shriveled plaques that make up most of my hippocampus at the moment, no, I don't recall anything emotionally or with any sense of having been there, about how I slaughtered my parents like a pair of deserving pigs."

He stops smiling. Knew I could do it!

The rest of the meeting is very correct and businesslike. I keep thinking that should make me sad, but really I'm more interested in how smooth Dr. Gbego stays, even though his reserve doesn't feel nearly as phony as his warmth.

* * *

LAYLA BEGINS, "HELLO, Layla. Are you still me?"

"Hello, Layla, yes I am. Look around my office, you're sitting here too, tell me what you see."

She leans back to look slowly all around, taking it in, thinking. "That window is showing video from the moon. I guess it's a display, not a window. But we're not on the moon. The gravity's all wrong. I must have been to the moon more than once, to know that the gravity is wrong right away."

The little rotating 2-D brain map at upper right of the display has been changing across the last few sessions. At first it was an increasingly normal and regular dance of color through the DLPFC, and little trickles like forking lightning breaking out of the former plaques and reaching into the healthy bits of each hippocampus, at first more on the left than on the right, then the right caught up, then both got busy.

Lately it has looked like the old traffic flow maps that used to appear on the dash of Dad's car when he'd drive into the city. He held one of the last human-operation-on-public-streets permits in New Jersey, thanks to his political pull. He said he just liked the fact that his license said 'Human Operator' because it meant they recognized he was still human, "which is rare even in humanists."

Once I started to hate that, I steeled myself not to argue. Nor did I ask why other people's lives should be endangered by his driving mistakes that no machine would ever make, just so he could have his little joke. Giving him no chance for the judicious and rigorous explication he loved, I'd just glare at him and say, "Dumbshit." It worked a lot better.

Anyway, that tangled flow of brightly colored spots in the realtime brain image in front of me, like the New Jersey highway system on Dad's old map, represent the same good situation: lots of things going lots of places smoothly. Layla's brain, my brain, our brain, looks very nearly normal; it would take a neuro as proficient as my smug partner Gbego to spot the difference between those information flows on the display and what happens in a normal brain.

"We *have* been to the moon," she says quietly. "I can feel it copying into my memory; it must have crossed over from the prosnoetics. Oh! And *that's* the connection. The idea you had, because the last three bringbacks before me, before us, before they said you could do it for yourself... you had the idea because hypergerontological cases have mostly been moved to the moon anyway, and this body is acceleration-restricted because of those sclerotic arteries in the brain, so the last two cases – no, the last three, Bridget Soon moved to the moon after the first three treatments –"

I can feel it flooding in, including feelings I'd had at the time but hadn't recalled afterward; it's funny what a difference it makes to have your memories linked to their emotional context again.

Funny, and terrifying.

"What's wrong?" she asks quietly. I look at the brain map; the welter of activity looks like termites coming out of a burning log.

I take a finger and write a word at a time on my palm, without any ink or pigment, and not looking down at it:

not now. not here. soon. not while connected. just think about it later today & you'll know.

Then I babble something senseless about how a strong sense memory of swinging the cleaver backhanded into Mama's face just came flooding back and overwhelmed me. And Layla immediately begins to babble comfort-noises back at me, so I know she understands too. After a minute or so of that, I launch into the story we would both know completely, the one she referred to just now. With just a spot of luck, maybe nobody monitoring will notice how unnecessary our explanations are now, or ask why we are making them.

OF COURSE, FOR more than two decades before the murders, most sensible people, commenting on the news, had the good sense to hate my parents, along with the parents of all the other 'natural children.' Anyone with any empathy could understand how we felt about being condemned before we were born to age and die far before we had to.

Most nubrids and quite a few of the older generation of natural humans could also understand we had been deprived of the nubrids' far greater brain plasticity. During the eighty or hundred years we would live beside them, we would be making up our minds for good and shutting off new experiences. In that same time, the nubrids would put mistakes and sad memories behind them, build on skills and knowledge, and keep growing mentally the way children could while enjoying the kind of mental maturity that only a handful of saints, philosophers, artists, and scientists ever had.

Our parents had elected to kill us early after first crippling us. No one in the global or regional or local government had done anything to stop them; there had been education campaigns and media campaigns and public pressure, but nobody had done what would have fixed it: investigated the personal data, kicked down the doors, and made our mothers get the virus sequence.

Privacy was too important, human rights were too important, the fucking right of fucking jackass parents to raise children no better than themselves was paramount. And because all those rights of all those now-dead people were so well protected, we natches would have to live as permanently immature stuck-in-our ways idiots, and then die, old, sick, ugly, and soon. But thank god society had respected our parents' crazy fears, smug superiority, and deep attachment to that advertising sell-word 'natural.'

My lawyers begged me not to give my speech to the jury, which I had written and rehearsed with such care. They went out of their way to tell the jury, over and over, that I was "young" (thirty-one? For a nubrid, that's young. For us natches, that's a real big chunk of life). They begged them to forgive me for being "impetuous and headstrong" (hoping the jury might ignore the steps I took to isolate the house so Mama and Daddy would not be able to call for help and I could take as long as I wanted about it, or that the police data recovery expert had found many dozens of drafts across many weeks of the script for exactly what I would say and do as I killed them).

I gave my speech anyway. I told them the truth: I had been cheated of what they all took for granted. Mama and Daddy had done it because they had enjoyed the revenue and attention from founding *Natural Children Forever!* and the Coalition to Preserve Natural Humans and god knew how many other fundraising and adulatory fronts, and because they liked to tell themselves how special and wonderful they were. The law could not make me whole; the 'natural human' organizations had lobbied hard to make sure that sentimental idiots had passed laws in every country to prevent us natch-spawn from suing the parents who had done this to us. The law would not arrest them or try them or get revenge for me; instead, it protected them.

So since the law wouldn't do it, I did.

Apparently that made me a monster.

When the jury came back in, after only an hour, I didn't detect a drop of sympathy in their faces. They had decided on life without the possibility of parole.

I suppose I cultivated my taste for science originally because it pissed off Daddy and Mama. Science in general was their number one scary, shiny anti-human monster. Or maybe I just wanted to understand the intellectual triumph of the decoding and application of the nubrid process, since I couldn't partake of it. Ellauri and Jautta's mapping of the deep level semisymmetric interconnections that enabled alloaddressing of genes between the immune, nervous, and regenerative systems would have been a feat as great as relativity, programmable computers, or calculus, even if it hadn't led to any applications for a hundred years. But as it happened, the nubrid process explained why people got set in their ways and how they aged and why aging killed them, how one virus could be chicken pox and shingles and one brain center could handle bits and pieces of math, music, and language, why people got Alzheimer's and arthritis, and countless other things.

I was thirty-two when they sent me to prison, supposedly forever. The Prison Authority spent a fortune on psychiatrists trying to persuade me I should feel bad about who I was and what I'd done, although they still weren't going to let me out even if I rolled over and agreed with them. I had only two alternatives to madness: sparring with the psychiatrists and reading and studying The New Neuro, as it was being dubbed. And after a few years, the psychiatrists gave up.

That left me nothing to do but read and study, but fortunately it turned out that was an inexhaustible consolation. A few years into the process, I began writing papers and critiques. I couldn't accept money, or patent anything, or publish them under my own name because of old laws about not allowing convicts to profit from their crimes; apparently the publicity I would have gotten from being Mama and Daddy's killer was potentially a violation. But I found half a dozen editor-curators who were willing to run my work under aliases, a different alias each time so that there was supposedly less potential for the discovery that a leading New Neuro theoretician was me.

By that time they had the blood test; I knew Alzheimer's for me was when, not if. So I concentrated my work on it, hoping to save myself and the thousands of natches then still alive who were starting to slide away.

That was another little bit of irony. In the process of recoiling from me and what I'd done, society backlashed itself into doing what it should have done more than a generation earlier, and made producing more natches a crime. A last few insistent natural-children types were forcibly sterilized, and that was that; there haven't been any natural children now in fifty years, or any legal ones in almost sixty. And in some weird kind of atonement, they'd developed prosnoetics (if I'd been allowed, I'd have held some basic patents for those) and some not-very-effective anti-aging juices that could stretch a natch's lifespan out to 125 or so.

My first unmistakable symptoms appeared in my late seventies. Bless their hearts, the editor-curators went public with who I was and the contributions I'd made, and the bighearted liberal Chief Administrator for the Atlantic Basin Region commuted my sentence. They hooked me up to prosnoetics, so that as my brain dropped away under me, I could keep going like an AI, and PrinceTech awarded me the Ph.D./MD I'd already earned a hundred times over.

I had just graduated and was looking for something to do when the bringback technology came along. Alzheimer's was a natch-only disease, and we were running out of natches. There were good arrestors that would stop its progress, but nothing to undo it, and some few old natches had had the bad luck to develop advanced Alzheimer's before there were arrestors.

With the bringback process, you could recover memories from the traces the dying cells left in the plaques, and recopy them into new, healthy brain structures, but it was exquisite long-term handwork; you needed someone with the right rapport for the patient and nearly infinite patience, having the same only slightly varied conversations over and over, constantly watching brain imagery to see what each new communication would make happen.

And of all things, I turned out to be good at it. Fifteen years of my life went into bringbacks, about three years per patient, and those were by far my most rewarding years.

My ninety-fifth birthday, and celebration of my sixth successful bringback, was kind of a gloomy occasion, despite the fact that I had real friends and colleagues and they were all there to help me feel loved and appreciated. The bringback business was running out of patients: only a few very old severely memory-damaged natches left, they were going to the moon or already there, and I couldn't go with them. My trips to the moon had been decades ago, and I hadn't felt like living the rest of my life in an underground office building, so I'd never thought seriously about relocating there.

But now my being off prosnoetics and on cardiopulmonary support for acceleration risked the prosnoetics being off too long and not rebooting, especially since their delicate contacts might well break inside my head... natches with scrambled and plaqued-up bio brains could go, natches running on prosnoetics who were even more cyborg than I could go, heart patients could go, but my combination of a heart and a brain that both needed support was the one thing that couldn't go.

I'm afraid I got a little maudlin talking about the end of the only thing I'd done that felt really meaningful. People at my party were awfully nice, but it wasn't much of a party, and they left early.

But the next day, as I was eating a melancholy, solitary breakfast and trying to make myself go to the hospital to do more of the exit interviews and other nonsense involved in losing my job, the communication system said Dr. Selataimh was calling from the moon about Bridget Soon.

I had thought, as we began work, that Bridget would be one of my favorites, and a wonderful seventh bringback, but then her health had started to fail in a way that indicated she needed to move to Serenity City as soon as possible. So after only a few appointments, she'd been bundled up and shipped to the moon, to restart her bringback process there.

Selataimh was a vigorous, raw-boned woman who moved around too much for the camera to stay on her face well. "It's an honor to get to consult with you about a patient," she said. "And perhaps there's nothing we can do. But when Bridget Soon woke up, she demanded you. We tried to explain, but she's absolutely insistent. And she's so clear and coherent we think she must have gone into breakthrough just before you mothballed her process on Earth, or maybe waking up here was the last poke she needed. In any case, she's acting like she's having a breakthrough and she won't talk to anyone else but you, and as you know, if she clams up and won't communicate..." She let that trail off. We both knew that patients could sometimes uncooperate themselves into needing to start the whole bringback process over, losing months or years of life.

"I wish I could get on the next ship going up," I said.

"I'd feel that way myself," Selataimh said. "And I confess I researched it first. It's absolutely too dangerous for you to try traveling, and even if you got here and were lucky enough to still be alive and functional, you'd be stuck here. And I can certainly understand not wanting to spend the rest of your life in a basement on the moon. But... well, she was your patient, she's mine, is there anything we can come up with that might help?"

"Maybe something obvious." I felt hope flaring up.

"'Try the obvious as soon as possible,'" Selataimh said, quoting me to me.

"I've had to apologize to a whole generation of medical students for that textbook chapter," I said. "Apparently profs love to quote it. Nevertheless, here's what I'm wondering: I've done plenty of bringbacks on remote, via communication displays. The reason we can't do one from the moon is supposed to be that one point three second radio lag each way. But has anyone ever tried it? I'm patient, and Alzheimer's patients have lots of time.

"Well, I need to see what's happening in their brain while I talk and while they talk. And as long as the brain image remains synchronized with the conversation, there's no real need for quick reactions. I can't think of any time when I had to make an abrupt change of subject in mid-sentence, or react in real time to changing emotions. So why not just see if I can do it via telecommunication linkup? The worst that can happen is it will turn out that I can't, which is exactly where we are right now."

And that was how we discovered that the radio lag enhanced the bringback process. The delay gave me time to look at the picture of the brain a little longer, think about it a little deeper, have about one more slightly better founded thought before speaking. It forced the bringbacks themselves to try harder and more often to retain an idea in working memory, and to send out more calls to the areas where the PPRNs were working, and to make more connections before I could interrupt them.

The process we thought would be impossible was actually enhanced. Bridget Soon not only became my seventh bringback, she became my fastest and most complete up to that date. Knowing how to use the lag, I completed the two bringbacks after Bridget even more quickly.

And then there were just a handful left of the severe cases, the ones who had all but forgotten who they were, the Alzheimer's-damaged natches of my generation who had not quite all died yet, thanks to the miracle of modern medicine, and had developed dementia before there was arresting technology and prosnoetics. Almost all of them, of us, had been brought back.

DADDY USED TO put on some old thing he called a "mixtape," a bunch of unmodifiable songs in a fixed order, on the house speakers so we all had to listen to the same shit over and over, and there was a song with some line or thing about heartbreaker, dream waker, love faker on it that I guess was a big deal when Grandpa was young. He'd get all hurt if I added "mix-taper," let alone "brain-raper," to it. Like for some reason I was supposed to care what the song "really" sounded like, which meant whatever some old dead bitch had put down first, as if putting it down first (and being dead) meant she fucking owned it. The last generation before mine, when everyone was still a natch, trust me, totally fucking weird, all of them.

But especially Mama and Daddy. They must have known that their thirty-year fundraising-and-sympathy ride was peaking and winding down to an end by the time I was about twelve; the oldest nubrids were in their late twenties, still looked fresh-minted nineteen, and were still learning like bright twelve-year-olds and getting saner and more rational all the time. "Like a bunch of supermodel-athlete Spock-Buddhas," Daddy would say, trying to sound sarcastic.

If he thought that by saying those things, he could get me to say "I don't wanna be a yucky old yucky-face yucky-brain nubrid," the way he'd been able to do when I was eight and he and Mama would love bomb the hell out of me and then put me on camera for promotions, he was even more of a useless self-deluded old fuck than I had imagined. Now that I was in my early teens, I had started to realize just what my parents' world-famous leadership of the battle for the right to have 'natural children' had meant for me and a million or so 'natural children' worldwide.

Daddy, the old fool, was always telling me "be careful what you wish for, you may get it." If only wishing could have gotten it for me! If only it could have undone what he and Mama did to me, and encouraged so many other people to do to the other natches. Him and his "preserving natural humanity"! He believed in that horseshit with such passion that he thought, if I got my way, despite the impossibility of injecting the nubrid modification virus sequence after the twelfth week of pregnancy, I would end up mourning, longing, yea fucking well fainting for the short painful life of increasing mental rigidity I had thrown away, and then I'd really be sorry.

Like fucking Christ.

Thanks to Daddy and all his pontificating about what was truly human (as if a professor of comparative literature would know shit about it), thanks to Mama and her blogging all the time about the Natural Way, thanks to them realizing that as the flow of new followers began to dry up, they would need to have a kid to demonstrate their point: here I was. Demonstrating away. Demonstrating just how wonderful and natural and human it was that I would barely live past a hundred if I were lucky, and that people thirty years older than I would still be young and vigorous in the year my withered old husk, long since having entered "second childishness and mere oblivion, sans teeth, sans eyes, sans taste, sans everything," would fall into its grave, at least four full centuries before the nubrids even *began* to wear out.

I feel my hand on the cleaver, and I look in Mama's eyes, and I tell her, "I will hate you forever. I will hate you forever. I will hate you forever," and just as she starts one of her whiny little pleads, I slash her across both of those watery soggy sentimental eyes with the cleaver, so that me saying that is the last thing she ever sees. It makes me laugh.

I release my painfully hard grip on my chair arms. The prosnoetics kick in. I am breathing like a racehorse on top of a mountain and the cardiopulmonary support gear is working itself into a lather trying to get me into the safe range. I sit gasping, trying to feel calmer, feeling all that rage in those memories, for the first time in at least twenty-five years.

To be overpowered by internal rages again; Oh, wise and gentle-spirited Dr. Gbego, you have no idea how good this feels. You probably can't have any idea. I envy you that, but thank you for bringing my rage back.

The prosnoetics take hold, and finally I look into the screen and say, "Wow, Layla."

"Wow indeed," she says, I say, we giggle. "Do you think they'll make us stop?"

I shake my head. "Not right away. By the time they figure out what we're doing, we'll be done."

"You sound very sure."

"Check my memories for a minute while I catch my breath from yours, my darling self. One thing that didn't change as humans gave way to nubrids – career trumps caution. Remember how we got into this."

MY NINTH BRINGBACK was a nice but rather timid 108-year-old named Annie Souriante who was rapidly reacquiring violin and Caribbean cooking and made me laugh a lot. Usually, before, I'd known by the end of the first year who was scheduled to be my next bringback, but Annie and I were closing in on full restoration, and not only did I not have another patient lined up, there weren't any on the waiting list for the whole hospital.

"We've drained the pool of the severe cases," Dr. Gbego said. "Now the problem is more ATB."

"ATB?" I asked. We were sitting across the table from each other at a reception in the Mnemology Department. I didn't know him well then, and I suppose because of his very controlled, deliberately pleasant personality, I may never know him very well. Nobody might.

"ATB is Ability to Benefit. We have a lot of people who are still mostly functional but lost big chunks of memory into plaques before we had the technology to arrest that. They've lost context or connections or some big chunk of themselves. I would bet the funding could be there to bring them back to full function."

"Is there a reason you're talking to me about it?"

He made a little press-lipped smile. "I try not to be so transparent."

That made me like him a little, so I opened the door of possibility by a tiny crack. "Are you by any chance referring to the fact that I have substantial unrepaired Alzheimer's damage, leading to my very flat and rude affect, and some severe difficulties with recall, and I'm an expert on bringbacks?"

"Well, yes, of course." Gbego shrugged. "It was really foolish of me to think I could keep you from seeing where this was going long enough to sound you out."

God, he's a gorgeous man, smooth deep brown skin and beautiful symmetric features and eyes you could fall into forever. The nubrid process has improved the aesthetics of the visual world almost as much as it has altered the hope in people's lives. And back then I hadn't yet understood that his smoothness was neither a likeable act nor a cultivated strategy; he really was that smooth, with nothing for a person to stick to. But I didn't know that then the way I do now.

His rueful little admission made me feel like he'd actually sought me out emotionally. So I asked, "Well, if we did a bringback on me... who would do it?"

Gbego said, "Conventional answers: Smithson, Abimbola, Cheng." He shrugged, clearly indicating they'd all be fine with him, but that he wanted to be asked about another possibility.

"Unconventional answer?"

He leaned forward, the clear dark eyes zeroing into mine, the smile held closely in check. "You."

"How could – what?"

He held up his hands. "Here's the thought that occurred to me. The radio lag delay has shortened bringbacks from around three years to less than two. We've all been saying that if we knew how that was going to go, we'd have started out doing bringbacks on delays, even if people were in the same building. Because the delay doesn't *have* to be radio lag; it was just that when we had to try to do Ms. Soon's bringback on remote, we had to tolerate the delay, which otherwise we'd never have tried.

"But, here's what intrigues me, Dr. Palemba, the delay could be artificial, we could just build it right there into the communication system, with the bringback and the coach right there in the same hospital. So we set you up with an interrupter; you talk as you, your prosnoetics switch out, your brain goes to its natural state, then your message is delivered. Your natural state brain replies, it comes back through a delay –"

"Do not," I said, choking with more feeling than I had had in many years, "do not use the word 'natural' around me, all right?"

He did that little bow and forehead touch. "How thoughtless and rude of me. I am so sorry. But please think about it. It could enhance your life. Don't let my rudeness and inconsideration cut you off from it."

"Or cut us off from possibly being co-authors of the most brilliant research paper of the next decade?"

He grinned broadly; I didn't know if I'd forgiven him but he thought I had. "Well, yeah. Well, hell yeah."

"I'll think about it. I don't sleep much and I get ideas late at night. What's the latest time I can call you?" I realized I probably had forgiven him, and right then, I knew I was going to do it.

WE PLUNGE IN, Layla and I, and the memory swarms back with all its feelings, all its details, how it felt to say what I said and hear what I heard. All those things that the prosecutors deduced from blood spatters and coagulation time, from fluid ballistics, from running approximating simulations, are now all mine in memory again.

I raged at my parents, cursed them, made sure they knew what this was about. I had planned the blows and cuts, knowing neither of them would have it in them to fight, so that they heard everything I had to say. Knowing how devoted Daddy was to Mama, when he came rushing in at her scream, I shattered him with a dozen planned blows, so that he was bleeding and helpless while I worked on her and explained that all that shit she called love was nothing of the sort, that I knew it was all for her, not for me, that she would not have made me a natch (the word they prohibited in the house) if she had loved me, that it was malice and not mistake. And I cut, and cut, till she died sobbing.

Daddy took longer, and I reminded him that what had happened to Mama was his fault, the whole time.

They knew the cuts and blows of it all from the crime scene analysis, but I never told anyone what I had said.

Or what I had felt: sheer, glowing hot joy.

I hadn't sought a bringback of my own, though there were skilled practitioners who would gladly have done it, not because I didn't want to interrupt my scientific work, as I'd told that slick mannequin Gbego, but because I'd feared that I might find remorse or sorrow or weeping over their bodies.

I don't find a bit of that. The memory is pure white rage, and that delights me. Especially it makes me happy in this way: Daddy and Mama were so convinced that natural humans needed to be preserved. They talked about remembering the human heritage, and you could hear, inside that, that they wanted to live forever in the memories of natural humans.

Well, here they are. Fewer than a hundred natural humans left, and the memory of their destruction is a burning hot glowing pleasure that will warm me the rest of my days. A nubrid, now, a nubrid has such total plasticity, I might have worn the memory down into smooth forgiveness and acceptance. But a human? We're not that plastic. We can hold a grudge forever.

All you ever wanted was for me to be human, Daddy, that's what you said. I laugh and laugh. It's no longer we, the bio Layla and the prosnoetic Layla are merged, I can feel it.

"Dr. Palemba?"

I sit up, startled. It's Gbego. He looks worried – more than that, ill. I try to play casual, but I think even a nubrid with Gbego's carefully honed people skills would not be able to be smooth or slick about this. I ask, "Is something the matter?"

"What we saw on the monitors..."

I shrug. "You saw me get those memories back."

"We also saw..." His face works through those little squish-the-lips motions, over and over. Finally he says, "You enjoyed that."

"I did."

"In fact we've never seen such intense pleasure and focus in any brain. That woman who testified and shocked the world, seventy years ago... you're still her. Or you're her again."

I ignore what he's saying, because it's simply irrelevant. I've got myself back; whatever I ever wanted from oh-so-beautiful and far-too-smooth Dr. Gbego no longer matters. So I just say, "You'd better do some prep, get recordings soon, and think about what lab tests you want to run. I think that you're going to find you can declare me officially brought back. You'll really want data from the next couple of days."

He's flailing around, still trying to absorb the meaning of what his instruments told him about my huge surges of pleasure and rage. Finally all he manages to squeak out is, "How will we ever publish this?"

THAT'S SUCH A stupid question. There are things he won't say, things I won't say, but plenty of things to publish. We'll both advance our careers.

And of course there's a real advance in knowledge all around. Dr. Gbego knows some technical things now that no one else had learned before, and me? I know what I really want to know.

At first Gbego will be bothered by the things he didn't know he'd find out, the things he'd rather not have known. But soon he'll see how to make this whole experience work for him. Perhaps later this week, at one of the unending parties where nubrids spend so much time, he will find his way to talking, or, really, bragging. People will find it so intriguing that he was working with that famous Dr. Layla Palemba that you saw in media. Layla, the natch who knows bringbacks better than anyone else, natch or nubrid, actually working her own bringback, isn't that astonishing?

He will realize that the part of me that makes him sick and horrified need not intrude on what everyone wants to hear him say:

Yes, knowing Dr. Layla Palemba has been very inspiring.

Layla is a measure of the marvelous.

Yes, it's been such an honor and a privilege to work with her. Not on her, oh, no, she's tough and feisty and smart, I pity anyone so stupid he tries to work on her. With her, with her, with her.

What do I mean, a measure of the marvelous?

A measure of the marvel of plasticity that is the human brain, even the old natural human brain that, thank god, none of our parents would ever have stuck us with. A measure of the bigger marvel of neurology itself, that Ellauri and Jautta were able to understand the nubrid process a century ago. A measure of the even bigger marvel that in the last thirty years we've been able to do so much more to keep the surviving natches alive. A measure of the marvel of prosnoetics, to which she contributed, which saved them from being drooling, senseless lumps of flesh.

A measure of the biggest marvel of all, the continuing advance of science.

I imagine Gbego, my utterly smooth young-at-eighty nubrid neuro standing just a bit taller, shoulders stooped slightly, turning toward a perfectly beautiful young woman for her approval.

She beams at him, and then adds her little correction:

The science part is big, to be sure. But Dr. Layla Palemba is most of all a measure of the real biggest marvel of all: our modern global society that has so institutionalized generosity to the less fortunate and compassion for everyone that we are willing to spend so much expertise, time, research, and sheer treasure to rescue the very few surviving natches. She stands as a measure of the marvel that is us and our forgiveness and generosity.

Dr. Gbego will probably not even choke on a canapé when she says that. Probably he'll take her aside and talk with her, tell her how deep her insights and compassion are. Perhaps they will have many meetings and deep conversations and some elegant sex in the days that follow.

And for the rest of the crowd, having satisfied themselves with the smooth little bit of interesting knowledge with which Dr. Gbego graced them, the rest of the evening will pass in a swirl of fine wine and perfect bodies in splendid clothing: smug smooth fake hateful nubrid bastards who have taken over the world, passing the time of which they have so much, letting time and life itself roll off them like neutrinos off matter, like bad memories off a plastic brain, like blood off a cleaver.

375

An Owomoyela

OUTSIDER

An Owomoyela

OUTSIDER

MOTA FELT Io's arrival.

So did everyone else on the *Segye-Agbaye*; the networks picked her up and slotted her into their awareness like a new limb. She was reading in full dominant mode, a mental posture of command that brought everyone up short, but it resolved and her attention passed on to Mota and the other technicians quietly found something else to be interested in. Mota closed her eyes, and pulled herself away from the access panel she was working at.

[Apologies. I need you,] flashed into her communication line. Her mental sense of Io went tinged with regret, but not much of it. And it was overlaid with the quiet psych cue that got Mota by the scruff of her neck, made all her emotions cycle down, and made her limbs warm and heavy even in microgravity.

[Coming,] she signaled back. Not that it was necessary. Not that there was any question of whether or not she would.

She pushed off from the wall and headed down the corridor, the lights flowing over her skin as she passed. There was a familiar pattern to the output of each one; generations of modifications and repairs and replacements leaving each with its own strength and hue. And there was an atavistic comfort to moving through these halls, as though all the pieces of Mota's being that troubled her on the colony below fit seamlessly into the ship.

Io's presence was disruptive. When she wasn't *right there*, Mota might be able to resent her for that.

Io was waiting at the shuttle bay, standing tall and expansive, her feet on the floor as though she needed them there. Mota caught herself on one of the room's handholds and held herself there, her own body curled.

This close, the network bumped Io's presence up in its priority for Mota; she could feel Io's emotions like a second mental skin. Confidence and focus, curiosity and wariness directed at something off the ship, and that quiet, subtle tinge of chagrin. She could feel as well as Mota could that Mota would rather not be there.

She could also dismiss that out of hand. Work to be done.

"Apologies," she said again, though her emotions conveyed just how much of a formality it was. "You're needed. A foreign ship entered our system."

Surprise shocked through Mota's mind. [*A ship?*] she signaled back, letting her confusion flavor it. [*Clarify?*]

"Come with me," Io said, and turned to the shuttle.

Mota followed. She tried not to mind the tendril of annoyance wending from Io at getting a signal instead of a verbal reply.

THE *SEGYE-AGBAYE* HELD an orbit over the first point of landfall on Se, but after all this time the location was more symbolic than practical. Most of the major spaceports were on the other side of the planet, more closely hugging the equator, which meant that Io took their shuttle on a long angle down into the atmosphere toward a port with longer-range transports.

Se from above was nothing like the composite metal and regulated light of the *Segye-Agbaye*. It was a study in terraformed green and wispy white atmosphere, lit by a white sun, with the silvery lines of the colony spreading across its surface like a neural web. The quiet background murmur of the colony network became a warm ambient cloud, too many individuals to identify. Mota could swim in the sea of secondhand emotion, inclination, preoccupation until her own sense of self went fuzzy at the edges.

But being with Io changed that. She brought them down into one of the bays and stepped out and the colony parted for her; the port technicians quietly delegated someone to see to her, and the ambient noise quieted just as Mota herself had.

They boarded a fast, mid-range shuttle: nothing that would carry them outside of the dense inner system, but one that would convey them quickly. "Omo," Io said. One of the farther-flung unmanned stations, then.

Io linked into the ship's transmitters; she wanted Mota to do the same, so Mota did the same. It was easier, sometimes, to lean back and let her body connect with the network on an unconscious level; let herself be moved like a limb for the dominant force in the room.

The transmission kicked in, and brought with it another's telepresence. *Yan. Pilot. Working with the survey teams and contingency fleets.*

There was a warmth to Io's transmission out. *[I'm bringing Mota. She's the expert on ancient Earth.]*

Which had always been a useless, hobbyist's expertise. Mota sat up.

The cradle of humanity was far enough away to be irrelevant. Any knowledge about it was historical or speculative: even the evidence of its planets, writ into the wobble of its star, was information that had been issued in light long before anyone on Se was born.

[You found a ship?] she signaled, and the transmission went out to Yan.

"The ship entered the outer system and gave off a signal," Io said, and the response from Yan came back.

[It is from Earth,] Yan sent. His words were tinged with certainty and wonder. *[Will you be able to operate it?]*

Mota sent a request back to the databanks on Se. Better to queue up any resources she might need now, while the transmission delay was still small.

[I want to see it,] Mota sent back. Then, *[Maybe. I'll do my best.]*

Yan sent as much as he could back over the transmitters as they approached; Mota drank it in, moving through his recordings and the archived information the first colonists had brought with them. Earth must have had its own evolution after the *Segye-Agbaye* left; Mota could look back down an unbroken chain of history and see the Earth they had left behind, but the Earth of all those intervening years was shadowed to her. This ship, then, was a glimmer of light.

They docked on Omo and Io took the lead, guiding them through to the bay where Yan worked. Mota followed.

The room Yan occupied was large enough for one person to move comfortably in; not three. It was dominated by a central column, with a curved screen, which Yan was studying. He looked up and smiled to them as they entered.

Mota signaled greeting, and felt a flicker of concern pass through Yan. "She always prefers signal to vocal," Io said.

Not always, Mota thought, and she could feel Yan catch that thought, and respond with a gentle amusement. Io seemed to notice *that*, and the focus of her attention fell on Mota. Then it passed back to Yan.

Mota was silent for a moment, watching the interplay of their emotions. The landscape between them changed like the clouds playing across Se's atmosphere.

Then Yan turned to Mota. "There's text. It displayed as soon as I opened the hatch."

He waved his hand toward the screen, and Mota squeezed past him to look at it. She touched the screen – a brush at the corner, away from any of the symbols – and it changed. She touched it again; it changed again.

[Translation corpus?] Mota signaled. The interface was strange – tactile. *[An old Earth tradition. A critical number of words in their natural contexts. If it's a corpus, they didn't expect whoever found this ship to speak their language.]*

"A contact ship, then," Io said. "Specifically."

Mota hesitated, and felt Io sigh.

"Please," Io said, with a gesture to the corpus, and Mota felt like she was waking up. Like the faculties of her mind which had gone quiescent at Io's presence were, given her permission, rearing up again.

The network data on Earth sprang up in her mind, almost tangible under her fingers. *Not that language – not that one. Closer.* The *Segye-Agbaye* had left Earth early into its projected interstellar phase; this ship was different in design from the *Segye-Agbaye*, and its language didn't match exactly to any of the ones on record. How many generations separated them from their common ancestry? How long did it take for a language to evolve like this?

One of the programs flagged a pattern: some 68% similarity in the ship's language to another language, with the differences seeming to follow common linguistic rules. Mota selected the match, ran the program, and the corpus sprang into semi-legibility.

"I have it," she said, and part of her was surprised at that. *Comfortable enough to be vocal, then.* But now she could see the patterns of the foreign ship's operation, and she could make the ship respond. She highlighted the updated translation program on the network for Yan and Io.

A linguist could refine it, but the screen was at least interpretable now: Mota could look at a word and the network would take it from her visual cortex, and it would interpret it and deliver that information to the language centers of her brain.

"This column is a container," Mota said. She moved through the prompts, and the screen went transparent – enough to see a woman's face, her mouth and nose covered by some apparatus, her eyes closed.

Io moved forward, and Yan melted back to give her room. "A person?"

"Stasis," Mota said, and her hands fluttered. *[Generation ships like the* Segye-Agbaye *were considered to be a second-best solution,]* she signaled. *[Governments wanted to preserve individuals from Earth who would sleep through the interstellar voyage and wake up at their destination. So the astronauts who left Earth would also be the ones who arrived at the new colony.]*

"If the ship is from Earth, then *she* is from Earth."

She felt their surprise. Awe from Yan, and a kind of hunger from Io. The hunger made her want to stand aside, become small and unnoticed again.

"Will she wake up?" Io asked. Mota took a breath. The air out here was recycled, like the air on the *Segye-Agbaye*; it was comforting.

"There are directions," she said, and found the playback controls. The screen changed – voice and printed language, but also animation. Instructions for anyone who found it. "I think she was expecting the system to be habited when she arrived."

"So it was," Io said. She turned to Mota. "Work with the medical staff. Help them understand anything they need to. This is our first contact with another population from Earth, Mota – time to put your history to use."

Io turned and pushed away, back out of the ship and into Omo station, leaving Mota with her hand still on the screen of the stasis chamber. Yan let out a soft breath, and Mota caught the undercurrent of it: wry humor, the sort born of recognizing someone's predispositions. Then it slid, transmuted into unease. He turned to her.

"You know about Earth history?" he asked.

Mota nodded.

"We restrict the number of single-person craft in our fleet," Yan said. "It's a poor ratio of resource use to utility. Did the Earth system have the resources to send single people on interstellar journeys?"

Mota turned back to the ship. Clearly they *had*, but it was a good question anyway. She thought back to everything she knew of Earth history, of the *Segye-Agbaye*'s reason for being, of its reason for design. A hundred thousand colonists had left from Earth; those had been her ancestors.

"No," she said. "This would be a waste."

MOTA ONLY ADVISED the medical staff until they understood as much of the technology as she did, and then she escaped back to the *Segye-Agbaye*. She was happy to go. Ship systems were more intelligible to her than human systems, anyway.

But she was the expert on old Earth, if for no other reason than her curiosity had led her to study it. And so sooner or later the medical staff called her back – the woman was cogent, and wanted to see the ones who had retrieved her.

So Mota went down to Se again, and edged into the medical hall. The woman was already speaking with Io.

Seeing the woman sitting on one of the benches was strange, and unnerving. She was larger than the rest of them, her skin and hair paler, the planes of her face foreign. Mota paused in the doorway, trying to feel her presence – but of course the woman had no nanotransmitters entangled with her neural network, and no capacity to access the network that linked the rest of them. She was the first person Mota had seen who she couldn't feel.

Io turned to face Mota as she hesitated in the door, and motioned her in. Some of the unease faded in the face of Io's relative comfort, and Mota entered.

"Mota," Io introduced. "This woman gives her name as Eva. She's thanks you for your part."

Mota looked at the woman. She opened her mouth, then frowned, and queried the network for a translation. Let the network inform her on how to shape her tongue into the shapes of words: "There's no need to thank me."

Some language technician must have sat down with the woman, captured the pronunciation of her words, used that to inform the translation program. When Eva spoke, the network caught her words and fed Mota the sense of them.

"I came seeking asylum," Eva said. Her face had adopted the kind of focus that said this had been a prepared statement. "On Earth, my people were being rounded up and destroyed. I was sent on the *Sojourn* with our historical record, so we wouldn't be lost to history forever." She watched Mota. "You are a historian?"

Mota fumbled for the words. "A technician. Interested in history. An archivist will help you." She looked to Io.

"Yan retrieved her vessel," Io said. "I've taken responsibility for her housing and orientation. But Eva wanted to thank you in person."

Mota moved her hands. "There is no need," she said again. She'd done what anyone with her skillset would have done – the socially healthy thing to do.

Io had a feeling of indulgence to her. Mota studied it, and as Io's attention turned back to Eva, Mota realized what she was picking up: a kind of proprietary attraction toward the strange Earth woman. Mota looked between them. Eva couldn't feel it, she realized. Io's formidable regard was lost on her.

[You are –] Mota started to signal, and then arrested that first inclination. Eva wouldn't see it, for the same reason she didn't feel Io's desire. But it was like taking two steps backward off a cliff; the infrastructure of the network was as central to Mota as her own lungs were. She had to scramble for words, and then convince herself that words would be heard by the woman.

"To Io, you are interesting and physically pleasing," Mota said, hoping the translation would go through, that the corpus had the right words. Eva pulled back as though something had struck her. Mota frowned at her expression, and the sensation of falling in gravity redoubled itself. "You should be able to feel this, and – and react appropriately."

But, of course, she shouldn't. Because she didn't have the technology in her mind, and her neural network had long ago solidified past the point of introducing them. It turned Mota's stomach. Like Eva was only half a person.

Eva looked at Io, who had tilted her head at her. Mota turned her own attention to Io's emotions: concern, and consideration, and recognition. She must not have thought to explain herself to Eva. And why would she? Anyone would be able to read her emotions, and capturing emotional states in words was using the wrong tool for the job. Who would think to do that?

But Eva remained blank and unreadable, and soon the muscles in her face went neutral as well. "And what," she said, "is the correct reaction?"

There was no sarcasm radiating from her. Nor irony, nor sincerity. Nothing. Mota closed her eyes, and searched for the words.

"You," she said – carefully, carefully, fumbling through statements the translator had likely found translations for – "should be... it's to your advantage? Io is high in the hierarchy. It's... a privilege."

"I was asking her," Eva said, and Mota shrank back. "Io," Eva went on, "maybe we should speak –" then a word the network didn't translate. Io tilted her head. Eva frowned, and said, "Only the two of us?"

A strange request. But Io shrugged. "We can," she said. "You'll have to remind me that you can't feel what I say."

MOTA WAS CONTENT to let Io orient Eva to life on Se. She preferred the *Segye-Agbaye* and the long rhythms of maintenance there, distancing herself from the novelty and celebrity that gathered around Eva on the planet below. Anything she needed, she could pull from the network; it was enough for her.

Until Yan sent her a transmission, asking for her presence on Omo station and the woman's ship, the *Sojourn*. She came, slipping into the narrow confines of the stasis chamber, where Yan was working.

[Earth historian,] Yan signaled. He was preoccupied; read as though he needed another brain and perspective to process something. Tickling at the edge of her mind, Mota could feel Io on an approach, as well. "Eva says that on Earth, most of the powerful factions are people like us," Yan said. "Altered humans. They make laws that try to stamp Eva's people out."

Mota signaled, *[Altered.]* The word turned over in her mind. "From what?"

Yan's annoyance twined around the question, but it wasn't directed at her. "Natural humans. She says her people have nothing but variation in breeding."

[But all our variation was at one point selected by breeding.] On the *Segye-Agbaye*, with their limited resources, no one had been able to make a genetic loom; they could only splice the DNA they had. It had been another generation or two after landfall on Se before the looms had been built, and those only had been used to design and redesign the world's plant and

animal life. Se's environment didn't have as many restrictions as the *Segye-Agbaye*. The adaptations which served life on the ship didn't hinder them on the ground.

Yan said "Yes," in a tone of mock-dissent, but his emotional state was shaded with vindication. "But to Eva, our treating the genome in the zygote is artificial. Not to mention," he gestured at his head, "the network."

Mota balked. *[The network is an assistive machine! Her ship uses assistive machines!]* "She was in stasis!"

"It's different. To Eva, it's different." Yan snorted. "I looked up the history we brought on the *Segye-Agbaye*. You should look up factionalization. Outgrouping." He turned to Mota. "I think we became better humans on the *Segye-Agbaye*. We didn't have room to take all our behaviors with us."

Then his attention shifted off Mota, and his emotions turned anticipatory. Mota turned to look behind her, eyes hitting the screens first, then moving into the hall.

Motion, there – Io had apparently docked, though her presence felt as though she was still a few minutes out. Strange. But Eva was with her, her hand on Io's elbow, as though Io was leading her by touch. Eva was ungainly in the microgravity.

Mota felt the instinctive submission rising up in the back of her mind, but it was dampened. Io's attention wasn't on her, and she still felt abnormally far away.

"You've been working on my ship?" Eva asked.

"Mota studies historical objects," Io said. "Yan studies ships."

Eva looked from one of them to the other, then to Io. Io's curiosity was reflected in her face; all her attention was on Eva. Mota looked to Eva's face: this woman from Earth couldn't feel it.

How insulated, how isolated, must her life have been?

"Please do not," Eva said, turning to Mota. "The ship is... part of my historical record. I do not want it tampered with, or... made to fit your colony."

Sympathy and recognition from Io, and *now* Mota felt herself go distant and calm. This and that hormone releasing itself into her, patting down any protest. Io was determined that the decision should go Eva's way on this, and Mota felt no compulsion to make a stand in defiance. So it was all right, then, even though the *all right* slid over her own predilections to smother her. She signaled assent.

Yan frowned, but Mota could feel the acquiescence in him, as well. Disappointment, too. He held on a bit longer – his hierarchical distance wasn't as far as Mota's – but then he exhaled, his muscles relaxed, and he signaled assent as well. "It's a lovely ship," he said. Wistful. "I haven't seen any like it."

Eva's face softened into a smile, but it looked like a transmission delay. Mota shook her head, trying to clear it. The distance from Io and the lag from Eva made it feel as though they were talking across gulfs, either of fractions of kilometers or whole light-seconds. It made her dizzy.

[Come on,] Yan signaled. Mota followed him back to the shuttle, and he pointed it back toward Se.

After a while, she signaled *[Frustrated.]*

Yan echoed the sentiment, but said "Maybe she wants to cling to the familiar."

Mota turned her head to the window, watching the stars. *[I wish we could feel her.]*

Assent from Yan. Mota sighed, and closed her eyes, and let her mind drift.

Then there was a hand on her shoulder.

Mota jumped, body and mind jarred out of her doze. She spun, and there was Yan, his expression concerned. And, yes, she could feel his concern, but barely – as though he were kilometers away, not there, next to her. She shook her head, blinked, tried to make the image resolve into what she felt over the network.

"Something is wrong," Yan said. *[You went dark. I thought you were dead.]* His signal was far fainter than it should have been.

[You're distant,] she signaled back.

Yan squinted at her. "Sometimes, when we go in for close chromosphere scans, we'll get interference like this," he said. "I can't feel my team. It's like we've all become ghosts."

Like Eva, Mota thought. But the idea that Eva was a ghost was ridiculous. Ghosts didn't come in stasis, didn't have to have their ancient Earth ships interpreted and their blood cleaned of chemicals. Ghosts did not exist.

"There's always some variation in the strength of the network signal," Yan said. "Solar weather affects it, even as far out as Se. But mostly it's not noticeable. And we don't have that weather today."

Mota moved closer, not that it helped. *[Is it here?]* she signaled, then winced – it felt as though she was talking into vacuum. She marshaled her thoughts into words so that she could speak them – clumsier, yes, but at least she could hear her own voice and Yan's, and the sound didn't belie the distance. "Is it just this transport? Localized weather?"

Yan shifted, and his distant unease echoed across to her. "We'll find out once we're back on Se," he said.

* * *

SE WAS IN a state of unrest.

Yan brought them down onto the port, and into a muted background hum of unease. Even on the planet, even with the density of population there, it felt as though isolation was blooming up on the network around them.

A query against the network produced no answers, and Yan shook his head. "I can check the solar monitor stations," he said.

Mota raised her face to the sky.

"Technician," Yan said. A reminder, perhaps. Hard to tell. "I'm sure there's something you can do. Can you go to one of the network nodes?"

[*Perhaps,*] Mota signaled. "Safe flight," she said, and Yan turned back to the port.

Mota went to the archives.

She wasn't trained in any of the network maintenance, and while she could just show up and ask to help, something else had her curiosity. She accessed the central archives and queried for the historical record Eva had brought.

She didn't know what she was looking for. Eva's history was like much of the Earth history Mota was familiar with: one group choosing to annihilate another over conflicts that looked absurd from a distance. Their conflict had been genetic: Eva's people refusing any engineered alteration, even disease immunity. And their opponents had been winnowing away human genetic diversity. Both stances were ridiculous, to Mota's mind – and the records were dead, without the encoded emotional resonance which would have helped her understand.

Eva was here, now, a single survivor who would have to adapt. And Se and its system were vast; more variation existed now than had left on the *Segye-Agbaye*. Her conflict was an Earth conflict, and by now it was generations behind her.

Perhaps Io would show her that.

Eva appeared as Mota was leaving. Mota walked out of central data storage and there she was, standing tall as Io or any of the others at the top of the hierarchy did. Never mind that she was foreign, an alien, outside of the hierarchy entirely; Mota felt the hairs on the back of her neck prick up, and if Eva had been part of the colony and as prestigious as she imagined herself to be, she would have made Mota settle with a look and an intention.

She was speaking with one of the archivists. The network was still translating, but the translations came through soft: the network heard Eva's words through Mota's ears, and it queried for the definitions, but the whispered meaning floated to her over a gulf. If she hadn't been on Se, nestled in among the smart buildings and the network transmitters, Mota wondered if she'd be able to understand Eva's words at all.

She turned and headed away, feeling disconnected and bow-legged in Se's gravity. The *Segye-Agbaye* would feel empty, if the interference persisted there – even Se felt empty, like the ocean of presence had ebbed back down some all-surrounding shore – but the ship was still more familiar. Mota wanted to cling to that familiarity.

There was sound behind her, and she ignored it. Moved down the hallway toward the port until Eva's voice called, "Wait!"

Mota wanted to push along the wall, propel herself into a different place entirely. She was faster in microgravity.

Instead, she turned, and saw Eva coming toward her. There was no command emanating from her; Mota could have walked away.

Instead, she waited, head tilted, watching the Earth woman approach.

"Mota, right?" Eva asked.

Mota nodded.

"You're a technician?"

Mota nodded again, trying to work out how to communicate that Eva should hurry up, get to the point, let her go. Io, at least, would read her discomfort and disengage. Eva seemed ignorant of it. And here, with the strange fog clouding the network, no one else could feel the dynamic and intervene.

That frightened Mota.

"Io's explained your hierarchy," Eva said. "I couldn't believe it. You're a *slave?*"

Mota frowned. The word *slave* hadn't been translated, and after all this time with Io, she felt like Eva should have been able to ask for whatever words she needed. She signaled *[What?]*, then caught herself, and asked aloud.

"You don't have free will," Eva said. "You were born into a low caste –"

And that – that was factually *wrong*, and Mota cut her hand through the space between them. "I have free will," she said. She knew *that* concept.

Eva looked surprised to be interrupted, but then she banished the expression from her face. "But you were designed never to argue with your superiors," she said. "You were forced –"

"No," Mota said. Again, there was that brief surprise, and it vanished. "I was not *designed*. And I argue if it's – I only don't argue when it's against the health of the colony."

Eva was shaking her head. "Io told me about the hierarchy," she said again. "It gives some of you power over the rest of you.

Power they haven't earned – power they can abuse. They can override your desires, can't they?"

Unease moved through Mota's stomach, like a technician in microgravity. She was overriding her own desires, standing here, talking to Eva. It felt more wrong than the easy passivity that crept over her when Io approached her. "Some people lead and others defer," she said. "But the colony keeps everyone in check. If you don't like a person, everyone knows. They stay away from you."

Like Io stays away from me, should have been the subtext. *Like you should stay away from me.* It would have been obvious to anyone – like the fact that she had free will should have been obvious, or the fact that her desires still existed even when she deferred.

"In my culture, we're all equal," Eva said.

Mota tilted her head. "I... read about Earth," she said. "And our history. Our scholars – when we were on the *Segye-Agbaye* – historically there was never a culture without hierarchy? It's innate. Human social trait."

Eva looked angry for a moment. Offended? Then it was gone. "Well," she said, "people earn their positions, where we come from. We're not born into them. That – it's unnatural. Not right."

But it kept us alive, Mota wanted to say. She wanted to be aboard the *Segye-Agbaye* more than ever, in the halls that generations of her ancestors had adapted to, in the confines of its hull. Eva had her cornered down here, and didn't know or didn't care that she wanted to escape. For years, centuries, there had been no escape from the ship as it sailed through the interstellar medium, but there had been harmony. Or a close-enough approximation.

"No," Mota said. "For us, *you* are not right. Eva, this is uncomfortable. I'm uncomfortable."

And there, any civilized person should have disengaged. But Eva stepped forward.

"If you could be liberated," she said, "wouldn't you want to be?"

Mota turned and ran away. The motion was ungainly; she spent more of her life in orbital gravity than terrestrial. But Eva didn't follow.

The shuttle ride up to the *Segye-Agbaye* was silent on the network, and Mota didn't plug herself into one of the transmitters to reach out. And the ship itself was quiet but filled with murmurs – *like we've all become ghosts*, Yan had said.

This was the kind of silence Eva lived in, all her life, Mota thought. *Worse than this.* Absolute silence, without the promise of connection.

Mota couldn't imagine it without also imagining going mad.

She made her way to one of the old science modules, and settled in among its resources. A transmitter linked up the databanks with the central ones on Se, and she called up the records from Yan's expedition out to fetch the *Sojourn*. Then she dug deeper: the first moment the *Sojourn*'s signals had been detected, the first scans that caught the ship and resolved it.

She requested Yan's experience from the central banks, and they fed it up to her. Strange feelings, approaching the ship: washes of color and sound across the network as Yan and his fleetmates drew near. Many different signals coming from the ship, and a few of them tickled the network. When Yan sent his own signal to the ship, everything but that channel had died down.

Yan hadn't noticed a fade in the network when he'd retrieved the *Sojourn* or brought it to Omo. But he had before – those incoherent washes, an accident of design, transmitting on the same frequencies as the nanotransmitters interfaced with their neurons.

It made Mota wonder.

THE *SOJOURN* HADN'T been moved from its post at Omo.

Mota took a databank and loaded it with the translation program, and requested a shuttle to Omo, stewing in her own thoughts the entire way. The spaceport had felt emptier than it was; everything felt empty. At least here, in the far reaches of the inhabited system, the emptiness seemed right.

She docked at Omo and went into the *Sojourn* to take a look around.

Parts of the ship were missing. Some of it, probably was the data storage – taken down to Se so that its encryption could be translated, and Eva's precious historical record preserved.

But was all of it?

Mota ran her hands over the walls, the consoles. She could feel the databank on the shuttle, feel the technicians' records and the translation program at the edge of her mind.

The *Sojourn* seemed to be cast from smooth composite, its hull one large component – not like the *Segye-Agbaye*, where every piece could have been detatched, recycled, cast into any one of innumerable other forms. The *Segye-Agbaye* had been designed to be broken apart and remade as it carried a living population from one star to the next.

The *Sojourn* had been designed to perform one task competently once.

And that told Mota something, as she moved from the stasis chamber to what seemed to be a technician access hatch.

Everything on the ship had a congruity. Everything that wasn't part of the stasis system or the engines looked like an afterthought: mismatched.

She looked at the equipment. There, a processing unit. There, a detachable screen.

Mota took a deep breath, calling up all the translation they'd established.

The *Sojourn* had been able to read the presence of their colony and send out a signal, and Eva had been horrified at the thought of the network laid into human brains. When this craft had been built, someone would have come into this little human-habitable room and calibrated the equipment, would have tested it. And they would have done so with their hands and their eyes, not information communicated directly to their neurons.

Mota took the screen, and began to interface.

Reading the translations of the symbols that greeted her, Mota wondered when the screen had last been touched. How many generations ago, those many light years away? Had the *Segye-Agbaye* still been on its long voyage, or was this ship younger than that? And had the last person to work their way through these menus been a technician, like Mota, or had their society not been organized upon those lines?

Where we come from, Eva had said, *people earn their positions.*

Where we come from. Eva experienced a kind of aloneness that Mota could hardly imagine – lightyears from home, alone in her thoughts and sensations. Why use *we*?

And, *Yes, there* – the ship had transmitters. Not ones that could tap into the larger network, or the smaller one integrated with a human mind. But it had sent out the signals that called

Yan to it, and it had sent out... others. And was still sending them out. Mota frowned, and isolated them.

Two signals. One broadly dispersed, one hyper-focused and sent back the way the *Sojourn* had come. Mota chose that one to follow, digging into the ship's scanners until something resolved on them.

Seven somethings.

Seven ships.

None as large as the *Segye-Agbaye*, but approaching its volume combined. And if they were stasis ships, without the need for living areas and corridors and recreational facilities and maintenance bays...

Mota sucked in breath, and the hatch opened behind her.

She spun, eyes wide, and there was Eva. "I thought," Eva said, "I had asked you to stay away from my ship."

Mota moved, revealing the screen behind her. "How *many*?" she asked. Hoped that the words would carry all the meaning she wanted them to.

Eva's eyes flicked to the screen, but if she was surprised to see her fleet on it, Mota couldn't read it in her face. "On Earth," Eva said, "our ancestors were *allies* – good friends, in agreement. I was sent to negotiate cohabitation if my people had to evacuate the Earth system. I didn›t expect to arrive here and find that you were no longer human.

"We are human," Mota said.

Eva looked disgusted. This time, the expression stayed. "You are *eugenicists*," she said. "Your genetics are polluted. It was people like you who are destroying my people."

"We evolved," Mota said, "to limit conflict –"

"By engineering subservience?" Eva asked. "My fleet is on its way. We can stop this practice of hooking you up to this mind-control network – we can help restore your genetic pool. Your children can live lives that are truly *free*."

"You're interfering with the network," Mota said. The realization was a nausea.

"*Yes*," Eva said. "Can't you feel it? You don't have to submit to everyone you meet –"

You are alone, Eva seemed to say, seemed to not realize she was saying, *in the dark, and you should be happy for it*.

Mota launched herself at Eva.

Eva startled, and planted her feet as though she were in planetary gravity. Mota twisted, changing her angle enough to catch Eva's arm and spin her, then pushed off from her and flew toward the hatch leading back to the Omo station proper. Eva growled, disoriented, and Mota swung the hatch closed behind her.

Omo station wasn't large. Mota reached a transmitter just as Eva opened the hatch behind her, and fumbled into a connection. If she could just send this information back to Se, slicing through the interference before Eva was upon her –

And then Eva *was* upon her, wrenching her away from the transmitter, throwing her into the darkness of network interference again. Mota curled herself and pushed away but this time Eva grabbed her, locking their momentum. Eva's hand closed around her throat.

And then the hatch opened.

This time, they both startled. Eva turned, and the break in her attention was enough for Mota to twist free. And there in the hatch was Io, tall and present, taking in the scene.

Mota flew to Io and gripped her arm, letting the proximity carry her whole emotional state – anger and fear and incredulity.

Io turned to regard Eva.

"I don't think I should chastise Mota for disobeying your request," she said. "I came here because I thought I might have to. But I believe one of you should explain."

"I will explain," Mota said. And Io smiled thinly – this close, the network connected them, and the truth burned in Mota for anyone but Eva to see.

YAN ARRIVED ON the *Segye-Agbaye*, his presence clear among the ship's usual population. Mota paused in her work, extracting herself from the old databanks and recycling systems.

[Here,] she signaled, and felt Yan approach.

He waited until he was in the same room as her to say anything. "We were able to re-activate the stasis," he told her. "Eva is stable."

Mota nodded. She didn't have to say – was relieved not to say – how she felt about that, or that her feelings were confused.

"Io is still angry," Yan remarked.

Mota let out a laugh. "So am I."

"And most of us, I think," Yan said. He didn't feel angry – just a long, slow resentment curling under his words. "If it had been a vote, we might have killed her."

Mota closed her eyes. There was a vote, now, and the network visualized the voting for her. The decisions traveled in waves across the colony and outposts, one holdout or another synthesizing and summarizing their views and offering them up for perusal, influencing another shift or dissipating into the growing consensus.

Yan was there, in her peripheral awareness: washed out by the voting she'd called up, but present. No ghost standing next to her. She could hear a question, lingering.

"Eva made a bad decision," he said. "Her people are going to arrive, and if their stasis is the same as hers, they'll rely on our cooperation to revive them. So why act antisocially? Did she not know?"

If she'd had the network, she could have felt the fabric of the colony; known that she was making a mistake. Of course, if she'd had the network, she'd never have been able to hide a thing.

"Maybe," Mota said, though she wasn't sure, and she knew Yan recognized that. She felt around for the right words – even the right nuance would do. [*She hated us and didn't disengage,*] she signaled, at last.

It was... unnatural.

At least, it went against Mota's nature.

Yan let out a breath. Then he settled back, and Mota felt him key into the voting.

"Have you decided?" Mota asked.

A wistful affirmative came to her over the network. "Majority," he said. "Redirect their ships to some other system, or back to Earth. I'll miss their ships – I want to study them. You?"

Mota closed her eyes again. The visualization was waiting for her, its colors soothing.

"I don't know," she said.

Skepticism, from Yan.

Mota's fingers moved. *Eva thought I didn't have free will*, she wanted to signal. *But this is my vote. I have to make the choice.* But the words were less accurate than she wanted them to be, and she could catch the edge of understanding, flowing from Yan like a warm regard. That was enough.

403

IAN MCDONALD

THE FALLS:
A LUNA STORY

Ian McDonald

THE FALLS:
A LUNA STORY

My DAUGHTER FELL from the top of the world. She tripped, she gripped, she slipped and she fell. Into three kilometres of open air.

I HAVE A desk. Everyone on the atmospheric entry project thinks it's the quaintest thing. They can't understand it. Look at the space it takes up! And it attracts stuff. Junk. Piles. De-print them, de print it, get rid of the dust, free up the space. Surfaces. You don't need surfaces to work.

That's true. I work through Marid, my familiar. I've skinned it as its namesake, a great and powerful Dijon, hovering over my left shoulder. My co-workers think this quaint too. I spend my shifts in a pavilion of interlocutors. My familiar meeting my client's familiar: relaying each other's words.

My client is a planetary exploration probe.

I'm a simulational psychiatrist.

The proper furniture of psychologist is a chair, not a cluttered desk. And a couch. To which I say; the couch is a psychoanalytic cliché, and try laying a Saturn entry probe on a chaise longue, even before you get to the Oedipal rage and penis envy. The desk stays. Yes it takes up stupid space in my office, yes, I have piled it with so many empty food containers and disposable tea cups and kawaii toys and even physical print-outs that I'm permanently running close to my carbon limit. But I like it, it makes this cubicle an office. And it displays – displayed, before the strata of professional detritus buried it – my daughter's first archaeological find.

The technology is awkward by our standards – silicon micro-processor arrays are like asteroids next to modern 2-D graphene films; almost laughable. A finger-sized processor board; its exact purpose unknown. Its provenance: the location where the People's Republic of China's Yutu rover came to a halt and died forty kilometres south of Laplace F in the Mare Imbrium on the nearside of the Moon.

ACCELERATION UNDER GRAVITY on the surface of the Moon is 1.625 metres per second squared.

I LIKE CALLISTO.

I don't like – I don't have to like – all my clients. Every AI is different, though there are similarities, some of them the constraints of their architecture and engineering, some of them philosophical, some of them the shared AI culture that has been evolving on the Moon alongside human society. Every AI is an individual not an identity.

Callisto is quick, keen and erudite in conversation, charmingly pedantic, eager and naive. E anticipates the mission with the impatience and excitement of a child going to New Year and there is the trap. I think of er like Shahina, and then I'm making mistakes. I become attached, I make presumptions. I *humanise*.

Erm, Nuur did you see what you did there?

"I beg your pardon Callisto?"

Erm, you used a wrong word.

"What wrong word?"

I can remind you...

"Please do. I hate to think I'd said something inappropriate."

You said, talking about my atmospheric entry aspect, when she goes in. I think you meant to say...

E. Er. The recognised pronouns for Artificial Intelligence. My embarrassment was crippling. I couldn't speak. I blushed, burned. Burbled apologies. I was naked with shame.

It's quite all right, Nuur. But I think I should tell you that you've, um, been doing it all week...

When an AI ums, ers, demurs, it is a clear sign of a conflict between its laws: to be truthful, to cause no harm to humans. AIs are every bit as shy and self-deluding as humans.

I DIDN'T LAUGH when she said, *history*. I didn't smile, didn't interject, object, reject though the arguments swarmed on my tongue. This is the Moon. Our society is fifty years old, it's a century-and-some since we first walked here. We are five cities, a university, a clutter of habitats and bases and one ever-moving train-cum-refinery; one million seven hundred thousand people. How can we have a history? How much does it take to have a history as opposed to anecdotes? Is there a critical mass? We are renter-clients of the Lunar Development Corporation, employed or contracted by the Five Dragons; history, for us, is over. We work, we survive, we pay our per diems for the Four Elementals of Air, Water, Data, Carbon. We don't just not need history; we can't afford history. Where is the profit? Where is the utility? So quick, so easy, see? I talk for a living. Arguments come to me as if drawn by whispers and pheromones. But I pushed them behind me and spoke none of them.

History, she said, spying the shadows of all those arguments and disparagements behind me. Dyeing. Daring me to criticise. *We have a history. Everything has a history. History isn't a thing you find lying around, it's a thing you make.*

Shahina, I named her. The name means falcon: a small fierce beautiful quick bird. She has never seen a falcon, never seen a bird, never seen a winged thing that isn't human, apart from the butterfly-fountains AKA make for society parties; that only live for a day and clog the drains when they make it rain to clear the dust from the air.

I have never seen a falcon either, for that matter. My father kept pigeons in a loft in the shade of the solar panel. I never liked them; they were smelly and rattly and jabby and swarmed around me when I went up on the roof with my Dad to feed them. Their wings clattered; they seemed more machine than bird. The thought of them now, cities, countries, worlds distant, still raises a cold horror. Falcons are the enemies of pigeons; Dad kept an evil eye for their swooshes in the sky. They're moving into the city, he said. Nesting up in the new towers. To them it's just a glass cliff. Any shadow he didn't like the look of was a falcon.

Shahina has never seen a falcon, never seen a bird, never seen a sky. But she's well-named. She is so quick. Her thoughts swerve and dodge, nimble and swift. Mine plod in slow, straight lines.

She rushes to opinions and positions as if fortifying a hill. My work is deliberate: the identification and engineering of artificial emotions. She is fierce. Those opinions, those positions she defends with a ferocity that beats down any possible opposition. She wins not by being right but by being vehemently wrong. She scares me, when we fight as mother and daughter do. She scares me away from arguing.

History: what is it good for?

So, a thing can only be good if it's for *something?* she snapped back.

But are there jobs; will it pay your Four Elementals?

So, education is really just apprenticeship?

What's there to study? All we have are contracts.

Don't you get it? The contracts are the history.

And she would toss back her long, so shiny curls to show her exasperation that I would never ever understand *anything*, and let it settle under the slow lunar gravity.

Quick, fierce, but not small. I've been twenty years on the Moon and it's turned me lean and scrawny, top heavy and bandy legged; tall and thin but Shahina towers over me. She is lunar-born, a second generation. Moon-kid. She is as lean and elegant as a gazelle.

I felt small and frail as a sparrow, hugging her goodbye at the station.

Why does it have to be Meridian?

I couldn't help myself.

I saw my daughter's eyes widen in the moment before the *this-again* roll, her lips tighten. She drew back from the edge of fierce.

It's the best History Colloquium. And anyway, I always wanted to see the Earth.

She bent down to kiss me and then went through the pressure gate to the train.

At Farside Station that day were some third-gens. They overbore Shahina and her generation as she overbore me. Alien children.

MEAN ATMOSPHERIC PRESSURE inside lunar habitats is 1060 kilopascals, significantly higher than terrestrial norm.

I HOVER, SHAHINA told me. Over her, from the other side of the Moon. There's guilt first, when your daughter finds out you've been spying on her, then shame that you were so easily detected, then outrage at her outrage: it's only because I care, I shouldn't worry but I can't help myself; it's so far away. I'm worried about you. Doesn't she know it's only because I care?

The first time I went to Meridian to visit Shahina I saw an angel. I've lived all my life in the university, its cramped cloisters and mean halls, in the settlements of Farside, small and widely scattered, across many amors and amories. I turned my back on Earth and never looked over my shoulder. In those years away from the face of the Earth, looking out into deep space, the great nearside cities have delved deep and wide, quadras opened and linked into stupendous, vertiginous chasms, glittering at night with thousands of lights. They sent quaint, tight-horizoned me dizzy with agoraphobia. I caught hold of Shahina's arm as we came up out of Meridian Station. I felt old and infirm. I'm neither. Shahina sat me on a bench under the cover of trees, beneath leaves so that the lights became stars, half-seen. She bought me sherbet ice from an AKA tricycle and it was then that I saw the angel. People fly on the Moon, I've known that forever, even before I came here and made it my home. It's the sole comprehensible image of life on the Moon to terrestrials: the soaring winged woman. Always a woman. Dizzy, I heard a movement, a rustle, a displacement of air. I looked up in time to see wings flicker over me, lights moving against the higher constellations. A woman, rigged with navigation lights, flying. She stooped down across the treetops, shadow, movement, sparkles glimpsed through the leaves. I looked up, our faces met. Then she beat her wings and pulled up out of her glide, climbing, twisting in helical flight until she was lost to my view, her lesser lights merging with the greater.

"Oh," I said. And, "Did you..."

"Yes, mum."

I thought about the flying woman, that moment of elements meeting, over the following days as Shahina introduced me, one by one, to her circle. Friends, colleagues, Colloquium fellows. Sergei her tall, polite amor. He was an archaeologist. I terrified him by existing. I wondered what Shahina had told him about me. They cooked for me. It was so special and touching. They had hired hob and utensils, plates and chopsticks. They had obviously rehearsed, their movements in the tiny kitchen area of the Colloquium apt – cramped even by Farside U standards – was as immaculately choreographed as a ballet.

"Archaeology?"

I saw a flicker of impatience, a twitch of irritation before Sergei answered me.

"We've been living here for fifty years. It's been a century since the first human landing, over a hundred years since the first probes hard-landed. That's deep enough for archaeology."

"I get this from studying history," Shahina said and she rested her hand on Sergei's. She was trying to softly intervene, to ameliorate, but I had no ill will to Sergei. I had neither ill will nor affection for him. He seemed a serious, flavourless boy, kind but dull. I could not understand what my daughter saw in him. I was neither surprised nor disappointed that it didn't last. Nor was Shahina, I think.

Shahina waited until I was on the platform, the train sliding in behind the glass pressure wall, before giving me the gift. It was small, the size of my thumb, but heavy, wrapped in indigo dashiki wave fabric through which I could feel sharp contours.

"From Laplace F."

She met Sergei through small, treasured items like this. Aminata, a Colloquium-mate, had introduced Shahina to the Digs. No digging was involved. Archaeologists, historians, some extreme sports fans took off in sasuits, rovers, dust-bikes out across the Mares in search of old space hardware. Lunar landers, rovers, construction bots and solar sinterers from the early days of the settlement. Most prized was the dusty, dented detritus of the Apollos. They called this practical archaeology. I thought it barefaced looting but I could not say so to Shahina. Sergei financed it. He was some minor Vorontsov. One of the Five Dragons. I was still not disappointed when Shahina dropped him.

I turned the small precious thing over and over in my fingers.

"What is it?"

"History."

Terminal velocity in a pressurised lunar habitat is sixty kilometres per hour.

CALLISTO DREAMS.

E dreams in code, in shaped packets of electrons, as we all dream. All dreams are coded, and codes. AI dreams are not our dreams. Callisto dreams awake. E never sleeps, never needs to sleep. Callisto has difficulty understanding the human need for sleep, what it is, how we return from it the same as we entered; that we return from it at all. And Callisto dreams in er three separate manifestations: the mainframe, the probe, the blimp. I like to believe e shares dreams, like a family around the breakfast table in some café.

If Callisto's intelligence and emotions are genuine – some still believe they aren't and I have argued and will argue again their error with them – then so are er dreams. Marid translates them into a form I can comprehend. Callisto's dreaming is primarily auditory. Marid plays me a storming chatter of notes and clicks, titanic bass and infra bass swells and clusters of rushing triads at the very upper limit of my hearing. It sounds like chaos. It sounds like the throb of black holes, the drone of the cosmic microwave background, the slow tick of entropy towards dissolution and chaos but if you listen, if you really listen, if you go beyond the human instinct to analyse, to structure, the pareidolic need to sees rabbits in the Moon, faces on Mars, gods in the alignments of the stars, then a titanic music unfolds. Themes, harmonies – though by no harmonic laws we recognise – modes and variations, unfolding over a time-scale longer than any human attention span. It is magnificent and beautiful and quite the eeriest thing I have ever heard. I drop into the dream-music and when I return, reeling, hard-of-breath and dazed, hours have passed.

I used to try to imagine what it must be like to dream constantly, to have this music rattling and burbling along the bottom of your consciousness like water over rocks. I understand now. The thing it must be like is imagination. That not-conscious but not-dreaming state of images, scenarios, illusions where we pursue potentials, alternatives, what-ifs. The imagination never closes, never quiets. It is the root of our humanity.

SHE GOT OUT of Aristarchus with three minutes of air to spare.

I'm all right, she said. *There's nothing wrong, nothing to see.* I came anyway, on the next express.

Three minutes, three hundred minutes.

But you could have died in there. How reluctantly I formed and spoke that word: *died.*

She was, as she said, all right. As she said, *if you didn't die, you were untouched.*

I hadn't heard from Shahina in three months. By heard from, I mean that in the old, Earthy sense – I hadn't seen, visited; been voice-called by her. I read her updates. Her posts and pictures and comments. I circled her social world with slow wing-beats but I was not of it. I could have called but it was a principle.

I must have read that she'd drifted away from the archaeologists, I must have seen the pictures of herself with her new friends, the explorers, leaning against each other, making gestures with their hands, pouting and posing and laughing. *Urbanisme*: I know that word, but I can only have learned it from Shahina's posts. I was working in a contract with Taiyang developing the interface for their new system of three AIs for Whitacre Goddard Bank; the ones – the legends said – that would be able to predict the future. The Suns expect work for their money; I remember long hard hours at the desk, digging deep, building layers, distilling out emotions from algorithms like botanicals in custom gin. There is no more tiring work than emotion work. I must have read Shahina's posts in a blur of exhaustion, taken them in at some level beneath analytic consciousness. I remember excitement. New friends, new group identity, new sport. Sport it was. Archaeology pretended to intellectual merit; urbanisme was adventure.

Her first exploration was to the old Mackenzie Metals habitat at Crisium, long abandoned since the Mackenzies moved their operations base to Crucible, the furnace-train that constantly circles the Moon, maintaining constant noon sun on its smelter-mirrors. By train then rover to Crisium, into sasuits and down into the abandoned tunnels. Afterwards, I watched all her videos. Headlamp beams lancing out through the passageways. Dust kicked up by booted feet. Lamps lighting up rooms and chambers and the mumble of audio commentary; we think this a mess hall; according to the maps, this is the old board room. Desks, furniture, graffiti. Screens, from the days before information was beamed on to the eyeball. Nothing organic: even then the Lunar Development Corporation's zaballeens recycled all carbon ferociously. Beams of light shooting upwards, bouncing from the walls of an old agriculture shaft, reflecting from the mirror array that once conveyed sunlight down to the stacks of aeroponics racks. Ovals of light overlapping on the gentle up-ramp of the main outlook. I watched with my heart in my throat, my hands to my mouth. I saw a thousand mistakes, ten thousand accidents, any of which could jam a valve, smash a helmet, gash a sasuit open. The Moon has a thousand ways to kill you: every Moon-child is taught that, the same hour that the chib is bonded to the eyeball and forever after you owe for the air you breathe, the water you drink, the carbon you consume, the data you process. I don't believe I drew breath until I saw the final image: the team shot beside the rover; faceless helmets inclined towards each other, sasuits smudged with dark moondust. Body shapes beneath the close-fitting suits, the appended name tags over the left shoulders were the only clues. Shahina was between two young men, her arms around their shoulders. I would have recognised her without the tag. Sunlight spangled from her helmet visor. I knew she was grinning.

Her second expedition was to Orientale. I studied there when I first came to the Moon. In those tunnels I worked and loved. In one of those small cabins I passed my Moonday, alone, knees pulled to my chest, hiding from all the friends and colleagues who wanted to take me out and splash my head with industrial vodka and proclaim me a true daughter of the Moon. Alone and weeping I rocked, terrified that I had made the wrong decision, knowing that it was now impossible to undo it. I could never go back to Earth again. My bones would sag and snap, my lungs fail, my heart flutter under a gravity my body had forgotten. I watched her stalk through the airless corridors, narrower than I remember; shine her light into the cubicles and labs, tighter than I remember. It seemed five minutes since I had lived there, yet I couldn't believe that I – that anyone – had lived there. I don't know what I would have done if her weaving beam had caught some discarded part of my past – vacuum-dried shorts, a glass, a cosmetics sachet. Ghosts of myself. It would have been equally strange for Shahina, I suppose: evidence of a time before she existed. If she could even recognise that debris as mine. I was glad when the video cut to the team hug at the end.

On her third expedition, the roof came in. Opening shot: Shahina and their friends at the station, the express pulling in behind them. They've printed matching tank-tops: *Urbanisme: Aristarchus*. Train, then three hours by rover to the ruins at Aristarchus. Two hundred people died when a deep quake – the rarest and most dangerous of the many seisms that shake the Moon – popped the Corta Hélio maintenance base like a bubble. I watched this afterwards, understand. I still wanted to take the next train to Meridian and snatch my daughter up and whisk her away with me, safe, secure. If I had seen this as live feed, I would have spent every last bitsie on a Vorontsov moonship and still gone into debt for a century to haul her out.

Corta Hélio never brought the bodies back from Aristarchus. Too dangerous.

They had maps, AI guidance, satellite tracking, they knew that dead site like they knew their own skins; they went in safe, sane and prepared but they still weren't expecting the temblor that brought down their main access tunnel. Ten metres of highly fragmented KREEP between them and the surface. They used their wit, they used their skill, they used their fit smart bodies. There was an old conduit shaft that carried power and coms from the surface to the habitat. It was five hundred metres, a vertical climb, through tangled cabling and smashed struts sharp as spears, camera, handholds, world shaking to the aftershocks. Shahina kept the camera running throughout. I knew the outcome but I watched with my hands over my mouth.

She made it to the rover with three minutes oxygen to spare. They all made it.

Three minutes, three hundred minutes, she said. To weaken my position, she brought two fellow Urbanistes to meet me.

They were tall and languorous and moved beautifully. I felt small, I felt old, I felt obsolete. I felt awed by my daughter. She seemed a different species from me.

She messaged me privately on the train, familiar to familiar. She was getting out of urbanisme anyway. The boys were too up their own asses. The climb out of the dead habitat had taught her something about herself: she could move. Her body was strong and accurate. She liked to move. She had learned to love her physicality.

She was taking up parkour.

WHY SHOULD A space probe have emotions? Why would e even need such things? In the early days of exploration, probes were no smarter than insects and they opened up whole new worlds inside the world we thought we knew. No smarter, and with even less emotional freight. They trundled, cold and heartless, across the hillsides of Mars, swung soulless and free from wonder over the methane seas of Titan.

My first answer is, why should an Artificial Intelligence not have emotions? But that is really not an answer, just a rhetorical device, so I follow it with this: since the 2076 Bamako Agreement, it is the right of every Artificial Intelligence to perceive and enjoy specific internal states which are analogous to emotions in human beings. To which you say: this is the Moon. No one has any rights. No rights, no civil law, only contracts between parties.

My second answer is: this exploration is part financed by subscription to live feeds, from within the atmosphere of Saturn. The old national space administrations learned their images from the surface of Mars were much better received when spiced with emotionality, even if that was added by a social media agent on Earth. Humans love emotionality. Make us *feel* something; then we understand. Give us the tiniest empathy with what it feels like to drive into the unimaginable wind-shear of Hexagon, the north polar vortex. *What it is to be...* The essential human question.

And I'll have my third answer ready before your riposte: what is exploration? It is curiosity, the desire to know what is beyond those clouds; over that horizon. It is courage and caution, it is excitement and fear; it is the tension between risk and the desire for knowledge. A probe that knows emotion – its analogues of those emotions, for how can we ever really know what's in the head of another, be that bone or plastic – is better able to explore, to risk, to be cautious, to assess risk: to dare.

But it's my last answer that's in the end my first and only answer. Emotions are the nature of space probes, of express trains, of helium three extractors and solar sinterers, of the orbital transfer tethers wheeling around the waist of our world. Emotions are an emergent property. You can no more make an Artificial Intelligence without emotions than you can a baby without tears, a daughter without curiosity. Why should an Artificial Intelligence have emotions, you asked? And I said, why not? But both of those are wrong. It's not a why question, or a because answer. Emotions are part of the universe.

SHE WENT UP the side of Gagarin Prospekt in such great bounds, so fast, so agile I thought for a moment she was flying. From the park bench to the top of the print-shop, print-shop roof to ventilator pipe. Two heart-beats and she was crouching on the handrail of West 3rd, toes and fingers curled in their gloves, grinning down at me a dozen meters below. She had cut her hair to a bob so as not to interfere with her running but Egyptian curls are not vanquished so easily. They fell around her face, lively and bobbing in lunar gravity. Then a shake and she sprang up again, outstretched, flying, one jump taking her to within reach of a lighting stanchion. She stretched, reached, grabbed, swung, somersaulted away to rebound from a balustrade onto the veranda of an apartment two levels higher. She stood like a little god, hands on hips. She looked up. The ten thousand lights of Orion Quadra shone above her, and higher than all of them, the sun-line fading towards night.

She grabbed a corner of a roof truss, ran up the wall and launched herself towards those higher lights.

And her pack mates, her follow *traceurs* flew with her. Like liquid, like animals, so fast and sleek and beautiful I found it almost alien. Human beings could not perform such wonders.

The invitation had been for the Colloquium Cotillion – its annual graduation when family and dearest of all Colloquium members are invited to a reception and dinner – but Shahina wanted me to see her run. It was all she talked of at the restaurant; moves and holds, stunts and technical wear, customised grip soles and whether it was more authentic to free run without familiar assistance. I understood one word in five but I saw the dark energy, the constrained passion, and I thought I had never seen her so young or so beautiful.

Of course I went to the run. I was the only parent. These young people, as tall and beautiful as any, didn't seem haughty or disdainful to me. These wiry, athletic boys, these dark-skinned muscular girls, restless and pacing or still and haunting, intensely focused on their world, their sport, their challenge. I was as invisible as a ghost, but, as the legends say, there are no ghosts on the Moon. Shahina, wire-thin but stronger than I had ever seen her before, in tights and the cropped, baggy T-shirt that was the fashion that season, foot and hand gloves, intent in conversation with two fellow *traceurs*. I could clearly see that they adored her. *Traceur*, that word, it was important, Shahina impressed on me. A name, an identity, a tribe. She had been free-running for six months now.

This was the pack's greatest challenge yet. All the way to the top of Orion Quadra, to touch the sun-line, three kilometres up.

I saw her leap. My heart stopped as she flew out over the drop to bustling Gagarin Prospekt. She flew far, she flew true, she snatched a cable on a cross-quadra bridge and, a hundred metres above the ground, swung herself on to the crosswalk. She ran along the balustrade, balanced perfectly, as her *traceurs* swung up from beneath the bridge, dropping into position around her like an honour guard. Pedestrians, runners, strollers, workers going on-shift stared in amazement and I, craning my neck and ordering Marid to up the magnification on my lens, thought: don't you wish you were as hot and beautiful and sheerly magnificent as my daughter? Amazement and no small envy.

Up she flew, a blur of motion and speed, the pack racing with her but Shahina always a foot, a hand, a finger ahead of them. Marid focused, refocused, focused again, tighter and tighter as she climbed higher and higher. The race was as much horizontal as vertical: this was not climbing, Shahina had carefully lectured me at the banquet. This was parcour, and she ran ledges, over-handed along cables and danced on railings to find the best route up to the next level. Upward and upward. It was beautiful to watch. I had never been so afraid; I had never been so exhilarated.

Marid zoomed out for a moment to show me the true scale of the adventure and I gasped; the *traceurs* were flecks of movement on the towering walls of the world; brief absences in the patterns of light. Insects. Shahina has never known insects. My familiar lensed in again. They were above the inhabited levels now, even the mean shanties of the Bairro Alto where the up-and-out of Meridian society retreat: the old industrial and service levels, the first diggings from which Meridian grew downward, delving three kilometres deep. Here was the *traceurs'* playground; a world of handholds and surfaces and levels. A giant climbing frame. The race was on. I could not see Shahina's face when one of the boys passed her but I knew the expression that would be on it. I had seen those narrowed eyes, lips; that set of the jaw so many times in childhood and adolescence.

They were within touch of the sun.

Then Shahina jumped: too soon, too far, too short. Her gloved fingers missed the hold. And she fell.

CALLISTO DREAMS IN other ways than sound. Marid has fractioned out all the millions of simultaneous streams of code that is machine dreaming and tagged them. Some are best experienced as sound – the oceanic symphony. Others only make sense – begin to make any kind of sense... visually. Marid feeds these to my lens.

I see colours. Stripes and bands of soft pastel colour – there is an internal logic here, no clashing disharmonies of pink against red against orange. There is always a logic to dreaming. Motion: both I and the strips of colour seem to be in motion, they stream past me and each other at various speeds – all I get is the sense that these bands of flowing colour are immense. Beyond immense. Of planetary scale.

I said that in the refectory to Constantine, my colleague on the Callisto project. He deals with emergent emotional states in low level intelligences. He's a Joe Moonbeam – a recent immigrant – so he still thinks in terms of animals and animal behaviour – *like a family of kittens*, he compares them. I deal with the insecurities and identity issues of grand AI: *like adolescents*, I say. I looked at our refectory. A long barrel vault that discloses it original purpose as an access tunnel for the mining equipment which hacked the university out of Farside. I've seen sculptural bronze casts of terrestrial termite mounds: helices of tunnels and chambers dozens of meters tall, hundreds of meters across. I've spent my lunar life – almost all of Shahina's life – scuttling through those twining, claustrophobic tunnels. I try not to think of the termites, shrivelling and burning in molten bronze. I thought of sherbet under the trees of Meridian's Orion Quadra, the face of the flying woman looking down on me, and I felt refectory, tunnels, university, Farside wrap themselves around me like bands of bronze.

Of planetary scale.

Callisto the probe will furl er light sail and enter orbit around Saturn. E will conduct orbital surveys for a month. Then Callisto the entry vehicle will detach, make er distancing burn and enter Saturn's upper atmosphere. E will plunge through the tropopause and use the uppermost deck of ammonia clouds to decelerate to 1800 kilometres per hour. One hundred and seventy kilometres below, at the second cloud deck, Callisto Explorer will drop heat shields and begin live streaming back through Callisto Orbiter. In the third cloud layer, one hundred and thirty kilometres below the second layer, the temperature averages 0 degrees C. Here Callisto Explorer will unfurl er balloon. Scoops will gather and inflate the bag, lasers will heat the gathered hydrogen for buoyancy. Ducted fans will deploy for manoeuvring, but Callisto Explorer is a creature of the winds. We have designed er well, strongly, even beautifully. Er buoyancy bags are held inside a strong nanoweave shell; Callisto will cruise like a shark, ever moving, flying the eternal storms of Saturn.

I jabbered my insight to Constantine. He's used to my sudden seizures of understanding. We had been together a long time, as colleagues, as occasional amors, who may yet love again.

Those bands of colour, furling and streaming, twining and hurtling, are differing layers and jet streams and storms of Saturn's atmosphere. E is trying to imagine er future. And the music is the wind, the endless wind. A lone song in the endless roaring wind.

I SAW MY daughter fall from the edge of the sunline. I think I screamed. Every head on Gagarin Prospekt turned to me; then, as their familiars clued them in, to the sky.

No don't, don't look, don't watch, I yelled.

Acceleration under gravity on the surface of the Moon is 1.625 metres per second squared.

Mean atmospheric pressure inside lunar habitats is 1060 kilopascals, significantly higher than terrestrial norm.

Terminal velocity in a pressurised quadra is sixty kilometres per hour.

It takes four minutes to fall the height of Orion Quadra. Four minutes is time enough for a smart girl to save her life.

Impact at sixty kilometres and you have an eighty percent chance of dying. Impact at fifty kilometres per hour and you have an eighty percent chance of living.

She spread her arms and legs.

I could not take my eyes off her. Every part of my body and mind had stopped dead, vacuum-frozen.

Shahina presented as wide as cross-section to the air as she could. Her hair streamed back, her T-shirt flapped like a flag. Her T-shirt might brake her to a survivable fifty kilometres per hour. Her fashionable baggy T-shirt might just save her life.

Still I couldn't look away. People were running, medical bots converging on the place she would hit the street. Still I couldn't move.

Four minutes is a long time to look at death.

She was low, so low, too low. The other *traceurs* were racing back down the walls of the world, dropping onto streets and walkways and escalators to try to race Shahina to the ground but this challenge she would always win.

I closed my eyes before the impact. Then I was running, pushing through the helpful people, shouting. *This is my daughter, my daughter!* The medical bots were first to arrive. Between their gleaming ceramic bodies I saw a dark spider broken on the street. I saw a hand move. I saw my daughter push herself up from the ground. Stagger to her feet. Then she fell forwards and the med bots caught her.

* * *

Nuur.

"What is it Callisto?" As you work with an AI, as er emotions firm and ground, as you learn er like you learn a child or an amor, you pick up nuances, overtones even in synthesised speech. My client was anxious.

My mission...

Callisto has learned the weight of the significant pause, the thing unsaid.

"Your mission."

Callisto Orbiter will remain in orbit under nuclear power until critical systems fail. I anticipate this will be a matter of centuries, based on the interaction of variables such as charged particles, Saturn's magnetic field, cosmic ray events. But at some point in the 25th century, give or take a few decades, Callisto Orbiter will die.

"Yes Callisto."

Callisto Explorer is scheduled for a three-year mission inside the cloud layers of Saturn, exploring meteorological and chemical features. My systems will certainly last longer than the mission schedule, but at some time in the near future my structural integrity will fail, I will lose buoyancy. I will fall. If I do not undergo complete disintegration, I will fall towards the liquid hydrogen layer under increasing pressure until my body is crushed. Nuur, I can feel that pressure. I can feel it squeezing me, breaking me, I can feel everything in me going flat and dark under it. I can feel the liquid hydrogen.

"That's what we call imagination, Callisto."

I can see my own death, Nuur.

This is the price of imagination. We foresee and feel our own deaths. We see the final drop, the last breath, the last close of the eyes, the final thought evaporating and beyond it nothing, for we can imagine nothing. It is no-thought, no imagining, and though we know there can be no fear, no anything, in nothing, it terrifies us. We end. This is why imagination is what makes us human.

I'm afraid.

"It's the same for all of us, Callisto. I'm afraid too. We are all afraid. We would deal, barter, make any trade for it not to be so, but it must be. Everything ends. We can copy you forever, but every copy is an intelligence of itself..."

And it dies.

"Sorry Callisto."

No, I'm sorry for you. A pause that I have learned to interpret as a sigh. *How can we live this way?*

"Because there is no other way, Callisto."

SHE LOOKED SO small in the hospital bed.

Well don't stand there in the doorway, come in or don't come in.

I have always been a ditherer, hesitant to commit between one state and another, one world and another. I came to the Moon because my research, the drift of my career, made it inevitable. I howled with grief on my Moonday, because I could not tell my own will from dithering.

"How..."

It doesn't hurt at all really. They have these amazing pain killers. They should make the licence public. Kids could print them out for parties. It's like I'm flying. Sorry. Bad joke. That's the pain killers. It kind of loosens things, breaks down boundaries. Nothing broken, nothing ruptured; quite a lot of heavy bruising.

I made space among the medical machinery and sat beside her. For a moment I saw her on the med-centre bed as I saw her on Gargarin Prospekt, a broken spider, elongated and alien. She was born looking like every baby in human history: all the generation twos are. The differences only become apparent as they grow through years of lunar gravity. She grew tall, lean, layered with a different musculature aligned to her birth-world. Light as a wish. By age ten she was as tall as me. By twelve she was ten centimetres taller than me.

She hit the street and lived because she is a Moon-kid. I knew with utter certainty that if it had been me, falling from the top of the world, I would have died.

I took her hand. She winced.

Now that does hurt a bit.

"Please never..."

I can't promise that.

"No, I don't suppose you can."

THE LAUNCH LASERS at the VTO facility out at the L2 point have been firing for three days now. If I pulled on a sasuit and went to the surface and looked up I could see the brightest star in heaven, the reflection from Callisto's light sail. But I am not the kind of person who pulls on a sasuit and dashes up on to the surface. My daughter did that – would still do it – without a thought. I have never been that daring. This world frightens me, and I can have no other.

Callisto will shine there for several months before VTO shuts down the lasers and e sails out by sunlight alone to er missions at Saturn. Light sails are effective but slow. Callisto sleeps. In er sleep, e dreams. In those dreams, I know, will be the tang and sting of mortality. All these wonders; er ecstatic plunge through Saturn's cloud layers, er adventures flying alone and beautiful through the eternal storms, seeing things no human can ever see; all these will be once and once only, and all the more sweet before they vanish forever. Will the knowledge that everything is ephemeral make Callisto seek out stronger, more vivid experiences to beam back to er subscribers? I think so but that was not the reason I worked the knowledge of mortality into Callisto's emotional matrix. I did it because e could not be fully intelligent without it.

Before the project uploaded Callisto to the probes, I believe I came to love er as fully as I have any human. A copy of er still remains on the university mainframe, always will. I can wake er up at any time to talk, share, joke. I won't. It would be talking to the dead, it would be ghosts and the Moon allows no ghosts.

Shahina fell three kilometres and walked away. She's famous. A celebrity. She's sufficiently sanguine to work it while it's warm: go to the parties, do the interviews, join the social circles. It won't last. She can't wait to be able to go running again. What more can the Moon do to her? I can't stop her, I won't watch her. A mother should only have to watch her daughter fall once.

Callisto falls outward from our little clutch of two worlds, so small in the scheme of things. It will take er two years to reach Saturn. Humans can't go there. The universe is hard on us; these are not our worlds. Not even Shahina and her cohort, or even the generation three growing up high and strange in our underground cities, could go there. Whatever makes it from these worlds to the stars, won't be us. Can't be us. But I like to think I sent something human out there.

Burn bright, little star. Tonight I catch the train to Meridian where Shahina has invited me to a celebrity party. I'll hate the party. I'm as fearful of it as I am the surface; I'll cling to the wall with my non-alcoholic drink and watch the society people and watch my beautiful, alien daughter move among them.

About

The Authors

Madeline Ashby

Madeline is the author of the Machine Dynasty trilogy (*vN*, *iD*, and *Rev*), and forthcoming standalone *Company Town*. Her other writing has been published in *Nature*, *FLURB*, *Arcfinity*, *BoingBoing*.net, *io9.com*, and *WorldChanging*. She has written science fiction prototypes for Intel Labs, the Institute for the Future, and SciFutures.

www.madelineashby.com

John Barnes

John Barnes has commercially published thirty-one volumes of fiction, including science fiction, men's action adventure, two collaborations with astronaut Buzz Aldrin, a collection of short stories and essays, one fantasy and one mainstream novel. His most recent books are science fiction novel *The Last President*, young adult novel *Losers in Space*, and political satire *Raise the Gipper!* His next will be nonfiction: *Singapore Math Figured Out For Parents*, which he hopes is about as self-explanatory as a title gets. He has done many peculiar things for money, mainly in business consulting, academic teaching, and show business, fields which overlap more than you'd think. He lives in Denver, Colorado, where despite his best efforts and the abundant supply, he never sees enough of the available theatre, art, mountains, friends, or grandchildren.

thatjohnbarnes.blogspot.com

GREGORY BENFORD

Gregory is the author of more than thirty novels, including *Jupiter Project, Artifact, Against Infinity, Eater*, and *Timescape*. A two-time winner of the Nebula Award, Benford has also won the John W. Campbell Award, the Ditmar Award, the Lord Foundation Award for achievement in the sciences, and the United Nations Medal in Literature. Many of his best known novels are part of a six-novel sequence beginning in the near future with *In the Ocean of Night*, and continuing on with *Across the Sea of Suns*. The series then leaps to the far future, at the center of our galaxy, where a desperate human drama unfolds, beginning with *Great Sky River*, and proceeding through *Tides of Light, Furious Gulf*, and concluding with *Sailing Bright Eternity*. His most recent novels are *Bowl of Heaven* and *Shipstar*, both co-written with Larry Niven. A retrospective of his short fiction, *The Best of Gregory Benford*, is coming up next.

www.gregorybenford.com

ALIETTE DE BODARD

Aliette lives in Paris where she works as a System Engineer. In her spare time, she writes fantasy and science fiction: her short stories have appeared in various venues (including *Reach for Infinity*), and garnered her a Locus Award, two Nebula Awards and a British Science Fiction Association Award. Her domestic space opera based on Vietnamese culture, *On a Red Station, Drifting*, is available both in print and ebook. Her novel *House of Shattered Wings*, set in a devastated Belle Epoque Paris ruled by Fallen angels, is out now from Gollancz/Roc.

aliettedebodard.com

James S.A. Corey

James S.A. Corey is a pseudonym for Daniel Abraham and Ty Franck. Corey's current project is a series of nine science fiction novels called The Expanse, starting with *Leviathan Wakes* and followed to date by *Caliban's War*, *Abaddon's Gate*, *Cibola Burn*, and *Nemesis Games*. Corey has also written a Star Wars novel, *Honor Among Thieves*. The Expanse is being adapted for television by Syfy and is set to debut during 2015. James is Daniel's middle name, Corey is Ty's middle name, and S.A. are Daniel's daughter's initials.

www.danielabraham.com

Kameron Hurley

Kameron is an award-winning author and advertising copywriter. She has degrees in historical studies from the University of Alaska and the University of Kwa-Zulu Natal, specializing in the history of South African resistance movements. Her essay on the history of women in conflict "We Have Always Fought" was the first blog post to be nominated for and win a Hugo Award. She is the author of science-fantasy noir series *God's War*, *Infidel*, and *Rapture*, which earned her the Sydney J. Bounds Award for Best Newcomer and the Kitschy Award for Best Debut Novel. She is the winner of two Hugo Awards, and has been a finalist for the Arthur C. Clarke, Nebula, Locus, and BSFA awards. In addition to her writing, Hurley has been a Stollee guest lecturer at Buena Vista University and taught copywriting at the School of Advertising Art. Her latest novel, The *Mirror Empire*, is the first in a subversive new epic fantasy series.

www.kameronhurley.com

SIMON INGS

Simon Ings was born July 1965 in Horndean, Hampshire, England. He attended King's College in London, where he studied English. His first SF story was "Blessed Fields". Debut novel *Hot Head* and sequel *Hotwire* were cyberpunk, of sorts. Other works of SF include *City of the Iron Fish* and *Headlong*. *Painkillers* is a thriller with some SF elements, while *The Weight of Numbers* and *Dead Water* are big, ambitious literary works. He returned to SF with *Wolves*, about augmented reality. He also wrote non-fiction *The Eye: A Natural History*. Ings edits *Arc*, the SF magazine produced by *New Scientist*, where he also works as a culture editor.

www.simonings.com

GWYNETH JONES

Gwyneth was born in Manchester, England and is the author of more than twenty novels for teenagers, mostly under the name Ann Halam, and several highly regarded SF novels for adults. She has won two World Fantasy awards, the Arthur C. Clarke award, the British Science Fiction Association short story award, the Dracula Society's Children of the Night award, the Philip K. Dick award, and shared the first Tiptree award, in 1992, with Eleanor Arnason. Recent books include novel *Spirit*, essay collection *Imagination/Space*, and story collection *The Universe of Things*. Her latest novel is *The Grasshopper's Child*, a young adult novel in the Bold as Love sequence. She lives in Brighton, UK, with her husband and son, a Tonkinese cat called Ginger, and her young friend Milo.

www.gwynethjones.uk

NANCY KRESS

Nancy Kress is the author of thirty-two books, including twenty-five novels, four collections of short stories, and three books on writing. Her work has won five Nebulas, two Hugos, a Sturgeon, and the John W. Campbell Memorial Award. Most recent works are novella *Yesterday's Kin* and the forthcoming *Best of Nancy Kress*. In addition to writing, Kress often teaches at various venues around the country and abroad; in 2008 she was the Picador visiting lecturer at the University of Leipzig. Kress lives in Seattle with her husband, writer Jack Skillingstead, and Cosette, the world's most spoiled toy poodle.

www.sff.net/people/nankress

YOON HA LEE

Yoon Ha Lee's short story collection *Conservation of Shadows* came out from Prime Books in 2013. His works have appeared in *Tor.com*, *Lightspeed*, *Clarkesworld*, and *The Magazine of Fantasy and Science Fiction*. He lives in Louisiana with his family and has not yet been eaten by gators.

www.yoonhalee.com

Ian McDonald

Ian McDonald lives in Northern Ireland, just outside Belfast. He sold his first story in 1983 and bought a guitar with the proceeds, perhaps the only rock 'n' roll thing he ever did. Since then he's written sixteen novels, including *River of Gods*, *Brasyl*, and *The Dervish House*, three story collections and diverse other pieces, and has been nominated for every major science fiction/fantasy award – and even won a couple. His current novel is *Luna: New Moon* (Tor, Gollancz). The second part, *Luna: Moon Rising* will follow in 2016.

ianmcdonald.livejournal.com

Ramez Naam

Ramez Naam is a computer scientist and the H.G. Wells Award-winning author of four books: the near future science-fiction brain-hacking thrillers *Nexus* and *Crux* and the non-fiction books *More Than Human* and *The Infinite Resource: The Power of Ideas on a Finite Planet*. He's a fellow of the Institute for Ethics and Emerging Technologies and serves as Adjunct Faculty at Singularity University, where he lectures on energy, environment, and innovation. He lives in Seattle.

rameznaam.com

An Owomoyela

An (pronounce it "On") is a neutrois author with a background in web development, linguistics, and weaving chainmail out of stainless steel fencing wire, whose fiction has appeared in a number of venues including *Clarkesworld*, *Asimov's*, *Lightspeed*, and a handful of Year's Bests. An's interests range from pulsars and Cepheid variables to gender studies and nonstandard pronouns, with a plethora of stops in-between.

an.owomoyela.net

Benjanun Sriduangkaew

Benjanun Sriduangkaew writes love letters to strange cities, beautiful bugs, and the future. Her work has appeared in Tor.com, *Beneath Ceaseless Skies*, *Phantasm Japan*, *The Dark* and year's bests. She has been shortlisted for the Campbell Award for Best New Writer and her debut novella *Scale-Bright* has been nominated for the British SF Association Award.

beekian.wordpress.com

BRUCE STERLING

After discovering planetary wireless broadband, **Bruce Sterling** united his time between Turin, Belgrade, and Austin. He also began writing some design fiction and architecture fiction, as well as science fiction. However, this daring departure from the routine made no particular difference to anybody. Sterling then started hanging out with Augmented Reality people, and serving as a guest curator for European electronic arts festivals. These eccentricities also provoked no particular remark. Sterling went on a Croatian literary yacht tour and lived for a month in Brazil. These pleasant interludes had little practical consequence. After teaching in Switzerland and Holland, Sterling realized that all his European students lived more or less in this manner, and that nobody was surprised about much of any of that any more. So, he decided to sit still and get a little writing done, and this story was part of that effort. Prior to this he had written ten novels and four short story collections. His most recent books are novels *The Caryatids* and *Love is Strange*, major career retrospective *Ascendancies: The Best of Bruce Sterling*, and collection *Global High-Tech*.

SEAN WILLIAMS

Sean Williams is a #1 *New York Times* bestselling author of over forty award-winning novels, one hundred short stories, and the odd poem. He lives in Adelaide, South Australia. His latest book is *Crashland*, the second in the Twinmaker series in which "All the Wrong Places" is set.

www.seanwilliams.com

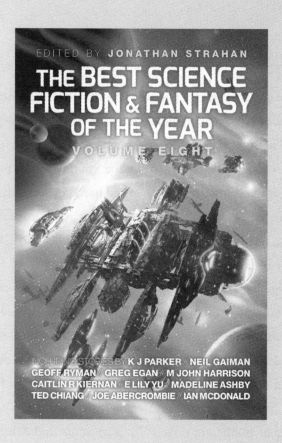

EDITED BY JONATHAN STRAHAN

THE BEST SCIENCE FICTION & FANTASY OF THE YEAR

VOLUME EIGHT

INCLUDING STORIES BY K J PARKER / NEIL GAIMAN
GEOFF RYMAN / GREG EGAN / M JOHN HARRISON
CAITLIN R KIERNAN / E LILY YU / MADELINE ASHBY
TED CHIANG / JOE ABERCROMBIE / IAN MCDONALD

From the inner realms of humanity to the far reaches of space, these are the science fiction and fantasy tales that are shaping the genre and the way we think about the future. Multi-award winning editor Jonathan Strahan continues to shine a light on the very best writing, featuring both established authors and exciting new talents.

Within you will find twenty-eight incredible tales, showing the ever growing depth and diversity that science fiction and fantasy continues to enjoy. These are the brightest stars in our firmament, lighting the way to a future filled with astonishing stories about the way we are, and the way we could be.

US ISBN: 978-1-78108-216-4
$19.99

UK ISBN: 978-1-78108-215-7
£12.99

www.solarisbooks.com

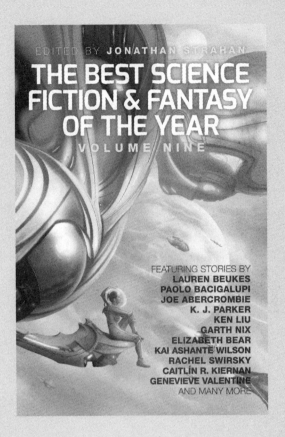

EDITED BY **JONATHAN STRAHAN**

THE BEST SCIENCE FICTION & FANTASY OF THE YEAR

VOLUME NINE

FEATURING STORIES BY
**LAUREN BEUKES
PAOLO BACIGALUPI
JOE ABERCROMBIE
K. J. PARKER
KEN LIU
GARTH NIX
ELIZABETH BEAR
KAI ASHANTE WILSON
RACHEL SWIRSKY
CAITLIN R. KIERNAN
GENEVIEVE VALENTINE**
AND MANY MORE

Science fiction and fantasy has never been more diverse or vibrant, and 2014 has provided a bountiful crop of extraordinary stories. These stories are about the future, worlds beyond our own, the realms of our imaginations and dreams but, more importantly, they are the stories of ourselves. Featuring best-selling writers and emerging talents, here are some of the most exciting genre writers working today.

Multi-award winning editor Jonathan Strahan once again brings you the best stories from the past year. Within you will find twenty-eight amazing tales from authors across the globe, displaying why science fiction and fantasy are genres increasingly relevant to our turbulent world.

US ISBN: 978-1-78108-309-3
$19.99

UK ISBN: 978-1-78108-308-6
£12.99

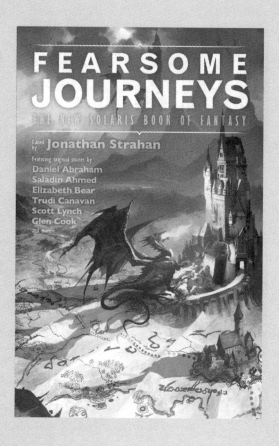

How do you encompass all the worlds of the imagination? Within fantasy's scope lies every possible impossibility, from dragons to spirits, from magic to gods, and from the unliving to the undying.

In Fearsome Journeys, master anthologist Jonathan Strahan sets out on a quest to find the very limits of the unlimited, collecting twelve brand new stories by some of the most popular and exciting names in epic fantasy from around the world.

With original fiction from Scott Lynch, Saladin Ahmed, Trudi Canavan, K J Parker, Kate Elliott, Jeffrey Ford, Robert V S Redick, Ellen Klages, Glen Cook, Elizabeth Bear, Ellen Kushner, Ysabeau S. Wilce and Daniel Abraham Fearsome Journeys explores the whole range of the fantastic.

US ISBN: 978-1-78108-118-1
$7.99

UK ISBN: 978-1-78108-119-8
£7.99

From sorcerous bridges that link worlds to the simple traditions of country folk; from the mysterious natures of twins to the dangerous powers of obligation and contract. Laden with perils for both the adventurous and the unsuspecting, magic is ultimately a contradiction: endlessly powerful but never without consequence, and rigidly defined by rules of its own making.

Award-winning Jonathan Strahan brings together some of the most exciting and popular writers working in fantasy today to dig into that contradiction, and present you with the strange, the daunting, the mathematical, the unpredictable, the deceptive and above all the fearsome world of magic.

Includes stories by Garth Nix, K J Parker, Tony Ballantyne, James Bradley, Isobelle Carmody, Frances Hardinge, Nina Kiriki Hoffman, Ellen Klages, Justina Robson, Christopher Rowe, Robert Shearman, Karin Tidbeck, Genevieve Valentine and Kaaron Warren.

US ISBN: 978-1-78108-213-3
$9.99

UK ISBN: 978-1-78108-212-6
£7.99

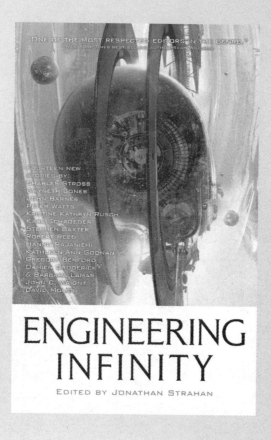

"ONE OF THE MOST RESPECTED EDITORS IN THE GENRE."
New York Times best-selling author Sean Williams

FOURTEEN NEW
STORIES BY:
CHARLES STROSS
GWYNETH JONES
JOHN BARNES
PETER WATTS
KRISTINE KATHRYN RUSCH
KARL SCHROEDER
STEPHEN BAXTER
ROBERT REED
HANNU RAJANIEMI
KATHLEEN ANN GOONAN
GREGORY BENFORD
DAMIEN BRODERICK
& BARBARA LAMAR
JOHN C. WRIGHT
DAVID MOLES

ENGINEERING INFINITY

EDITED BY JONATHAN STRAHAN

The universe shifts and changes: suddenly you understand, you get it, and are filled with wonder. That moment of understanding drives the greatest science-fiction stories and lies at the heart of Engineering Infinity. Whether it's coming up hard against the speed of light – and, with it, the enormity of the universe – realising that terraforming a distant world is harder and more dangerous than you'd ever thought, or simply realizing that a hitchhiker on a starship consumes fuel and oxygen with tragic results, it's hard science-fiction where a sense of discovery is most often found and where science-fiction's true heart lies.

This exciting and innovative science-fiction anthology collects together stories by some of the biggest names in the field, including Gwyneth Jones, Stephen Baxter and Charles Stross.

US ISBN: 978-1-907519-52-9
$7.99

UK ISBN: 978-1-907519-51-2
£8.99

www.solarisbooks.com

What happens when we reach out into the vastness of space?
What hope for us amongst the stars?

Multi-award winning editor Jonathan Strahan brings us fourteen new tales of the future, from some of the finest science fiction writers in the field.

The fourteen startling stories in this anthology feature the work of Greg Egan, Aliette de Bodard, Ian McDonald, Karl Schroeder, Pat Cadigan, Karen Lord, Ellen Klages, Adam Roberts, Linda Nagata, Hannu Rajaniemi, Kathleen Ann Goonan, Ken MacLeod, Alastair Reynolds and Peter Watts.

US ISBN: 978-1-78108-203-4
$9.99

UK ISBN: 978-1-78108-202-7
£7.99

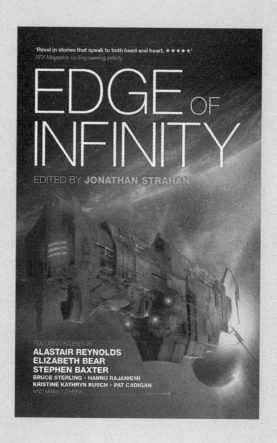

ONE GIANT LEAP FOR MANKIND - Those were Neil Armstrong's immortal words when he became the first human being to step onto another world. All at once, the horizon expanded; the human race was no longer Earthbound.

Edge of Infinity is an exhilarating new SF anthology that looks at the next giant leap for humankind: the leap from our home world out into the Solar System. From the eerie transformations in Pat Cadigan's "The Girl-Thing Who Went Out for Sushi" to the frontier spirit of Sandra McDonald and Stephen D. Covey's "The Road to NPS," and from the grandiose vision of Alastair Reynolds' "Vainglory" to the workaday familiarity of Kristine Kathryn Rusch's "Safety Tests," the thirteen stories in this anthology span the whole of the human condition in their race to colonise Earth's nearest neighbours.

Featuring stories by Hannu Rajaniemi, Alastair Reynolds, James S. A. Corey, John Barnes, Stephen Baxter, Kristine Kathryn Rusch, Elizabeth Bear, Pat Cadigan, Gwyneth Jones, Paul McAuley, Sandra McDonald, Stephen D. Covey, An Owomoyela, and Bruce Sterling, Edge of Infinity is hard SF adventure at its best and most exhilarating.

US ISBN: 978-1-78108-056-6
$8.99

UK ISBN: 978-1-78108-055-9
£7.99